*Everyman, I will go with thee,
and be thy guide*

THE EVERYMAN
LIBRARY

The Everyman Library was founded by J. M. Dent
in 1906. He chose the name Everyman because he wanted
to make available the best books ever written in every
field to the greatest number of people at the cheapest possible
price. He began with Boswell's 'Life of Johnson';
his one-thousandth title was Aristotle's 'Metaphysics',
by which time sales exceeded forty million.

Today Everyman paperbacks remain true to
J. M. Dent's aims and high standards, with a wide range
of titles at affordable prices in editions which address
the needs of today's readers. Each new text is reset to give
a clear, elegant page and to incorporate the latest thinking
and scholarship. Each book carries the pilgrim logo,
the character in 'Everyman', a medieval mystery play,
a proud link between Everyman
past and present.

Fyodor Dostoyevsky

NOTES FROM UNDERGROUND

Lev Tolstoy

A CONFESSION

Edited by

A. D. P. BRIGGS

University of Birmingham

EVERYMAN
J. M. DENT · LONDON
CHARLES E. TUTTLE CO.
VERMONT

Chronology, introduction, textual editing and endmatter
© J. M. Dent 1994

This edition first published in Everyman in 1994

J. M. Dent
Orion Publishing Group
Orion House, 5 Upper St Martin's Lane, London WC2H 9EA
and
Charles E. Tuttle Co. Inc.
28 South Main Street, Rutland, Vermont 05701, USA

Typeset in Great Britain by
ROM-Data Corporation Ltd, Falmouth, Cornwall, England
Printed in Great Britain by
The Guernsey Press Co. Ltd, Guernsey, C.I.

British Library Cataloguing-in-Publication Data
is available upon request

ISBN 0 460 87448 9

CONTENTS

NOTE ON THE AUTHORS AND
EDITOR

FYODOR MIKHAILOVITCH DOSTOYEVSKY was born in Moscow in 1821. The son of an army physician, he studied at the St Petersburg Academy of Military Engineering before achieving literary fame in 1846 with his first novel *Poor Folk*. His second novel, *The Double* (also 1846), was not well received and his reputation declined. In 1849 he was arrested and imprisoned in the Peter and Paul Fortress for membership of a secret political society and conspiracy against the Tsarist regime. At his trial he was sentenced to death, a sentence commuted only at the very last moment to one of hard labour and Siberian exile. He did not return to St Petersburg until December 1859. During his period in Siberia Dostoyevsky found himself among the dregs of humanity and underwent a profound spiritual change. He also began to suffer from epilepsy, a disease that afflicted him for the rest of his life. Dostoyevsky resumed his literary career convinced that modern Europeanised Russian man had lost his native roots, but that these were intact in the simple Russian peasant and the teachings of the Orthodox Church. After a period spent travelling in Europe, he started, along with his brother Mikhail, two periodicals, *Time* (1861–3) and *Epoch* (1846–65), devoted to the popularisation of his ideas. Dostoyevsky's prison memoirs *The House of the Dead* were serialised in *Time* throughout 1861–2. In 1864 he published *Notes from Underground*, a sort of introduction to the great philosophical novels that were to follow in the final two decades of his life: *Crime and Punishment* (1866), *The Idiot* (1868), *The Devils* (1871–2), *A Raw Youth* (1875) and *The Brothers Karamazov* (1880). By 1880 Dostoyevsky had achieved the status of a prophet amongst the reading public, particularly after his speech at the unveiling of a Pushkin memorial in summer 1880. He died of emphysema in January 1881, just two months after the completion of *The Brothers Karamazov*.

LEV NIKOLAYEVICH TOLSTOY was born at Yasnaya Polyana, south of Moscow, in 1828. His mother died in 1830 before he was two years old and his father in 1837, the year the family moved to Moscow for their children's education. He was brought up by his aunts. After a couple of unproductive years at Kazan University (1844-7) he spent some time on the estate before joining the army. He served in the Caucasus and fought at Sevastopol in the Crimean War. To this period belong his first publications, *Childhood* (1852) and the *Sevastopol Stories* (1855), with which he made his name as a writer. He travelled abroad twice, in 1857 and 1860-1, returning with advanced ideas on education which he began to put into practice on his estate. In 1862, at the age of thirty-four, he married a girl of eighteen, Sofya Andreyevna Behrs. Over the years she would bear him thirteen children and assist him with massive transcription of his writings. During the next two decades he wrote *War and Peace* (1863-9) and *Anna Karenina* (1873-6), but this period took its toll. His health worsened, his relationship with Sonya deteriorated and he became increasingly worried about religious and philosophical questions. The story of his spiritual crisis, which brought him to the brink of suicide, is told in *A Confession* (1879-81). He regained stability by returning to a religion of love based on the Sermon on the Mount. From now on all his works carried a didactic burden, though several of them (such as *The Death of Ivan Ilich* (1886), *Master and Man* (1894-5) and *Hadji Murat* (1904)) are nevertheless literary masterpieces. His last major novel, *Resurrection* (1899), written for money (to finance the emigration of a persecuted religious sect, the Dukhobors), lacks the subtlety of its two great predecessors. Tolstoy's ideas and way of life after his conversion put an even greater strain on his family life. His views on the evil of property, his decision to hand over all his works into the public domain and his growing closeness with a spiritual brother, Vladimir Chertkov, increasingly alienated Sonya. He ran away from her in November 1910, was taken ill on the journey and died at the railway station of Astapovo.

A. D. P. BRIGGS, Professor of Russian Language and Literature at the University of Birmingham, is a specialist in modern Russian literature, mainly of the nineteenth century. Among his many publications are half a dozen books, three of them devoted to Alexander Pushkin.

CHRONOLOGY OF DOSTOYEVSKY'S LIFE

————————

Year	Age	Life
1865	44	Closure of *The Epoch*. Severe financial difficulties. Starts work on *Crime and Punishment*
1866	45	Publishes *Crime and Punishment*. Writes *The Gambler* in twenty-six days with the help of stenographer Anna Grigoryevna Snitkina
1867	46	Marries Anna Grigoryevna. Flees abroad to escape creditors. Meets Turgenev in Baden. Visits Dresden and Geneva
1868	47	Still abroad. Birth and death of infant daughter. *The Idiot*
1869	48	Returns to Dresden. Birth of daughter Lyubov
1870	49	*The Eternal Husband*
1871	50	Returns to St Petersburg. Birth of son Fyodor
1871–2	50–1	*The Devils*
1872	51	Becomes editor of *The Citizen*
1873	52	Starts *The Diary of a Writer*
1874	53	Resigns from *The Citizen*. Visits Bad Ems for treatment for emphysema
1875	54	*A Raw Youth*
1878	57	Death of son Alexey. Visits Optina Monastery with Vladimir Solovyov
1879–80	58–9	*The Brothers Karamazov* (completed November 1880)
1880–81	58–9	Final issues of *The Diary of a Writer*
1880	59	Delivers speech at Pushkin celebrations in Moscow
1881	59	28 January: dies in St Petersburg. 1 February: funeral in Alexander Nevsky Monastery attended by over thirty thousand people

CHRONOLOGY OF TOLSTOY'S LIFE

Year	Age	Life
1828		28 August: born at Yasnaya Polyana
1830	2	Death of mother
1837	9	Family moves to Moscow. Death of father
1847	19	Leaves university. Inherits Yasnaya Polyana
1848	20	Dissipated life in Moscow and St Petersburg
1851–3	23–5	Serves as army volunteer in the Caucasus. *Childhood* (1852)
1854–5	26–7	Commissioned, serves at Sevastopol. *Sevastopol Sketches*
1857	29	Travels in Europe: France, Germany, Switzerland
1859	31	*Three Deaths, Family Happiness*
1860–1	32–3	Another European trip. Death of brother Nikolay. Quarrels with Turgenev
1862	34	Marriage to Sofya Andreyevna Behrs
1863	35	*The Cossacks, Polikushka*. Birth of first child
1863–9	35–41	*War and Peace*. Three more children
1869–71	41–3	Studies Schopenhauer. Learns Greek
1873–7	45–9	*Anna Karenina*
1878	50	Spiritual crisis, resolved by reversion to Christian principles
1879–81	51–3	*A Confession*
1879–83	51–5	Theological studies and writings about Christianity (works banned)
1883	55	Meets Vladimir Chertkov
1885	57	Writes parable stories for the peasantry
1886	58	*The Death of Ivan Ilich, The Power of Darkness*
1888	60	Birth of thirteenth and last child
1889	61	*The Kreutzer Sonata* (banned in 1890). Begins *Resurrection*
1891	63	Renounces rights to all his works published after 1881. Famine relief work
1893	65	*The Kingdom of God is Within You*
1894–5	66–7	*Master and Man*
1897	69	*What is Art?*
1898	70	Organises aid for Dukhobors
1899	71	*Resurrection* completed

CHRONOLOGY OF THE TIMES

Year	Artistic Events	Historical Events
1823–31	Pushkin, *Eugene Onegin*	
1825		Decembrist Revolt and accession of Nicholas I
1830	Stendhal, *Le Rouge et le Noir*	July Revolution in France
1834	Pushkin, *The Queen of Spades*	
1835	Balzac, *Le Père Goriot*	
1836	Gogol, *The Government Inspector*	
1837	Death of Pushkin in a duel Dickens, *The Pickwick Papers*	
1839	Stendhal, *La Chartreuse de Parme*	
1840	Lermontov, *A Hero of Our Time*	
1841	Death of Lermontov in a duel	
1842	Gogol, *Dead Souls* and *The Overcoat*	
1847		Emigration of Herzen
1848	Death of Belinsky Thackeray, *Vanity Fair*	Revolutions in Europe Publication of Communist *Manifesto*
1849		Russia invades Hungary
1850	Dickens, *David Copperfield* Turgenev, *A Month in the Country*	
1851	Great Exhibition: Crystal Palace, London	
1852	Death of Gogol Turgenev, *A Sportsman's Sketches*	Louis Napoleon becomes Emperor of France
1853–6		Crimean War
1855		Death of Nicholas I; accession of Alexander II Hopes of social and political reform in Russia
1856	Turgenev, *Rudin*	

Year	Artistic Events	Historical Events
1857	Flaubert, *Madame Bovary* Baudelaire, *Les Fleurs du Mal*	Indian Mutiny
1857–61	Buckle, *A History of Civilisation in England*	
1859	Turgenev, *A Nobleman's Nest* Goncharov, *Oblomov*	Publication of Darwin's *The Origin of Species*
1860	Turgenev, *On the Eve* Birth of Chekhov Eliot, *The Mill on the Floss*	Abraham Lincoln elected 16th President of the United States Garibaldi captures Naples and Sicily
1861		Emancipation of the serfs Formation of the revolutionary organisation *Land and Liberty* Start of the American Civil War
1862	Turgenev, *Fathers and Children* *The Contemporary* suspended; arrest of Chernyshevsky Hugo, *Les Misérables*	Tense revolutionary mood in St Petersburg Bismark becomes President of Prussia
1863	Chernyshevsky, *What is to be Done?*	Polish uprising Emancipation of American slaves
1864	Dickens, *Our Mutual Friend*	First Communist International Student unrest in Kazan Legal reforms in Russia
1865		Assassination of Abraham Lincoln
1866		Attempted assassination of Alexander II by Dmitry Karakozov
1867	Turgenev, *Smoke*	
1869		Murder of student Ivanov by Nechayev's political group Opening of Suez Canal
1870		Defeat of France in Franco-Prussian War Death of Herzen Birth of V. I. Ulyanov (Lenin) Death of Dickens
1871		Defeat of the Paris Commune
1872	Leskov, *Cathedral Folk*	Trial of Nechayev Marx, *Das Kapital* published in Russia
1874		Attempts by thousands of Russian students to provoke revolutionary unrest among the peasantry
1875		Political strikes in Odessa
1877	Turgenev, *Virgin Soil*	Russia declares war on Turkey

Year	Artistic Events	Historical Events
1878		Death of Nekrasov
		Arrest and trial of Vera Zasulich
1879		Birth of Stalin
1881		Assassination of Alexander II;
		accession of Alexander III
1883	Nietzsche, *Thus Spake Zarathustra*	
1885	Zola, *Germinal*	
1886	Hardy, *The Mayor of Casterbridge*	
1891	Hardy, *Tess of the d'Urbervilles*	
1894–1904		Dreyfus affair in France
1895	Wilde, *The Importance of Being Ernest*	
	Fontane, *Effi Briest*	
1896	Chekhov, *The Seagull*	
1899	Chekhov, *Uncle Vanya*	
1900		Boers attack Ladysmith
1901	Chekhov, *Three Sisters*	
	Mann, *Buddenbrooks*	
1902	Gorky, *The Lower Depths*	
1904	Chekhov, *The Cherry Orchard*	Outbreak of Russo-Japanese War
1905		Revolutionary activity in Russia
		Bloody Sunday massacre in St Petersburg
		Election of the first Duma (elected legislature)

INTRODUCTION

The two most serious writers in Russian literature are, by common consent, Fyodor Dostoyevsky (1821–81) and Lev Tolstoy (1828–1910). In life they disliked each other and never met, but that has not prevented them from standing side by side in posthumous reputation as two of the world's greatest novelists and men of ideas who happened to write at about the same time, and in Russian. The titles of their finest achievements, *Crime and Punishment*, *The Brothers Karamazov*, *Anna Karenina* and *War and Peace*, trip off the tongue of every educated reader as examples of the most substantial and rewarding of all the world's novels.

Both writers produced other long novels and, besides them, a fair number of shorter works which vary a good deal in quality and significance. The two presented in this volume, Dostoyevsky's *Notes from Underground* and Tolstoy's *A Confession*, have not normally been linked together. This is perhaps surprising, since they have much in common and, more importantly, each of them may be said in some way to epitomise both the general thinking and the literary method of its writer. Both are accepted as being of vital importance for an understanding of the author concerned and – the most curious thing of all – when you look at them closely, beyond the strong dissimilarities which first strike the eye, it is hard to escape the impression that they are actually very similar indeed – particularly in their philosophical conclusions, which matter more than anything else.

At first sight, perhaps, a comparison of these two works does not look promising. *Notes from Underground*, written in 1864 as a kind of prelude to the four great novels soon to follow, is fiction, with much psychological interest and some social satire. Its 30,000 words are, for the most part, hostile and discouraging; sometimes they are confusing and almost impenetrable. Their style is best described as poetic, since much is presented through paradox, contradiction, metaphor and other such rhetorical devices. Could any work be more different from all of this than

A Confession? One third shorter, it is an autobiographical essay rather than fiction, written in 1879–81 as a kind of epilogue to the author's great novels. Its purpose is spiritual, its manner accommodating, its style lucid, straightforward and, apparently, logical to a fault. An irrational, rambling story seems to have been supplanted by a manual of closely argued discourse. But these first impressions are false. For instance, relentless logic turns out to be a fundamental characteristic of the *Notes*, despite outward appearances, and the reverse is true of *A Confession*, in which the best ideas are communicated not by reasoned argument but through fable and metaphor.

Notes from Underground

The title of this work has been mistranslated in more ways than would seem possible. These are notes (*zapiski*) and they issue from a place best known as 'underground'. They are certainly not letters, and they are much more than memoirs. They have nothing to do with the 'Underworld' (the classical realm of Pluto or the criminal world of Fagin), or with *the* Underground, a phrase which makes us think of France with its Resistance movement or its metro. *Notes from Underground* is the only acceptable English version. Incidentally the term 'underground' should be understood both literally, as the dismal basement-flat into which the writer has retreated for the last couple of decades, and figuratively, as a dark, largely submerged region of the human mind having something in common with Freud's concept of the Id.

The notes are set down in quite the wrong order, according to the normal expectations of a reader of fiction. Throughout Part I runs the suggestion that there is no story at all, merely a series of weird jottings by the 'Underground Man' about life in general. But Part II puts this right by describing three or four incidents in his life which, as well as confirming much of what we have half-understood so far, also make a coherent narrative. This determines the first and most important feature of the work; it turns out to be a remarkably successful bonding together of three different strands: an interesting story, an unusual psychological case-book and a most original philosophical treatise.

Notes from Underground is a rather complex work which reveals its secrets slowly. Perhaps it has to be re-read in order to be fully understood. Certainly it must be considered retrospectively, working back from the events of the last couple of chapters through the preceding incidents to the utterances of Part I. The story and the psychology are bound closest together. When Liza arrives at the Underground Man's apartment in the penultimate chapter and the two of them play out their squalid little drama with its inevitably negative outcome, we receive final confirmation of all that we have learned about him and his inadequacies. Working backwards through his encounters with old school 'friends', his bitter reminiscences about the 'penal servitude' of his days at school and his outpourings of self-revelation in Part I, we can piece together a psychological profile which is not only coherent in itself, but is also a strong reminder of another inadequate 'anti-hero' of Russian letters, Grigoriy Pechorin in Lermontov's *A Hero of Our Time*.

Both of these men are incapable of living anything like a normal life because of their inability to establish conventional relationships with anyone, male or female. This combined character (Dostoyevsky's Underground Man is clearly modelled on Pechorin) was born unwanted, rejected when very young, forced into early isolation and introspection, convinced of his superiority over all the other boys at school (especially in regard to intellect), filled with a desire for love which, when frustrated, turned into bitter hatred and a longing for domination, and ultimately condemned to dream of heroic status by seeing himself as, and trying to behave like, a dashing character in fiction. Much of this, in the case of the Underground Man, can be gleaned before the appearance of Liza, but her entry into the story locks everything into place. The Underground Man is drawn to her for a number of reasons – perhaps at first he is even trying to get rid of his life-long inhibitions and allow himself into a fairly normal loving relationship – but the old attitudes soon reassert themselves. As long as he can dominate Liza he can accept friendly relations with her and derive pleasure from their association. However, her initiative in visiting him (itself worth thinking about in terms of its motivation) is too much for him to bear. Before long it is she who plays the dominant role, thus confirming his worst fears. His full inadequacy as a human being is revealed. He cannot dominate even the most vulnerable people, the dregs of society; he cannot love without domination and he therefore cannot live, in any recognisable sense of the word. All the impulses which might be regarded as natural in most people have suffered total inversion in the Underground Man; love has turned into malevolence, the search for caresses into a longing for pain, gentleness into violence, sociability into reclusiveness, openness into agoraphobia, an attraction towards purity and beauty into a love of degradation and squalor. We must remember that the incidents described at the end of the story took place a decade and a half before Part I came to be written. They are the explanation and vindication of what went before. The story is touching, the psychology is complete and convincing; the two blend together and give final coherence to a mass of material which, ten chapters before, looked unfinished, puzzling and only half-satisfactory.

This difficult material, the whole of Part I, is the great glory of the work. Those words are hardly excessive. *Notes from Underground* is undoubtedly one of the most original and trenchant philosophical statements of the entire nineteenth century. As George Steiner puts it, 'Had Dostoyevsky written nothing else, he would have been remembered as one of the master builders of modern thought.' However, his message may not come across clearly at a first reading, and for a good reason. The author is attacking rationalism as the basis for human behaviour; in order to do that he can hardly proceed in a rational manner. The Underground Man simply pours out a long diatribe consisting of personal recollections, challenging observations and assertive statements, some of them contrary to common sense, some of them self-contradictory. What is he doing and why would he want to attack rationalism in the first place?

Dostoyevsky was disturbed by the general trend of thinking in mid-century Europe, which he saw as naive, inhuman and dangerously seductive. The modern view of the world was that reason and science held the keys not only to prosperity but also to human happiness. You only had to look at the glorious technological achievements housed in the Crystal Palace in London for the Great Exhibition of 1851 to realise how bright the future was for humanity. The scientists would solve all our problems, removing the need for drudgery, eliminating poverty and issuing in an epoch of plenty, during which all warfare would cease because men and women would come to see that there was no profit in enmity and violence. This was confirmed by writers such as the English historian Henry Thomas Buckle, who claimed that the laws of human history would soon be exposed as clearly as those of the natural sciences. The same kind of claims were made by a fellow-Russian, Nikolay Chernyshevsky, in a popular novel (execrable in style, characterisation and dialogue), *What is to be Done?*, which created a utopian vision of a happy world based on utilitarian, socialist and essentially rationalistic principles.

All of this was seen by Dostoyevsky as rampant materialism, a terrible danger to humanity. Even if it were true and capable of delivering its seductive promises (which was not the case), Dostoyevsky believed that it contained the seeds of disaster. The materialist philosophy, with all its offshoots into positivism, socialism, etc., left out of account the things that really mattered – human personality, spiritual values and especially the overriding need for freedom in all directions, including the freedom to make mistakes, go off the rails, ignore one's own interests. The ideas of Chernyshevsky, were they to take root, would lead inevitably to a totalitarian society in which rules for human behaviour were worked out according to scientific formulae and imposed upon the population for their own good. If this sounds like the twentieth century, not only in the real-life seventy-year experiment with Soviet rule but also in the frightening visions of possible future societies evoked as further warnings by Zamyatin, Huxley, Orwell, Bradbury and many others, then that is a measure of Dostoyevsky's foresight and influence.

The Underground Man was created as a fictional refutation of all such thinking and principles. For him human freedom is all that matters. That such a positive idea should emerge from the mind of a man with an irredeemably negative personality is one of the many paradoxes of *Notes from Underground*. Many of his utterances seem at first sight to go against reason and common sense, but they turn out on reflection to have an inner truth that is irrefutable. More than that, time after time the Underground Man digs deep into some of the most impenetrable regions of the human mind and the human condition. Most of his controversial revelations on human history and psychology, on the nature of the universe and its physical structure, have been vindicated in surprising ways during the twentieth century.

To refute Buckle and Chernyshevsky was only the beginning, and not too difficult a task. Their shallow optimism could be disposed of in a few caustic sentences (especially in Part I, 7). Nevertheless, Dostoyevsky was swimming against a strong tide of materialist confidence, and he deserves much credit for his brave exposure of their fallacies. He points out that, although man has made material progress, he has not changed his fundamental animal nature, which remains aggressive, predatory and often gratuitously cruel. His argument predicts that the next century, far from marking a decline in this nastiness, would watch with horror as it continued to determine human affairs on an increasing scale. More than a century later, with Stalin, Hitler, Pol Pot, Idi Amin and other such monsters behind us, who will dare to suggest that he was wrong?

In psychology he was also ahead of his time. As well as depicting characters with an unusual, but strangely consistent, psychological profile, he also draws attention to general aspects of human behaviour which were not widely accepted or understood in his day. For instance, where his positivist contemporaries would have taken it for granted that the achieving of a long-desired goal was a source of the greatest human happiness, he points out the reverse – that it is usually the *process*, not the achievement, which satisfies (I, 9). Beyond that, his comments on such recondite matters as perversity and masochistic delight are undeniably accurate, however abnormal they may at first appear to be. His revelations on repression (I, 11) are exceptionally acute. It is easy to see why Dostoyevsky is regarded as Russia's greatest psychological writer, and why the science of psychology, in the twentieth century, has acknowledged him as a vital precursor of modern theory. His name is mentioned in direct connection with those of Freud, Jung, Adler and other such practitioners.

However, Dostoyevsky's probings go much deeper than this. In his bold refutation of pure reason, mathematical certainties and the entire concept of primary causes, in his wonderful assertion that $2 \times 2 = 4$ is not a reliable formula, he anticipates twentieth-century ideas about the nature of matter, space and time of which no other contemporary writer could have dreamt. When Einstein's Theory of Relativity (1905) overturned the neatly structured Newtonian universe, and when subsequently scientists were able to confirm his proposals empirically, it became clear that Underground Man had been right all the time. The formula $2 \times 2 = 4$ may be a useful device for us in our everyday lives, but it has no absolute meaning. It is not true on all occasions, in all circumstances and at all times, and our view of reality is occluded if we think that it is. What seemed like paradoxical, or even nonsensical, assertions in the early 1860s now look like accurate predictions of mysterious principles newly revealed to us in the depths of quantum mechanics and the heights of astrophysics, to which the old-fashioned scientific laws are utterly inapplicable. In the realms of antimatter, quarks, dark matter, gluons, Schrödinger's cat, black holes, neutrinos and baby universes, the formula $2 \times 2 = 5$ is not only alive and well; it mocks us for ever having doubted its existence.

From all of this it is easy to understand why people get excited about *Notes from Underground*. Perceptive, accurate and original, this work shows up the emptiness of contemporary thinking, leaves it floundering, far behind, and leaps forward over several generations with one triumphant flash of inspired insight after another. In what he said about human nature and history, politics, psychology and physical reality Dostoyevsky proved to be, by a wide margin, the most incisive and original thinker of all the great Russian creative writers. Many of his ideas would be fully worked out only in the four subsequent novels, but the important ones are to be discovered, at least in embryo, in *Notes from Underground*.

A Confession

Tolstoy's mature work *A Confession* works the other way round. Preceded by the great novels, it casts a retrospective glance over the author's life, works, ideas and principles. It is short and easily read, despite the fact that it asks the profoundest questions, not stopping short of demanding a meaning to life itself. It approaches these issues with shocking directness. They are always related to Tolstoy himself, though the reader feels personally affected by the writer's agonising quest for explanations in the face of his own mortality. When other writers discuss, or hint at, mortality, the subject may well be treated safely in the abstract, as if it applied only to someone else; by contrast, Tolstoy makes you painfully aware of your own impending death. His direct confrontation of this concept has earned him rich praise: Prince Dmitriy Mirsky ranked this work alongside the books of Ecclesiastes and Job, calling it 'the greatest piece of oratory in Russian literature, one of the greatest and most lasting expressions of the human soul in the presence of the eternal mysteries of life and death'. Derrick Leon agreed: 'Its place is amongst the great religious writings . . ., and it should be read by everyone who wishes to understand Tolstoy and his thought.'

This is a work so carefully constructed that it looks even more cerebral and schematic than it actually is. It reads almost like the skeletal outline of a multi-volume treatise on human spirituality, the massive details of which we have been spared. (To work out its ideas in close detail, the reader should peruse the many religious tomes by Tolstoy which followed *A Confession.*) The signal quality of the work is forthright intellectualism. Tolstoy was a man of the strongest intelligence; here he gathers all the force of this faculty for a massive onslaught on the challenging secrets of our finite human condition. Needless to say, they will not yield to this battering, but the author has done his work well. *A Confession* is arguably the last serious attempt to exert human reason in the hope of explaining human destiny.

The work is measured out in tidy, roughly equal chapters of 1200–1500 words – sixteen of them in all – and it describes a neat, cyclic curve, beginning with the author's experience of the Russian Orthodox Church and returning him, if not to that organisation itself, at least to Christian principles and an idea of faith, at the end of a long, despairing spiritual odyssey which brought him at one time to the brink of suicide. Tolstoy takes us through his own life, describing how he abandoned religion and sought personal fulfilment through realising all the promising possibilities open to a young man of his time – sensual pleasure, including all the vices, soldiery, literary success, travel, teaching, journalism, marriage and family life. Nothing satisfied; everything led to deepening disillusionment. Faced with the idea that the only thing worth doing with a human existence was to end it, Tolstoy turned for guidance to the great thinkers of the past, but found them unhelpful; they seemed to emphasise the futility of it all. One of these thinkers happened to be the pessimistic Schopenhauer, much in vogue in Russia at the time. His ludicrously negative view of existence ought to have been neutralised by listening to half an hour of Mozart or reading a few dozen lines from Pushkin, but Tolstoy seems to have been more determined to torment himself increasingly than to balance one school of ideas against another in the interests of objectivity. This lays him open to the charge, which is often made, of intellectual dishonesty, and it is certainly true that he manipulates the course of his argument through selectivity and oversimplification. What keeps him on the rails, however, is the directness of the questions asked and the energy with which they are relentlessly pursued. The reader may feel some dissatisfaction with particular examples and conclusions as they pass by, but he or she will not lose interest, because the issues are so tremendously important.

Eventually Tolstoy solves his own problem. The nadir of his sorrowful adventure comes, neatly enough, about half-way through the work, after which steady progress is made towards a spirit of reconciliation enough to make life worth living and apparently purposeful. Again, the way that this is done will not please everyone. On the one hand, he was obviously correct in his (all too belated) conclusion that sheer thinking, however effortful, was not going to provide any solutions to his problems or relief from his anguish. No one should quarrel with this. On the other hand, in turning to the broad mass of the Russian people for solace, since they knew, instinctively and collectively, how to live and die, he was indulging in the kind of extreme oversimplification which may annoy more readers than it will satisfy. Tolstoy's strange idea that moral goodness, healthy living and a sensible acceptance of mortality all fly out of the window the moment anyone acquires a modicum of education, wealth and sophistication is both patronising to the working masses and insulting to those who do not have the 'advantage' of their lowly status. Even a wonderful story like *The Death of Ivan Ilich* (1886) is devalued by this kind of simplistic thinking, which ignores the rich diversity of the human personality within and between individuals from all levels in society. Nevertheless, that story is rightly hailed as a masterpiece which succeeds despite itself; it has tremendous narrative energy as well as an inbuilt capacity for shocking the reader into serious thinking. So it is with *A Confession*.

Tolstoy returns to the religion which he abandoned when still young with a new certainty in God, the goodness of life and the need for faith. His last obstacle to spiritual contentment is removed by a further decision to renounce the dogma and ceremony of entrenched religious institutions. He can live with the spirit of Christianity, though not with its outward symbolism. Human reason has its limitations and must be transcended if any kind of understanding of the meaning of life is to be achieved. Religious knowledge is not scientific knowledge and cannot be understood in the same way. Tolstoy's enjoinder for us to consider such issues and to remind ourselves that it is futile to insist upon ultimate explanations may seem both obvious and ponderously expressed, but it remains a salutary lesson, especially in an age of continuing (perhaps accelerating) materialism which, many would say, enriches and impoverishes in almost equal measure.

Above all, it is the intensity of this writer's pursuit of deeper understanding that is likely to command attention and win sympathy.

In rejecting the scientific way of solving life's problems Tolstoy allows the message to dictate the style. Carefully ordered and lucid reasoning is steadily subverted by its opposite, the language of legend, story, poetry and fable. The two methods co-exist throughout the work, a constant and uncomfortable reminder of the divided mentality which is striving to communicate with us. On the one hand, we have Tolstoy the logician. He uses lists, schematic programmes, arithmetical formulae. Reason proves only that $0 = 0$ (chapter 9); a man with 1000 wives equals 1000 men without wives (7); the truth cannot be avoided any more than the equation $2 \times 2 = 4$ (11; a curious correspondence with *Notes from Underground*); Socrates said . . . , Schopenhauer said . . . , Solomon said . . . , the Buddha said . . . (6); my contemporaries, faced with the ultimate questions, fall into four categories: a) . . . , b) . . . , c) . . . , d) . . . (7); and so on. This is the language and method of a *raisonneur*. But it is interpenetrated with something quite different, and, in the last analysis, much more persuasive: an oriental fable (4); a story by Solomon (6); a parable concerning a naked, hungry beggar (11); the remarkable analogy of a man sailing downstream, almost out of control (12); a memorable dream (16, conclusion). The author scarcely needs to *tell* us that logical discourse is letting him down; the collapse of reason is made more evident with every passing chapter.

A famous anecdote from Tolstoy's childhood recounts his belief in the existence somewhere of a little green stick on which was inscribed a formula for the eradication of evil and the conferring of great blessings. Most children do not play such soulful games; most adults lose their capacity to believe in such comforting simplicities. Tolstoy's incorrigible yearning for them pursued him well into middle age, and probably beyond. This mature work describes the agonising struggle which he had to endure in order to prove to himself something known instinctively to most people: he who looks for a little green stick is sure to be disappointed.

Two Confessions, One Conclusion

It will already be clear that certain characteristics are emerging as common to both *Notes from Underground* and *A Confession*.

There are many more, a surprising number of them. To begin with, both works were written at a time of personal crisis for the author, perhaps what we should now describe as a 'mid-life crisis'. Dostoyevsky was nursing his wife and watching her die. He had also just turned forty; so has the Underground Man, whose multiple references to that number (from the second paragraph onwards) suggest a deep preoccupation with his age. As for Tolstoy, his first real mental crisis, verging on madness, also came at the age of forty, when, in the remote town of Arzamas, he suffered a terrifying vision of death. He got over it somehow, and, although his spiritual anxiety continued to intensify over a number of years, he staved off the next real crisis until he was fifty, perhaps an even more critical age. Obsessed with personal anguish exacerbated by a sharp awareness of ageing, both authors emerge, particularly at the outset of these two works, as monstrous egoists. Each narrative begins with the strong, lonely word 'I'. Each first page is bespattered with first-person pronouns and first-person-singular verbs. Dostoyevsky's Underground Man makes one hundred uses of the first person in the first chapter of one thousand words. Every single chapter of Tolstoy's confession uses the first person in the opening sentence, five of them as the first word. First-person narrative, in both cases, extends from start to finish. Incidentally, *both* works are confessional and could be entitled as such. In Part I (11) the Underground Man compares himself to Rousseau, with particular reference to the latter's *Confessions*. When Dostoyevsky described (to his brother) the original conception of *Notes from Underground* as 'a confession – a novel about everything . . . I have had to live through myself', he is thinking in terms applicable also to Tolstoy's later work which would actually call itself a confession. One further egotistical preoccupation common to both pieces is the assertion of other men's inferiority because of their inability, or unwillingness, to face up to stark truths.

Both works are shockingly thought-provoking, challenging, disturbing – each in its way a *tour de force* of rhetorical discourse. Deeply spiritual, both explore reality for its ultimate meanings, looking for an acceptable attitude to the great mysteries which surround us and which most people are happy enough to disregard, since they appear to be more frightening than reassuring. Comforting certainties are swept away from us, leaving behind a dreadful agony of spirit. Little or no consolation is offered by these works, since they studiously avoid references to the nicer aspects of art, religion or just life itself; there is no mention of spontaneous joy, celebration, awe, happy love, the delights of poetry or music.

In all of these respects the two works come together. But the relationship goes even deeper. When closely compared, they yield a double secret. In the first place, far from being antithetical in form and style, they turn out to be remarkably similar. Within the apparent ramblings of the Underground Man are hidden dozens of passages argued through with relentless, convincing logic. Conversely, as we have seen, Tolstoy's carefully measured arguments continually collapse into irrationality. Thus both works may be said to consist of a strange concoction: a mixture of logical argument and rhetorical persuasion, with one of them ostensibly disavowed. The overall manner, because of the continuing use of the first person, is direct, even conversational. Questions are asked on all sides, direct, oblique and rhetorical. Numbers, symbols, formulae and equations come into both arguments, as do abundant references to outside authorities, figures and writers from history and the contemporary world.

The other part of the secret is that these two works, for all their differences in attitude, intention and style, actually come to conclusions which are also remarkably similar. Here, for instance, are two quotations, one from chapter five of each work, which are difficult to differentiate:

> a) It is only necessary for experimental science to introduce the question of a final cause for it to become nonsensical.
> b) Men of independence and action . . . mistake approximate and secondary causes for primary ones . . . Well, my advice is . . . to leave first causes alone.

For the record, the first is from Tolstoy, the second from Dostoyevsky. Here are two more; this time Dostoyevsky comes first:

> a) See here: reason is an excellent thing . . . , but reason is reason and no more, and satisfies only the reasoning faculty in man, whereas volition is a manifestation of all life.
> b) Rational knowledge, presented by the learned and the wise, denies the meaning of life, but the enormous masses of man . . . receive that meaning in irrational knowledge.

These latter quotations (which could be multiplied from both sources) are most important, because each amounts to a summation of the work in which it appears and also the general pattern of thinking of the author. Both of these men, for all the things that separated them, stood for spiritual, and against material, values. Tolstoy and Dostoyevsky, individually and together, remind us of what we should know, but choose to overlook: the limits of reason, the inadequacy of science, philosophy, arithmetic. They tell us, both openly and obliquely, that faith is the only satisfying answer to our human needs. The message of faith is much more clearly enunciated in *A Confession*, but only because the censors wrecked the tenth chapter of *Notes from Underground*, which was to have contained an overt statement of the need for faith. Here the two authors were trampling over territory jealously patrolled by the Church, and, naturally enough, both fell foul of that Church. Dostoyevsky yielded up most of the religious content of his story. Tolstoy retained his, but was soon to be excommunicated as a direct consequence of it.

Dostoyevsky and Tolstoy may be shown to stand closer together in these works than most people have imagined. They themselves would never have acknowledged it. In general, their considerable dissimilarities may have had too much attention; what they have in common is both fascinating in itself, and a powerful message for all future readers. Perhaps their closeness has been underestimated. There is even an intriguing suggestion that, despite himself, the younger writer was more closely drawn towards the older than he realised. 'It may be', says A. N. Wilson, 'that part of the unconscious, motivating force for the conversion of Tolstoy was a panic-stricken longing not to be Dostoyevsky.'

A. D. P. BRIGGS

NOTE ON THE TEXTS

The original idea of the work which was to become *Notes from Underground* occurred to Dostoyevsky at the end of 1862. His intention was to write a long novel rejecting the principle of reason as the basis of human conduct, entitled (curiously, in the present context) *A Confession*. Part One was written in the early months of 1864. The first edition (in his journal *Epokha*) not only contained hundreds of misprints and errors, it had also been savaged by the censor. Dostoyevsky was particularly distressed by the fate of the penultimate chapter, which he saw as the very kernel of his work. Ironically, the censor had accepted passages where, for effect, he had indulged in desecration and blasphemy, but had struck out his references to the need for faith and for Jesus Christ. The omissions were never restored, and the plan for a long novel was not realised. Part Two appeared also in *Epokha*, later the same year. The full text was published in 1865, never to be re-issued during the author's lifetime. The present translation has been adapted from an early one by C. J. Hogarth.

The religious crisis suffered by Konstantin Levin at the end of *Anna Karenina* was actually Tolstoy's own experience. Its detailed story is told in *A Confession*, which he began in the autumn of 1879. After much reworking, the final text was completed by mid-1881. Precautions taken to satisfy the religious censor were insufficient; it was banned in 1882, and again in 1885. First published in Geneva, in 1884, under the title *The Confession of Count L. N. Tolstoy: Introduction to an Unpublished Work*, it went through four editions before the end of the century, and was finally published at home in 1906. Tolstoy disliked the title, *A Confession*, which did not appear on the manuscript or first proofs; the author wanted no association with St Augustine or Rousseau. Nevertheless, it began to be used by several correspondents and Tolstoy finally approved it, probably as late as 1885. The present translation is by his English biographer, friend and editor, Aylmer Maude.

NOTES FROM UNDERGROUND

superstition is inconsistent w/ education –
but prevails

PART I

Underground[1]

psychosomatic illness?

I

I am ill . . . I am full of spleen and repellent. I conceive there to be something wrong with my liver. Not that I have any real idea what's wrong with me, or where the illness is. Medicine I cannot, I never could, take, although for medicine and doctors I have much reverence. Also, I am extremely superstitious, which is probably why I cherish such respect for the medical profession. (I have enough education not to be superstitious, but superstitious I am.) No, sir, it is spite that makes me refuse treatment. I suppose you cannot understand this? Well, I can understand it although it would puzzle me to tell you exactly whom I hope to hurt with my spite. I only know that I cannot hurt the doctors by telling them that I am unable to accept their treatment; I know better than anyone that in all of this I am only going to harm myself, and nobody else. Nevertheless, if I do refuse treatment, it is out of spite. What if my liver is giving me trouble? Let it get worse!

I have been living like this for a long while now – fully twenty years. I am forty years old, and, in my day, I have been a civil servant. But I am a civil servant no longer. Moreover, I was a bad civil servant at that. I used to offend everyone, and to take pleasure in doing so. Yet never once did I accept a bribe, though it would have been easy enough for me to have feathered my nest in that way. (This may seem to you a poor sort of a witticism, yet I will not erase it. I had written it down in the belief that it would wear rather a clever air when indited, yet I will not – no, not even now,

[1] It need hardly be said that both the writer of these notes and the 'Notes' themselves are creatures of the imagination. Nevertheless, in view of the circumstances under which, in general, our society has been formed, such men as the writer in question not only may, but are bound to, exist. I have tried, therefore, to set before the public, in more striking guise than usual, a character which is peculiar to a very recent time, representing a generation which has not yet passed away. In this section entitled 'Underground' this individual presents himself and his views on life, and purports to explain the causes which have created him, as a matter of inevitability, just as he is, given our *milieu*. In the next section you will find the actual 'notes' written by this person concerning certain incidents in his life.

FYODOR DOSTOYEVSKY*

when I see that I was but playing the buffoon – alter the *mot* by a single iota).

Whenever people approached my office table to ask for information, or what not, I used to grind my teeth at them, and invariably to feel pleased when I had offended their dignity. I seldom failed in my aim. Men, for the most part, are timid creatures – and we all of us know the sort of men favour-seekers are. Of such dolts there was one in particular – an officer – whom I could not bear, for he refused to defer to me at all, and always kicked up a most disgusting clatter with his sword. For a year and a half we joined battle over that sword; but it was I who won the victory, I who caused him to cease clattering his precious weapon. All this happened during my early manhood.

Do you wish to know wherein the sting of my evil temper has always lain? It has always lain (and therein also has always lain its peculiar offensiveness) in the fact that, even at moments of my bitterest spleen, I have been forced to acknowledge with shame that not only am I not at all bad-tempered, but also I have never received any real cause of offence – that I have been but roaring to frighten away sparrows, and amusing myself with doing so. Foam though I might at the mouth, I needed but to be given a doll to play with, or a cup of sweet tea to drink, and at once I sank to quiescence. Yes, I have always grown calm for the moment – even though, later, I have gnashed my teeth at myself, and suffered from months of insomnia. Such has invariably been my way.

For a long time past I have been belying my own personality by calling myself an irascible fellow. It has been pure rancour that has made me tell that lie against myself. As a matter of fact, I only played, so to speak, with my office callers, and with that officer, while all the while it was impossible for me to lose my temper. Every day I keep discovering in myself elements of the most opposite order conceivable, and can feel them swarming within me, and am aware that, to the very end of my life, they will continue so to swarm. Yet, often as they have striven to manifest themselves outwardly, I have never allowed them to do so. Of set purpose I always prevent that from happening, even though they torture me shamefully with their presence, and sometimes throw me into convulsions of *ennui* – ah, of how much *ennui* indeed! . . . Would not all this lead you, gentlemen, to suppose that I am expressing a sort of regret – that I am asking, as it were, your pardon? I am sure that you think so? Well, I can only say that I do not care a rap for your opinion.

No, I am not really bad-tempered. Rather, the fact is that I have never succeeded in being anything at all – whether kind-hearted or cruel, a villain or a saint, a hero or an insect. I just crouch here in this den of mine, and worry myself with the irritating, the useless, reflection that, after all, a man of parts cannot become anything; for only a fool does that. Yes (I say to myself), a man of the nineteenth century is morally bound, above all things, to be a colourless being, since a man of character, a man of action, is a being who is essentially limited. Such is the conviction which forty years have forced upon me. Forty years have been the span of my life, and forty years are a life-time – they are the most extreme limit of old age. To live longer than that seems indecent, base, immoral. Who would want to live longer than that? Answer me – sincerely, and from your heart. Well, *I* will tell you who want to live longer. Only fools and rogues. This I say to all old men in the world – to respected old men, to silver-haired old men, to old men of repute. Yes, I say it to the whole universe. And I have the right to say it, for I myself am going to live to be sixty, or seventy, or even eighty! . . . Wait a minute. Give me a moment to recover my breath. . . .

Probably you think that I am trying to amuse you? If so, you are wrong. I am not such a merry fellow as you suppose, or as you *may* suppose. At the same time, if, in irritation at my fooling (and I suspect that you *are* so irritated), you were to ask me exactly what sort of a man I am, I should reply that I am a collegiate assessor who, for my living (and for that purpose alone), served the State for a season, but who last year, on the death of a distant relative who left me six thousand roubles, retired from the service, and settled down in this den which you see. I used to live in it before, but since then I have taken up my abode in it for good. It is a mean, shabby room on the outskirts of the city, while for servant I have an old country-woman whose stupidity makes her crusty, and whose person smells to heaven. They tell me that the climate of St Petersburg is doing me harm, and that, in view of my insignificant means, it is sheer extravagance for me to go on living in the capital. Well, I know all that. Yes, I know it better than all the wisest and most experienced counsellors and tossers of heads in the world could possibly do. Yet I remain in St Petersburg, nor do I intend to leave it. No, I intend to remain where I am . . . Ah!

As though it matters one way or the other whether I stay here or take my departure!

By the way, what is it that all respectable men talk about most readily? Answer – about themselves. So I too will talk about myself.

2

I wish to tell you, gentlemen (no matter whether you care to hear it or not), why I have never even been able to become an insect. I solemnly declare to you that I have often *wished* to become an insect, but could never attain my desire. I swear to you, gentlemen, that to be overcharged with sensibility is an actual malady – a real, a grievous malady. For humanity's daily needs mere ordinary human sensibility ought to suffice, or about one-half or one-quarter of the sensibility which falls to the lot of the average educated man of our miserable nineteenth century, if he has the additional misfortune to reside in St Petersburg (the most abstract, the most contrived city on this terrestrial sphere of ours, where towns, in their psychology, may be contrived or uncontrived). At all events such sensibility as falls to the lot of (for instance) the generality of so-called independent persons and men of action ought to suffice. I dare wager, now, that you think that I am writing this with my tongue in my cheek, and solely to make fun of men of action; that you think that it is sheer bad taste that is making me rattle my sword in the way that that officer used to do? Yet, to tell the truth, gentlemen, who would be vain of one's weaknesses while at the same time one is using them as a means for poking fun at others?

Yet why should I *not* do this? All men do it. All men are proud of their weaknesses, and I, perhaps, more so than my fellows. Let us not quarrel about it. It may be that I have used an awkward expression. Yet I am persuaded that not only is excess of sensibility, but also sensibility of any kind whatsoever, a malady. Of that I have not the smallest doubt in the world. For the moment, however, let us drop the point. Tell me this: how is it that always, and of set purpose, as it were, and at the very moment – yes, at the very moment – when I have appeared to be most in a position to appreciate the finer shades of 'the great and the beautiful' *(to use the term once current amongst us), I have not only invariably failed to recognise as unseemly, but also have never failed to commit, actions which – well, in a word, actions which all men commit, but which I have always perpetrated just when I was most acutely sensible that I ought not to do them? The more I have recognised what is good and what constitutes 'the great and the beautiful', the deeper I have plunged into the mire, and the more I have been ready to smear myself over with the sticky stuff. But the most curious point of all is this – that the mood which I have described never seemed to be a mere fortuitous happening with me, but my permanent, my normal, condition, and therefore neither a weakness nor a vice. Consequently I have gradually come to lose all desire to combat this failing of mine. Indeed, things have reached the point that I almost believe (I might almost say, I *wholly* believe) that it is my normal condition. At first, however – i.e., at the actual beginning of things – I suffered terrible pangs in the struggle against my weakness, for I never could bring myself to believe that other men were not in the same position as I. Yet I kept the fact a secret close-locked in my breast, for I was ashamed of it then, and am ashamed of it now – yes, ashamed of the fact that I used to experience a sort of mysterious, abnormal, base gratification in recalling to my memory (say) some filthy nocturnal revel in St Petersburg, and in recognising that once again I had acted foully, but that what had been done could never be undone. Inwardly and secretly I often licked my lips at the thought of these revels, and chewed the cud of my recollections until their bitterness turned to a sort of base, accursed sweetness, and then to an actual, an assured, sensation of delight. Yes, I say of delight, of delight. I insist upon that. I often told myself that I would greatly like to know whether the same delight fell to the lot of other men. First of all, however, let me explain to you wherein that delight lay. It lay in a clear consciousness of my degradation – in a feeling that I had reached the last wall, and that the whole thing was base, and could never be otherwise, and that no escape therefrom was to be looked for, and that it was not possible for me to become a different man, and that, even if I still retained sufficient faith and energy to become a different man, I should not wish to become so, but that I would rather do nothing at all in the matter, since to undergo such a change might not be worth my while. And the chief thing about it was that one felt that the process was ruled by the normal, the fundamental, laws of acute sensibility, added to the inertia which arises from the working of those laws;

wherefore one was never likely to alter, nor yet to lift a finger to effect an alteration. Hence may be deduced the fact that over-sensibility causes a villain to hug his villainy to himself if he really *perceives* that he is a villain. . . . However, enough of this. Have you understood all that I have said? Can you explain to me what that delight of mine consisted of? No; so I will explain it myself. I will pursue the matter to the end, seeing that I have taken up my pen to write.

I am extremely self-conscious. Also, no hunchback, no dwarf, could be more prone to resentment and to offence than I. I have been through moments when, had I happened to receive a blow in the face, I should have been glad! Yes, I say it in all seriousness, that I should have derived the greatest possible gratification from a blow – the gratification of being able to feel desperate (since it is in desperation that one finds one's most glorious moments, especially when one has recognised that one cannot possibly draw back from the position taken up). Yes, a blow, and nothing but a blow, can wholly erase the consciousness of the grease in which one has been rubbed. Yet, averse though I am to scenes, it has always befallen me that *I* have been the offending party; as well as that (a still more shameful thing) I have been at fault without actually having transgressed – I have been, as it were, guilty through the mere working of the laws of nature. In the first place, I have often been at fault in that I have thought myself cleverer than anyone else with whom I have come in contact. Such has always been my way. Sometimes, though – would you believe it? – I have felt sorry for this. At all events I know that, all my life long, I have preferred to look people under the eyes rather than in them. And in the second place, I have often been at fault in that, if there lies within me any nobility of soul, such ability has never been able to do anything for me beyond torment me with a conscious-ness of the utter uselessness of possessing it. I have never been able to *do* anything with that nobility, for the reason that, however much an offender might strike me in obedience to the laws of nature, it is not feasible to forgive laws of nature, nor yet to overlook them, while, despite the existence of those laws, an insult still remains an insult. Hence, were I able to divest myself of all magnanimity, and to take revenge upon each and every person who offended me, I should never really be able to revenge myself upon such persons, for the reason that, in all probability, I should never be able finally to make up my mind to any given course of action, even if I had the power to carry it out. Why should I be so unable to make up my mind? On that subject I have a word or two to say.

3

People who are able to wreak vengeance upon an assailant, and, in general, to stand up for themselves – how do they do it? It can only be supposed that, momentarily, their whole being is possessed by a desire for revenge, and that no other element is, for the time being, within them. A man of that sort goes as straight to his goal as a mad bull charges with lowered crest; and nothing but a stone wall will stop him. (*Apropos*, such persons – that is to say, independent persons and men of action – make no bones about *yielding* to the wall. For them a wall is not an excuse for turning aside [as it is for us, the men of thought, and therefore the men who do nothing]; it is not a pretext for swerving from the path [a pretext in which, as a rule, no one – not even oneself – believes, but for which one is nevertheless thankful]. No, they just come to a halt before it. For them a wall connotes something calming, something morally decisive, final, and even mystical. . . . But about the wall later.) I do not consider an independent man of that type to be the real, the normal, man as his fond mother, Nature, who has borne him upon earth, would have him be. Yet I envy such a man with all the power of my spleen. True, he is gross – but then the normal man may *have* to be gross. How, indeed, do you know that his grossness is not one of his very best points? Anyway I daily grow more and more confirmed in my suspicion that if he were to take the antithesis of the normal man – that is to say, the man of acute sensibility, the man who hails, not from Nature's womb, but from a chemical retort (this approaches a little nearly to mysticism – a thing which I also suspect) – the man born of the retort would sometimes feel so conscious that he was outclassed by his antithesis, the man of action, that he would come to look upon himself, despite his acute sensibility, as a mouse rather than as a human being. A very sensitive mouse, it is true (he would say to himself), yet none the less a mouse; whereas the other is a man, and therefore, et cetera, et cetera. Above all things, it would be he – he, the man of sensibility – who, of his own volition, would dub himself a mouse. He would ask no one else's opinion on the matter. This is an important point. Next let us observe the mouse in action. Suppose, for example, that it receives an insult (and it nearly always *is* so receiving an insult), and that it wishes to revenge itself. Perhaps it will be capable of harbouring malice in its breast to an even greater extent than *l'homme de la nature et de la vérité*. Yes, a mean, debased little yearning to repay the offender in his own coin might wax in that mouse's bosom in an even meaner way than it would do in that of *l'homme de la nature et de la vérité*, since the innate grossness of the latter would cause him to look upon revenge as bare justice, whereas the mouse, with its hypersensibility, might very possibly deny the existence of such justice. Lastly we come to the act itself – to the actual deed of revenge. By this time the unfortunate mouse will have augmented the original insult by surrounding itself, through doubts and questionings, with such a number of other insults – it will have added to the main question such a string of questions which are still undecided – that involuntarily it will have collected about itself a fatal quagmire, a stinking morass, of misunderstandings, emotions, and, lastly, spittle discharged at it by the independent persons, judges, and dictators who are solemnly standing around it in a ring, and saluting the little animal with full-throated laughter. Naturally nothing will be left for the mouse to do but to make a disdainful gesture with its little paw, indulge in a smile of deprecatory contempt wherein even the smiler itself will have no belief, and retire shamefacedly into its hole. There, in its dirty, stinking underworld, our poor insulted, brow-beaten mouse will soon have immersed itself in a state of cold, malignant, perpetual rancour. For forty long years (so it may very well be) it will continue to recall to its mind the most minute, the most shameful, details of the insult which it has sustained, and to add to them, as it does so, other details more shameful still, and to taunt and worry itself with its own fancies. Of those fancies it will be ashamed, yet it will nevertheless remember them all, exaggerate them all, and even imagine to itself things which have never happened, on the mere pretext that one day it may obtain its revenge, and that therefore it must, in the meanwhile, forget nothing. Or perhaps it *will* actually embark upon a scheme of revenge; but if it does so the thing will be done only by fits and starts, and from behind a stone, and incognito, and in a manner which makes it clear that the mouse distrusts alike its right to wreak vengeance and the ultimate success of its scheme, since it knows in advance that its poor attempts at retribution will bring upon its own head a hundred times more suffering than will fall to the lot of the person against whom the vengeance is aimed, but upon whom not so much as a scratch will be inflicted. Yes, upon its very deathbed the mouse will again recall the whole story, with compound interest added.

Now, it is just in this same cold, loathsome semi-mania, this same half-belief in oneself, this same conscious burying of oneself in the underworld for forty years, this same voluntarily imagined, yet privately distrusted, powerlessness to escape from one's position, this same poison of unsatisfied wishes that for ever penetrates inwards, this same fever of vacillation, of resolutions adopted for all eternity, and of regrets that come upon one in a moment, that there lies the essence of the strange delight of which I have spoken. So subtle is this delight, so elusive to the senses, that merely limited persons, or persons who merely possess a strong nervous system, cannot grasp a single one of its features. 'Perhaps, too', you may add with a simper, 'persons who have never received a blow in the face cannot understand it?' – thereby implying that, at some date or another during my life, I have received such a blow, and therefore am speaking as an expert. Yes, I dare wager that that is what you are thinking. Do not disturb yourselves, gentlemen. Never once have I received a blow in the face – though I do not care a pin what *your* imaginings on the subject may be. My only regret is that I have dealt so few blows in my life. . . . But enough of this. Suppose we say no more concerning this theme which you seem to find so extraordinarily interesting? Let me quietly continue what I was saying about strong-nerved individuals who do not understand the higher refinements of the pleasure which I have described.

Good people who, under other circumstances, bellow as loudly as bulls (of course, we must suppose that the performance does them infinite credit) at once become mute in the face of the Impossible. By the Impossible I mean the stone wall of which I have spoken. What stone wall, do you say? Why, the stone wall constituted of the laws of nature, of the deductions of learning, and of the science of mathematics. When, for instance, people of this kind seek to prove to you that you are descended from an ape,* it is of no use for you to frown; you must just accept what they say. When, again, they seek to prove to you that a single drop of your fat is of more essential value to you than the bodies of a hundred thousand men who resemble yourself, and that by this deduction there become finally resolved the so-called virtues and duties and other inventions of unreason and prejudice, you must just accept what they tell you, and make up your mind to do nothing at all, since the formula that twice two make four is mathematics. To that find an objection if you can!

'Pardon us', so these people bawl, 'but you simply *cannot* refute what we tell you. Twice two make four; Nature does not ask *your* leave for that; she has nothing to do with *your* wishes on the subject, no matter whether you approve of her laws or not. You must just take her as she is, and, with her, her results. A wall still remains a wall', – and so forth, and so forth. . . . Good Lord! What have *I* to do with the laws of Nature, or with arithmetic, when all the time those laws and the formula that twice two make four do not meet with my acceptance? Of course, I am not going to beat my head against a wall if I have not the requisite strength to do so; yet I am not going to *accept* that wall merely because I have run up against it, and have no means to knock it down.

Does a wall, forsooth, constitute a full-stop, a signal for a cessation of the struggle, for the mere reason that it and the formula that twice two make four are one? Oh, blindness of blindnesses! What, rather, we should all do is to comprehend everything, to envisage everything – to comprehend and to envisage every impossibility and every stone wall; to accept no single impossibility, no single stone wall, if we do not feel inclined to accept it; to attain (in spite of the most inevitable combinations and the most refutative conclusions of logic) to the eternal truth that one may be at fault even in regard to a stone wall, no matter how much one may *seem* not to be at fault; lastly, on recognising that fact, to subside silently, and with lips compressed to resignation, and with a bitter-sweet feeling in one's heart, into a state of inertia, there to dream that one need not *really* be angry with anyone, since one's reasons for being so never existed, and never will exist, and have become changed, and shuffled, and substituted for one another, and half obliterated (though how, or by whom, one cannot think, except that those unknown factors and changes cause one's head to ache more and more as the mysteries in the question remain unsolved).

4

'Ha, ha, ha! Then we presume that you would find pleasure even in toothache?' you say to me with a grin?

'Well, why not?' answer I. 'Even toothache may afford one gratification. I myself have had it for a month, so I know what it means. When one has toothache one does not, of course, sit glowering in silence; one groans aloud. But those groans are not candid ones – they are uttered with suppressed venom; and in such a venomous state as that anything may turn to a jest. In reality those groans express the sufferer's *delight*. If he found no pleasure in them, he would not groan.'

Yes, you have suggested an excellent theme to me, gentlemen, and I will hasten to exploit it. Those groans express, firstly, the degrading futility of one's complaint, a legalised tyranny of nature which one despises, but from which one, unlike nature, is bound to suffer. They also express a sense of the fact that at the moment one has no other foe than the pain; a sense of the fact that one is utterly at the mercy of one's teeth; a sense of the fact that Providence is in a position either to will that your teeth shall cease on the instant to ache or to will that they shall go on aching another three months; and, lastly, a sense of the fact that if you do not agree with, but, on the contrary, protest against, the situation, your only resource, your only comfort, will be either to cut your throat or to go on beating the walls of your room ever harder and harder with your fists, since there is nothing else for you to do. Now, all these dire self-insultings, self-mockings, at length lead to a pleasure which often attains to supreme heights of voluptuousness. Let me beg of you, gentlemen, to seize the first opportunity of listening to the groans of a cultured man of the nineteenth century who is suffering from toothache. But this you should do only on the second or the third day of his malady, when he is beginning to groan in an altogether different manner from what he has done on the first day (when he will groan simply from the pain); when he is beginning to groan, not as a rude peasant, but as a man who has felt the touch of European progress and civilisation; when he is beginning to groan as a man who has 'divorced himself from the soil and from vulgar principles' (to use the phrase now current). Well, by that time his groans will have become malicious and meanly irascible; and though he may continue them whole nights and days at a stretch, he will be aware all the time that he is doing himself no good by his utterances, but merely uselessly angering and annoying himself and others. Better than anyone else will he be aware that his family, as also the public before whom he is cutting such a figure, have for a long while been listening to him with disgust; that they think him an utter rascal, and have it in mind that he might just as well have groaned in a simpler manner (that is to say, without any turns or roulades), since his present style of groaning is due simply to temper, and is leading him to play the fool out of sheer viciousness. Now, all this self-expression, all these insults to others, connote a certain voluptuous delight. 'I am disturbing you', you can say to your friends, 'and driving you to distraction, and preventing everyone in the house from sleeping. Very well. Pray do not sleep, but join me in my constant recognition of the fact that I have got the toothache. I am no longer the hero whom I have hitherto seemed, but only a public nuisance. Very well; be it so. I am very glad that you have found me out. Do you dislike having to listen to my villainous groans? Then go on disliking it, and I will execute a few more of these infernal roulades.' Do you understand it *now*, gentlemen? No, I wager that you do not. It is clear that I must develop and expound my theme much further if you are ever to comprehend all the ins and outs of the pleasure which I mean. You laugh, do you? Then I am delighted. If my jests are in bad taste, and rude, and obscure, and halting, that arises from the fact that I have no self-respect. Indeed, what man of sensibility could possess self-respect?

5

How could any man respect himself who wilfully takes pleasure in a consciousness of his self-abasement? I do not say this out of any feeling of puling regret, for never at any time have I found it possible to say, 'Father, forgive me, and I will sin no more.' This is not so much because I have actually felt myself *incapable* of uttering the words as because they have always come too easily to my lips. And whenever I have said them, what has happened next? Why, that, as though bound to fall, I have plunged straight into sin, when all the time I have been innocent both in thought and intent. A worse thing could not be. Next I have felt softened in heart, and shed tears, and reproved myself, and seen things as

they were, and felt unclean of soul. Yet for this I cannot very well
blame the laws of Nature, since to offend against them has been
the chief, the constant, occupation of my life. It is a degrading fact
to have to recall, but the fact remains. Then, a moment or two
later, I have always angrily reminded myself that my whole
conduct has been false – horribly, gratuitously false (by 'it', of
course, I mean all my regrets, my softenings of heart, my vows of
regeneration). So I would ask you, gentlemen – what caused me
to rack and torture myself in this way? Well, the answer is that I
always found it irksome merely to sit with folded hands. That is
why I have given myself up to so much wrongdoing. Mark what
I say, gentlemen, for what I say is true, and will give you the key
to the whole business. Of set purpose I used to devise oppor-
tunities for ordering my existence in such a way as to – well, as at
least to see a certain amount of life. For instance, I have often been
careful to take offence at something – not for any good reason,
but merely because I wanted to. Gentlemen, you yourselves know
that if one takes causeless offence – the sort of offence which one
brings upon oneself – one ends by being really, and in very truth,
offended. I have been at pains, all my life, to play tricks of this
sort; with the result that I have come to be destitute of any sort of
self-control. Also, I have twice tried to fall in love; but I can assure
you, gentlemen, that I suffered greatly in the doing so! One's heart
may not *seem* to be suffering as the smiles pass over one's face,
yet one *is* in pain all the while, and that in a very real, a very
demonstrable, fashion, since at such times one is jealous, and
above oneself. The sole cause of it all, gentlemen, is *ennui*; yes,
the sole cause of it all is *ennui*. The fact is that one comes to feel
crushed with the tedium, the conscious folding of the hands in
contemplation, which is the direct, the inevitable, the automatic
outcome of sensibility. Of this I have spoken above. . . . I repeat,
therefore, I earnestly repeat, that all men of independence and
action – men who are men of action because they are *prone* to
action – are both gross and limited in their purview. How is this
to be explained? Thus. Such men are led by their limitations to
mistake approximate and secondary causes for primary, * and so
to persuade themselves, more easily and more readily than other
men do, that they have an assured basis for their action, and
therefore may cease to trouble themselves further. That is the
truth, and the whole truth, of the matter. To embark upon action
one must first of all feel perfectly sure of oneself, so that no doubts

as to the wisdom of that action may remain. But how does a man like myself bring himself to the requisite state of assurance? Whence do I derive my primary causes? Whence my bases? Well, first of all I begin thinking things over; which has the effect of leading each original cause thought of to attract to itself some cause a good deal more primary, more original, still. And it is in this that there lies the essence of self-realisation and thought (though perhaps it is also the law of Nature). What is the result? Always one and the same thing. You will remember that, just now, I spoke of revenge (though perhaps you did not altogether follow me?). I said that a man may wreak vengeance because he believes it to be justice; wherefore he has found his original cause for action in justice, and may feel sure of himself, and proceed to wreak his vengeance quietly, and with success, since he is persuaded that what he is doing is altogether right and honourable. But, for my part, I never can perceive either justice or virtue in such a course: wherefore, if I embark upon a scheme of revenge, I do so, rather, out of malice. Of course, malice *may* succeed in overcoming one's doubts – it *may* serve (and with perfect success, too) as a first cause for action (though it is nothing of the sort); but what am I to do if even malice be wanting in me (which is the point whence I originally started)? Under the accursed laws of sensibility, malice becomes subject to a process of chemical disintegration, since it always happens that if a given object of action be volatile, the reasons for such action easily turn to gas, and responsibility disappears, and the offence ceases to have been an offence at all – it becomes merely a delusion wherein (as in toothache) no one is guilty, and wherefrom there is no other way of escape than from toothache – namely, by beating one's head against the wall. Perhaps, in despair of finding a first cause for action, one shrugs one's shoulders? Well, my advice is blindly and unthinkingly to leave first causes alone, and to give oneself up to one's impulses, and, for once in a while, to let volition lie altogether in abeyance. That is to say, either hate or love, but in any case do anything rather than sit with folded hands. If you do this I wager that by the day after tomorrow (at the very latest) you will have come to despise yourself for having ever got into a fluster at all; with the result that once again you will relapse calmly into inertia and the blowing of soap-bubbles. Ah, gentlemen, at least I can look upon myself as a wise man in that I have never succeeded in beginning or ending *anything*. Grant that I am a foolish, useless, troublesome chatterer, as we all are – yes, grant that: yet may not the one true function of every man of sensibility be to act as a chatterer – to act, that is to say, as a dissipator of airy trifles into space?

6

If only I had never done anything but out of sheer laziness! How I should have respected myself! Yes, I should have respected myself for the reason that I *was* capable of being lazy – that in me there *was* at least one positive quality of which I could rest assured. If you were to ask me, 'Who are you?' I should be thankful to be able to say, 'A lazy man.' Yes, I place it beyond doubt that I should like it to be said of myself that I am a sluggard. 'A lazy man' – in that there is connoted a whole calling, a whole destiny, a whole career! Do not laugh at me. What I say is true. Once upon a time I used to belong to a leading club, and to cultivate the art of self-respect; and among my club acquaintances there was a man whose lifelong boast it was that he was an infallible judge of 'Chateau Lafitte'.* Upon this accomplishment he looked as a positive merit, and was never in doubt about it; with the result that he died, if not with a quiet conscience, at all events respectably. And he was right in his way of life. I, too, used to wish to have a similar career. I, too, longed to become a sluggard and a glutton – though not *merely* a sluggard and a glutton, but a sluggard and a glutton who could sympathise with 'the great and the beautiful'. Does that meet with your approval? It is a long time now since I had such fancies; yet all through my forty years of subterranean life that craze for 'the great and the beautiful' has remained as an obsession. Once upon a time things were different. Once upon a time I longed for a congenial sphere of activity in which I should be able ceaselessly to drink to the health of 'the great and the beautiful'. Yes, I used to seek every possible opportunity of dropping a tear into my cup before emptying a bumper to the health of 'the great and the beautiful'. I used to refer everything in the world to that standard, and, even in regard to the most damnable and indisputable rubbish, would first of all consult 'the great and the beautiful', and be as ready with my tears as a wet sponge. For instance, an artist would paint some picture or another, and I would hasten to drink to the health of the artist who had painted that picture, since I loved only 'the great and the beautiful'. Or an author would write some book or another, and again I would hasten to drink to the health of the author who had written that book, since I loved only 'the great and the beautiful'.

Also, I was firmly persuaded that I ought to be looked up to for this; so that at any time I was ready to put a man through his paces who refused to show me that respect. To live in peace, and to die with *éclat* – yes, that constituted my whole aim and object in life. I even dreamed of growing a fat stomach, developing a triple chin, and fashioning for myself a purple nose, in the hope that everyone who met me would exclaim as he gazed upon my figure, 'See, there goes something *substantial*, something *positive*!' Well, they might have said that as much as they liked; for, in this negative age, gentlemen, it is always pleasant to hear of anything positive.

7

But these are mere golden dreams. Who was it first said, first propounded the theory, that man does evil only because he is blind to his own interests, but that if he were enlightened, if his eyes were opened to his real, his normal interests, he would at once cease to do evil, and become virtuous and noble for the reason that, being now enlightened and brought to understand what is best for him, he would discern his true advantage only in what is good (since it is a known thing that no man of set purpose acts against his own interests), and therefore would of necessity also *do* what is good? Oh, the simplicity of the youth who said this! Oh, the utter artlessness of the prattler! To begin with, since when, during these thousands of years, has man ever acted solely in accordance with his own interests? What about the millions of facts which go to show that only too often man knowingly (that is to say, with a full comprehension of what is his true advantage) puts that advantage aside in favour of some other plan, and betakes himself to a road, to risks, to the unknown, to which no agent nor agency has compelled him, as though, unwilling to follow the appointed path, he preferred to essay a difficult and awkward road along which he must feel his way in darkness? Would it not almost seem as though the directness, the voluntariness, of such a course had for him a greater attraction than any advantage? Advantage, indeed? What, after all, *is* advantage?

Would *you*, gentlemen, undertake exactly to define wherein human advantage consists? What if human advantage not only *may*, but *does*, consist of the fact that, on certain occasions, man may desire, not what is good for him, but what is bad? And if this be so, if this really be so, the rule falls to the ground at once. What is your opinion about it? Can it be so? I see you smiling. Well, smile away, gentlemen, but also answer me this: Can human interests *ever* be properly reckoned up? May there not always remain interests which never have been, never can be, included in any classification? You, gentlemen, take your lists of human interests from averages furnished by statistics and economic formulæ. Your lists of interests include only prosperity, riches, freedom, tranquillity, and so forth, and anyone who openly and knowingly disagreed with those lists would, in your opinion (as in mine also, for that matter), be either an obscurantist or a madman. Would he not? But the most surprising point is this – that statists, savants, and lovers of the human race never fail, in their summing up of human interests, to overlook *one interest in particular*. This interest is never taken into account in the shape in which it ought to be taken; and this fact vitiates all their calculations. Yet, were they to add this interest to their summaries, no great harm would be done. The mischief lies in the fact that this particular interest declines to fall under any particular heading, or to enter into any particular schedule. For instance, I might have a friend – as also might you yourselves, gentlemen (for who has not?) – who, when about to embark upon a given piece of work, might tell one, clearly and grandiloquently, that he intends to proceed strictly on lines of truth and reason. He might even go so far as to speak with emotion and enthusiasm of the nature of true, normal human interests, and with a smile to inveigh against short-sighted dolts who do not understand either their own interests or the proper meaning of virtue. Yet within only a quarter of an hour, and without any sudden, unforeseen event having arisen – merely in accordance with something which is stronger than all his other interests put together – this same man may cut straight across what he himself has said – that is to say, cut straight across both the dictates of reason and his own true interests and everything else! Yet this friend of mine is but one of a type; wherefore the fault cannot be laid at his door alone. May there not, therefore, exist something which to most men is even dearer than their true interests? Or, not to infringe the logical sequence, may there not exist some supreme interest of interests (the additional interest of which I am speaking) which is greater and more absorbing than any other interest, and for which man, if the need should arise, is ready to contravene every law, and to lose sight alike of common sense, honour, prosperity, and ease – in a word, of all the things which are fair and expedient – if haply he can gain for himself that primal, that supreme, advantage which he conceives to be the dearest thing on earth?

'Ah well, there are interests and interests', you might interrupt me at this point. Pardon me, gentlemen, but I ought to make it clear that, not to juggle with words, this interest of which I am speaking is a notable one, and escapes all classification, and shatters every system which has ever been established by lovers of the human race for that race's improvement. In short, let it be understood that it is an interest which introduces general confusion into everything. Before naming to you that interest I should like to damn myself for ever in your eyes by telling you bluntly that all those fine systems of, and schemes for, demonstrating to mankind its true, its normal, interests, and for explaining to it that, so long as it strives to attain its true interests, it will ever grow better and more noble, are so much dialectic. Yes, I say so much dialectic. To maintain theories of renovating the human race through systems of classification of true interests is, in my opinion, about the same thing as – well, about the same thing as to maintain that man grows milder with civilisation, and, consequently, less bloodthirsty, less addicted to fighting. Logically, perhaps, that *does* happen; yet he is so prone to systems and to abstract deductions that he is for ever ready to mutilate the truth, to be blind to what he sees, and deaf to what he hears, so long only as he can succeed in vindicating his logic. Of this let me give an example which will be clear to all. Look around you at the world. Everywhere you will see blood flowing in streams, and as merrily as champagne. Look at our nineteenth century; look at Napoleon – the great Napoleon and the modern one;* look at North America,* with its everlasting 'Union'; look at the present caricature of Schleswig-Holstein.* What has civilisation done to instil greater mildness into our bosoms? Civilisation develops in man nothing but an added capacity for receiving impressions. That is all. And the growth of that capacity further augments man's tendency to seek pleasure in blood-letting. Nothing else has civilisation conferred upon him. You may have noticed that the most enthusiastic blood-letters have almost invariably been the most civilised of men – men whose shoes even Attila* and Stenka Razin* would have been unworthy to unloose; and if such men as the former have not bulked in the public eye quite so largely as have Attila and Stenka Razin, it is only because the former have been too numerous, too transitory. At all events civilisation has rendered man, if not more bloodthirsty, at least a worse (in the sense of a meaner) thirster after blood than before. Once upon a time he considered blood-letting to be just retribution, and could therefore, with a quiet conscience, exterminate anyone whom he wanted to; but now we account blood-letting a crime – and indulge in that crime even more than in former days. Which, then, is the worse of the two? Well, judge for yourselves. It is said that Cleopatra* (if I may take an instance from Roman history) loved to thrust golden pins into the breasts of her slaves, and took pleasure in the cries and contortions of her victims. Possibly you may say that all this happened in a comparatively barbarous age – that even at the present day the times are barbarous – that golden pins are still being thrust into people's breasts – that though man, in many things, has learnt to see clearer now than he used to do in *more* barbarous ages, he has not yet learnt to act wholly as reason and science would have him do. Yet all the while, I know, you are persuaded in your own minds that man is bound to improve as soon as ever he has dropped some old, bad customs of his, and allowed science and healthy thought alone to nourish, to act as the normal directors of, human nature. Yes, I know that you are persuaded that eventually man will cease to err *of set purpose*, or to let his will clash with his normal interests. On the contrary (say you), science will in time show man (though, in our opinion, it is superfluous to do so) that he does not possess *any* will or initiative of his own, and never has done, but that he is as the keyboard of a piano, or as a sprig inside a hurdy-gurdy. Above all, science will show him that in the world there exist certain laws of nature which cause everything to be done, not of man's volition, but of nature's, and in accordance with her laws. Consequently, say you, those laws will only need to be *explained* to man, and at once he will become divested of all responsibility, and find life a much easier thing to deal with. All human acts will then be mathematically computed according to nature's laws, and entered in tables of logarithms* which extend to about the 108,000th degree, and can be combined into a calendar.* Better still, there will be published certain carefully revised editions of this calendar (after the manner of modern encyclopedias) in which everything will be enumerated and set down so exactly that henceforth the world will cease to know wrong-doing, or any occasion for the same.

Then (I am supposing *you* still to be speaking) there will arise new economic relations – relations all ready for use, and calculated with mathematical precision, so that in a flash all possible questions will come to an end, for the reason that to all possible questions there will have been compiled a store of all possible answers. Then there will arise the Crystal Palace.* Then – well, *then*, in a word, there will dawn the millennium! . . . Of course, though (it is *I* who am now speaking), you cannot very well guarantee that things will not have come to be excessively dull, seeing that there will be nothing left for us to do when everything has been computed beforehand and tabulated? By this I do not mean to say that things will not also be excessively *regular*. I only mean to say, is there anything which dullness will not lead men to devise? For instance, out of sheer *ennui*, golden pins may again be inserted into victims' breasts. That is all. It is shameful to have to think that into everything which is goodly man loves to thrust golden pins! Yes, he is a gross animal, phenomenally gross. Rather, he is not so much gross as ungrateful to a degree which nothing else in the world can equal. For instance, I should not be surprised if, amid all this order and regularity of the future, there should suddenly arise, from some quarter or another, some gentleman of lowborn – or, rather, of retrograde and cynical – demeanour who, setting his arms akimbo, should say to you all: 'How now, gentlemen? Would it not be a good thing if, with one consent, we were to kick all this solemn wisdom to the winds, and to send those logarithms to the devil, and to begin to live our lives again according to our own stupid whims?' Yet this would be as nothing; the really shameful part of the business would be that this gentleman would find a goodly number of adherents. Such is always man's way. And he might act thus for the shallowest of reasons; for a reason which is not worth mentioning; for the reason that, always, and everywhere, and no matter what his station, man loves to act as he *likes*, and not necessarily as reason and self-interest would have him do. Yes, he will even act straight against his own interests. Indeed, he is sometimes *bound* to do so. Such, at least, is my notion of the matter. His own will, free and unfettered; his own untutored whims; his own fancies, sometimes amounting almost to a madness – here we have that superadded interest of interests which enters into no classification, which for ever consigns systems and theories to the devil. Whence do savants have it that man needs a normal, a virtuous, will? What, in particular, has made these pundits imagine that what man most needs is a will which is acutely alive to man's interests? Why, what man most needs is an *independent* will – no matter what the cost of such independence of volition, nor what it may lead to. Yet the devil only knows what man's will——

8

'Ha, ha, ha!' I can imagine you interrupting me with a chuckle. 'Whether you choose to think so or not, there is no such thing in the world as human will. Science has so far dissected man as to make it absolutely clear that his volition and so-called freewill are but——'

Wait a moment, gentlemen. I was just going to say the same thing myself, though I confess that I was feeling a little nervous about it. I was just going to observe that the devil only knows what man's will depends upon, when suddenly (the Lord be thanked!) I recalled that precious science of yours, and broke off short. However, you have now said it for me. As a matter of fact, if ever there shall be discovered a formula which shall exactly express our wills and whims; if ever there shall be discovered a formula which shall make it absolutely clear what those wills depend upon, and what laws they are governed by, and what means of diffusion they possess, and what tendencies they follow under given circumstances; if ever there shall be discovered a formula which shall be mathematical in its precision, well, gentlemen, whenever such a formula shall be found, man will have ceased to have a will of his own – he will have ceased even to exist. Who would care to exercise his will-power according to a table of logarithms? In such a case man would become, not a human being at all, but an organ-sprig or something of the kind. What but the sprig of a hurdy-gurdy *could* a human being represent who was devoid either of desires or volition? Is it not so? Reckoning all the possibilities, could things ever come to be thus?

'Hm', you might conceivably reply, 'our wills mostly err

through adopting false views of our interests. Sometimes we will what is sheer rubbish, for the reason that in such rubbish we foolish fellows perceive the easiest way to the attainment of some presupposed advantage. But if all were to be tabulated and set forth on paper (which it would be quite an easy thing to do, seeing that to assume that man is incapable of learning a few laws of nature is senseless and absurd), there would, of course, be an end to our so-called power of volition. If, on the other hand, our volition were always to march with our reason, we should invariably exercise that reason in preference to our freewill, since such exercise of one's reasoning powers would prevent us from ever again desiderating foolish things, or wilfully cutting across our own judgment by desiderating for ourselves what would be harmful.' Well, *if* all desires and resolutions (of course, it is *I* who am now supposed to be speaking) can be exactly computed, for the reason that they are revealed to us beforehand by the laws of our so-called freewill, I do not really see that I am jesting when I say that something after the manner of tables *might* be compiled, and that we should be forced to exercise our volition only according to what might be found in them. Yet were those tables to tell me, to reckon for me, that, should I (say) point with my finger to an object, I should be doing so simply because it would have been impossible for me to do otherwise, or even to point to the object in question with any other finger than the one I used – well, in that case what element of freedom would remain to me, even though I were an educated man, and had gone through a course of science? In short, if things were so arranged, I might be able to forecast my life for (say) the next thirty years, and there would be nothing left for me to do, and I should not so much as require an intelligence. All that I should need to do would be to keep on reminding myself that never, and under no circumstances, will nature ask me what I *desire* to do, but must be taken just as she is rather than as what we would have liked her to be. Therefore, if our tendency is towards tables and calendars – yes, or even towards retorts – we shall just have to accept them. Nature is always herself, and therefore requires her retorts to be taken with her.

For me, however, all such matters are bagatelles. Pardon my philosophising like this, gentlemen, but it is the fruit of forty years underground, and you must not mind my building castles in the air. See here: reason is an excellent thing – I do not deny that for a moment; but reason is reason, and no more, and satisfies only the reasoning faculty in man, whereas volition is a manifestation of all life (that is to say, of human life as a whole, with reason and every other sort of appendage included). It is true that, in this particular manifestation of it, human life is all too frequently a sorry failure; yet it nevertheless *is* life, and not the mere working out of a square root. For my own part, I naturally wish to satisfy *all* my faculties, and not my reasoning faculty alone (that is to say, a mere twentieth portion of my capacity for living). For what does reason know? Reason only knows that man possesses a certain capability of apprehension. Anything else, believe me, it does *not* know. This may be poor comfort, yet why should it not be said? On the other hand, human nature acts as a whole, and with all that is contained in it; so that, whether conscious or unconscious, sane or mad, it is always human nature. Now, I suspect, gentlemen, that you regard me with pity, for you keep telling me that man can never be really enlightened or developed – he can never be what the *future* human being will be – through the fact that he knowingly desiderates for himself what is harmful to his best interests. This is mathematical deduction, you say. I do not dispute it. It *is* mathematical deduction. Yet *I* tell *you* (and for about the hundredth time) that there is one occasion, and one occasion only, when man can wilfully, consciously desiderate for himself what is foolish and harmful. This is the occasion when he yearns *to have the right* to desiderate for himself what is foolish and harmful, and to be bound by no obligation whatsoever to desiderate anything that is sensible. It is his crowning folly; it is wherein we see his ineradicable waywardness. Yet such folly may also be the best thing in the world for him, even though it work him harm, and contradict our soundest conclusions on the subject of interests. This is because it is possible for his folly to preserve to him, under all circumstances, the chief, the most valuable, of all his possessions – namely, his personality, his individuality. Yes, it is not I alone who maintain that this is the most priceless asset whereof man can boast. Of course, he *may* make his volition march with his reason, and the more so if the former does not abuse the latter, but uses it with moderation. Such a proceeding is expedient, and may, at times, even be praiseworthy; but only too often do we see volition clashing with reason, and – and—— Yet, do you know, gentlemen, *this too*, at times, may be both expedient and praiseworthy. For suppose man *not* to be innately foolish (in reality this could never be said of him, except in so far as that it might be urged that, if he be foolish, who in the world is wise?); yet, though he may not be foolish, he is at least monstrously ungrateful, phenomenally ungrateful. In fact, I believe that the best possible definition of man would be 'A creature which walks on two legs and is devoid of gratitude'. And this is not all – this is not his principal failing. No; his greatest failing is his constant immorality, which began with the Flood, and has lasted up to the present Schleswig-Holstein period of human history. Consequently, immorality being his leading weakness, so also is unreason, for it is an axiom that unreason arises from immorality. Try if it does not. Glance at the history of mankind, and tell me what you see there. Immensity? Well, what availed even the Colossus of Rhodes?* Not for nothing did some people maintain that it was the work of human hands, while others asserted that it had been fashioned by nature herself. Variety? Well, in all ages and in all nations, what has been the use of discriminating between certain uniforms worn by military men and civilians, so long as there were no non-uniformed people, nor yet any men of learning? Uniformity? Well, in history men fight and fight, and are fighting now, and have always fought, and fought again. I should imagine that *here* you see an *excess* of uniformity! Everything, therefore, which could possibly enter into the most disordered of imaginations might well be said of the history of the world. Yet there is one thing which could *not* be said of it – and that is, that it affords much of a spectacle of reason. If one were to state the contrary one would choke at the very first word. In particular, we are continually confronted, in history, with the diverting circumstance that there continually figure in its pages large numbers of moral, sensible men and scholars and lovers of the human race who make it their prime object in life to behave as morally and as sensibly as possible – to, as it were, enlighten their neighbours by proving to them the possibility of leading, in this world, both a moral and a sensible existence. Yet what is the good of all this? We know that, sooner or later, many of these philanthropists undergo a change, and display phases of a most unseemly order. Consequently, I would ask you – what are we to expect from man, seeing that he is a creature endowed with such strange qualities? You may heap upon him every earthly blessing, you may submerge him in well-being until the bubbles shoot to the surface of his prosperity as though it were a pond, you may give him such economic success that nothing will be left for him to do but to sleep and to eat dainties and to prate about the continuity of the world's history; yes, you may do all this, but none the less, out of sheer ingratitude, sheer devilment, he will end by playing you some dirty trick. He will imperil his comfort, and purposely desiderate for himself deleterious rubbish, some improvident trash, for the sole purpose that he may alloy all the solemn good sense which has been lavished upon him with a portion of the futile, fantastical element which forms part of his very composition. Yes, it is these same fantastical dreams, this same debased stupidity, that he most wishes to retain in order to feel assured of the one thing with which he cannot dispense – namely, of the knowledge that men are still men, and not keyboards of pianos over which the hands of Nature may play at their own sweet will, and continue so to play until they threaten to deprive him of all volition, save by rote and according to calendars. Moreover, even if man *were* the keyboard of a piano, and could be convinced that the laws of nature and of mathematics had made him so, he would still decline to change. On the contrary, he would once more, out of sheer ingratitude, attempt the perpetration of something which would enable him to insist upon himself; and if he could not effect this, he would then proceed to introduce chaos and disruption into everything, and to devise enormities of all kinds, for the sole purpose, as before, of asserting his personality. He would need but to launch a single curse upon the world, and the mere fact that man alone is able to utter curses (the one privilege by which he is differentiated from the other animals) would, through the very act of commination, effect his purpose for him – namely, the purpose of convincing himself that he really *is* a man, and not the keyboard of a piano. But if you were to tell me that all this could be set down in tables – I mean the chaos, and the confusion, and the curses, and all the rest of it – so that the possibility of computing everything might remain, and reason continue to rule the roost – well, in that case, I believe, man would *purposely* become a lunatic, in order to become devoid of reason, and therefore able to insist upon himself. I believe this, and I am ready to vouch for this, simply for the reason that every human act arises out of the circumstance that man is for ever striving to prove to his own satisfaction that he is a man and not an organ-sprig. And, however devious his methods, he *has* succeeded in proving it; however troglodyte-like his mode of working may have been, he *has* succeeded in proving it. So in future, perhaps, you will refrain from asserting that this particular interest of his is nugatory, or that his volition depends upon anything at all?

Also, you often tell me (or, rather, you tell me whenever you deign to favour me with a single word) that no one can deprive me of my freewill, and that I ought so to arrange matters that my freewill shall, of its own volition, coincide with my normal interest, and with the laws of nature, and with arithmetic.

Ah, gentlemen! How much freewill should I have left to me when we had come to tables and arithmetic – when only the rule that twice two make four had come to hold the board? However much twice two might make four, my will would, to the end, remain my will.

9

Gentlemen, I need hardly say that, so far, I have been jesting. Yet, poor as my jests may have been, not everything which I have said has been uttered in mockery: for some of my jests have been spoken through clenched teeth. Certain questions are disturbing my soul, and I beg of you to solve them. For instance, you say that you desire man to unlearn certain of his old customs, and to regulate his will according to the dictates of science and of sane thought. But how do you know that man not only *can*, but *must*, change? What leads you to suppose that the human will stands in need of being regulated? In short, how do you come to feel certain that such regulation of man's will would bring him any advantage, or that if he refrained from flying in the face of his real, his normal interests (as guaranteed by the deductions of reason and of arithmetic) such a course would *really* be good for him, or require to be made the law for all humanity? So far all this is only a proposition put forward by yourselves – a mere law (we must suppose) that has been made by logicians rather than by humanity as a whole. Perhaps you think me mad, gentlemen? Well, if so, I plead guilty; I quite agree with you. Man is essentially a constructive animal – an animal for ever destined to strive towards a goal, and to apply himself to the pursuit of engineering, in the shape of ceaseless attempts to build a road which shall lead him to an unknown destination. But that is just why man so often *turns aside* from the road. He turns aside for the reason that he is *constrained* to attempt the journey; he turns aside because, being at once foolish and an independent agent, he sometimes takes it into his head that, though the road in question may eventually bring him to a destination of some sort, that destination always lies ahead of him. Consequently, as an irresponsible child, he is led at times to disregard his trade as an engineer, and to give himself up to that fatal indolence which, as we know, is the mother of all vices. Man loves to construct and to lay out roads – of that there can be no question; but why does he also love so passionately to bring about general ruin and chaos? Answer me that. First of all, however, I myself have a word or two to say about it. May not his passion for bringing about general disorder (a passion which, we must admit, allows of no dispute) arise from the fact that he has an instinctive dread of *completely* attaining his end, and so of finishing his building operations? May it not be the truth that only from a distance, and not from close at hand, does he love the edifice which he is erecting? That is to say, may it not be that he loves to create it, but not to *live* in it – only to hand it over, when completed, to *les animaux domestiques*, in the shape of ants, sheep, and so forth?

Ants are creatures of quite a different taste. They are constantly constructing marvellous edifices, but ones that shall be for ever indestructible. From the antheap all respectable ants take their origin, and in it (probably) they meet their end. This does credit alike to their continuity and to their perseverance. On the other hand, man is a frivolous, a specious creature, and, like a chess-player, cares more for the process of attaining his goal than for the goal itself. Besides, who knows (for it never does to be too sure) that the aim which man strives for upon earth may not be contained in this ceaseless continuation of the process of attainment (that is to say, in the process which is comprised in the living of life) rather than in the aim itself, which, of course, is contained in the formula that twice two make four? Yet, gentlemen, this formula is not life at all; it is only the beginning of death! At all events men have always been afraid to think that twice two make four, and I am afraid of it too. Can it be, therefore, that, though man is for ever working to attain this formula, and though, in his search for it, he sails all the seas and sacrifices his whole life to the acquisition of his end, he fears *really* to succeed in the quest, for the reason that, if he were suddenly to come upon the formula, he would feel that he had nothing left to look for? Workmen, on completing their weekly tasks, receive their wages, and betake themselves to the tavern to make merry. Such is their weekly diversion. But whither can man in the mass betake himself? It is plain that he feels ill at ease when the end of his labour has really been reached. That is to say, he loves to attain, but not *completely* to attain; which, of course, is an exceedingly ridiculous *trait* in his character, and would appear to contain a paradox. In any case the formula that twice two make four is the factor which, of all others, he cannot stomach; nor do *I* look upon it in any other light than as an abomination, since it is a formula which wears an impertinent air as, meeting you on the road, it sets its arms akimbo, and spits straight in your face. True, I agree that, in its way, it is well enough; yet I also beg leave to say (if I must apportion praise all round) that the formula 'Twice two make five' is not without its attractions.

Why, then, are you so absolutely, so portentously, certain that one thing, and one thing only, is normal and positive – in a word, good – for mankind? Does reason never err in estimating what is advantageous? May it not be that man occasionally loves something besides prosperity? May it not be that he also loves *adversity*? And may not adversity be as good for him as is happiness? Certainly there are times when man *does* love adversity, and love it passionately; so do not resort to history for your justification, but, rather, put the question to *yourselves*, if you are men, and have had any experience of life. For my part, I look upon undivided love of prosperity as something almost indecent; for to cause an occasional catastrophe, come weal come woe, seems to me a very pleasant thing to do. Yet I am not altogether for adversity, any more than I am altogether for prosperity; what I most stand for is my personal freewill, and for what it can do for me when I feel in the right mood to use it. I know that adversity is not thought acceptable in vaudeville plays, and that in the Crystal Palace it would be a thing quite unthinkable, for the reason that, since adversity connotes a denial and a doubt, no edifice of the kind could exist wherein a doubt was harboured. Nevertheless, I feel certain that man never wholly rejects adversity (in the sense of chaos and disruption of his schemes); for adversity is the mainspring of self-realisation. When beginning these notes I said that, in my opinion, self-realisation is, for man, a supreme misfortune; yet I am sure that he loves it dearly, and that he would not exchange it for any other sort of delight. For example, adversity is immeasurably superior to the formula that twice two make four; for if the latter were ever to be found, what would there remain for us to do or to realise? All that there would remain for us to do would be to muzzle our five senses, and to relapse into a state of perpetual contemplation. The same result (namely, that there might remain nothing for us to do) might arise from self-realisation; yet in that case one could at least give oneself an occasional castigation, and revivify oneself. This might be a retrograde course to take, yet at least it would be better than nothing.

10

You believe, do you not, in a palace of crystal which shall be for ever unbreakable – in an edifice, that is to say, at which no one shall be able to put out his tongue, or in any other way to mock? Now, for the very reason that it must be made of crystal, and for ever unbreakable, and one whereat no one shall put out his tongue, I should fight shy of such a building. For do you not see that if the edifice were not a palace, but a hencoop, and rain were to begin falling, I might take refuge in that hencoop, yet should hardly be likely, out of mere gratitude for its shelter, to mistake it for the residence of a king? At this you may laugh, or you may even go so far as to say that, in such a matter, a hencoop would do as well as the most stately fane. If so, I should retort, 'Yes – provided that one's sole object in life is to avoid getting wet.'

But how if I were to take it into my head that one need not live for that purpose alone, and that if one *must* live, it were best done in a palace? I am supposing such to be my will, my desire. In that case you could not rid me of my desire by any method save that of abrogating my will-power. And even supposing such abrogation to be possible for you to accomplish, and that you had some counter-attraction to offer me, and that you could provide me with a new ideal, I might *still* decline to mistake a hencoop for a palace. And even if a palace of crystal were only a thing of dreams and, by the laws of nature, a sheer impossibility, and even if only my individual folly, added to certain old-established, irrational customs of my generation, had made me imagine it, what, even then, should I care if it *were* an impossibility? Would it not be all one to me whether it existed or not – or, rather, whether it existed or not so long as my desire for its existence ceased? . . . Again I see you smiling. Well, smile away. I take your smiles for what they are worth, for at least I am not in the habit of saying that I am surfeited when I am hungry, or that I do not know that my hopes are based upon something better than a mere compromise, an ever-recurring nought, which the laws of nature may (and, indeed, *do*) allow to exist. The crown of my desires is not a block of flats, with its tenements let as offices to dentists, or as homes to poor lodgers on thousand-year leases; but if you were to annul my volition, to erase my ideals, and to show me something *better*, I might then come to fall in with your views. To this you might reply that to convince me would not be worth your while; whereupon I might make a similar retort: after which we might solemnly discuss the matter a little further, until finally you decided that I was not deserving of your attention. I should not greatly care. For me there will always remain the underground.

Meanwhile, I go on living, and exercising my volition: and may my hand wither ere ever I use it to add so much as a brick to any block of tenements! Never mind that only a short while ago I rejected the idea of a crystal edifice, for the sole reason that I should not be able to put out my tongue at it. What I then said I did not say because I am fond of putting out my tongue at things, but because, of all buildings, an edifice whereat no one can mock is the only one that has not yet come into existence. On the contrary, of sheer gratitude I would cut out my tongue if matters could be so arranged that I should never at any time feel a desire to protrude that member. What care I that an edifice of such a kind is impossible, and that I must rest content with my present lodgings? Why should such desires occur to me at all? Merely in order that, eventually, I may come to the conclusion that my whole organisation is a fraud? Is that the object of it all? I do not believe it.

Yet of one thing I am certain – namely, that a denizen of underground ought always to ride himself upon the bit; for although for forty years he may sit silently in his den, let him once issue into the light of day, and straightway he will take the bit in his teeth, and continue talking, and talking, and talking. . . .

II

So at length, gentlemen, we have reached the conclusion that the best thing for us to do is to do nothing at all, but to sink into a

state of contemplative inertia. For that purpose all hail the underground! True, I said above that I profoundly envy the normal man;
yet, under the conditions in which I see him placed, I have no wish
to be he. That is to say, though I envy him, I find the underground
better, since at least one can—— Yet I am lying. I am lying because,
even as I know that two and two make four, so do I know that it
is not the underground which is so much better, but something
else, something else – something for which I am hungry, but which
I shall never find. Ah no! To the devil with the underground!

At least, though, I should find things better if I could bring
myself to believe a single word of all that I have written. I swear
to you, gentlemen, that not a single syllable of what I have been
jotting down enjoys my confidence. That is to say, I *believe* it all,
but at the same time I suspect – somehow I feel – that, throughout,
I have been lying like a bootmaker.

'Why, then, have you written it?' you might ask me; to which
I should reply –

'Supposing I were to submerge *you* somewhere for forty years,
and that you had no occupation to beguile the time, and that,
during the whole of those forty years, you were forced to keep
peering out from underground, what would become of *you* under
such circumstances? Can a man spend forty years alone, yet do
nothing at all?'

'But it is no shame, no degradation, to you', you might retort,
with a toss of the head. 'It is only natural for you to hunger for
life, but the mischief is that you seek to decide the *questions* of life
by a mass of logical tangles. How daring, how insolent, are your
sallies, though all the while you are shaking with fear! You talk
arrant nonsense, yet you are delighted with it. You give vent to
impertinences, yet you are afraid of them, and hasten to beg our
pardon. You assure us that you care for nothing, yet in the same
breath you come cringing to us for our opinion. You declare that
you speak through clenched teeth, yet the next moment you
attempt witticisms in order to make us laugh. In short, though
well aware that your witticisms are not witty, you appear to rest
perfectly satisfied with their literary merit. Possibly, in your time,
you have had to suffer, but at least you do not show any respect
for your suffering. A grain or two of truth may lie in you, yet not
an atom of reticence, since your petty vanity leads you to make a
show of everything – to befoul it, and to air it in the market-place.
You try to speak concisely, yet your nervousness leads you to spin

a perfect web of words, for the reason that you have not a particle of self-confidence, but only a sort of pusillanimous knavery. You keep praising self-knowledge, yet at the same time you continue to vacillate, for the reason that, though your mind be working, your heart is befogged with corruption. Without a pure heart there can be no full, no true, realisation of self. And what an impudent way you have with it all! What strings of questions you ask, and what fearful grimaces you make! Yet all of what you say is lies, lies from beginning to end.'

This speech I have, of course, invented for you out of my own head – another trick which living underground has taught me. You must remember that for forty years I, through a chink, have been listening to the kind of stuff which you usually utter. Yes, I have been listening to it, and thinking it over, until it is no great marvel that I have learnt it all by heart, and can set it down in more or less literary form.

But are you actually so credulous as to suppose that I intend to have it all printed, and to give it to you to read? True, I myself am rather puzzled to know why I keep on calling you 'gentlemen', and addressing you as though you were destined to be my readers. Confessions such as mine should never be printed, nor handed to others for perusal. At all events *I* have not sufficient self-confidence for that course, nor do I think it necessary. My reason for writing must be that the idea of it has entered my head and stuck there. That is how it must be.

Every man's reminiscences include things which he reveals, not to all men and sundry, but to his friends alone. Again, every man's reminiscences include things which he does not reveal even to his friends, but to himself alone, and then only under a close seal of secrecy. Lastly, every man's reminiscences include things which he hesitates to reveal even to himself. Of this latter category there soon becomes accumulated in the mind of every decent man a large store. The more decent he be, the larger will his store of such recollections become. Recently I decided to recall to my memory certain of my old experiences, but until now have always deferred doing so, through a feeling of uneasiness even at the idea. Now, however, that I am minded, not only to recall things, but to write them down, I wish, in particular, to try whether one can *ever* be really open with oneself – *ever* be really fearless of any item of truth. *En passant*, Heine* has said that a true autobiography is practically impossible, since every man lies to himself. In his

(Heine's) opinion, even Rousseau,* in his *Confessions*, lied – partly out of set purpose, and partly out of vanity. And I believe that Heine is right. I myself know how vanity may lead a man to impute whole crimes to himself; of the working of such vanity I have a good idea. But Heine was speaking of men who write their confessions *for the public eye*, whereas I wish to write but for myself alone. Let me therefore state, once and for all, that, though I may seem to be writing for the eye of a reader, I do so out of mere show, and for the reason that I find that that kind of writing comes easier. It is all mere form – all a mere empty form, for I shall never have a reader. This I have explained before.

Moreover, I do not wish to be restricted in the scope of my writing. Consequently I intend to observe therein no order or system. What I remember, that I shall write down.

Upon this you might catch me up, and say: 'If you do not count upon being read, why is it that you make these compacts with yourself, and set them down on paper? – the compacts, we mean, that you will observe no order or system in your writing, and that you will write down just what you remember, and so forth? To whom are you speaking? In whose eyes are you seeking to excuse yourself?'

I should merely reply: 'Wait and see.'

For it may be that there is a whole psychology of reasons for what I do. Possibly I am simply a coward. Or possibly it is that I have purposely imagined to myself a public in order to cut the better figure when I *really* come to write for the public. In short, there may exist a thousand reasons for my action.

Again, for precisely what reason, for precisely what purpose, do I desire to write? If not for the benefit of the public, why cannot I remember things without committing them to paper?

Certainly I *could* adopt that course; but on paper my reminiscences are more likely to come out regularly and in order. Besides, in doing so there will be something inspiring, and I shall be able to keep a better rein over myself, and to add a word or two here and there. Again, it is possible that I shall gain from the mere labour of writing a certain *relief*, for one oppressive reminiscence in particular is weighing heavily upon my mind – a reminiscence which recently came back to me, and remains in my thoughts like a musical *motif* which refuses to be banished. I must banish it somehow! A hundred others like it there are, yet at times this one in particular persists in standing out from the rest, and troubling me. Somehow I feel confident that, once it were written down, it would vanish for ever. Why should I not try the experiment?

Lastly, I wish to write because I am *ennuyé*, and have nothing in the world to do; whereas writing is at least work of a kind. They say that labour renders man good-hearted and honourable; wherefore I wish to avail myself even of *that* chance.

Today half-melted, yellow, dirty snow is falling. It was falling yesterday, and it does so nearly every day. I believe that it is that same half-melted snow which has once more recalled to me the episode of which I cannot rid my thoughts; so here goes for my confession *apropos* of the falling sleet.

PART II

Apropos of the Falling Sleet

When from the abyss, the darkness,
   A word of earnest prayer
Plucked your soul for an instant –
   For an instant dulled its care;
Wringing your hands, black curses
   You heaped upon your sin
As memory, that dread rider,
   Spurred with the rowels in.
Then did you, weeping, tell me
   The secrets of the past,
Till, torn, at bay, shame-stricken,
   Your soul stood bare at last . . . etc., etc., etc.

From a poem by Nekrasov*

I

I was then only twenty-four years old, and, so far, had lived a dull, ill-regulated existence that was wellnigh as solitary as that of a savage. I had no friends or intimates, and was gradually coming to confine myself more and more to my lodgings. In the same way, when working in my office, I never even looked at those around me, for I knew that my colleagues not only regarded me as an eccentric, but also felt for me a distinct distaste. Often I would ask myself why *I*, of all men, should excite such aversion. For instance, one of my comrades had a repellent, pox-riddled face that was almost ruffianly in its expression; it was a face of the kind (so it always seemed to me) with which no man would care to face the world; while another of my office-associates was so dirty in his person that he smelt aloud. Yet neither of these two gentlemen seemed in the least put about by this. They seemed to care not a pin about their faces, their clothes, or anything else. Neither the one nor the other of them seemed to think that he was detested; or, if he thought so, at least he did not care, so long as his superiors approved of his work. On the other hand, *I* was led by my *poltroon*

boundless vanity and pretentiousness to look upon myself with a dissatisfaction that, at times, amounted almost to loathing. Consequently I attributed to everyone the view of my personality which I myself took. For instance, I detested my face because I thought it had a knavish expression. I even suspected it of looking a little vicious. The result was that, while working in our office, I used to make constant and desperate attempts to look as 'pure' as possible, in order to escape any imputation of viciousness, while I would also endeavour to make my face express the utmost possible refinement. 'Even if I *have* an ugly face', I used to say, 'at least I will force it to look distinguished, speaking, and, above all things, clever.' Yet I knew, I knew only too painfully well, that my face would never come to express any one of those things. Worse still, I would take it into my head that my countenance looked positively stupid, and feel overwhelmed with despair. Indeed, I would not have minded its vicious expression if only I could have ensured its also being thought extremely clever.

Of course I hated and despised my colleagues. Yet somehow, also, I was afraid of them, and at times felt them to be my superiors. Yes, though I despised them, there were times when I rated them above myself. In fact, a man of the nineteenth century who is at all educated and refined cannot be vain without alternating between boundless self-assertion and envious self-depreciation. Contemptuous or respectful, I lowered my eyes before persons with whom I was brought in contact; and though sometimes I would try to outstare them, I always proved the first to avert my gaze. Also, I was desperately afraid of appearing ridiculous, and paid slavish heed to routine, and to everything that partook of an external nature. Yes, I took great care to walk always in the general rut, and dreaded lest I should discover in myself anything that savoured of eccentricity. But how was I to keep this up? I was a man of advanced tendencies, as befits a gentleman of the nineteenth century, whereas my comrades were men of dull habit, and as like one another as a flock of sheep. Probably I was the only man in our office who thought himself a poltroon and a slave because he was also a gentleman. Moreover, not only did I *think* myself a poltroon and a slave, but I was so in very truth. I say this without the least tinge of shame. Every educated man of the nineteenth century is, and must always be, a poltroon and a slave; it is his normal condition. Of that I, in those days, felt perfectly certain. Modern man is fashioned and constructed to that end and no other. Nor is it *now* only, and owing to fortuitous circumstances, that an educated man is bound to be both a coward and a bondsman; but for all time, and generally. Such is the law of nature for every educated man on this earth. If there should be anything upon which a man of refinement has cause to congratulate himself, he will derive no comfort or solace therefrom, since in all other matters he will still have to truckle to his neighbours. It is the inevitable, the eternal, result of his being what he is. Only the asinine family and its derivatives practise self-congratulation; and that only to a limited extent. But *them* we need not heed, since they signify precisely nothing.

One circumstance in particular used to torment me – namely, the circumstance that no one else was like me, and that I was like no one else. 'I am a person to myself, whereas they are *everybody*', was my usual thought whenever I engaged in meditations on the subject. From this you will see that I was also extremely young.

In some ways, too, I was inconsistent, for though at times I would find my office work perfectly abhorrent – so much so that I often returned home from it ill – at other times I would fall into an unexpected vein of scepticism and indifference (this often occurred), and laugh at my own impatience and distaste, and blame myself for what I called my 'romanticism'. At such times I would talk with anyone, and not only argue with him, but also consort with him on terms of friendship. Yes, my dislike of my fellow men sometimes disappeared entirely. Possibly I never really possessed that dislike, but derived it from books. Even to this day I cannot quite decide the point. However, no sooner had I broken the ice then I used to visit these friends of mine, to play cards with them, to drink vodka, and to talk 'shop'. . . . Here let me make a slight digression.

Generally speaking, we Russians have never gone in for that stupid transcendental romanticising of German and, still more, French origin in which nothing is ever done by anybody, though the ground be shaking beneath one's feet and all France be going to pieces at the barricades, so long only as decorum forbids one to change, and one can go on singing transcendental songs in what I might call the grave of one's existence, for the reason that one is a fool. In the Russian land there *are* no fools. That is a fact, and one that distinguishes us from all the other Germanic countries. Consequently, Russia contains no transcendental natures in the pure meaning of the term. Yet many of our publicists and critics have been in the habit of imagining that our romanticists are similar to those of France and Germany! On the contrary, the qualities of our romanticists are directly opposed to the transcendental-European standard, and not a single stanza in the European style finds acceptance here. (You must not mind my using the term 'romanticism'. I do so only because it is an old and a respected one, and has seen much service, and is familiar to everybody.) The nature of *our* romanticists is to comprehend everything, to see everything, and frequently to see everything incomparably more clearly than do more practical intellects; not to accord offhand acceptance to anyone or anything, but nevertheless to be squeamish of nothing; to skate around everything, to yield politic way in everything; never to lose sight of the useful and the practical (as represented by such things as lodgings at the State's expense, pensions, and medals); to keep that end in view through all the enthusiasms and depressions of lyrical poetry; to cherish always within themselves 'the great and the beautiful'; and to devote their own personalities, like so many precious jewels, to the furtherance – no matter in what trifles – of 'the great and the beautiful'. Yes, our romanticist is a man of wide sympathies, and the chief rogue whom we possess – that I can assure you from personal experience. Or at all events he is so if he is a wise man. But what am I saying? The romanticist is *in any case* a wise man. Rather, I mean that, though we used to have some mad romanticists among us, we need not take *them* into account, since, when just in the flower of their vigour, they became converted into Germans, and, the better to safeguard their treasures, went and settled in Weimar or Schwarzwald or some other German town. For my part, I used to have a sincere contempt for my official work, over and above the necessity which compelled me to sit on a stool and receive money for that work – an obligation, mark you, which I did *not* so greatly regret. On the other hand, if the ordinary foreign romantic were to lose his senses (though this does not very often happen) he would not feel in the least distressed at the prospect of having to be taken to the madhouse as 'the King of Spain'* or some such personage (that is to say, if he had gone *sufficiently* out of his mind); whereas with us only frail and aged romantics lose their reason. Moreover, the number of romantic writers could never be computed; which fact has led to their being divided into hosts and hosts of grades. Also, their many-sidedness is astonishing. For instance, what a faculty they possess for combining within themselves the most opposite of qualities! I used to derive great amusement from the fact – from the fact, that is to say, that among us there are numbers of 'broad-minded' writers who never lose their ideals, and who, though unwilling to stir a finger on behalf of those ideals, or to cease to be anything but declared robbers and brigands, continue, to the point of weeping, to cherish their original aspirations, while at the same time showing extraordinary singleness of heart. Yes, it is only in Russia that the most abandoned of rascals can be wholly, even splendidly, honourable men, while also continuing to be rascals. Therefore I repeat that the ranks of our romantics have given rise to bands of such absolute scoundrels (I use the term 'scoundrels' with particular pleasure) – to bands of men who display such a sense of the realities, such a knowledge of the practical – that a bewildered Government and public can but stand and gape at them!

Yes, their many-sidedness is astonishing, and God only knows whither at the present day it is being bent and developed, or what it promises for the future. Yet, after all, it does not make bad material. I do not say this out of patriotism, nor in a sour or sneering way, though I have an idea that once more you will believe me to be poking fun at you. Well, I greatly value and appreciate your opinion, and would ask you to pardon me if I have offended.

With my comrades I, of course, maintained no intimacy, and soon grew tired of them. Indeed, my then youthful inexperience led me not to curse them, but simply to drop them. At home I read a great deal, in a vain endeavour to drown in a flood of external impressions what was seething within me. The way to attain this lay, so far as I could see, only in reading. Books helped me, for by turns they soothed, stimulated, and pained my intellect. Yet at times I grew terribly weary of it all, and felt that, come what might, I must embark upon some kind of activity. Hence I would suddenly plunge into the lowest depths of foul, dark – well, not so much debauchery, as lewdness, for at that time my passions were keen, and derived all the greater heat from the aching, perpetual discontent with the world of which I was full: and to these bouts there would succeed intervals of hysteria which threw me into convulsions of weeping. I had no resource beyond reading. That is to say, there was nothing in my daily life which attracted me, or which I could respect. Above all things, constant depression seethed within me – a depression which, causing me to thirst for something different, for some sharp contrast, plunged me into vice. This I am not saying merely out of self-justification—— But again I have lied. I *am* saying it merely in order to justify myself. I make this confession for my own eyes alone, since I do not wish *you*, gentlemen, to think me a liar.

Stealthily, and by night, I used to indulge in solitary rounds of dissipation, but always with a timid, blackguardly, shamefaced sort of feeling which never deserted me even in my moments of greatest abasement (though at such times, true, it caused me to curse myself). It was the fruit of my long carrying of the underground within me. Always, too, I had a great dread of being seen, or met, or recognised by anyone; wherefore I would frequently change the venue of my dark proceedings.

One night, when passing a tavern, I saw, through some lighted panes, a party of gentlemen playing at billiards. Presently they fell to fighting one another with their cues, and one of their number was thrown out of the window by his companions. At any other time I should have felt only disgusted at this, but on the present occasion I conceived a sort of envy of the expelled individual – so great an envy that I entered the tavern, and approached the billiard-room. 'Come', I thought to myself, 'let me but pick a quarrel, and they will expel me too.' I was not drunk; I was merely ready for anything – to such a pitch can hysteria and depression eat into a man's soul. Yet nothing happened. Seeing that I could not, if necessary, spring from the window, I was on the point of departing without joining in the brawl when I was brought up short by an officer. At the moment, all unwittingly, I was blocking the door of the room, and he was trying to pass out of it. Taking me by the shoulder, and saying not a word of warning or explanation, he pushed me aside, and pursued his way as though he had not noticed me. Under ordinary circumstances I should have apologised to him, but, as it was, I felt that I could not do so, seeing that he had not only thrust me out of his path, but also departed without deigning me a single glance.

The devil only knows what, at that moment, I would have given to pick a real, a regular, a more decent, a more (if I might use the term) literary quarrel! I had been treated like a fly! Whereas the officer had been a man of six feet, I was only a thin, mean little fellow; yet the quarrel had lain entirely in my hands, and, had I protested, I too could have been thrown out of the window. But

I had wasted time in a mass of thinking and proposing, and so had incurred the shame of seeing myself snubbed!

So angry and disturbed was I that when I left the tavern I went straight home, and next day continued my course of dissipation – but in an even more timid, cowed, and lugubrious manner than usual. Indeed, I did so with, as it were, tears in my eyes. Yet I *did* continue it. Do not think that I was *afraid* of that officer. I have never yet been a coward at heart, however much I have been so in action. No, you need not smile; I have an explanation for this, even as I have, you may rest assured, an explanation for everything else.

Oh, if that officer could have been one of those who will fight duels! But no, he was essentially one of those gentlemen (now, alas! a vanished race) who prefer to take action with billiard cues, or, like Gogol's Lieutenant Pirogov,* in obedience only to orders. Such men do *not* fight duels; a duel even with a fellow fire-eater they consider inexpedient, since they look upon the duel as a senseless, free-thinking institution which savours of Frenchism. Consequently they remain ever ready to insult others – especially if they (the aggressors) can boast of six feet of stature!

No, it was not out of cowardice that I held my hand, but through boundless vanity. I feared neither six feet of stature nor the fact that I might be beaten and thrown out of the window. *Physical* courage has never been wanting in me: what I then lacked was *moral* courage. I was afraid lest everyone present, from the head marker to the lowest official, with his blotched and pimpled face and greasy collar, would fail to understand me, and laugh when I protested and addressed them in really literary language. For of the point of honour – not of honour pure and simple, mind you, but of the *point* of honour – it has never been the custom to speak in any but the most refined and literary diction. No ordinary words have I ever heard spoken concerning that same point of honour. Therefore I felt certain (it was due to the practical sense in me, as distinguished from the romantic) that everyone present would burst their sides with laughter, while the officer would not merely – that is to say, inoffensively – thrash me, but also trip me in the back with his knee, lead me a dance around the billiard-table, and, finally, have sufficient pity upon me to expel me through the window. But of course I could not let this wretched episode end where it was. Frequently in after days I met the officer in the street, and took the most careful note of him. I do not know whether he recognised *me*, but I think that he did not. None the less I always regarded him with hatred and envy. Thus things continued for several years, my grudge against him growing ever deeper and stronger as the years passed on.

Early in the proceedings I tried to make some cautious inquiries about the man, but found the task very difficult, for the reason that I knew no one. At last one day someone spoke to him in the street (I was then following him as closely as though I were tied to his person), and I learnt his name. Another time I followed him home to his flat, and for the sum of one *grivennik** ascertained from the porter what number the officer lived at, on which floor, and whether alone or with someone else – in short, all that *could* be ascertained from a porter. Another morning, though it was my first essay in literature, I took it into my head to indite this officer a letter, in the form of a caricature embodying a story. With great zest I wrote it, and, making it fairly scurrilous, at first appended to my enemy a name which he was bound to recognise at first sight; but later I decided to change it for another one, and then sent the whole to *Notes of the Fatherland*.* But, to my grief, it never got into print. Sometimes my wrath almost stifled me; so much so that at length I decided to challenge the foe to a duel. To this end I composed a beautiful, a most attractive letter, wherein I adjured him to expiate his fault, and hinted that, in case of refusal, I should call him out to fight me. Yet the missive was couched in such terms as would lead the officer, if he were at all capable of comprehending 'the great and the beautiful', to at once seek me out, fall upon my neck, and proffer me his friendship. 'And how splendid that would be!' I said to myself. 'We will have such a time of it together – yes, such a time of it! He shall hold over me the aegis of his professional position, and I shall give him the benefit of my refinement – er – and – and of my ideas. Much, much will come of it!' You must remember that it was now two years since he had offered me the insult, and my challenge was simply a gross anachronism, without mentioning the added *gaucherie* of my letter, which at once disclosed and concealed that anachronism. However, thank God! (even to this day I can never bless the Almighty without tears) I failed to send the letter. Indeed, whenever I think what *might* have happened, had I sent it, I turn cold. In the end it befell that I wreaked vengeance in the most simple, the most genial, of fashions, for a brilliant idea suddenly occurred to me. You must know that, at four o'clock on the afternoon of festival days, I would go for a walk along the sunny side of the Nevsky Prospect;* or, rather, I would not so much go for a walk as go to indulge in a series of annoyances, humiliations, and outpourings of spleen – things which seemed to me an absolute necessity. Like a lamprey, I would, in uncouth fashion, go wriggling my way through the throng, and give room, now to a general, now to an officer of the Horse or of the Foot Guards, now to a civilian, and so on. Yet all the while there would be spasms of pain at my heart, and shivers running down my back, at the mere thought of the wretched appearance that my costume and figure must be presenting. To me it was sheer misery and degradation – sheer, ceaseless, unbearable misery and degradation – to have to think, always and *apropos* of everything, that, in the eyes of this shining world, I was no more than an unclean and useless fly. True, the fly was one that was much cleverer, better educated, and better born than those who were jostling him, yet none the less it was a fly that had to give way to everyone, to be looked down upon by everyone, to be scorned by everyone. *Why* I should voluntarily have incurred the misery which I used to suffer on the Nevsky Prospect I do not know. I only know that I found myself drawn thither on every possible occasion.

It was at that period that I began to experience the species of delight to which I have referred in Part I; and after the incident with the officer I began more than ever to be attracted to the Nevsky Prospect, for it was there that I most often encountered and found myself obsessed by him. He, like myself, walked there mostly on festival days; he, too, stepped aside to make room for generals and bigwigs; he, too, wormed his way along like a lamprey, while common folk like myself he merely jostled, or else walked straight into, as though the space in front of him were perfectly clear. Never did I see him make way for such people, and as I gazed at him I used to feel perfectly drunk with rancour – though I gave him room with the rest whenever I met him. How it hurt me to think that even in the streets I was powerless to get on even terms with him. 'Why the devil *do* you step aside?' I would ask myself in a sort of idiotic, hysterical way when I awoke, say, at three in the morning. 'Why is it always *you*, not *he*? Is there no law for such a man – no precept? Supposing that we were to meet on equal terms, in the usual way that gentlemen meet one another, what would happen? Well, he would yield me half the path, and I the same to him, and we should pass one another with mutual respect.' Yet never did this befall. Always I turned aside for him, whereas *he* – he never even seemed to notice that I had done so. It was then that there first occurred to me the brilliant idea of which I have spoken. 'What', was my thought, 'if I were to meet him and *not* leave the path – to *purposely* not leave it, even though my not doing so should entail a collision?' This daring notion gradually obsessed me until I could not rest. Ceaselessly, deeply I pondered over it, while of set intent I patrolled the Prospect more frequently than ever, so as to realise the more clearly what I ought to do when actually I *did* come to make the attempt. All the while I was in transports, for more and more it was dawning upon me that my scheme was not only feasible, but a very good one. 'Of course, I shall not actually *push* him', I would add to myself, anticipatorily considerate in my joy, 'I will simply omit to turn aside, so that without coming into violent contact with him, I may rub shoulders with him so far as the conventions ordain. Exactly as he jostles *me* so will I jostle *him*.' At length my mind was made up, though the preparatory process had taken a long time. In the first place, I felt that at the moment of execution I should need to be looking my best, and therefore must take some thought for my raiment, seeing that, if a public scene should ensue (the public itself, of course, did not matter, but promenading there would also be the Countess A. and the Prince B. and the whole of the literary world), I should require to be at least *decently* dressed. To be so would inspire respect, and at once place myself and my antagonist on an equal footing in the eyes of society. Accordingly I drew some salary in advance, and bought, at Churkin's, a pair of black gloves and a smart hat. Somehow black gloves seemed to look more respectable, more *bon ton*, than the yellow ones which I first tried on. 'Coloured gloves are too loud, and make a man look too conspicuous', said I to myself as I rejected the yellow articles referred to. As for a shirt, I had long had one ready – one that was not only in pretty good repair, but also was fitted with white bone studs. The only thing that gave me pause was my overcoat. In itself it was not a bad one, for it was at least warm; but it had a wadded lining and a raccoon collar, and both of those things were the height of flunkeyism. Consequently it would be necessary to change the collar for a beaver one, such as all the officers wore. For this purpose I made the round of the shops, and at length lit upon a piece of beaver of cheap German extraction. Though German beaver soon comes to wear shabby and present a miserable appearance, it easily passes muster at first, if properly furbished up. Consequently a piece of it would do well enough for this occasion only. On asking the price, however, I found that it was too dear; so, after further grave consideration, I decided to sell my raccoon collar, and to borrow the deficit from the head of my department, Anton Antonych Setochkin. The latter, though an easy-going man, was of serious and opinionated bent, and anything but a moneylender; wherefore, despite the fact that on my entry to the service I had been highly recommended to his favour by the gentleman who had procured me my nomination, I dreaded the prospect of begging a loan of him. Somehow it seemed such a monstrous, such a shameful, thing to do that for three whole nights I never slept, little though my fevered condition had for some while past inclined me to slumber. By turns my heart would sink to nothing and turn to throbbing and throbbing and throbbing. At the first blush Anton Antonych seemed surprised at my request; then he frowned, considered the matter again, and, finally, handed me the cash in exchange for a note of hand which empowered him to recoup himself, in two weeks' time, out of my salary. Thus I had everything prepared. The beautiful beaver had now dethroned the miserable raccoon, and I could set myself to the work in hand. No rash decision must be come to, I felt; the affair was one which called for gradual and guarded management. Yet it must be confessed that, though I made many attempts to carry out my enterprise, I soon found myself beginning to despair of ever coming into actual contact with the enemy.

For instance, on one occasion I was not ready; on a second occasion I had not properly thought the matter out. More than once the officer and myself were on the point of colliding when – again I stepped aside, and he passed me by without looking at me. Sometimes I even went so far as to mutter fervent prayers as I approached him – prayers that God might steel me to the effort. At length I had really made up my mind to jostle him when, at the very last moment, when only a couple of paces from him, my breath failed, and I tripped and fell under his feet. Nonchalantly he stepped over me, and I rolled away out of the throng like a ball. That night fever again seized me, and I became delirious. However, the affair ended in the best way possible, for it struck me, the next afternoon, that I might as well desist from my abortive enterprise, and accordingly I made my way to the Nevsky Prospect for the last time, to see whether I really could effect my purpose.

Suddenly, when my foe was within three paces of me, I came to a sudden decision, put on a ferocious scowl, and – and came into violent collision with his shoulder! Not an inch did I budge, but continued my way with unshaken stride. Again he did not look at me, again he did not appear even to have noticed me; yet I felt certain that he was shamming. Yes, to this day I am sure of it. In any case it was I who had gained the most from the encounter. Though he might remain the stronger of the two, that did not matter. What really mattered was that I had attained my end, I had upheld my dignity, I had not yielded to him an inch, and I had publicly placed myself on an equality with him in the eyes of society. I returned home revenged, revenged! I felt transported with delight, and trolled an Italian aria as I proceeded. I need not tell you how I spent the next three days. Those of you who have read my *Underground* will be able to guess it for themselves. Later, the officer was transferred to another station, and it is fourteen years since I last saw him. What has become of my idol? Whom is he now bullying?

2

After this my phase of dissipation came to an end, and I found the time hanging heavy on my hands. Occasionally repentance would seize me, but I always drove it forth again, for I was too weary to do aught but fall in with – rather, put up with – whatsoever chanced to happen. Yet all the while there was a way of escape which reconciled me to everything – namely, the way of escape contained in my visionary cult of 'the great and the beautiful'. I did nothing but dream and dream of it; for three whole months on end I, crouching in my den, did nothing else. You may be sure that at this period there was nothing in common between myself and the individual who, in chickenish perturbation of heart, had sewed a piece of German beaver onto the collar of his overcoat. No; of a sudden I had become a hero. Even my six-foot colonel I would not have deigned to admit to my rooms. As a matter of fact, I had forgotten all about him. What my dreams were, and how I was able to rest satisfied with them, it is difficult, at this distance of time, to conjecture, but at all events they *did* give me pleasure. Moreover, they always came to me with greater strength and sweetness after a bout of dissipation; they came in company with tears and regrets, transports and curses. Indeed, such moments of rapture, of happiness, had I that, thank God, it never entered into my head to deride them. Ah, how full they were of faith and hope and love for my fellow men! That is to say, I had a sort of blind belief that one day some miracle, some external circumstance, would suddenly cause the present to break and become widened, and that suddenly there would dawn before me a horizon of congenial, productive, fair, and, above all things, *instant* activity (though in what manner *instant* I did not know), and that at last I should issue into God's world, mounted on a white horse, and crowned with laurels. Any secondary role I found myself unable to envisage, and that is why I thought so much about the subject. Whether a hero, or whether a groveller in dung, for me there could be no medium. Hence my undoing; since, when grovelling in dung, I always comforted myself with the reflection that at other times I was a hero, and that the hero overlaid the dung-groveller; for, thought I, though a man is usually ashamed when he bathes in mire, a hero stands on too lofty a plane ever to be wholly immersed in the stuff; wherefore he may grovel as he pleases. It is curious that my aspirations towards 'the great and the beautiful' should always have come to me precisely in moments of dissipation – on the very day that a bout of debauchery had occurred. Yes, they always came to me in isolated bursts, as though to remind me of their existence, but without repairing the dissipation by this manifestation of themselves. On the contrary, they seemed, through the mere force of contrast, to revivify my debauched instincts – to arrive, as it were, in time to make a sauce for those instincts. Of that sauce the ingredients were remorse and a sense of contradiction, added to torturing self-analysis; all of which pains and torments communicated to my degradation a sort of piquancy, and even a meaning. In short, my aspirations towards 'the great and the beautiful' fulfilled all the functions of a relish. Yet behind this there was something else; for how, otherwise, could I have reconciled myself to debauchery that was worthy only of an underclerk, or have covered myself to such an extent with mire? What was there in it all to attract me, or to lead me to cheat the night out on the street? Ah, I had a good excuse for everything. . . .

How much love – my God! how much love – I used to expend in those dreams, in those yearnings for 'the great and the beautiful'! – yes, even though my affection was of a fantastical order which could not possibly have been applied to a human being, but the abundance of which was such that I never felt any need so to apply it, seeing that, throughout, it was love of a superfluous, luxurious kind. Fortunately, it usually ended by turning to an indolent, sensuous cult of art, in the shape of beautiful forms of life which I borrowed ready made from poets and romanticists, and then adapted to every possible use and requirement of my own. In those visions I would rise superior to all mankind; all men were in the dust before me, and forced to recognise my perfection as I extended to them my pardon. Rapturously I would imagine myself to be a famous poet or courtier, or the fortunate possessor of untold millions which I was devoting to the benefit of the human race, while confessing to the latter my sins – though not sins in the actual sense of the word, but, rather, acts which partook of 'the great and the beautiful' (something after the Manfredian style).* Yes, I would picture the whole world weeping and embracing me (it was bound to do so if it were not wholly gross), and myself walking abroad, barefooted and hungry, to preach my new ideas, and to deal with reaction at Austerlitz.* Then a grand march would sound, and a general amnesty would be issued; after which the Pope would consent to leave Rome for Brazil, and a ball to which all Italy would be invited would be held at the Villa Borghese (the said Villa Borghese being situated, for that occasion only, on Lake Como, which, also for that occasion only, would have been transferred to the neighbourhood of Rome). Then, again, the scene would become shadowy—— But does not everyone know the kind of thing? Not long ago you said that it is wrong for a man to expose his all in the market-place – to expose such tears and raptures as those to which I have confessed. But why? Do you really think that I am ashamed of them, or that any of them were a whit worse than is anything in your own lives? Moreover, not *all* my ideas were badly conceived; not *all* of them centred around Lake Como. However, you may be right; they *may* have been low and degraded. The lowest thing of all is that I should have sought to justify my conduct in your eyes. A lower thing still is the fact that I have said so. . . . However, enough of this, or I shall never have finished with it. Always one thing lower than the last will keep occurring to me.

Yet I had not spent more than three months upon these ecstasies of mine when I began to feel a renewed inclination for intercourse with my fellow men, although, for me, the social round meant only an occasional visit to the house of my official superior, Anton Antonych Setochkin. Indeed, he was the one friend whom ever I have permanently retained; and to this day I marvel at the circumstance. Even him, however, I never visited except when one of my curious moods had come over me, and my dreams had reached a pitch of delight which impelled me forthwith to embrace humanity at large (which I could not well do without having at hand at least one concrete, one existing, human being). Also, since my calls upon Anton Antonych had always to be paid on a Tuesday (such being his reception day), I had to make my yearnings towards humanity also fall upon the second day in the week. His abode consisted of four rooms on the fourth floor of a block at Five Corners – rooms poorly furnished, and charged with the most penurious, the most jaundiced, air conceivable. With him lived two daughters and an aunt; the last-named of whom always poured out tea. At that time the daughters were thirteen and fourteen respectively, and had flaxen hair; while their habit of whispering and giggling together used greatly to embarrass me. As for the master of the house himself, he usually passed the time on a horsehair sofa near his study table, while beside him would sit a grey-haired guest who was one of the officials of our (or, possibly, some other?) office. In all, I never encountered more than two or three guests at these gatherings, and their conversation invariably turned upon the Stock Exchange, the last debate in the Senate, salaries, routine business, the Minister of our Department, and the best means of winning that Minister's favour. For some four hours or so I would sit stupidly beside these people, and listen to them without either a smile or a chance of joining in the conversation. Very dull I found it; but since, at times, I became so stricken with shyness that I would actually break out into a sweat, the whole thing did me good, since on the way home I would find no difficulty whatever in temporarily ridding myself of any desire to fall upon the neck of humanity.

Also, I had an acquaintance named Simonov, an old schoolfellow of mine. At that time many of my old schoolfellows were residing in St Petersburg, but in most cases I had dropped them, and ceased even to salute them in the street. Moreover, I had gone so far as to procure my transfer to another department, for the sole purpose of severing all ties with my hateful boyhood. Yes, a curse upon the school at which I studied, and upon its horrible years of servitude! In short, from the moment when I regained my liberty I broke with the majority of my old comrades, save two or three. Of these, Simonov was one, since his retiringness and docility had saved us from any serious difference at school, and I could discern in him a certain amount of independence and uprightness of character. Nor did I look upon him as wholly a limited man; wherefore I spent many a friendly hour with him, and it was only comparatively recently that these reunions had ceased to be, and a mist had descended over their brightness. The truth was that suddenly he seemed to have grown weary of exchanging confidences, and to have taken fright lest we should again slip into the old footing. Yet, despite the fact that I gathered that I was no longer a *persona grata* with him, I still continued to pay him occasional visits.

So, one Thursday evening, when I felt unable any longer to bear my loneliness, and knew that on Thursdays Anton Antonych's door would be closed to me, I bethought me of Simonov.* As I mounted the stairs to the fourth floor where he lived I remember I felt more than ever assured that he had grown tired of me, and that I had come in vain; but considerations of this sort invariably ended by drawing me on the more to fill ambiguous positions, and I therefore entered his apartments. It was now almost a year since I had last seen him.

3

With him I found two other old schoolfellows of mine who were discussing what appeared to be a very important subject. On my entry neither of them paid me the least attention: which seemed to me an odd thing, seeing that I had not seen either of them for the space of a year. Evidently they looked upon me as some kind of ordinary fly. Even at school, much as, in those days, they had disliked me, they had not treated me so. I, for my part, felt sure that their contempt was due to my unsuccessful career in the service, my social descent, my shabby clothes, and such other things as, in their eyes, would constitute signs of my incompetence and low standing. Yet I had not expected quite such a lack of ceremony as this. For his part, Simonov seemed surprised to see me enter – though it had always been his way to appear so (a circumstance which had never failed to annoy me). Consequently

I seated myself in rather a dejected mood, and set myself to listen to the conversation.

A grave, and even heated, discussion was in progress concerning a farewell dinner which these three gentlemen wished to offer, the next evening, to a friend of theirs named Zverkov, an officer in the army, who was about to leave for a distant post. He too had been a companion of mine at school, but during our latter days he had led me to conceive an intense dislike for him. Even when we were juniors I had envied him because he was a gay, good-looking young fellow whom everyone liked. Yet he had never done his lessons aught but badly, and the more so as time went on. Indeed, that he passed his examinations at all was due to the fact that he had some influence behind him, for during his last year at school he had inherited a legacy of two hundred souls; and since nearly all of us, his schoolfellows, were poor, he had taken to assuming rather grand airs over us. Yet, though in the highest degree vicious, he was also good-natured, even when swaggering his worst; with the result that, despite our purely external, fantastic, stilted forms of honour and *esprit de corps*, we all of us, except a few, grovelled before him, and the more so in proportion as he played the lord. Nor was it altogether out of self-interest that he was fawned upon; it was equally because he was so favoured of nature. Moreover, it was, with us, an accepted axiom that he was a specialist in good manners and deportment. But the latter assumption simply maddened me. I could not bear either the grating, boastful intonation of his voice, or his admiration of his own stupid witticisms, or the sight of his vapid, handsome face (gladly though I would have given in exchange my own supposed-ly 'clever' one), or his free and easy assumption of the manners of an officer of forty years' standing, or his talk about his intended conquest of the fair sex (which, since he had decided to leave it unentered upon until he had assumed an officer's epaulets, he was the more eager to initiate), or his everlasting prattle about his future prowess in duels. Once, when, out of school hours, he was holding forth to his comrades about the property which was one day to be his, and sporting at the prospect of it like a young puppy in the sun, and stating that he meant to take stock of every serf girl on the estate (he asserted that this would be no more than his *droit de seigneur*), and that if the peasants dared to utter a protest he would flog them all, greybeards included, and impose double tithes upon their holdings; when, as I say, he was declaiming all this, I suddenly dropped my customary role of silent auditor, and joined issue with him. Some of our fellows clapped their hands at this; which made me fasten upon my antagonist the more, since my prime motive was not so much pity for the serf girls and their fathers as rage at the thought that such a louse of a fellow should ever have his utterances applauded. True, on this occasion I won the day, but Zverkov, though foolish, was also proud and good-tempered, and contrived to laugh off the affair in such a manner that I was partly cheated of the fruits of victory, and forced to see the laugh remain on the other side. Several times afterwards he managed to turn the tables upon me in the same way, but this he did without malice, and merely in jest, or in passing, or with a smile, though I felt too angry and contemptuous to respond. Nay, when our school days were over, he even made overtures of friendship which I did not altogether resist, since they rather attracted me; but soon we drifted apart again. Next, I heard of some doings of his in barracks, and of the dissipated life that he was leading there; subsequently of the fact that he was getting on in the service. Yet whenever he passed me in the street he used to give me the cut direct; wherefore I suspected that he was afraid of compromising himself by being seen in converse with such an insignificant individual as myself. Also, on one occasion I saw him in a third-tier box at the theatre – already adorned with shoulder-knots, and engaged in bowing and scraping to the daughters of an old general. During the last three years, however, he had become much thinner in the face, though he was still handsome and engaging; his body had grown bloated, and it was clear that by the time he had reached the age of thirty he would have come to be a mass of wrinkles. Such was the Zverkov to whom the farewell dinner was to be given by my fellow guests at Simonov's. For the last three years these gentlemen had been his constant companions; although, as I could easily discern, they in no way considered themselves his equals.

Of Simonov's two guests one was Ferfichkin – a Russo-German of dwarfish stature and ape-like face, who, in his stupidity, laughed at everybody, and had, from our earliest school days, been my bitterest foe. Yet, though a vicious, conceited *farceur*, he aspired to the nicest sense of honour – he a man who, all the while, was essentially a coward! Lastly, he was one of those panderers of Zverkov's who openly flattered him, and secretly borrowed of him money. The other of the two guests was a military nonentity named Trudolyubov – a man of tall stature and frigid mien, but possessed of a certain notion of honour, even though he worshipped success in every form, and could talk only 'shop'. In addition, he could trace a certain relationship to Zverkov; which fact, I am ashamed to state, conferred upon him a certain standing in our circle. Me, however, he seemed to rate very low, for he treated me, if not with actual rudeness, at all events with the barest toleration.

'Seven roubles apiece', said Trudolyubov. 'In all, that will make twenty-one roubles, and provide us with a very good dinner indeed. Of course *Zverkov* need not pay his share.'

'Of course not, seeing that he is the guest', agreed Simonov.

'But do you suppose', put in Ferfichkin, with all the insolence of a valet who is flaunting his master's, the general's, medals, 'do you suppose that he will *permit* us to pay his share? In all probability he will accept the invitation rather than hurt our feelings; yet he will be sure also to contribute at least half-a-dozen of champagne.'

'Then how are we to apportion the other half-dozen among ourselves?' asked Trudolyubov – his attention now riveted upon the wine question.

'I propose that the three of us (each of us contributing seven roubles) meet Zverkov at the Hôtel de Paris at five o'clock tomorrow evening', said Simonov, who appeared to be the prime organiser of the feast.

'What? Only twenty-one roubles?' I put in, in as excited a tone as though I were offended. 'Then accept me also as a guest, and we shall raise the total to twenty-eight roubles.'

The truth was that there had suddenly come to me an idea that to cut in unexpectedly in this fashion was a clever thing to do, and would be sure to win the respect of all present.

'So *you* wish to take part in it?' exclaimed Simonov, though without looking at me. He always avoided my gaze, because he knew me by heart, and I felt furious that he should do so.

'Why not?' I spluttered. 'I also am a comrade of Zverkov's, and might well have taken offence at being passed over like this.'

'We did not know where to find you', said Ferfichkin brusquely.

'Besides, Zverkov and yourself are not exactly *friends*', added Trudolyubov, with a frown.

Nevertheless, I stuck to my idea, and retorted with a stutter –

'I – I do not consider that anyone has the right to judge between

Zverkov and myself. It is precisely because we *have* been on bad terms that I now wish to meet him again.'

'Oh, who could understand *your* fine ideas?' said Trudolyubov, with a sneer.

'Well, well', decided Simonov, 'you *shall* form one of the party. Tomorrow, then, if you please, at the Hôtel de Paris, at five. And mind you come.'

'And mind you bring the money, too', added Ferfichkin gruffly, with a wink at Simonov. Further than this he did not venture, for even Simonov looked confused at what he (Ferfichkin) had just said.

'All right', said Trudolyubov, rising. 'If he wants to come, *let* him come.'

'But the affair is a private party, not an official reception', persisted Ferfichkin as he too rose and reached for his hat. In leaving the room he omitted to accord me any salute whatever, and Trudolyubov gave me only a very faint one as he averted his eyes. Simonov, too, seemed annoyed when he found himself left *tête-à-tête* with me, and kept throwing stealthy glances in my direction.

'Hm! Yes, tomorrow', he stammered. 'Er – by the way, would you mind handing me your contribution *now*, so as to make quite sure of it?'

For the moment I felt beside myself with rage; but the next minute I remembered that for a long while past I had been owing him fifteen roubles, which, though never paid, I had not wholly forgotten.

'Surely', I replied, 'you yourself see that I could not be expected to know what was in the wind when I came? Of course I regret my negligence.'

'Very well, very well. You can pay me tomorrow, after dinner. I merely wanted to know; that is all. Pray do not——'

Without finishing his sentence he began to pace the room with an air of ever-growing annoyance, and a constant clicking of his heels.

'No', he went on. 'That is to say, yes. . . . However, I must be off now. I am not going far.' This last he said almost apologetically.

'Why did you not tell me before?' I cried, as I seized my hat.

'Oh, it is not very far – merely a couple of steps', he repeated, as he escorted me to the door with a preoccupied air which did not sit well upon him. 'Tomorrow, at five', he cried for the last time, as I was descending the staircase – doubtless signifying that he was only too glad to see me go. I felt furious.

'May the devil take the lot of them!' I thought, as I wended my way home. 'Why on earth have I gone and mixed myself up in the affair? Why, indeed? And to entertain an idiotic pig like Zverkov, too! Good Lord! Of course, I *need* not go. But how am I to get out of the engagement? Tomorrow I shall send Simonov word that——'

What really maddened me was the knowledge that I *should* go to the dinner. The more tactless, the more out of place it seemed to me to go, the more was I bent upon going. Yet one difficulty confronted me: I had no money. True, I had nine roubles in my possession, but, tomorrow, seven of these would need to be paid over to my servant, Apollon, who received from me, as wages, board and lodging and the monthly sum specified. Not to pay his wages punctually was, for me, a thing impossible, owing to his character. But of this brute, of this plague of my life, more anon.

All the time I knew that I should *not* pay those wages, but, on the contrary, go to the dinner.

I had terrible dreams that night – a not very remarkable thing, seeing that I had spent the evening in company with memories of my servitude at school – memories which I could not banish. To that school I had been sent by some distant relatives in whose care I had been, and of whom I had long since lost sight. They had sent me to that school an orphan whom they had cowed with scoldings until I had become a prematurely silent, introspective, curiously observant boy; and there I had been saluted by my comrades with nothing but cruel, pitiless jeers, owing to the fact that I was not like any of them. Those jeers I could not stand; I could not get on good terms with my companions in the easy way which *they* could with one another, but conceived an instant grudge against them, and shut myself up in a world of nervous, sensitive, boundless pride. My comrades' roughness was a sheer torture to me, for they never grew tired of making cynical jests on the subject of my face and ungainly figure. Yet how stupid their own faces were! Indeed, our school fostered a sort of facial expression that was unique for its innate, ever-growing dullness. However good-looking a boy might be when he first came to us, a few years would succeed in making him look simply repulsive. Even at sixteen I found myself astonished at the pettiness of my companions' thought, and at the inanity of their pursuits, games, and subjects of conversation.

They did not understand even the most ordinary things of life, while things that were at all striking or inspiring aroused in them no interest whatever. Consequently I had no choice but to regard my fellow students with disdain. Yet it was not mere wounded vanity that impelled me to do so, so for the love of God do not pounce upon me with the sickeningly hackneyed phrase that 'you were then only a boy of dreams, whereas *they* knew what life meant.' I tell you that these boys knew simply *nothing*, whether of life or of anything else: and this incensed me all the more against them. On the other hand, the plainest, the most evident, actuality was viewed by them in fantastically stupid fashion, for they were already accustomed to worship only success. Everything which, though of good report, was also lowly and unassuming they flouted with insults and cruelty. Rank they mistook for brains, and even at the age of sixteen they could speak familiarly of places of bad resort. Of course, much of this *may* have arisen from the crass, debased conditions which surrounded their early boyhood and adolescence; yet, even so, it must be said that, taken as a whole, they were almost monstrously vicious. True, that viciousness may, in its turn, have been largely cynical and external, for at times a certain youthful freshness glimmered amid the vice; yet even that freshness was devoid of all attractiveness, and showed itself mostly in a sort of premature pruriency. In short, I had the greatest horror of them all, even though I myself may have been the worst of the lot; and this detestation they repaid – and very openly, too – in kind. However, I did not want their liking. On the contrary, my one desire was to see them humbled to the dust. As a means of escaping their ridicule I set myself earnestly to pursue my studies, and soon had risen almost to the top of the school. This *did* make a certain impression upon them, for it gradually dawned upon them that I could read books which they could not even decipher, and that I understood things (beyond the school curriculum) which they had never so much as heard of. Of this they took their usual derisive, barbaric view, but, morally, it gave me the whip hand over them – and the more so since the circumstance led the tutors themselves to pay me some respect. Thus the sneers died away, but there still remained a feeling of hostility which caused cold, constrained relations to subsist between my schoolfellows and myself. Indeed, the situation was too irksome to be borne, and as the years passed on I developed a yearning for *real* comrades, *real* friends. But, try though I might to form some extraneous intimacies, the latter always seemed unnatural, and soon came to an end of their own volition. True, I had *one* school friend for a while, but at heart I was tyrant enough to try to exercise an excessive sway over him as, in an endeavour to inspire him with dislike for our environment, I demanded of him a final, an unconditional divorcement from everything. The result was that I only frightened him with my passionate friendship, and reduced him to tears and sullenness. By nature he was unspoilt and of a yielding disposition; yet no sooner had he surrendered to me his all than I disliked him as much as I did his companions, and drove him from me as though he had been congenial to me only so long as I could hector him and keep him in subjection. Yet it was not *all* my companions that I could bully in this way, for my friend was unlike the rest of the gang, and constituted a bright exception. On leaving school, my first act was to refuse the post to which I had been nominated; my object being to sever all ties with the past, and to bury it wholly in the dust. . . . And God only knows what, later, drew me towards the man Simonov of whom I have just spoken!

Early next morning I sprang out of bed in as agitated a state as though something important were soon about to happen. Somehow I had an idea that some radical change in my life was approaching, inevitably approaching. All my life it has been my way, on the least external occurrence, to feel that some fundamental break in my existence is at hand. However, I went to my office as usual, and slipped away home again two hours before the usual time, to prepare myself for the dinner. 'Above all things', I thought to myself, 'I must not be the first arrival, or I shall be thought over-eager about the thing.' Important points like this seemed to multiply by thousands, and worried me until I almost fainted. Next with my own hands I cleaned my shoes, for Apollon would never have done them twice in the same day; he would have thought such a proceeding quite irregular. That done, I swept the hall clear of the litter which I had made, in order that he should not afterwards see the remains and despise me for what I had done. Then I looked through my wardrobe in detail, and found that it was old and worn and creased. Yes, I had grown very slovenly in my dress. True, my uniform* looked decent, but one cannot very well go out to dinner in a uniform. Worst of all, my trousers had a large yellow stain on one of their knees, and I felt that that stain alone would deprive me of nine-tenths of my dignity, well though

I knew it was beneath me to feel like that. 'Come, come', I thought to myself with a sinking of the spirits, 'enough of what I may or may not think. I have now to deal with *reality*.' Yet, though well aware that I was exaggerating everything to a perfectly monstrous degree, the thought of what lay before me shook my soul as with ague. Distractedly I pictured to myself the cold, superior manner in which 'that rascal' Zverkov would greet me; the dull invincible contempt with which 'that blockhead' Trudolyubov would eye me; the rude, insulting giggles which 'that skunkish' Ferfichkin would vent at my expense (if by so doing he could curry favour with Zverkov); the manner in which Simonov would size me up, and despise me for my wretched vanity and want of spirit; and, lastly, the degree to which the affair, from start to finish, would be sordid and shameful rather than 'refined'. Of course, it would be best for me not to go, but this was impossible, since no sooner do I take a thing into my head than it drags my head along with it. That is to say, it is always *after* the event that I reproach myself. 'But why', was my reflection, 'should I be afraid of, play the coward before, reality?' Yet, passionately desirous though I was of showing all this riff-raff that I was not the coward whom I imagined myself to be, it was in a perfect storm of pusillanimous agitation that I fancied myself getting the better of the company – first snubbing them, then attracting them, then forcing them to like me for 'the elevation of my thoughts and my undoubted wit'. Zverkov I should first of all displace from his perch, and then force to sit in shame and silence while I simply *crushed* him. Lastly, if you please, I should have pity upon him, and drink his health, and address him in the second person singular. None the less, the cruellest and most shameful thought of all was the knowledge – yes, the certain knowledge – that none of these things would *really* happen; that, as a matter of fact, I had no desire to crush, or to get the better of, or to attract my fellow guests, and that for such a result (were it even attainable) I should be the last man in the world to care. Oh, how I prayed God that the evening might pass as quickly as possible! Finally it was in inexpressible anguish that I went to the window, opened the sliding pane, and looked out into the dim swirl of wet, falling snow. . . .

At length my shabby wall clock whirred, and struck the hour of five. Instantly I seized my hat, and, trying not to catch Apollon's eye (ever since the morning he had been awaiting receipt of his wages, yet had been fool enough never to speak of them), I darted past him through the door, and, in a cab which I had ordered beforehand, drove in state (and in return for my last half-rouble) to the Hôtel de Paris.

4

As long ago as the previous night I had known that I *should* be the first to arrive. Yet that did not greatly matter. What really mattered was that I had great difficulty in finding our room. Nor, as yet, was the table even laid! What could this mean? After many inquiries of the servants, I learnt that dinner had been ordered for six o'clock, not for five; and this the attendants in the buffet confirmed. It was bad enough even to have to ask them! As yet the clock showed twenty-five minutes to six. If the change of hour was in any way due to my fellow guests they ought to have let me know by post rather than have lowered me in my own eyes and in those of the servants. However, I sat down, and a waiter began to lay the table – greatly embarrassing me by his presence as he did so. Towards six o'clock candles were brought in, to aid the lamps, though the waiter evidently had not thought it worth while to bring them in when I first arrived. In a neighbouring room there were dining two sombre-looking customers who appeared, from their mien, to be out of temper and disinclined to talk; while in a room further on a considerable noise, and even some shouting, was in progress – the chattering of a whole party of people being audible, with stray little exclamations in French. Evidently the company included ladies. In short, I found the time of waiting excessively tedious – so much so that when (exactly at six o'clock) my fellow guests arrived *en masse*, I felt momentarily so delighted (as if they were my deliverers) that I almost forgot my role of an offended personage.

Zverkov entered at the head of the band, as their manifest leader. At the moment he and his companions were laughing loudly, but when he became aware of my presence he straightened his face, came forward slowly, and with a sort of coquettish wriggling of the waist, gave me his hand with a faintly benevolent, yet faintly reserved, air in his manner, as though, even in the act, he desired to guard himself against something. On the other hand, I had expected him to break into his old thin, high-pitched laughter, and, at the first word, to lapse into his old way of cracking sorry jests and witticisms. Indeed, ever since the previous evening, I had been looking for this to happen. Consequently I was the more dumbfounded by his condescending and superior *bonhomie*. Could it be that he conceived himself immeasurably above my level in all the relations of life? If so, and if his design was only to insult me by his patronage, it did not greatly matter, since I could get even with him somehow; but what if, without actually intending to offend, he really cherished in his sheep's brain the idea that he was the better man of the two, and therefore in a position to treat me with condescension? The very supposition made me gasp!

'I have learnt with pleasure of your wish to join us', he began, with a drawl and a lisp and an even greater mouthing of his words than in the old days. 'Somehow we never seem to meet one another now, for you keep so much to yourself. Yet you need not do so, for we are not nearly such queer creatures as you think. At all events I am very glad to renew your acquaintance now', and he turned away with a slighting air to lay his hat upon the window-sill.

'Have you been waiting long?' Trudolyubov asked me.

'Yes', I replied in a voice which presaged a coming explosion. 'I arrived exactly at five o'clock, as warned to do yesterday.'

'Then did no one let him know that the hour had been changed?' cried Trudolyubov, turning to Simonov.

'No; I forgot to do so', answered the latter in an unrepentant tone, as, without a word of apology to myself, he departed to order dinner to be brought in.

'So you have been here an hour, my poor fellow!' cried Zverkov with a laugh (naturally it would seem to him a laughing matter). In imitation of his patron, Ferfichkin also burst into a shrill, mean chuckle like the barking of a small dog, for he too evidently thought my position an extremely ridiculous and absurd one.

'There is nothing to laugh at', I exclaimed to Ferfichkin, growing more and more exasperated. 'It was somebody else's fault, not mine. No one ever warned me. It was, it was – well, it was simply rude.'

'Not only rude, but something else', remarked Trudolyubov, naïvely taking my part. 'You put things too mildly. It was simply an insult – though, of course, not an intentional one. How Simonov could have done it I—— Ahem!'

'If *I* had been played such a trick', said Ferfichkin, 'I should have——'

'Yes, you would have ordered up something to go on with, or simply have told them to lay dinner', concluded Zverkov for him.

'Certainly I *could* have so acted without anyone's permission', I rapped out. 'If I waited, it was only because——'

'Well, well; let us take our seats, gentlemen', said Simonov, at that moment re-entering. 'Everything is ready, and I will answer for it that the champagne is well iced. You see', he added to myself, 'I did not know your address, nor where to find you.' Again he avoided my eye, for he evidently bore me a grudge of some sort. After my experiences of last night I was determined to find out what it was.

Everyone – myself included – seated himself at the table, which was a circular one. On my left I had Trudolyubov, and, on my right, Simonov; while Zverkov confronted me, with, between him and Trudolyubov, Ferfichkin.

'Tell me, are you in a government department?' Zverkov said to me. Clearly, seeing that I was ill at ease, he had decided to interest himself in my affairs, and really thought that he ought to be kind to me – to, in a way, 'hearten' me.

'Does he want me to throw a bottle at his head?' thought I to myself. Somehow, the strangeness of the situation had made me unnaturally prone to take offence. But aloud I said drily, with my eyes on my plate –

'I am in the Ministry of ——.'

'And do you like it? Also, tell me – what led you to resign your former post?'

'What led me to resign my former post?' I re-echoed, involuntarily assuming a drawl thrice as pronounced as Zverkov's own. 'I resigned it simply because I wanted to.'

Ferfichkin giggled, and Simonov looked at me with an ironical air. As for Trudolyubov, his fork remained poised in the air, so petrified was he with astonishment.

Zverkov winced, yet he did not mean to show it.

'And what is your present income?' he continued.

'My present income?'

'Well, your *salary*?'

'Am I, then, to be put through a regular examination?' I retorted. However, I told him the amount of my salary, and grew very red in the face while doing so.

'Not much indeed!' he observed pompously.

'No, one couldn't afford good restaurants every night on *that*', added Ferfichkin mischievously.

'In my opinion it is sheer poverty', was Trudolyubov's comment.

'And how thin you have grown! You have changed a good deal since I last saw you', continued Zverkov, with a glance of impertinent commiseration at my person and clothes.

'Come', said Ferfichkin, with a snigger, 'we have put our good friend sufficiently out of countenance.'

'Sir', I retorted, 'it is not in your power to put me out of countenance. Do you hear? I am dining in this restaurant at my own expense, at my own expense, and not at that of someone else, Monsieur Ferfichkin.'

'What?' cried Ferfichkin, turning as red as a boiled lobster, and looking at me with fury. '*Which* of us is dining at the expense of someone else?'

'Never mind', I replied, feeling that I was in for it. 'We should do well to talk on some more intellectual topic.'

'Yes; to give you an opportunity of airing your wonderful gifts, eh?'

'No, not at all. That would be out of place here.'

'More so than in your *leper*-tment?'

'Enough, gentlemen, enough!' cried Zverkov imperiously.

'What folly this is!' murmured Simonov.

'Yes – and utter stupidity!' assented Trudolyubov. 'We have met here to spend a few friendly hours together, and to wish our friend *bon voyage*; yet *you*' – this was addressed to me exclusively – 'must start quarrelling! Since you invited yourself to the dinner, pray do not disturb the general harmony at it.'

'That will do, that will do', said Zverkov again. 'Let us drop the subject, gentlemen. Allow me to tell you how, three days ago, I came very near to getting married.' And he embarked upon a story which bore no relation at all to marriage, but only to the amorous exploits of some old generals, colonels, and court chamberlains, with the narrator himself as the leading spirit. A general chorus of laughter followed, and Ferfichkin fairly shrieked. No one noticed me any longer, and I sat crushed and humiliated.

'My God! Look at the company that I am keeping!' thought I to myself. 'Yet what a fool I must look to them all! And I used to forgive Ferfichkin so many things! Do these blockheads really imagine that they are doing me an honour by giving me a place at their table? Cannot they understand that it is *I* who am doing *them* an honour? I have grown thin, have I? I wear shabby clothes? Oh, the cursed clowns! Long ago Zverkov must have noticed the yellow stain on my knee. What then? I have a great mind to rise – yes, this very minute – from the table, and to take my hat, and simply go without another word. Yes, go out of sheer contempt. Tomorrow, perhaps, there will be a duel? Oh, the blackguards! But I do not think that they would miss my seven roubles very much. Perhaps they intend to—— Oh, the devil take them all! I don't care a hang for the seven roubles. I'll go this very instant.'

However, I stayed, and kept drinking glass after glass, both of claret and sherry. Lack of usedness to wine soon began to turn my head, and my anger increased with my fuddlement. Suddenly I felt as though I should like to insult everyone in the rudest possible fashion, and then go. I had an idea that I should like to seize a favourable moment to show myself in my true colours. 'Let them say what they like!' I thought to myself. 'Even if I *am* ridiculous, I have some brains in my head, and – and – in short, they can go to the devil!'

From time to time I glared at the company, but everyone seemed to have forgotten my existence, and to be merged in a din of shouting and merriment. Zverkov was holding forth, and I set myself to listen. His story related to a fine lady whom he had induced to confess to a passion for himself (of course the fellow was lying throughout), as well as to an intimate friend of his – a certain Prince Kolya, of the Hussars, the alleged owner of three thousand souls – who had rendered him valuable assistance in the affair.

I broke into the conversation. 'This Prince Kolya', I said, 'this owner of three thousand souls, how comes it about that *he* is not here to entertain you tonight?'

For a moment or two no one spoke; but presently Trudolyubov threw a contemptuous nod in my direction, and even went so far as to remark that for some time past I had been drunk. Zverkov, for his part, sat gazing at me like a cow, until I was forced to lower my eyes, while Simonov seized the opportunity to pour out fresh bumpers of champagne. As soon as he had done so, Trudolyubov raised his glass, and everyone except myself did the same.

'Your very good health, and a pleasant journey to you!' he cried to Zverkov. 'Let us drink to the years which are gone, and to the years which are coming! Hurrah!'

The whole company honoured the toast, and then rushed to embrace Zverkov. I alone did not stir, and my glass remained untouched upon the table before me.

'And are not *you* going to drink it?' rapped out Trudolyubov impatiently, as he turned to me with a threatening air.

'Yes; but first of all I wish to make a speech of my own, Monsieur Trudolyubov. When I have done *that* I will drink the toast.'

'Oh, the abominable cad!' muttered Simonov.

I straightened myself with the aid of the table, and feverishly clutched at my glass. I felt as though I were preparing to say something very important, yet had not a notion what it was going to be.

'Silence!' cried Ferfichkin. 'We are about to hear something worth hearing!'

Zverkov sat waiting gravely. He had an inkling of what was coming.

'Monsieur le Lieutenant Zverkov', I began, 'please to know that I detest phrases, phrasers, and fools with waists. That is my first point. Follows my second.'

There was a general stir of astonishment.

'My second point is that I detest blackguards and blackguardism, but more especially the former. My third point is that I love truth and frankness and honesty.' I was speaking almost mechanically, and beginning to shiver with apprehension at my own words. 'Yes, and I love high thinking, Monsieur Zverkov, and I love genuine good-fellowship and equality and—— No. Ahem! – I love – I love—— However, Monsieur Zverkov, I drink to your good health. May you conquer the whole Caucasus, and slay your country's enemies, and – and – here is your very good health, Monsieur Zverkov.'

He rose, bowed, and said, 'Thank you.' Plainly he was very much put about, for he had turned quite pale.

'The devil take it!' exclaimed Trudolyubov, striking his fist upon the table.

'That sort of thing ought to have been answered with a blow on the mouth', squeaked Ferfichkin.

'Let us throw him out', muttered Simonov.

'Not a word, gentlemen! Do not lose your tempers!' cried Zverkov, endeavouring to appease the general indignation. 'I thank you, but *I* shall know what value to set upon his words.'

'Monsieur Ferfichkin', I shouted at the top of my voice, 'tomorrow you shall make good to me what you have just said.'

'A duel?' he replied. 'Then I accept.' Yet so absurd did I look as I challenged him, and so ill did it consort with my figure, that everyone – Ferfichkin included – burst out laughing.

'Oh, leave him alone', said Trudolyubov disgustedly. 'He is drunk.'

'I shall never forgive myself for having included him in the party', added Simonov.

'Now is the time for me to throw bottles at them', thought I to myself. I seized up one, and – calmly poured myself out another glassful.

'I had better stay on to the end', I reflected. 'I dare say you fellows would be thankful to see me go, but I don't intend to do so. I intend, rather, to sit on here and drink, as a sign that I think you of no importance whatever. I intend to sit on here and drink because the place is a tavern, and I have duly paid my entrance money. I intend to sit on here and drink because I look upon you all as so many insubstantial dummies. I intend to sit on here and drink because – yes, and to sing too if I want to, and because I have the right to sing, and because – ahem!'

As a matter of fact, I did *not* sing that night, but exerted all my faculties to avoid meeting my companions' eyes, the while I struck attitudes expressive of independence, and impatiently waited for someone to be the first to address me. But, alas! no one was so. How I wished, how I wished that at that moment I could have made my peace with my companions! The clock struck eight, and then nine. Presently the revellers moved from the table to a divan, where Zverkov stretched his full length, and rested one foot upon a what-not. Also, more wine was handed round – he producing three bottles of his own, but omitting to include me in the invitation. Round him sat his admirers, who seemed to listen to him with such absolute veneration that it was clear they really liked him. 'But why, but why?' thought I to myself. From time to time, in their drunken rapture, they actually embraced him as they talked of the Caucasus, of the nature of true passion, of lucrative service posts, of the astounding income of the hussar officer Podcharzhevsky (whom none of them personally knew), of the marvellous beauty and grace of the Princess D—— (whom none of them had even seen), and of the immortality of Shakespeare.

I smiled contemptuously, and, placing myself in front of the divan, started to pace the length of the room – from the table to the stove, and back again. My one desire was to show my companions that I could get on without them; wherefore I purposely clicked my heels together, and stamped a good deal with my soles. Yet it was all to no purpose, for the party paid me no attention whatever. Thus, from eight o'clock to eleven, I tramped to and fro before the company, always keeping to the same beat (namely, from the table to the stove, and back again). 'Here I walk', was what my attitude expressed, 'and no one can prevent me from doing so.' Several times, when he entered the room, the waiter stopped to stare at me, while the frequent turning and turning made me giddy, and every moment I thought that I should have a fit, seeing that three times, during those three hours, I burst into a sweat, and then grew dry again. Also, every now and then there pierced my heart, with deep and venomous pain, the thought that ten, twelve, or, maybe, forty, years might pass, yet I should still remember, with horror and humiliation, the most ridiculous, the most degraded, the most disgusting evening of my life. More unconscionable, more gratuitous, my degradation could not have been, and I fully understood that as I paced up and down between the table and the stove. 'Oh, if you only knew what thoughts and feelings I am capable of, and what a man of refinement you have in me!' was my incessant reflection as I purposely turned towards the divan where my enemies were seated. But my enemies comported themselves as though I were not so much as present. Once, and only once, did they pay me the slightest attention – namely, when Zverkov was speaking of Shakespeare, and I gave a contemptuous laugh. So scurrilous, so mean was my snigger that, as with one consent, they stopped speaking, and for two or three minutes gazed at me gravely and in silence, the while I continued pacing the room, and making as though I had not noticed them. Yet nothing came of it. None of them spoke, and the next moment I was again forgotten. At length eleven o'clock struck.

'Gentlemen', cried Zverkov as he rose from the divan, 'let us now go to the place of which you know.'

'Of course, of course!' came the general exclamation.

Upon this I moved sharply towards Zverkov. I felt so tortured and shattered in mind that I could almost have cut my throat, and put an end to things then and there. A sort of fever had got hold of me, and my sweat-soaked hair was clinging to my forehead and temples.

'Zverkov', I said harshly, but firmly, 'I beg your pardon. Ferfichkin, I beg yours also, as I do that of everyone present; for I have done a wrong to each one of you.'

'Aha! So a duel is not in your line, after all?' hissed Ferfichkin venomously.

This cut me to the heart.

'Do not think that I fear a duel, Ferfichkin', I retorted. 'I shall be ready to fight you tomorrow, but only after a reconciliation. Upon the latter I insist, and it is not for you to refuse it me. Yet, to show that there is no duel of which I am afraid, I propose that you shall fire first, and that I shall fire in the air.'

'He is only playing the fool', remarked Simonov.

'Or clean gone out of his mind', added Trudolyubov.

'Please let me pass', said Zverkov contemptuously. 'Why do you block my way like this? What is it you want?'

Everyone was red in the face, with glittering eyes, for much wine had been drunk.

'I only seek your friendship, Zverkov', I replied. 'I have offended you, but——'

'Offended *me*? *You* offended *me*? Please to understand, my good sir, that never, and under no circumstances whatsoever, could you offend *me*.'

'Besides, we have had enough of you', growled Trudolyubov. 'Come on, you fellows. Let us be off.'

'Olympia for me, gentlemen!' cried Zverkov. 'That was a bargain.'

'Yes; we don't dispute it', came the laughing response.

I remained alone in my shame as the party left the room. Trudolyubov drawled out some idiotic song or another as they went. Only Simonov lingered a moment to tip the waiters. Suddenly I approached him.

'Simonov', I said in a tone of absolute despair, 'please to lend me six roubles.'

Extreme astonishment dawned in his stupid eyes (for he too was drunk).

'Do you also wish to go *there* with us?' he inquired.

'Yes.'

'Then I have no money to lend you', he retorted with a contemptuous smile as he moved towards the door.

I seized him by the greatcoat, for a sort of nightmare was upon me.

'Simonov', I remonstrated, 'I have just seen that you *have* some money. Why do you refuse me? Am I such a rascal? Besides, mind how you refuse me, for you cannot know the real reason why I make the request. Everything depends upon this – my future, my plans, my——'

Taking some money from his pocket, he almost threw it at me.

'Here you are, then!' he said in a hard voice, 'if you care to be such a cur.' Then he left the room at a run, to rejoin his companions.

For a moment or two I remained where I was – alone with the litter, the leavings, the dregs of liqueur, the spilt wine, the odds and ends of cigarettes: alone with the fumes and the fever in my head, and the aching depression in my heart; alone with the waiter, who, having seen and heard all, was now staring at me with intense curiosity.

'Yes; *I* will go there too!' I cried. 'Either they shall kneel to me, and clasp me by the feet, and beseech my friendship, or – or I will hit Zverkov full in the face!'

5

'So, at length, *this* is contact with reality!' I muttered as I tore down the staircase. 'Surely to learn *this* it was not necessary that the Pope should leave Rome and go to Brazil, or that a ball should be given on Lake Como?'

'You cur!' I went on, in objurgation of Zverkov. 'What if you should get the laugh of me even now?'

'No matter if he does', I cried the next moment, in answer to myself. 'By now you have lost everything.'

The scent of my quarry had now had time to grow cool, yet I knew where to find the man for whom I was seeking.

At the door of the hotel there was lounging a solitary night cabman, with his greatcoat dusted over with the moist – almost warm – snow which was still falling and making everything look dim and oppressive; while his shaggy little piebald pony also had a powdering of snow upon its back, and from time to time, I remember, kept coughing. Leaping into the rough bark sledge, I was in the act of bending my legs to sit down when the recollection of Simonov's recent loan of six roubles threw me into such a state of mind that I rolled backwards on to the seat like a sack.

'Yes, it will take a great deal to set all this right', I exclaimed as I did so. 'Yet I *will* set things right, or perish in the attempt. Forward!'

Off we started – I with a veritable whirlwind circling in my brain.

'Yet it is unlikely that they will go upon their knees to win *my* friendship', I reflected. 'It is all a mirage – a horrible, disgusting, romantic, fantastic mirage, like the ball on Lake Como. Consequently I shall have no choice but to strike Zverkov in the face. I shall simply *have* to. *That* at least is decided upon. Get on with you, cabman!'

The cabman gave his reins a jerk.

'I shall deal Zverkov the blow as soon as ever I enter the room. But ought I first of all to say a few words, by way of preface? No, I shall just enter and hit him. They will all be in the salon together, with Zverkov seated by Olympia's side, on the divan. That cursed Olympia! Once she refused me, and laughed in my face. I will pull out her hair by the roots, and Zverkov's ears as well! Or, rather, I will take him by one of those ears, and drag him about the room! Perhaps his companions will hurl themselves upon me, and beat me. At the very least they will throw me out of doors. What then? At all events I shall have dealt him the blow; I shall have taken the initiative, and branded him, and placed it beyond his power to efface my blow with one of his own – only with a duel. Yes, he will simply *have* to fight me. But suppose they should beat me first? Well, let them, the brutes! Trudolyubov would do the most in that way, for he is very strong, whereas Ferfichkin would probably steal up from behind, and hang on to my hair. However, be it so, be it so! I am going there for that very purpose. Yes, at last their sheep's brains shall be forced to taste the tragic note in this. And when they are dragging me to the door I shall cry to them that the whole gang is not worth my little finger. . . . Drive on, drive on!' I shouted to the cabman, who started, and then flourished his whip, for my shout had been a wild one.

'Yes, at dawn we shall fight', I went on. 'That is decided. Likewise, my work in the office is ended. I remember Ferfichkin making a joke about a department and a *leper*-tment. . . . But where am I to get pistols? Pshaw! I shall draw an advance of salary and purchase some. And powder and ball? Oh, *they* are the business of the seconds. But how is everything to be arranged by dawn tomorrow? And where am I to get seconds? I have not so much as a friend in the world. Pshaw! Why, the first person whom I meet in the street will be glad to act as my second, just as he would do if he were asked to come and save a drowning man. Extraordinary circumstances must be specially allowed for. Even if I were to ask the head of my department to second me to-morrow, he would consent out of very chivalry, and keep my secret as well. Anton Antonych is——'

At that moment I suddenly realised, with absolute and increasing clearness, the idiotic folly of my plans. Yes, I saw the reverse side of the medal. But——!

'Drive on, cabman! Drive on, you brute! Drive on, I tell you!'

'Aye, aye, sir!' responded that son of the soil.

Next, a cold fit seized me.

'Would it not be better', I thought, 'would it not be better if I were to go straight home now? Oh, my God! Why on earth did I ever invite myself to that dinner? It is impossible for me to go home after that three hours' walk between the table and the stove. They – yes, they and no one else – must reckon with me for that walk. They alone can purge me of my dishonour. Drive on, cabman!

'But what if they should give me into custody? No, they would never dare to do such a thing, for they would be afraid of the scandal. Again, what if Zverkov should contemptuously refuse to fight a duel? It is quite probable that he would do so. Well, in that case I should show him that—— But no; I should wait for him at his door tomorrow, and, just when he was coming out, and about to get into the cab, I should seize him, and tear the greatcoat off his back, and fasten my teeth into his hand, and bite him. "See, everyone!" I should cry. "See to what lengths a desperate man may be driven!" Yes, even though he were striking me over the head, and the rest of the gang were clinging to me from behind, I should still continue to cry to the public: "Look! Here is a young man going out to conquer the Caucasus! Look at the mark of my spittle on his face!" '

After this (so it seemed to me) all would be over, and my Department would, as it were, disappear from the face of the earth. I should be arrested, tried, dismissed the service, thrown into gaol, and, finally, sent to a penal settlement in Siberia. No matter! Five years later, when released from prison, I should set out – poor, and clad only in a shirt – to look for Zverkov. Probably I should find him in some provincial capital – a married man, happy, and with a young daughter just beginning to grow up; and I should say to him: 'Look, villain, upon my hollow cheeks and ragged clothes! Everything have I now lost – my career, my happiness, my art, my learning, the woman whom I love, and all because of you! Here are pistols. I had come hither to fight a duel with you, but – but now I pardon you.' Then I should fire in the air, and be seen and heard of no more.

I could almost have wept at the pathos of my own imaginings. Yet all the while I knew that every one of them came out of Silvio* or Lermontov's *Masquerade*,* or some such piece. Suddenly I began to feel ashamed of myself – so ashamed that I stopped the cab, got out of it, and stood in the snow, in the middle of the street, with the driver looking on in open-mouthed amazement.

'What am I to do?' was my reflection. 'It is clear that to go on is folly, while to stop at the present stage is impossible, now that I have got so far. Good Lord! I only wish that I could put an end to the matter! Yet how am I to do that after all the insults I have received?'

'No!' finally I shouted, as I sprang into the cab again. 'It is foreordained! It is fate! Drive on, cabman!' – and, beside myself, I struck him a blow on the back of his neck.

'What are you hitting *me* for?' cried the little peasant; but nevertheless the blow had the effect of causing him to whip his steed until it began to kick. Wet snow was still falling in large flakes, but I took no heed of the elements as I sat there with my coat unbuttoned. Everything was now forgotten save that I had finally decided upon dealing the blow. With horror, too, I realised that, come what might, the blow must be dealt, and that no power on earth could save me. In the streets the solitary lamps glimmered dimly through the mist, like torches at a funeral, while snow was drifting under my greatcoat, jacket, and scarf, and melting there. Yet I scorned to wrap myself up, for I felt that all was lost.

At length we arrived at our destination. Leaping from the cab, I ascended the steps at a single stride, and banged with feet and fists upon the door. It opened as quickly as though I had been expected. As a matter of fact, Simonov had warned the people of the house that another member of the party might soon be following, and in houses of that kind it is best always to give warnings, and to take precautions. The house was one of those *magasins de modes* which used to be so numerous, but have now been closed by the police. During the daytime it was a dressmaker's establishment, but at night only those who had the *entrée* could resort thither for entertainment.

Passing rapidly through the show-room (which was unlighted), I reached a *salon* to which I was not altogether a stranger, and where a solitary wax candle was burning.

'Where are they?' I found myself asking of someone; but it turned out that they had that moment departed.

Presently I perceived that the proprietress herself – a woman with a foolish, smiling face, whom I knew a little – was standing before me. Then a door opened, and another person entered. Without paying any attention to either of them, I started pacing the room, and muttering to myself as I did so. I felt as though I had been saved from death. Certainly and beyond all doubt I should have dealt the intended blow, but my antagonist, by leaving the place, had altered the whole situation. I kept throwing vague glances around the room, for I could not properly rally my thoughts. Then, in mechanical sort of fashion, I looked at the woman who had just entered, and saw before me a pale, fresh young face which, though a trifle sallow, had straight black eyebrows and a serious, an astonished sort of an expression. It was a face which pleased me at once, for I should have detested it if it had been a smiling one. As I looked at her with increased attention I could discern in that serious countenance – a countenance that was grave almost to the point of singularity – a species of good-humoured *naïveté*. Assuredly she was not the sort of woman to attract those sots, and probably had passed unnoticed by them. True, she could not be called exactly pretty, but her figure was tall, strong, and well-made, and she was dressed in quite simple fashion.

Then an evil impulse stirred within me, and I approached her. At that moment I caught sight of myself in a mirror, and could see that my face was pale and agitated, my expression sullen, repellent, and vicious, and my hair dishevelled.

'So much the better!' I thought. 'I would rather seem to her disgusting than attractive. It is just what I want.'

6

Somewhere behind the partition-wall, and with a strangled sound as though it were being violently squeezed, a clock emitted a prolonged whirring. Then, after continuing to do so for an almost unnaturally long time, it gave forth a thin, a mean, and, as it were, an unexpected stroke with its gong, as though someone had suddenly sprung at and hit it. The gong struck twice. Hitherto I had been dozing rather than sleeping – lying in a sort of half-comatose condition.

The room – a low, narrow, confined apartment in which there was a huge wardrobe, and which was littered over with little boxes, rags, and every sort of odds and ends of clothing – was almost dark, since a candle which had been burning on a table at the further end of the apartment had gone out, save for an occasional flicker. In a few moments the darkness would be complete.

Soon I recovered my faculties. At once, without the least effort, everything came back to my memory, as though it had been watching its opportunity to revive. Yet all through my slumber I had seemed to be conscious of some point which had never quite sunk into oblivion, and around which all the fantasies of my sleep had laboured in anguish. Another curious circumstance was that all the events of the previous day now seemed, at the moment of my awaking, to have happened a long while ago, and as though I had lived through them at some far distant period.

My head was filled with fumes, for something seemed to have come over me – to be catching at, exciting, disturbing me, until my old bilious depression began again to seethe within my breast and to search vainly for an outlet. Suddenly, by my side, I perceived a pair of widely opened eyes regarding me with intent curiosity. Their gaze was so cold, so detached, so sullen, that they seemed hardly to belong to a human being. Indeed, I found their inspection irksome to bear.

But presently a morose idea sprang to birth in my brain, and diffused itself over my body with a sort of unclean sensation which resembled what one experiences when for the first time one penetrates to the musty, fusty underground. Somehow, too, I thought it unnatural that those eyes should have chosen such a moment to scrutinise me. Also, I remembered that never once throughout the two hours since I had entered the room had I spoken to this creature beside me so much as a word. I had not thought it necessary to do so. Indeed, it had been a sort of pleasure to me to preserve the silence unbroken. Now, however, there suddenly rose to my mind an image as uncouth and repellent as a spider – an image of the debased passion which, destitute of love, begins, grossly and shamelessly, where true love ought to receive its final crown. For a long time we lay thus – looking intently at one another. Yet at last, since she neither lowered her eyes nor once changed her expression, I could stand it no longer.

'What is your name?' I asked brusquely, and the sooner to put an end to the situation.

'Liza', she replied in a half-whisper, and with a sort of reluctance. Then she turned her eyes away.

I remained silent for a moment.

'It is bad weather – snowy and horrible', I went on, though more to myself than to her, as I clasped my hands indolently behind my head, and lay staring up at the ceiling.

She said nothing. The whole thing was becoming unpleasant.

'Do you belong to St Petersburg?' I continued, almost angrily, with a slight turn of my head in her direction.

'No.'

'To where, then?'

'To Riga', she replied, with a very bad grace.

'You are German, then?'

'No; Russian.'

'And have you been here long?'

'Where?'

'In this house?'

'Two weeks.'

Her replies grew shorter and shorter. Soon the candle finally expired, and I could no longer see her face.

'Have you a father and a mother?'

'Yes – no – yes.'

'Where are they?'

'There – in Riga.'

'*Who* are they?'

'Somebody.'

'How "somebody"? What sort of people are they? What is their profession?'

'They are in business.'

'And have you always lived with them?'

'Yes.'

'How old are you?'

'Twenty.'

'Why did you leave your parents?'

'Because——' Her 'because' evidently signified: 'Leave me alone, for I am tired.' A silence ensued.

God knows why I did not seize the opportunity to get up and go, for I was growing more and more disgusted and depressed. In spite of my efforts to banish them, pictures of the happenings of the previous day would keep wandering through my brain. Suddenly I recalled an incident which I had witnessed in the street when leaving the office early in the afternoon.

'Yesterday', I said loudly, and as though I had not wished to begin the conversation again, 'I saw some men carrying a coffin. They very nearly let it fall.'

'A coffin?'

'Yes; in the Haymarket.* It had just been brought out of a cellar.'

'Out of a cellar?'

'Well, out of a basement – you know the sort of place – the basement of a brothel. There was mud everywhere and filth. The place simply stank. It was horrible.'

Another pause ensued.

'Bad weather for a funeral', I went on, in order at any cost to break the silence.

'That would make no difference', she remarked after a further pause.

'Oh, but it would', I replied, with a yawn.

'How so?' she inquired – again after a pause.

'Because it *would*. In the first place, it would wet the grave-diggers' jackets and make them swear, and, in the second place, it would fill the grave with water.'

'Why with water?' she asked, with a touch of curiosity, and in a sharper, rougher tone than she had hitherto employed. For some reason or another this irritated me.

'Because there is *always* a few inches of water. In Volkhovo cemetery it is impossible to dig a grave dry.'

'Why so?'

'Why so? Because it is a damp spot – marshy all over. They just tip the dead into the water. I have seen it done myself – yes, several times.'

(As a matter of fact, I had never once seen it done, for I had never been in Volkhovo at all – I was relying upon mere hearsay.)

'Does not that make you afraid to die?' I went on.

'*Why* should I be going to die?' she exclaimed, as though defending herself against some imputation.

'Well, you will have to die *some* day, and precisely as that woman in the Haymarket died. She, like yourself, was a young girl once, but now she lies dead of consumption.'

'A woman should go and die in a hospital.'

('Evidently she knows all about it', I thought to myself; 'for she said, "a woman", not "a young girl".')

'When that woman died she was deeply in debt to her mistress', I resumed aloud (for I was growing more and more cantankerous). 'Yet up to the very end she was forced to serve her old woman, despite the consumption. I heard some cabmen – probably they were old friends of hers – telling some soldiers about it. Lord, how they laughed! They were just about to repair to a neighbouring tavern to celebrate the funeral.' By this time I was inventing right and left.

There fell a silence – a profound silence. Not a sound came from the woman.

'Then it is better to go and die in a hospital?' at length I asked.

'It is much the same thing, is it not?' she asked irritably. Then she added: 'But *why* should I be going to die?'

'Not now; but, later on, will you not have to?'

'Perhaps – later on.'

'But look here. As yet you are young and fresh and comely; consequently you can still name your price; but remember that after another year of this life your good looks will have faded.'

'After *one* year only?'

'Well, after a year your value will at least have lessened.' Somehow I felt inclined to be captious. 'When that has come about you will be forced to leave this house, and to enter an inferior one, and then a third, and then a fourth, and so on, always descending lower and lower and lower, until, after some seven years of it, you will find yourself landed in a Haymarket cellar. That will be glorious, will it not? On the other hand, it is probable that some day you will catch a disease – pneumonia, or a chill, or something of the sort; and the kind of life that you are leading makes such an illness progress very rapidly. It will cling fast to you, and refuse to be shaken off until you die.'

'Ah, well – then I must die, that is all.' She spoke as though she were exasperated, and at the same time made a quick movement of impatience.

'But do you not at all regret it?'

'Regret what?'

'Your life?'

There came no answer.

'Have you ever had a sweetheart?' I resumed.

'What is that to you?'

'Oh, I do not wish to press you. Quite so; what is it to me? But why should you be so angry about it? However, probably you have your troubles like everyone else, and they are no business of mine. Only, I am sorry for——'

'Sorry for what?'

'For you.'

'You need not be', was her almost inaudible rejoinder, as again she made a movement of impatience.

This angered me the more. What? I had spoken to her kindly, and she——!

'Do you ever think?' I persisted. 'Do you suppose, for instance, that you are treading the right road?'

'No, I *never* think.'

'Ah, well, that is just where the evil lies. Open your eyes while there is yet time. There *is* yet time. As yet you are young and good-looking, and might fall in love, and marry, and——'

'But not all married people are happy, are they?' she interrupted in her old rough, rapid way.

'No, not all; but at least their life is better than yours. Indeed, in comparison with your life, immeasurably better. And if one loves, one can live even without happiness; and should sorrow come, such life is still good – it is still good to be alive and to live. But *here*, what is there but foulness? Pah!'

I turned away in disgust, for I could not reason with her coldly. Besides, I was beginning to feel the force of what I was saying, and to grow warm over it. Also, I was thirsting to expound certain ideas which I had long ago conceived in my solitary den. Something in me had suddenly caught fire; there had suddenly dawned before my vision a definite aim.

'Never mind the fact that I too am here', I said, 'for I cannot be taken as an example, even though I may be worse than you. As a matter of fact, when I came to this house tonight I was drunk' (it will be seen that I was in a very great hurry to justify myself), 'and in that respect a man is no example for a woman. You and I are different persons, for, however much I may bedaub and befoul myself, I am no slave. I come, I go, and it is as though I had not come. I can shake it off, and become, as it were, a new man. But you – you have been a slave from the beginning. Yes, a slave. For have you not surrendered your all, and even your freewill? Consequently, later on, when you may wish to break your chain, you will never be able to do so. It will fasten itself closer and closer upon you. And a right cursed chain it is, too! I know its nature only too well. But since, I suppose, you will not be able to understand me if I put it in any other way, I will ask you – Are you not in debt to your landlady? Ah! *Now* you see how it is; *now* you see your chain. Nor will you ever escape from it, for that is how it is done. The fact that your soul must go to the devil matters nothing to your employer. I, on the other hand, am an unfortunate who plunge into the mire simply out of despondency. Some men drink out of despondency, but I – well, I come *here*. Yet what good does it do? Here have we been lying together without a single friendly word to say to one another all the time. You have merely looked at me like a wild beast, and I at you. Is it *thus* that one should love? Is it *thus* that a man should mate with a woman? No, it is foulness, foulness, from start to finish.'

'*Yes*!' came a hasty confirmation of all that I had said. Indeed, I was astounded at the precipitancy with which she accorded her assent. Surely it meant that similar ideas had been wandering in *her* brain also while she had been looking at me? Surely, then, she was capable at least of *some* thought?

'Devil take it all, but this is curious, for we are akin', I thought to myself, as I almost rubbed my hands with joy. 'Why should I not probe a little further into this youthful soul?' By this time I was getting more and more excited with the game.

She turned towards me, and (so far as I could judge in the darkness) raised herself upon her elbow. How I regretted that at that moment I could not watch her eyes! Yet I could hear her deep breathing.

'Why did you ever come to this house?' I resumed, with something of an authoritative air.

'For a certain reason.'

'Would it not have been much better for you to have gone on living with your father? There you would have been at least safe and well. There you would have been, as it were, in the nest.'

'But what if things were *worse* there than here?'

'It still remains for me to find the right note', thought I in passing; 'for evidently she does not appreciate sentimentality.'

Yet this was only a momentary thought. I swear that she really interested me. Also, I was feeling weak and unstrung, and knavery goes all too easily with such a mood.

'Who can say?' I hastened to answer aloud. 'Such things often happen. Indeed, I feel sure that someone has ill-treated you, and that you have been sinned against rather than sinning. Of your history I know nothing, yet I *do* know that a girl of your type does not lightly enter a place like this.'

'What sort of a girl am I, then?' she whispered almost inaudibly: yet I heard it.

'The devil take it all!' I reflected. 'Here have I been actually flattering her! This is horrible. Yet it is possible that good may come of it.

'Look here, Liza', I went on; 'let me speak of myself a little. Had I, since childhood, had parents to live with, I should never have become what I am today. This often occurs to my mind, for, however miserable life at home may be, there one has at least one's father and mother, not enemies or strangers. Yes, and even though those parents show one love but once a year, still one knows that one is at home. On the other hand, I had to grow up an orphan: whence it has come about that I am what you see me now – a man of no feeling.'

Again I stopped and waited. 'Perhaps she does not understand me!' I thought. 'Perhaps all this moralising seems to her ridiculous!'

'If I were a father', I continued, 'and had a daughter, I should love her even more than I did my sons.' I confess to blushing as I said this.

'And why?' she inquired (she *had* heard, after all!).

'Because – well, I hardly know, Liza. I know a father – a stern, grave man – who adores his daughter, and often kisses her hands and feet, and never grows tired of looking at her. For a whole evening he will sit and follow her with his eyes as she dances. In short, he is absolutely mad about her, and I can understand his being so. When night time comes she may be weary, and goes to rest. Then the father arises, and folds her in his arms as she lies asleep, and makes the sign of the cross over her. He wears but a threadbare coat, for he is a miser; yet for her no gift is too costly – for her he will spend his last coin, and feel happy if, in return for the gift, he receive but a smile. A father is always fonder of a daughter than a mother is. Yes, young girls are indeed fortunate to be living at home with their parents. For myself, I think that I should never have allowed any daughter of mine to marry.'

'Why not?' she asked, with a faint laugh.

'Because, by heavens, I should have been jealous. What? She to kiss another man – to love a stranger more than she did her own father? It hurts me even to think of it! Certainly, many follies are committed, and all men come to their senses at last; but I believe that to the very day of my death I should have hated giving my daughter away. On the other hand, I would have put every suitor in the world through his paces to ensure that she should fall to the man she loved. Unfortunately, the man whom the daughter loves is generally the man who cuts the worst figure in the father's eyes. 'Tis always so, and causes much trouble in families.'

'Some parents prefer to *sell* their daughters rather than give them honestly away', she broke in quickly.

'Ah, ha!' I thought. 'So *this* is how the wind lies!' Aloud I said, with some heat: 'Liza, that happens only in families which are unfortunate enough to be destitute either of love or of God. Where there is no love there can be no wisdom. True, I know that such families exist, but it was not of them that I was speaking. To judge by your words, I think that you yourself cannot come of a very loving family – that you have been made to suffer. On the other hand, conduct of that kind sometimes arises from poverty.'

'Are things any better in gentle families? There are plenty of poor people who live honourably.'

'Yes – perhaps. But, Liza, man loves to count his misfortunes, and to forget his blessings. If he were a little juster he would admit that everyone has an equal share of both – that, so long as all goes well in a family, God distributes His benefits to each member alike. The father will be jovial, affectionate, and faithful – a man who makes everyone around him happy. Even in times of trouble everything, through him, will come to seem cheerful. For where, in marriage, does one not find trouble? If ever you should marry, you too will know trouble. But how happy is the honeymoon of a girl who has wedded the man she loves! Everywhere and always she will be happy. Even the most trivial disputes will be hushed during those few blessed weeks. At the same time, there are women who, the more they love, the more they desire to quarrel. I assure you that it is so. Once I knew a woman of that type. "I love you", they say, "and it is *because* I love you that I wish to torment you. Do you not see how it is?" I wonder if you know what torture a man may be put to on this plea? Yes, there *are* such women. They think to themselves: "How I mean to love him afterwards! I will caress him for ever if only I may tease him a little now." Yet even *they* tend to happiness in the home – to the making of everything cheerful and comfortable and peaceable and in order. Then other women there are who are jealous. I myself used to know such a one. If her husband went out she could never rest quietly at home, but must go out (even in the middle of the night!) to see if he were not "*there*" – that is to say, in a certain house, or with a certain woman. Yet she knew better than anyone else that it was all a mistake on her part. Yes, she suffered from it more than anyone else could do. And that was her punishment. Yet such women love, and are all for love. How pleasant, too, are reconciliations after a quarrel! The wife of her own accord acknowledges her fault to her husband, and he and she pardon one another with equal delight. Both are so happy! 'Tis like a reproduction of their first meeting, a second nuptial, a rebirth of love. Nor has anyone in the world a right to know what passes between husband and wife if they really love one another. However much they may quarrel, the wife's mother should never be called in to act as arbitrator. That she should so much as suspect the *existence* of a quarrel is wrong, for husband and wife are their own best judges. Love is a secret of two, and should live hidden from all eyes, whosoever they be. It is better so, it is more religious, and it tends to develop self-respect. Now, from self-respect there spring many things, and if love has come at the right time – if it is for love that a man and a woman have married each other – why should that love ever pass? Cannot it be fostered? If so, why not? Very seldom is such a thing impossible. Why should love ever pass if the husband be kind and honourable? Of course, the fervid passion of the first few weeks cannot last eternally; but to that love there sometimes succeeds another and a better love. When that has come about, husband and wife are twin souls who have everything in common. Not a secret is there between them, and if children should result of the union, even the most difficult moments in life will have a sweetness of their own. It is sufficient to love steadfastly, and work becomes a pleasure. A married couple will then be happy indeed, and tell themselves that one day their children will repay them with love for all the present pain, and that therefore it is for themselves that they (the parents) are working. In time, too, the children will begin to grow up, and you will feel that you must set them an example, and be their support, and that when you are dead they will, for all their lives, preserve in their hearts your precepts and your thoughts as they have received them from you. In short, you will feel that your children will ever cleave faithfully to your remembrance. But what an onerous duty does that impose upon you! Therefore, for the better ordering of your conduct, is it not better to be united in as close a bond as possible? It is said that child-bearing is a painful thing. Who said that? On the contrary, it is the happiness of heaven. Do you love little children, Liza? For myself, I adore them. Think if you had a little child to dangle at your breast! What husband would harbour even a single bitter thought against his wife if he could watch her nursing her firstborn – a little, rosy, chubby thing that stretches itself, and rubs itself, with its tiny feet and hands all swelling with milk, and its nails clean and so small, so small, that it is laughable to see them, and its little eyes so full of intelligence that one could not say *what* they do not see? Yes, look at a baby sucking – how he shakes and plays with the breast! Presently the father draws near, and at once the baby drops the teat, and turns over upon his back, and, gazing at his parent, falls to laughing as though he would never stop. Then he takes up the teat again, and sometimes falls to biting it if he has got sufficient teeth to do so, while at the same time he looks at his mother, as much as to say, "See how I have sucked my fill of you." Yes; is it not perfect happiness when all three are united in one – husband, wife and child? What would one not give to attain such moments as they enjoy? No, Liza; first one must learn the lesson of life before proceeding to lay the blame upon fate.'

('By such pictures as these I shall certainly catch you', was my secret thought the while. Yet what I had said I had spoken in all sincerity.)

Suddenly I turned very red in the face, for it had suddenly occurred to me, 'What if I were to find that all this time she has been bursting with laughter at me?' The idea simply enraged me. Towards the end of my speech I had grown really heated; and to find that my conceit was in danger of being wounded! The silence continued until I had a great mind to nudge her with my elbow.

'What made you say it all?' she began, and then stopped.

Even that was sufficient for me. In a flash I understood the situation, for quite a new note could be heard quavering in her voice. No longer was there in it the old rude, brutal, obstinate intonation, but, rather, an intonation eloquent of gentleness and timidity – a timidity so great that even I felt touched, as well as (it must be confessed) a little guilty towards her.

'What do you mean?' I asked with intense curiosity.

'Well, you——'

'I what?'

'Well, one would almost think that you were speaking from a book', she said. In her tone I could detect the mocking note.

The speech irritated me – it irritated me greatly. Nor could I understand what point lay in that mockery, seeing that such an artifice is usually the last defence of a heart which is not only diffident of itself, but, as yet, free from vice; of a heart which is holding out to the last against rudely insistent efforts to penetrate its recesses; of a heart which is seeking to conceal its true feelings. As a matter of fact, it was from those stray silences, during the period when she was making feeble attempts to rail and failing to accomplish it, that I ought to have derived enlightenment; but *that* I was not clever enough to see; and, moreover, I was blinded by my ill-humour.

'Wait a little', I thought to myself.

7

'Really, Liza', I said aloud, 'had vice been foreign to me, I *might* have been speaking like a book; but, you see, it is *not* foreign to me. Consequently everything that I have said to you has come from my heart. Is it, then, possible that you are not conscious of the vileness of your present life? Truly, if you are not, then great must be the force of habit, and the devil only knows whither it can lead a human being! Do you in all seriousness think that you will never grow old – that you will always be comely, and allowed to stay here? I am not speaking of your infamy in general, but of the following consideration. As yet you are young and attractive and pretty, as well as not altogether devoid of feeling. Are you, then, aware that, no sooner had I recovered my senses tonight, than I felt disgusted at finding myself here by your side? To have the hardihood to enter such a den as this one needs to be drunk. But if you had been of a different kind, if you had been leading an honest life, I might have courted and fallen in love with you. Then your every look, your every word, would have been delightful to me. I should have watched at your door, and knelt to you when you came out, and it would have been my highest boast to proclaim that I regarded you as my sweetheart. Never should I have harboured – never *could* I have harboured – a single impure thought concerning you. But *here* I know that I have but to whistle for you, and that you will come, since I need not consult *your* pleasure, but, rather, *you* must consult *mine*. The lowest peasant who sells his labour is none the less not a slave, for the reason that he knows that one day his labour will have an end. But when, for you, will that end come? Think, then: what is it that you have surrendered? What is it that you have delivered over into bondage? Why, your very soul – the soul of which you had no right to dispose, but which you have none the less enslaved to your body! You suffer your love to be profaned by drunkards when all the while love is the whole world, love is the most precious of jewels, love is the cherished treasure of virgins, love is what men will give their souls, their very lives, for! But what is *your* love worth? You have sold it beyond redemption, for who would seek to attain love where everything may be attained without love's presence at all? What worse offence could a woman commit? Do you understand me? True, I have heard that you wretched women are given a certain amount of amusement, and, at times, are allowed to have particular lovers of your own. Yet that is a mockery, a mere make-believe. You take what is given you, and get laughed at for your pains. For what sort of a man would such a lover make? Would he be even capable of love? Never! How could a man love you when all the while he knows that at any moment you may be summoned to attend someone else? No, the whole thing, for him, would be a piece of indecency, and no more. And could such a man have any respect for you? Could there be anything in common between you and him? No, he would only laugh at you and plunder you. Such would be *his* way of loving. You might consider yourself fortunate if some day he did not kill you. Could you ever be sure that he would not do so? Why, at the merest hint that he should marry you he would laugh in your face, even if he did not also spit in it, and then put you to death. And all the while, save that you had grown used to him, you might not care for him the amount of a couple of cracked kopecks! To think of it! Then why have you buried your life here? Is it because you are given coffee and fed well? But for what purpose are you fed? Food of that kind would choke any honest woman, since beneath such generosity she would always discern the hidden motive. Besides, you are in debt to your landlady, and will always be so – to the very end, to the very moment when your customers have ceased to care about you. And that moment will soon come! Do not trust too much to your youth, since in this place one year counts as three, and you will soon find yourself outside, though not before there have been many intrigues against you, and disputes and revilings, even as though you had not already handed over your health and youth to your landlady, even as though you had not already lost your soul for nothing, even as though your task mistress had not already despoiled and beggared you and stolen your goods! No, do not trust to her always to keep you. And, to please her, your companions will never be backward in attacking you, for they are slaves like yourself, and have long since lost sight of conscience and pity. In your life the prize goes to her who is the most unclean, the most vile, the most abominable. In your life, too, they know how to inflict such injuries as are undreamt of elsewhere. All that you possess, all that you hold most dear – your health, your looks, your youth, your last remaining shred of hope – will soon be lost. At twenty-two you will be aged thirty-five; and if by that time you have not also become diseased you may think yourself lucky, and render thanks to God. Perhaps you suppose that at least you do not *work* here, that you are always "making holiday"? Wretched woman! I tell you that in all the world there is no more horrible trade than yours – in all the world there exists no form of forced labour which is even *comparable* to your existence. Ought not that one thought – let alone any others – to make your heart weep? And when you come to be turned out of this house not a word, not a syllable, will there be that you can say for yourself. For ever you will have to go your way an outcast. Yes, you will have to enter another brothel, and then a third one, and others, until at last you find yourself landed in the Haymarket. There you will often be beaten, for the place has its own endearments, and its *habitués* are apt to confound caresses with blows. Its horrors pass belief! Pay but a single visit there, and when you have seen it for yourself you will believe the evidence of your eyes. One New Year's Eve, when I was walking through that quarter, I saw a woman outside a door. Her companions had turned her out of the house because they could not bear to hear her weeping. Despite the fearful cold, they had closed the door upon her! There she sat at nine o'clock at night – drunken, dishevelled, half-naked, and almost dead with the beating which she had received. Terrible was the contrast between her painted cheeks and blackened eyes; her nose and gums were running with blood from a blow which had been given her by a cabman. In her hands she was holding a piece of salt fish, and as she sat there on the pavement, and wept bitter tears of pain, and lamented her lot, she kept striking this piece of fish against the doorsteps of the house, while a group of cabmen and soldiers on the kerb were engaged in egging her on. Surely *you* do not wish to become like that? Personally I do not think that you ever will; but how can any of us tell? Perhaps, some eight or ten years ago, even that woman with the fish came to this house as fresh as a cherub, and innocent, and pure, and ignorant of evil, and ready to blush at the least word. Perhaps she too was once proud, like yourself, and sensitive, like yourself, and different to all her companions, and full of the idea that nothing but happiness awaited her and the man who said he loved her, and whom she loved. Yet see the end to which she has now come! Ah, can it be that, when, drunken and dishevelled, she was striking that fish against the dirty door-steps, she was recalling to her memory her unsullied past, and her father's house, and her school days, and the road where the young man used to wait for her to swear that he would love her always and devote his whole future to her, and the moment when they decided that their affection would be eternal, and that they must marry as soon as ever they came of age? Liza, it would be a sheer blessing for you if you were to die tomorrow, in some cellar, some hidden corner, like the consumptive woman who died the other day in the Haymarket. You say you will go to the hospital, do you? But they would not receive you there, because of your debt to your landlady. Consumption is not a rapid sickness, like a fever, which to the last moment leaves the patient some hope of recovery. No, a consumptive woman goes on deceiving herself, and believing herself still strong and well, while all the time she is playing into her landlady's hands. Slowly and surely you will be dying, and seeing yourself dying, and gradually being cast aside; until, at last, what will there be left for you to say? True, you will have sold your soul; but you will still be owing your landlady money. Consequently you will be left alone, utterly alone, for what else could they do with you? Perhaps they will reproach you for not earning your keep, as well as for being so long a-dying! And should you be thirsty, they will give you water, and, with it, insults, and the words: "When are you going to get out of this, you slut? You keep us awake at night with your groans, and the customers do not like it." I myself have heard things like that said to a woman. And at length, when death has nearly come to you, you will be thrown into a corner of some stinking cellar, to lie helpless in the darkness and the wet. What will you have to think of during the long, long, endless nights? . . . And when death has come, some strange, some grudging hand will shroud you; and around your corpse there will be heard, not prayers, but vile oaths. No one will be there to bless you, no one to bewail you. You will be placed upon a bier similar to that which they allotted to the consumptive woman of the Haymarket, and when that has been done the bearers will repair to a tavern and talk of you, while your body will be left to lie in the mud and the filth and the half-melted snow. And what of your funeral rites? "Lower away at that end, Vanya. Even here she keeps up her heels in the air, just as she used to do when she was plying her trade. Yes, that is the sort she was." "Don't bear too heavily upon that rope there. Let it down a bit. Yes, that's the way." "No, no; you will upset her if you do that. After all, she was a human being like ourselves." "Well, so much the worse for her! On we go." Nor will they quarrel long over you. As quickly as it can be done they will throw over you a few shovelfuls of wet blue clay, and then betake themselves once more to the tavern. Such is the future before you. Other women are accompanied to the graveyard by children, fathers, or husbands; but for *you* not a tear will be shed, not a sigh will be heaved, not a regret will be uttered. Nor will any one come to pray over your grave, but your name will vanish as utterly as though you had never existed, as though you had never been born. "Dust to dust!" And at night, when the dead raise the lids of their coffins, you will cry aloud: "Suffer me to go and live a little longer in the world, good people. I lived, but I never knew life, for my life served but as a cloth for others to wipe their lust upon. All my existence was drunken away in the mire of the Haymarket. Suffer me to go and live a little longer in the world, good people." '

Here my own pathos began to get the better of me, and I felt such a choking sensation in the throat that I was forced to stop. Presently a nervous feeling also came upon me, and with beating heart I raised myself to listen. I had good reason to do so.

For a long while past I had been suspecting that my words would probably end by overwhelming Liza's soul, and breaking her heart; and the more assured that that would be so I had become, the more I desired to attain my end as quickly and as thoroughly as possible. It was a game which greatly attracted me. Yet it was not *all* a game.

Though I knew that, throughout, I had spoken in a sententious, stilted, bookish manner, and could not have spoken otherwise, the fact in no way disturbed me, since I was well aware, and had a sure presentiment, that she would end by understanding me, as well as that my very bookishness would help me to further my plans. Yet even in the moment of success I recoiled and stood aghast at what I had done! For never, never in my life have I witnessed such despair as now came upon her! She lay there with her head buried in the pillow, her face pressed into its folds, and her frame shaken from head to foot with convulsive tremors. And just at the moment when her sobs seemed to be passing altogether beyond control, she broke forth into shrill cries and moans as she glued herself still closer to the pillow, in the hope that she might prevent any other inmate of the house – indeed, any living soul in the world – from hearing her agony. Tearing the sheet with her teeth, she bit her hands until (as I afterwards saw for myself) the blood came, while she twined her hands convulsively through her disordered hair. Lastly she lay motionless, almost without breathing, and with her teeth tightly clenched together. At first I tried to speak to her, to calm her agitation, but I had not the requisite courage. Shaking from head to foot, I groped my way from the bed, with the intention of dressing myself and departing; but the room was so dark that, despite my efforts, my movements were greatly retarded. At length I found a box of matches and a new and unburnt candle. As soon as the flame had lit up the room Liza raised her form with a sharp contortion, seated herself – a sorry figure – upon the edge of the bed, and looked at me with a gaze which had in it almost the smile of a mad woman. Seating myself by her side, I took her hand. Instantly she appeared to recall all that had passed during the preceding hour, and, leaning in my direction, as though to embrace me, seemed suddenly to change her mind, and ended by gently kissing my head.

'Liza, my dear one', I began, 'I did not mean it. Pray pardon me.'

Upon that she clasped my hands with such force that in an

instant I understood that I had said the wrong thing. So for a moment I held my tongue. Then I went on –

'Here is my address, Liza. Come and see me.'

'Yes, I will come', she murmured, though a little irresolutely, and with her head drooping.

'Now I must go. Good-bye until we meet again.'

I rose, and she did the same. Suddenly I saw her start and blush. Then she seized a shawl which was lying on a chair, threw it over her shoulders, and muffled herself up to the chin. After that she threw me a half-whimsical glance – a sort of sickly smile. It hurt me so much that I made all the more haste to depart. I had a longing to be gone.

'Wait a moment', came her unexpected request when we had reached the entrance-hall, and were standing by the door while I put on my overcoat. Setting down the candle, she ran back into the house.

'She must have remembered something which she had wished to show me', thought I. 'When she left me her face was red, her eyes were shining, and her smile had quite a different air to what it had before. What can it all mean?' I waited. Presently she returned with a sort of petitioning or deprecatory look in her face. Nor was it the same face as a few hours ago, for it no longer had in it the mournful, suspicious, obstinate eyes which I had seen before. On the contrary, those eyes were now gentle, beseeching, full of confidence and tenderness, yet timid. It was the face of a child who is gazing at someone whom it loves, and from whom it is hoping to receive a gift. They were clear and grey; they were beautiful, animated eyes which could with equal intensity express either love or hate.

Without any explanation, but as though I had been some sort of a superior being who could divine everything, she tendered me a paper. As she did so her face looked brilliantly radiant – naïvely, almost childishly, triumphant. I unfolded the paper. It was a letter from a medical student (or someone of the kind) which, though florid in tone and highly coloured, expressed in an entirely respectful manner a declaration of love. I have forgotten its exact terms, but can remember that, despite its flowery diction, it contained between its lines a certain amount of genuine feeling of the sort which cannot be feigned. When I had finished reading it I chanced to encounter Liza's gaze. It was eager, full of curiosity, and as impatient as that of a child. Next, since I was slow to make a remark of any kind, she told me rapidly, and in a few words (as well as with a kind of joyous pride), that, some few days ago, she had been to a ball at 'a good house' where there lived people 'who knew nothing of what I am now – no, nothing at all', since she was then quite new to the brothel, and had once, only once, et cetera, et cetera, and had now no intention of remaining there, but was resolved to leave as soon as ever she could get clear of the place. Well, at this ball she had met the medical student, and they had danced and talked together the whole evening, and the student had known and played with her as a little girl at Riga, and had also known her parents. Of *this*, however, he had known nothing, nothing whatever – he had never even suspected it. And, the day after the ball (that is to say, three days ago), he had sent her this letter by the hand of a friend who had gone with her to the dance; and – and – well, that was all. She lowered her eyes in confusion.

Poor girl! So she had been keeping this letter as a precious thing, and had yearned to show me her poor little treasure because she would not have me depart without knowing that even *she* could win honest, sincere affection, and be addressed with respect. Doubtless the letter was destined to lead to no result, but only to grow old and faded in a casket; yet sure am I that she would have treasured it to the end, as at once her visible trophy and her visible excuse. And now, in this moment of pride and desire for extenuation, she had thought of bringing me this poor little missive, that she might naïvely parade her triumph before me, and rehabilitate herself in my eyes, and (perhaps) even earn my congratulations! . . . However, I said nothing; I only pressed her hand and departed. Somehow I was in a great hurry to depart.

Large flakes of snow were falling, but I walked the whole way home. Tired, overdone, astonished though I was, there was yet dawning in me a consciousness of the truth. And a sorry truth it was!

8

At first I could not bring myself to accept that truth; but, next morning, on awaking from a heavy sleep of several hours, I at once recalled all the events of the night, and felt astounded at the sentimentality which I had displayed towards Liza. 'What was the use of that horror and that pity?' I said to myself. 'Am I getting as nerve-diseased as an old woman? Pah! And why did I give her my address? What if she should avail herself of it? Well, *let* her come. It will not matter.' Evidently the point – the chief, the most important point of all – was to hasten to retrieve my reputation in the eyes of Zverkov and Simonov. Consequently for that morning, at all events, Liza escaped my anxious mind altogether.

First of all it behoved me to repay Simonov my debt of last night; and to effect this I decided upon desperate means – namely, to borrow fifteen roubles from Anton Antonych. As it befell, the latter was in an exceedingly good temper that morning, and acceded to my request at the first asking. This so delighted me that, in signing the promissory note, I told him negligently, but with some archness of bearing, that, the previous evening, I had 'dined with friends at the Hôtel de Paris.' 'The occasion', I went on, 'was a farewell dinner to a comrade – I might even say, to a friend of my boyhood – who had gone the pace right royally. Of good family and unexceptionable standing, he has also had a distinguished career, is clever and good-natured, and can boast of very great success among the fair sex. We drank champagne by the dozen' – and so on, and so on. Rubbish though it all was, it nevertheless came quite easily, disconnectedly, and unbidden to my lips.

On reaching home I at once wrote to Simonov; and to this day I am lost in admiration when I recall the truly gentlemanly, the perfectly frank and good-humoured tone of my letter. Easily and with grace – above all things, with no superfluous expenditure of words – I begged pardon for all that had happened, and justified myself – 'if I may be permitted to do so' – by the fact that, from the moment when, between five and six o'clock (that is to say, previous to my companions' arrival), I had imbibed a first liqueur at the Hôtel de Paris, sheer unusedness to wine had turned my head. Of Simonov I begged pardon by name, and then asked him to make my excuses to the rest of my fellow diners, but more especially to Zverkov, whom I declared that I 'remembered only as in a dream', but whom I must undoubtedly have offended. To this I added that assuredly I would have called upon each of my fellow diners in turn had not my head – still more, my conscience – been too sore to permit of my doing so. Upon this facile, this, as it were, careless (yet entirely becoming) touch which had suddenly manifested itself in my pen I particularly plumed myself, since, better than anything else, it would give my friends to understand that I took an absolutely independent view of 'my unseemly behaviour of last night', and that I did not look upon myself as the crushed individual whom 'you, my good sirs, may suppose me to be', but as a gentleman who knows how to respect himself. 'Let me not be blamed for my youthful indiscretions', I wrote in conclusion.

'What marquis-like playfulness!' I commented admiringly, as I read the document through. 'What a refined, what a well-mannered person it makes me appear to be! Others, in my place, would have been at a loss to extricate themselves from the difficulty, whereas *I* have wormed my way out, and can go to dinner again, simply through the fact that I am a refined, educated man of the nineteenth century. To think that all this should have arisen out of last night's wine! Hm! But no; it was not due to the wine, for, as a matter of fact, between five and six o'clock I never touched a single drop of vodka, and have therefore told Simonov a lie. Yes, I have lied to him most unconscionably; and to do so was wrong. No matter; the main thing is that I *have* got out of it safely.

With this letter I enclosed six roubles, and, having sealed the lot, requested Apollon to take it to Simonov's; whereupon, Apollon having learnt that the package contained some money, the rascal became more respectful, and consented to perform the errand. Towards evening I went for a walk, for the previous night's festivities had left me very bilious, and my head was swimming badly. The further the evening advanced, and the darker the shadows grew, the more did my reflections become varied and involved. In the recesses of my heart and conscience there seemed to be lurking something which would not die – a sort of mysterious feeling which hurt me even as a burn might have done. Generally, on such occasions, I directed my steps towards the most crowded spots and most populous thoroughfares – especially at dusk, at the hour when the throng of hurrying workmen and artisans (their faces worn almost to brutality) becomes denser, and the daily toil has reached an end. It was precisely the humble pursuits of these humble breadwinners – the blatant prose of life – that interested me most. Yet, that evening, the jostling of the pavements only served to exasperate me, and to prevent me from properly connecting my thoughts. Within me there was arising a carking uneasiness which would not be quieted. At length so unstrung was I that I betook myself homewards. Something like a crime seemed to be weighing upon my conscience.

Also, the thought that one day Liza might call upon me kept torturing my soul. It was strange that, of all my recollections of the previous night, the memory of her should disturb me with a kind of a special, separate force. Everything else had by this time escaped my mind, since everything else had been put right by my letter to Simonov. Only as regards the point of which I have spoken did I still remain uneasy. It was as though only Liza had the power to make me suffer. 'What if she *should* come?' was my constant thought. 'Well, it will not greatly matter. *Let* her come. Hm! Yet I cannot bear to think that she should see the way in which I live. Last night I must have seemed to her a perfect hero; whereas now——! Also, I cannot bear to think that I am so out-at-elbows. My rooms speak of nothing but poverty. Look at the suit in which I had to go out to dinner last night! Look at that deal sofa shedding its straw, and at the dressing-gown which barely covers me! What a set of rags! And to think that she should see all this, and see Apollon too! And the brute will be sure to insult her, and to pick a quarrel with her, if only he can do me a rudeness. And I, as usual, shall play the cad, and fall to prancing before her, and wrapping myself in the folds of my dressing-gown, and grinning, and telling endless lies. Oh, the foulness of it all! Yet even that would not be the worst thing that I should do, for in me there is something fouler, baser, more serious yet. Yes, in me there is something baser – something which will once more make me don the mask of falsehood and dishonour.'

The thought of this fired my anger the more. 'But why dishonour?' I cried. 'What is there so dishonourable in it? What I said last night I really meant, for I genuinely felt it. What I did was to try and arouse her to better instincts. The fact that she wept was all to the good, and may prove the saving of her.'

Yet somehow I could not reassure myself. Continually during that evening – even after nine o'clock, when (so my calculations told me) there was no chance of her coming that night – I could see her present before me, and always in the same attitude. For, of all the incidents of the previous night, one in particular was for ever graven on my memory. It was the moment when the light of the match had revealed to me her pale, wrung face and martyred expression. What a strangely pitiful, futile smile there had been playing on her lips! Nor did I know that, even so long as fifteen years after the event, she would still be present to my mental eye, with that strangely pitiful, futile smile of hers.

But next morning I felt disposed to look upon the whole affair as nonsense and a mere lapse of the nervous system – above all, as an 'exaggeration'. Of this latter weakness in me I had always recognised the existence, and was afraid of its effects. 'I invariably magnify things; wherefore I invariably come to grief', was what I kept saying from hour to hour.

At length I summed up my reflections in the thought that possibly she *might* come. Yet still the uncertainty annoyed me.

'Yes, she *will* come', I burst out as I paced the room. 'If not today, at all events tomorrow. Oh, the cursed romanticism of these "pure hearts"! Oh, the damnableness, the folly, the obtuseness, of pruriently sentimental souls like hers! Yet how is it that I do not understand her? How is it, indeed?'

I stopped in strange perplexity.

'To think', I resumed, 'that a few words, a mere fragment of an idyll (and a bookish, artificial, invented idyll at that) should bring about such a revolution in the life of a human being! It only shows of what a virgin, untouched soil, is capable.'

At times I even thought of going to see *her*, and telling her all, and asking her not to come; but at these times such wrath again seized upon me that I verily believe that, had she at that moment been within my reach, I should have fallen tooth and nail upon her. Yes, I should have insulted her, spat upon her, chased her out of the house, and beaten her black and blue!

However, another day passed, and then another one, and then a third; yet no Liza came, and I began to feel a little easier. Especially after nine o'clock did I feel cheerful as I went out for my walk. In fact, I came to take a brighter view of things altogether, and would say to myself: 'I will save Liza by having her to visit me, and talking to her. Yes, I will develop and shape her mind. I know that she loves me, and loves me passionately, yet I mean to pretend that I am unaware of it (though *why* I should so pretend I do not know, unless it be because she is comely). Then one day, with an air at once confused and beautiful, she will throw herself into my arms, in a transport of tears and tremors, and tell me that I have been her deliverer, and that she loves me more than all the world beside. Then I shall feign surprise, and say: "Liza, is it possible that you suppose that I have never divined your love? Why, I saw it, and understood it, long ago, but dared not, of my own initiative, lay siege to your heart, since I had an influence over you, and feared lest, should you ever become aware of it, you would think it incumbent upon you to respond to my passion, and to force a similar passion in yourself; which would never have been in accordance with my wish, since such a course would have been sheer despotism and indelicacy on my part." At this point I shall plunge into a sea of Western-European, George-Sandian subtleties,* and then continue: "But now you are *mine*, Liza. Now you are my own creation, a thing pure and beautiful, and my fairest of wives. So –

> Into my house, with daring step and free,
> Enter thou and reign.*

'From that point onwards we shall tread the road of life together, and travel abroad', et cetera, et cetera, et cetera.

But in the end I used to feel ashamed of myself, and to put out my tongue at my own folly.

'Perhaps', also I thought at times, 'they will not let this tiresome woman leave the house. I believe such women are *not* allowed to go out very much – least of all in the evenings' (for some reason I always thought that she would come at night, and precisely at seven o'clock). 'But', I suddenly remembered, 'she told me that, as yet, she was not completely a slave – that she still stood upon a special footing. That means – hm! well, what the devil *does* it mean? Nevertheless, she will come some day; infallibly she will come.'

Really I must think myself fortunate in that, throughout that time, Apollon's rudeness did much to distract me. He simply exhausted my patience. He was my prime cross, my constant plague, in life. For years we had been wrangling with one another, night and morning, until I had come positively to hate him. My God, how I hated him! Never before nor since have I so hated a human being! An elderly man of imposing aspect, he not only acted as my servant, but also did a little tailoring in his spare moments. Why he had such a contempt for me I do not know. For he *did* despise me, and that to an unreasonable extent. Yet, though he looked down upon me from heights of unspeakable superiority, he treated everyone in the same way. Merely to see his tow-coloured head, his excessively sleek hair, the tuft which he grew on the top of his forehead (and which he periodically greased with olive oil), his huge mouth, and his V-shaped lips, made one feel that one was in the presence of a being who was supremely sure of himself. Besides, he was an intolerable precisian – the most precise person on earth, and could boast of a conceit which would have presumed to patronise Alexander of Macedon* himself. Also, for every button on his coat, and for every nail on his fingers, he cherished an affection which positively amounted to adoration. Myself, however, he treated with a high hand. He always spoke to me very shortly, and, when looking at me, did so with invincible self-sufficiency, supreme hauteur, and a sort of rallying mockery which drove me nearly to distraction. Yet, though he made such a favour of his services, those services amounted to very little, for he appeared to think himself under no particular obligation to work. In short, there can be no doubt that he thought me an absolute idiot; and if for a single moment he endured my presence, it was only because he took pleasure in drawing, at my hands, the seven roubles per month which I awarded him for his idling. Much, much may be forgiven me on his account. Sometimes, owing to our mutual enmity, the very sound of his footsteps would make me feel as though an attack of nerves were imminent. But the feature in him which disgusted me most of all was a sort of whistling noise which he always made when speaking. Surely he must have had a tongue too long for his mouth (or some such deformity) to make him suck his lips and whistle as he spoke? Yet of this circumstance he actually seemed proud – probably because he believed that it gave him a distinguished air! Usually he spoke low, and very slowly, with one hand clasped behind his back, and his eyes cast down. Above all things he infuriated me when he was reading his nightly Psalms (between my room and his there was only a thin partition-wall), and we had many a battle over those devotions. Yet with him they were a sheer passion. Every day he would fall to conning them over in a voice that was as level and devoid of intonation as the voice of a man keeping vigil over a corpse. Curiously enough, the last-mentioned pursuit is the very trade that he has now come to, for at the present time he is a professional reciter of Psalms over the dead, while the rest of his time he divides between the professions of rat-catcher and bottle-washer. However, I was powerless to dismiss him; he was, as it were, chemically soldered to my existence. Besides, nothing in the world would ever have induced him to give me notice; while, for my part, I could not have endured life in a furnished tenement. My present tenement was an isolated one, and therefore my sheath, my box into which I could withdraw from all humanity; and for some infernal reason or another Apollon always seemed to form part of it. Consequently for seven whole years I found myself unable to make up my mind to dismiss him.

As for my retaining his wages for a day or two, I had always found the scheme impossible, for the reason that whenever I had attempted to do so he had told me tales which had made me wonder where best I could flee to hide my head. On the present occasion, however, I was so exasperated with the world that I resolved (never mind why) to punish Apollon by making him wait as much as a fortnight for his emoluments. For the last two years I had been vowing to do this thing, even if it were only to show him that he could not take a high hand with me, and that I was his master; but on the present occasion I decided to say nothing to him about it, and so force him to take the initiative in referring to his wages. As soon as he should do so (I decided) I would go to my cash-box, show him the seven roubles in order to let him see for himself that they had duly been set apart for him, and say that I did not choose, *I did not choose*, to hand them to him now. Yes, I would say quite simply that I *did not choose* to do so, since I had a mind to be master, although for a long time past he had been rude and overbearing in his manner. On the other hand, if he chose to come and ask me for them respectfully, I would (perhaps) pardon him: otherwise he would have to wait fifteen days longer, or perhaps three weeks, or, possibly, a whole month.

Yet, for all my resolution, he proved the victor, for I failed to maintain the struggle longer than four days. He began in the manner which he always adopted on such occasions, and, since I had been making the same sort of attempt for three years, I knew exactly what to expect. Yes, I knew all his villainous tactics by heart. He would begin by staring me in the face with long-drawn-out severity; more especially if he met me in the street, or if he were leaving the flat at the same moment as myself. If I bore the ordeal well, or if I seemed to be paying him no attention, he would embark upon other, though always silent, persecutions. Unsummoned, he would suddenly enter the room on noiseless tiptoe, at a moment when I was either reading or quietly walking up and down. Halting on the threshold, he would then lay one hand behind his back, advance one foot a step, and train upon me a look less of severity than of absolute, whole-souled contempt. If I asked him sharply what he wanted he would return me no answer, but continue to stare me in the eyes. Lastly, with a very special, a very meaning sucking of the lips, he would turn on his heel, and slowly – very slowly – retire to his den. Two hours later he would return. This time, unable any longer to contain myself, I would not ask him what he wanted, but raise my head with a sharp, imperious movement, and fix him with my gaze. In this manner we would remain staring at one another for two or three minutes; after which, with great dignity, he would once more turn on his heel (even as he had done the first time), and take his departure for another couple of hours.

In case even *that* did not suffice to bring me to terms, and I still had the hardihood to continue rebellious, he would begin sighing as he looked at me – sighing long and deeply, as though by his sighs he wished to make clear to me the measure of my moral abasement. It need hardly be said that this last stratagem had always worsted me. I might be beside myself, I might even foam at the mouth with rage, but in the end I had always had to take the road which he desired me to take.

On the present occasion, however, he had no sooner reached the stage of 'stern looks' than I issued from my fastness and attacked him (I was sufficiently irritated, you may be sure, for the deed).

'Stop!' I cried. 'Remain where you are!'

With slow, silent and dignified bearing he continued to leave the room, with his hand still clasped behind his back.

'Return!' I cried after him. 'Return at once!'

My voice must have reached an almost supernatural intensity, for he *did* return, and stood gazing at me in some astonishment. Not a word did he speak, however, and that angered me the more.

'How dare you enter my room without being sent for?' I shouted. 'And how *dare* you look at me like that? Answer!'

For fully half a minute he continued calmly to look at me. Then again he turned to depart.

'Stop!' I yelled as I made for him at a run. 'Do not move an inch! Stop where you are, and answer my questions! For what did you come here?'

'To see if you had any orders for me', he replied with gentle deliberation after a moment's silence; the interval having been employed in sucking his lips and poising his head, first upon one shoulder, and then upon the other. His voice, his attitude, his whole self exuded a lethargy which drove me to distraction.

'It is *not* so, you ruffian!' I cried in a voice which trembled with rage. 'I never sent for you at all. *I* can tell you why you have come here. You have seen that I have not paid you your wages; yet your vanity will not allow you actually to ask for them. *That* is what you have come here for, with those damned looks of yours. Yes, you have come here just to punish and to torture me, without having the sense, you brute, to understand what a damnable, damnable, damnable thing you are doing!'

Again he was on the point of turning on his heel when I caught him by the arm.

'Listen!' I cried. 'Here is your money. Do you see it? It is *there*!' (I drew the sum from a drawer). 'Yes, the seven roubles are *there*! But you are not going to have them until you choose, humbly and respectfully, to beg my pardon.'

'That is impossible', he replied, with almost a superhuman amount of assurance.

'Very well!' I shouted. 'Then I swear to you that you shall *never* have your wages at all!'

'There is nothing that I need beg your pardon for', he went on, as though he had not heard me. 'On the other hand, you have called me a rascal, and I intend to go and see the superintendent about it.'

'Go, then!' I yelled. 'Go at once! Yes, this very minute, this very second! Go, you rascal, you rascal, you rascal!'

Scarcely looking at me, he moved towards the door; whence, paying me no further attention, nor once glancing in my direction, he re-entered his own room.

'But for Liza, all this would never have happened', I reflected. I felt so agitated that my heart had well-nigh stopped beating as for a moment or two I preserved my solemn, dignified attitude. Then I pursued Apollon to his room.

'Apollon', I said in a voice the low, restrained tone of which was really due to the fact that I was half-stifled with rage, 'go at once for the superintendent of the buildings.'

Apollon had just seated himself at his table, after donning his spectacles, and begun to sew; but, on hearing my command, he burst into a loud snigger.

'Yes, go this instant!' I repeated. 'Go this instant, I tell you! If you do not go, more will happen than you have bargained for.'

'You yourself are not feeling very comfortable about it, I think', he observed. As he spoke he did not even raise his head, but sucked his lips in, and slowly threaded his needle. 'Is it usual for a man to go for a policeman to effect his own arrest? And as for frightening me, you might as well save yourself the trouble, for you will never succeed in doing *that*.'

'Nevertheless, I tell you to go!' Barking out the words like a dog, I had just seized Apollon by the collar when – the door opened, and slowly and softly a figure appeared, came towards us, and stood gazing in astonishment at the spectacle. I felt so overcome with shame that, diving hastily into my room, I seized hold of my hair with both hands, staggered back against the wall, and remained crouching there.

A couple of minutes later I heard Apollon's slow footsteps approaching.

'Someone to see you', he said, with a look of amazing severity. Then he stood aside for Liza to pass. When she had done so, he made no attempt to depart, but stood there with his mocking smile.

'Go, go!' was my frantic command.

At that moment the clock, emitting a laboured whirring and creaking, struck seven.

9

> Into my house, with daring step and free,
> Enter thou and reign.

I found myself standing thunderstruck – standing shamed to the core. Yet I have an idea that I smiled, and tried to dispose my dilapidated dressing-gown to the best advantage – even as, in previous moments of doubting, I had imagined that I *should* do. She too seemed greatly confused – a thing for which I had been in no way prepared; yet it was my embarrassment which eventually rose superior to the occasion.

'Pray sit down', I said in mechanical fashion as, placing a chair for her near the table, I withdrew to the sofa. She seated herself obediently, and gazed at me in evident expectation that I should continue. I strove to keep myself in hand, but must confess that this artless attention on her part nearly drove me mad, for I conceived that she must be merely *pretending* to have noticed nothing, merely *pretending* to be looking upon everything as the normal state of things; whereas all the time she——! Inwardly I swore that I would make her pay for this.

'You have surprised me under odd circumstances, Liza', I began, though somehow conscious that that was just what I ought *not* to have said. 'No, no', I went on (for I saw her face suddenly colour), 'I am not speaking of my *furniture*. I am not in the least ashamed of my poverty, but, on the contrary, am proud of it. I may be poor, but at least I am honourable. One *may* be poor and honourable, you know' (here I stammered a little). 'By the way, will you have some tea?'

'No, thank you', she began, 'but——'

'Wait a moment', I interrupted. Rising swiftly, I ran to Apollon's room, where, in default of any other resort, I was only too thankful to take refuge.

'Apollon', I stuttered, with feverish eagerness, as I threw him the seven roubles which I had been holding in my hand the while, 'here are your wages – do you see? Yes, I will give them you *now*, but, in return, I beg of you to run to a shop, and get me some tea and a dozen lumps of sugar. If you refuse to do this, you will render me a dishonoured man, for you do not know who this lady is. Yes, that will be all. Er – perhaps you are thinking things about her? That is only because you do not know who she is.'

Apollon, who had now resumed his work and spectacles, squinted at the money without even laying aside his needle. Then, according me neither word nor glance, he continued to wrestle with his thread, which somehow seemed to be finding it difficult to pass through the eye of the needle. For fully three minutes, with my hands crossed *à la* Napoleon, I stood waiting. My temples were damp with sweat, and I could feel that I was turning pale all over. But at last, thank God, he had some compassion upon me. Relinquishing his thread, he slowly rose, pushed his chair back in the same manner, took off his spectacles with equal deliberation, counted his money at a similar pace, and, after asking me over his shoulder how much tea he was to purchase, departed as lethargically as he had executed his previous movements. On the way to rejoin Liza I could not help debating whether my best plan were not to flee away, no matter whither, in my dressing-gown, just as I was.

In the end I reseated myself. As I did so she looked at me anxiously, and for a few moments silence reigned.

'I will *kill* him!' suddenly I exclaimed as I struck the table with my fist – struck it so violently that the ink fairly spurted out of the inkstand.

'What do you mean?' she asked, trembling all over.

'I will *kill* him, I will *kill* him!' I repeated, barking out the words like a dog and (keenly though I felt the absurdity of my behaviour) continuing to thump the table with my fist.

'Oh, Liza, you cannot think what a torment the man is!' I went on. 'You must know that he is my rascal of a servant. Just now he has gone out to get some tea and sugar. Oh, Liza!' – and I burst into tears.

Here was a situation! How ashamed I felt of my weakness! Yet, do what I would, I could not master myself.

Liza was terrified.

'What *is* the matter?' she exclaimed, as she came fluttering towards me.

'Some water! Give me some water!' I stuttered in a strangled voice (though, as a matter of fact, I knew that I had no real use for water, any more than there was any real reason for my stuttering). 'The water is over there.' *Per se* the situation was real enough, but at the same time it may be said that at that moment I was only playing a comedy, to keep up appearances.

In great agitation she fetched what I had asked for, and presently Apollon entered with the tea. It seemed to me that anything so *bizarre* and prosaic as tea was a terribly unsuitable commodity after all that had just happened. So I turned a little red in the face. Liza looked at Apollon with a timid air, but he went out without giving us even a glance.

'How you must despise me, Liza!' I said as I stared at her with an almost agonised anxiety to know what she was thinking. However, she was too confused to reply. Angry with myself though I was, I laid the bulk of the blame upon *her*. A horrible sort of resentment against her was rising in my heart, and I felt that I could even have killed her. To revenge myself I registered an inward vow that never again on this earth would I address to her a single word.

'*She* is the cause of everything', I reflected.

The silence continued for something like five minutes, while the tea remained untouched upon the table. Such was my perversity that I purposely refrained from drinking any, that I might make her feel the more uncomfortable (since it would not have been proper for her to take the initiative). But from time to time she kept throwing covert glances at me, with astonishment and distress in her looks. I remained obstinately silent. It was *I* now that was undergoing martyrdom, for, although I recognised the abominable baseness of my folly and rancour, I could not, for the world, help myself.

'I – I wish to leave that place for good', she began – probably her object having been, by some means, no matter what, to break the intolerable silence. Poor woman! She had begun, as I had, precisely as she ought *not* to have begun. To think of mentioning *that*, at such a moment, and to such a man! For a few seconds my heart contracted with pity for her clumsiness and futile frankness; but to this feeling there succeeded, almost instantly, a renewed access of spleen. Indeed, the slight instinct towards compassion which I had experienced only served to redouble my fury. 'Let everything go to the devil!' I said to myself; and again there followed a five minutes of silence.

Presently she rose; saying in a tone which was scarcely articulate –

'Am I in any way inconveniencing you?'

In her tone there were both weariness and offended dignity; whereat my anger burst all bounds, and I too rose – trembling and well-nigh suffocated with rage.

'Why did you come here?' I shouted. 'Tell me, if you please!'

The logical order of my words I did not heed, for I felt as though I must say *all* that I had to say at once, in a volley, and without caring in the least at what point I began.

'Why did you come here?' I repeated. 'Tell me, tell me! Ah, *I* will tell you, my good woman – *I* will tell you why you came here. You came here because, the other night, I said to you a few words of compassion which touched your heart, and made you long for more. Let me inform you, then, that I was only making fun of you that night, and that I am making fun of you *now*. Yes, I have only been amusing myself a little. At dinner I had been insulted by some friends of mine, and had gone to your house to challenge one of them, an officer, whom I thought to find at your house before me. But I happened just to miss him, and felt that I must revenge myself upon someone, and get my own back. *You* chanced to be at hand, and so I vented all my rage and venom upon *you*. I had been humiliated, so I humiliated *you*. I had been rinsed out like a rag, so I exerted my strength upon *you*. There you have the whole truth of the matter. Yet you – you actually thought that I had gone there to save you! Is it not so? Is not that what you are thinking?'

I guessed that, though some of the details of my harangue might escape her, she would nevertheless catch the main gist of it. Nor was I wrong. She turned as white as a sheet, and tried to speak, as, with lips twisting painfully, she fell backwards across her chair like a woman who has been felled with a hatchet. All the while that I continued declaiming she listened to me with her mouth open, her eyes distended, and her whole form trembling with horror. The utter cynicism of my words seemed simply to stupefy her senses.

'To save you, indeed!' I went on as I leapt from my chair and began pacing the room. '*Why* should I save you, seeing that, for all I know, I am even worse than yourself? Why did you not give me a slap in the face while I was doing all that moralising, and say, "Why have you come here, then? To read me a lesson!" . . . No, power, power over someone, is what I want. I wanted to play the game of forcing your tears, your humiliation, your hysterics. *That* was my object the other night. Yet I felt loathsome even to myself, for I knew that I was both a villain and a coward, and God knows why I gave *you* – yes, gave *you*, you wretched woman – my address. As soon as I reached home I fell to cursing you, for all I was worth, because I *had* given you the address. I hated you because I had lied to you; I hated you also because I had only juggled with words, and dreamed dreams, while all the while I wanted – well, what do you think? – to see you go hang! What I wish for is rest and quietness, and, to gain it, I would sell the whole world for a song. Indeed, if I were given the choice between the world coming to an end and my retaining my liberty to drink tea, I tell you that the universe might go to the devil so long only as I could go on drinking tea. Did you guess this the other night, or did you not? Of course I know that I am a brute, a villain, an egotist, a poltroon – so much so that for three whole days I have been trembling with fear lest you should come. And do you know what most disquieted me during those three days? It was the thought that I had seemed to you a hero, whereas at any moment you might come here and surprise me, looking dirty and out-at-elbows, in this old, torn dressing-gown! A little while ago I said that I am not ashamed of my poverty; yet I tell you that I *am* ashamed of it – more ashamed, more afraid, of it than of anything else in the world, even of being accounted a thief, since

I am so full of vanity that every moment I feel as though my skin were being stripped from me, and I were being exposed to the outer air. Surely, too, you have divined that I shall never be able to pardon you for having surprised me in this dressing-gown at a moment when, like a savage dog, I was flinging myself upon Apollon? To think that the saviour, the former hero, should be brawling with his servant like a scabby vagabond, and so give you the laugh over him! Nor shall I ever be able to pardon you for the tears which, like an old woman who has been put out of counte-nance, I was shedding just now in your presence, despite my best efforts to restrain them. Nor shall I ever be able to pardon you the reason why I am confessing this to you. For it is you, and you alone, who must answer for it all, since it is you who have chanced to cross my path – the path of the foulest, the most blackguardly, the most ridiculous, the most trivial, the most obtuse, the most ill-grained worm upon earth. Other worms may be no better than I am, yet at least, for some God-only-known reason, they seem never to look foolish as I do, who all my life shall have to be slapped on the cheek by lice, since that is my *métier*. But what does it matter to me whether you understand this or not? And what does it matter to me whether you meet your ruin in that house or not? And cannot you understand that, having told you all this, I shall for ever hate you for having heard it? Man but once in his life makes such confessions as mine, and then only when he is in a fit of hysteria. And, after it all, how is it that you are still here to flout and torture me, instead of taking your departure?'

At this point a strange thing happened.

I have such an inveterate habit of thinking and meditating in purely bookish fashion – of regarding persons as I may have previously pictured them in fancy, that at first I did not grasp the inwardness of this strange occurrence. Yet the poor outraged, insulted Liza had gauged the position of affairs with far greater accuracy than I had done. In spite of all that had passed, she had divined what at once becomes clear to every woman who truly loves a man. She had divined that the wretch who had spoken to her in such terms was himself desperately unhappy.

Instantly the look of fear and resentment in her face gave place to a sort of mournful sympathy; and when I called myself a scoundrel and a blackguard, as also when my tears began to flow (for I wept a good deal during the course of my harangue), I saw her features contract as she rose and tried to interrupt me. Even when I had finished she did not seem frightened at my violence, nor appear to hear my reproaches to her for lingering; on the contrary her face expressed nothing but the fact that she was aware how greatly I must be suffering to make me speak thus. Besides, the poor woman was feeling so crushed and cowed, and thought herself so immeasurably inferior to me, that it never occurred to her to grow angry or to take offence. With a sort of impulse at once shy and irresistible she advanced towards me. Then, not daring to approach any nearer, she held her arms out to me. For a moment my heart contracted, and as she saw my face change she threw herself upon me, clasped me round the neck, and burst into tears. I too could no longer restrain myself, and fell to sobbing as never in my life had I sobbed before.

'I cannot be – I have not a chance to be – a good man', I murmured brokenly as, sinking upon the sofa, I sobbed for a quarter of an hour in a perfectly hysterical way. She clasped me to herself, and, folding me in her arms, seemed to forget the whole world as she did so.

But in time (and therein lay the mockery of it all) the fit passed (I wish but to reveal the sordid truth, and nothing else) as, with my form prone upon the sofa, and my face buried in its shabby leather cushions, I began, little by little, yet involuntarily and irresistibly, to feel that it would be an effort to raise my head and look Liza in the eyes. Of what, then, was I ashamed? I do not know. I only know that I *was* ashamed. Also, my clouded brain had taken unto itself an idea that our respective roles had now changed; that she was now the heroine, and I the wounded, humiliated creature whom, four nights ago, *she* had appeared to be. All this passed through my mind as I lay there on the sofa.

My God! Is it possible that I *really* hated Liza? I do not know. Even to this day I have no clear idea of how things were. I only know that never at any time in my life have I found it possible to live without playing the tyrant over someone, and—— But reasoning is a useless pursuit; so why reason?

After a while I got the better of myself so far as to venture to raise my head. Yet I wonder whether it was precisely because I felt ashamed to look Liza in the face that there suddenly revived in me a sense of domination, of possession. All unexpectedly my eyes began to blaze with passion as I clasped her hands in mine.

Yet how (so it seemed to me) I hated her! And how strangely that very hatred drew me to her arms! The one feeling spurred the other, until both of them came to resemble a desire for revenge. At first she appeared overcome with surprise – a surprise which amounted almost to terror; but that lasted only for a moment. Almost before I was aware of it she had strained me to herself in a passionate embrace.

10

A quarter of an hour later I was pacing the room with feverish strides. At intervals I would approach the screen, and, through a crack in it, take a peep at Liza. Seated on the floor, with her head against the bed, she seemed to be weeping. Yet she had not gone away, and that irritated me. By this time she knew all. She knew that I had outraged her to the core, and that (how am I to express it?) my short-lived passion had sprung only from a desire for vengeance, from a yearning to subject her to a new indignity; that to my formless enmity there had succeeded a *personal* hatred which was founded upon jealousy. However, I do not say that all this was manifest to her. I only know that henceforth she was bound to look upon me as a man utterly vile and, above all things, incapable of loving her.

Yes, I am aware that I shall be told that to have acted with such blackguardism and cruelty was an impossibility. Perhaps you will even add that not to have loved such a woman as Liza – at all events, not to have appreciated her love – was also an impossibility. But wherein does the impossibility lie? In the first place, I could not love her, for the reason that, to me, love always connotes tyrannisation and moral ascendancy. No other love has ever come within my purview, and I have even gone so far as to arrive at the firm conclusion that, properly speaking, love lies in the peculiar right of tyrannisation which the fact of being loved confers. Even in my most secret soul I have never been able to think of love as aught but a struggle which begins with hatred and ends with moral subjection. And, in the second place, I did not know what to do with the woman after I had subjected her. Again, therefore, I ask – wherein does the impossibility lie? Was I not depraved beyond belief? Had I not so fallen out of touch with everyday life as to think of taunting Liza with having come to hear 'further words of compassion' when all the time she had come to me for *love* (for it is in love alone that woman can find salvation and refuge from shipwreck; it is in love, and love alone, that she can attain regeneration)? So once again I ask – was it hatred, and *nothing but* hatred, that I felt for Liza during the time that I was pacing the room, and stopping, at intervals, to peep at her through the screen? I do not think so. Rather it was that I could not bear to feel that she was there, for I wanted her to go, and was longing for peace and solitude. I had lost the sociable habit, and she disturbed me to such an extent that she hindered my very breathing.

A few moments passed, but still she did not stir from her profound stupor. At last I was callous enough to tap the screen, to recall her to herself; whereupon she gave a violent start, rose in haste, and resumed her hat, shawl and furs, as though her one desire were to get away from me, no matter whither. Two minutes later she issued slowly from behind the screen, and stood looking at me with sombre gaze. In return I smiled a smile which I forced for the occasion. Yet the moment that her eyes met mine I found myself forced to avert my gaze.

'Good-bye', she said as she moved towards the door.

I ran to her, took and opened her hand, put something into it, and closed the fingers again. Next, turning my back upon her, I retired precipitately into a corner, where at least I could not see her. . . .

I was going to have lied to you, my readers – to have pretended to you that it was without thinking, and purely through absence of mind and stupidity, that I put that something into her hand. Yet I will not lie. No; I will tell you frankly that it was out of sheer malice that I opened her hand and put the money into it. The idea had occurred to me while I was pacing up and down the room and Liza was seated on the floor behind the screen. At the same time I can honestly say that the factor which caused me to perpetrate that gratuitous insult was malice of the brain rather than depravity of the heart. True, the act *was* an insult, but only a calculated, *bookish*, unreal one; and the moment that it had been perpetrated I retired, as I have said, into a corner – thence almost as instantly to dart back again in a storm of shame and despair. But Liza had gone. I opened the door, and shouted down the staircase (nervously, and in an undertone): 'Liza, Liza!'

No answer came, though I thought I could hear her footsteps on the bottom flight of stairs.

'Liza!' I cried once more – this time a little louder.

Still no answer came, except that the glass entrance-door of the building opened with a creak, and then shut to with a bang. The sound reached me even where I stood at the head of the staircase.

She had gone!

I returned thoughtfully to my room. My heart was heavy within me, and for a moment or two I remained standing before the table at which Liza, on her arrival, had seated herself. I gazed with unseeing eyes. But suddenly I started. Lying right in front of me I had just discerned the crumpled bank-note for five roubles which I had a moment or two ago put into her hand! It was the same note, and no other, for it had been the only one that I had possessed. She had taken advantage of the moment when my back was turned to throw it upon the table!

Well, I might have foreseen that. Yet *could* I have foreseen it? No; I was too much of an egotist to have done that; I had too great a contempt for the world to have thought *her*, of all persons, capable of such an act.

The sight was unendurable to me. With all speed I dressed myself (taking for the purpose the first garments which came to hand) and darted off in pursuit. As yet she could not have covered more than two hundred paces.

The air was so still that snow was falling almost perpendicularly, and forming a thick coverlet upon the pavements of the deserted streets. Not a sound was there to be heard, nor a soul to be seen. The street lamps seemed to be burning with a curious sort of dimness. Running a couple of hundred paces to the nearest corner, I stopped.

Where could she have got to? And why was I running after her at all?

Ah, why indeed? To go upon my knees to her, to weep out tears of repentance, to kiss her feet, to ask of her pardon? Yes, all these things I, at that instant, longed to do. My breast seemed to be bursting with a longing to do them. Never to the end of my days shall I be able to remember that moment without a spasm of emotion.

'Yet what good would it do us?' I went on. 'Should I not, tomorrow, be hating her for the very reason that tonight I had kissed her feet? And should I ever be able to make her happy? Have I not tonight proved to myself – for about the hundredth time – what I am worth? Should I not be a constant torture to her?'

For a long while I remained standing in the snow – standing in the dark, shadowy street – plunged in meditation.

'Surely things are best as they are?' I continued as I regained my room and set myself to drown with fancies the terrible aching of my heart. 'Surely it is best that to the end she should carry the remembrance of her humbling? Of her humbling? May it not, rather, prove a cleansing – a painful, yet an intimate, reminder to her of her human dignity? Tomorrow I should only have soiled her soul and wounded her heart; whereas the insult will *never* fade from her recollection. Yes, despite the filth and the horrors of the end which is awaiting her, the offence will never cease to raise and purify her – through hatred of the offender. Hm! And through pardon too? . . . *Will* she be happier so?'

In philosophic style I next proceeded to put to myself the following question – to be studied at leisure: Which of the two is better – moderate happiness or splendid suffering? . . . Which of them *is* the better?

To the solution of that problem I devoted the remainder of that agonising night. I felt half-dead for the pain in my heart. Never before nor since have I suffered, have I repented, as I did then.

Yet I still believe that, at the very moment when I left my rooms to go in pursuit of her, I was aware that I should return after going two hundred paces!

Never since that night have I seen her, nor have I heard of her.

To this I may add that, though for a time I derived considerable pleasure from my formula concerning the respective uses of insult and hatred, the agitation which I had suffered brought me near to being seriously ill.

Even now, after all these years, I find these bitter memories to recall; and though I can recollect many another bitter memory, had I not better, at this point, bring these Notes to an end? For it seems to me that I have made a mistake in writing them at all. At all events I know that, from start to finish, I have felt ashamed while writing the story which I have just related. Truly its inditing has been, for me, not so much literature as a well-merited punishment! Nor can it interest anyone that I should spin long tales as to how I have wasted my life in moral corruption – wasted it in solitude and poverty and detachment from reality – wasted it in vainglorious searchings of heart in the underground. A romance requires a hero, and in me fate seems to have combined only the materials for an anti-hero. Consequently the whole thing is bound to produce an unpleasant impression, since all of us stand divorced from reality – all of us halt in greater or lesser degree. So unfamiliar with life have we become that at times we feel for reality a positive loathing, and cannot bear to have it brought to our notice. Indeed, so far have we advanced as to look upon real life almost as a burden, a term of servitude, and to agree that the better course is to live strictly in the bookish manner. But why do we also, at times, grow restless, captious and querulous? Even you do not know the reason. Yet if our querulous petitions were to be granted we should find ourselves in a far worse plight. For suppose we were given complete independence, and freedom to bestow our love where we willed, and a wider sphere of activity, and increased exemption from tutelage. Why, I assure you that we should very soon be asking to be taken in hand again! I know that you will be angry with me for saying this, and raise an uproar, and stamp your feet. 'Speak for yourself and your own miseries in the underground', you will cry; 'but do not dare to use the expression "*all* of us".' Well, gentlemen, heaven forbid that I should justify myself by seeking to include all my fellow men with myself; yet, so far as I am concerned, I have but carried to a finish, in my life, what you have never even dared to carry half-way, although you have constantly mistaken your cowardice for prudence, you have constantly cheated yourself with comforting reflections. The truth is that I have been more *alive* than you. That is all. But look a little closer. We do not even know where present-day reality is to be found, nor what it is called. Whenever we are left to our own devices, and deprived of our bookish rules, we at once grow confused, and lose our way – we know not what to do, nor what to observe, nor what to love, nor what to hate, nor what to respect, nor what to despise. We grow weary of being human beings at all – of possessing real, individual flesh and blood. We are *ashamed* of being human – we account it beneath our dignity. Rather, we aim at becoming personalities of a general, a fictitious type. Yes, all of us are still-born creatures, not children sprung of living fathers; and that fact is coming more and more to please us. Soon we shall have invented a way of being born of nothing but ideas! But enough of this: I intend to bring these 'Notes from Underground' to a close.

* * *

It may be added that the 'Notes' of this dealer in paradoxes did *not* end here, since the writer could not forbear continuing them. But this seems as good a place as any for us to stop.

A CONFESSION

I was baptised and brought up in the Orthodox Christian faith. I was taught it in childhood and throughout my boyhood and youth. But when I abandoned the second course of the university at the age of eighteen I no longer believed any of the things I had been taught.

Judging by certain memories, I never seriously believed them, but had merely relied on what I was taught and on what was professed by the grown-up people around me, and that reliance was very unstable.

I remember that before I was eleven a grammar school pupil, Vladimir Milyutin (long since dead), visited us one Sunday and announced as the latest novelty a discovery made at his school. This discovery was that there is no God and that all we are taught about Him is a mere invention (this was in 1838). I remember how interested my elder brothers were in this information. They called me to their council and we all, I remember, became very animated, and accepted it as something very interesting and quite possible.

I remember also that when my elder brother, Dmitri, who was then at the university, suddenly, in the passionate way natural to him, devoted himself to religion and began to attend all the Church services, to fast and to lead a pure and moral life, we all – even our elders – unceasingly held him up to ridicule and for some unknown reason called him 'Noah'. I remember that Musin-Push-kin, the then Curator of Kazan University, when inviting us to a dance at his house, ironically persuaded my brother (who was declining the invitation) by the argument that even David danced before the Ark. I sympathized with these jokes made by my elders, and drew from them the conclusion that though it is necessary to learn the catechism and go to church, one must not take such things too seriously. I remember also that I read Voltaire* when I was very young, and that his raillery, far from shocking me, amused me very much.

My lapse from faith occurred as is usual among people on our level of education. In most cases, I think, it happens thus: a man lives like everybody else, on the basis of principles not merely having nothing in common with religious doctrine, but generally opposed to it; religious doctrine does not play a part in life, in intercourse with others it is never encountered, and in a man's own life he never has to reckon with it. Religious doctrine is professed far away from life and independently of it. If it is encountered, it is only as an external phenomenon disconnected from life.

Then as now, it was and is quite impossible to judge by a man's life and conduct whether he is a believer or not. If there be a difference between a man who publicly professes Orthodoxy and one who denies it, the difference is not in favour of the former. Then as now, the public profession and confession of Orthodoxy was chiefly met with among people who were dull and cruel and who considered themselves very important. Ability, honesty, reliability, good-nature and moral conduct were more often met with among unbelievers.

The schools teach the catechism and send the pupils to church, and government officials must produce certificates of having received communion. But a man of our circle who has finished his education and is not in the government service may even now (and formerly it was still easier for him to do so) live for ten or twenty years without once remembering that he is living among Christians and is himself reckoned a member of the Orthodox Christian Church.

So that, now as formerly, religious doctrine, accepted on trust and supported by external pressure, thaws away gradually under the influence of knowledge and experience of life which conflict with it, and a man very often lives on, imagining that he still holds intact the religious doctrine imparted to him in childhood whereas in fact not a trace of it remains.

S., a clever and truthful man, once told me the story of how he ceased to believe. On a hunting expedition, when he was already twenty-six, he once, at the place where they put up for the night, knelt down in the evening to pray – a habit retained from childhood. His elder brother, who was at the hunt with him, was lying on some hay and watching him. When S. had finished and was settling down for the night, his brother said to him: 'So you still do that?'

They said nothing more to one another. But from that day S. ceased to say his prayers or go to church. And now he has not prayed, received communion, or gone to church for thirty years. And this not because he knows his brother's convictions and has joined him in them, nor because he has decided anything in his own soul, but simply because the word spoken by his brother was like the push of a finger on a wall that was ready to fall by its own weight. The word only showed that where he thought there was faith, in reality there had long been an empty space, and that therefore the utterance of words and the making of signs of the cross and genuflections while praying were quite senseless actions. Becoming conscious of their senselessness he could not continue them.

So it has been and is, I think, with the great majority of people. I am speaking of people of our educational level who are sincere with themselves, and not of those who make the profession of faith a means of attaining worldly aims. (Such people are the most fundamental infidels, for if faith is for them a means of attaining any worldly aims, then certainly it is not faith.) These people of our education are so placed that the light of knowledge and life has caused an artificial erection to melt away, and they have either already noticed this and swept its place clear, or they have not yet noticed it.

The religious doctrine taught me from childhood disappeared in me as in others, but with this difference, that as from the age of fifteen I began to read philosophical works, my rejection of the doctrine became a conscious one at a very early age. From the time I was sixteen I ceased to say my prayers and ceased to go to church or to fast of my own volition. I did not believe what had been taught me in childhood but I believed in something. What it was I believed in I could not at all have said. I believed in a God, or rather I did not deny God – but I could not have said what sort of God. Neither did I deny Christ and his teaching, but what his teaching consisted in I again could not have said.

Looking back on that time, I now see clearly that my faith – my only real faith – that which apart from my animal instincts gave impulse to my life – was a belief in perfecting myself. But in what this perfecting consisted and what its object was, I could not have said. I tried to perfect myself mentally – studied everything I could, anything life threw in my way; I tried to perfect my will, I drew up rules I tried to follow; I perfected myself physically, cultivating my strength and agility by all sorts of exercises, and accustoming myself to endurance and patience by all kinds of privations. And all this I considered to be the pursuit of perfection. The beginning of it all was of course moral perfection, but that was soon replaced by perfection in general: by the desire to be better not in my own eyes or those of God but in the eyes of other people. And very soon this effort again changed into a desire to be stronger than others: to be more famous, more important and richer than others.

2

Some day I will narrate the touching and instructive history of my life during those ten years of my youth. I think very many people have had a like experience. With all my soul I wished to be good, but I was young, passionate and alone, completely alone when I sought goodness. Every time I tried to express my most sincere desire, which was to be morally good, I met with contempt and ridicule, but as soon as I yielded to low passions I was praised and encouraged.

Ambition, love of power, covetousness, lasciviousness, pride, anger, and revenge – were all respected.

Yielding to those passions I became like the grown-up folk and felt that they approved of me. The kind aunt with whom I lived, herself the purest of beings, always told me that there was nothing she so desired for me as that I should have relations with a married woman: '*Rien ne forme un jeune homme, comme une liaison avec une femme comme il faut.*' Another happiness she desired for me was that I should become an aide-de-camp, and if possible aide-de-camp to the Emperor. But the greatest happiness of all would be that I should marry a very rich girl and so become possessed of as many serfs as possible.

I cannot think of those years without horror, loathing and heartache. I killed men in war and challenged men to duels in order to kill them. I lost at cards, consumed the labour of the peasants, sentenced them to punishments, lived loosely, and deceived people. Lying, robbery, adultery of all kinds, drunkenness, violence, murder – there was no crime I did not commit, and in spite of that people praised my conduct and my contemporaries considered and consider me to be a comparatively moral man.

So I lived for ten years.

During that time I began to write from vanity, covetousness, and pride. In my writings I did the same as in my life. To get fame and money, for the sake of which I wrote, it was necessary to hide the good and to display the evil. And I did so. How often in my writings I contrived to hide under the guise of indifference, or even of banter, those strivings of mine towards goodness which gave meaning to my life! And I succeeded in this and was praised.

At twenty-six years of age I returned to Petersburg after the war, and met the writers. They received me as one of themselves and flattered me. And before I had time to look round I had adopted the views on life of the set of authors I had come among, and these views completely obliterated all my former strivings to improve – they furnished a theory which justified the dissoluteness of my life.

The view of life of these people, my comrades in authorship, consisted in this: that life in general goes on developing, and in this development we – men of thought – have the chief part; and among men of thought it is we – artists and poets – who have the greatest influence. Our vocation is to teach mankind. And lest the simple question should suggest itself: What do I know, and what can I teach? it was explained in this theory that this need not be known, and that the artist and poet teach unconsciously. I was considered an admirable artist and poet, and therefore it was very natural for me to adopt this theory. I, artist and poet, wrote and taught without myself knowing what. For this I was paid money; I had excellent food, lodging, women, and society; and I had fame, which showed that what I taught was very good.

This faith in the meaning of poetry and in the development of life was a religion, and I was one of its priests. To be its priest was very pleasant and profitable. And I lived a considerable time in this faith without doubting its validity. But in the second and still more in the third year of this life I began to doubt the infallibility of this religion and to examine it. My first cause of doubt was that I began to notice that the priests of this religion were not all in accord among themselves. Some said: We are the best and most useful teachers; we teach what is needed, but the others teach wrongly. Others said: No! we are the real teachers, and you teach wrongly. And they disputed, quarrelled, abused, cheated, and tricked one another. There were also many among us who did not care who was right and who was wrong, but were simply bent on attaining their covetous aims by means of this activity of ours. All this obliged me to doubt the validity of our creed.

Moreover, having begun to doubt the truth of the authors' creed itself, I also began to observe its priests more attentively, and I became convinced that almost all the priests of that religion, the writers, were immoral, and for the most part men of bad, worthless character, much inferior to those whom I had met in my former dissipated and military life; but they were self-confident and self-satisfied as only those can be who are quite holy or who do not know what holiness is. These people revolted me, I became revolting to myself, and I realized that that faith was a fraud.

But strange to say, though I understood this fraud and re-nounced it, yet I did not renounce the rank these people gave me: the rank of artist, poet, and teacher. I naïvely imagined that I was a poet and artist and could teach everybody without myself knowing what I was teaching, and I acted accordingly.

From my intimacy with these men I acquired a new vice: abnormally developed pride and an insane assurance that it was my vocation to teach men, without knowing what.

To remember that time, and my own state of mind and that of those men (though there are thousands like them to-day), is sad and terrible and ludicrous, and arouses exactly the feeling one experiences in a lunatic asylum.

We were all then convinced that it was necessary for us to speak, write, and print as quickly as possible and as much as possible, and that it was all wanted for the good of humanity. And thousands of us, contradicting and abusing one another, all printed and wrote – teaching others. And without noticing that we knew nothing, and that to the simplest of life's questions: What is good and what is evil? we did not know how to reply, we all talked at the same time, not listening to one another, sometimes seconding and praising one another in order to be seconded and praised in turn, sometimes getting angry with one another – just as in a lunatic asylum.

Thousands of workmen laboured to the extreme limit of their strength day and night, setting the type and printing millions of words which the post carried all over Russia, and we still went on teaching and could in no way find time to teach enough, and were always angry that sufficient attention was not paid us.

It was terribly strange, but is now quite comprehensible. Our real innermost concern was to get as much money and praise as possible. To gain that end we could do nothing except write books and papers. So we did that. But in order to do such useless work and to feel assured that we were very important people we required a theory justifying our activity. And so among us this theory was devised: 'All that exists is reasonable. All that exists develops. And it all develops by means of Culture. And Culture is measured by the circulation of books and newspapers. And we are paid money and are respected because we write books and newspapers, and therefore we are the most useful and the best of men.' This theory would have been all very well if we had been unanimous, but as every thought expressed by one of us was always met by a diametrically opposite thought expressed by another, we ought to have been driven to reflection. But we ignored this; people paid us money and those on our side praised us, so each of us considered himself justified.

It is now clear to me that this was just as in a lunatic asylum; but then I only dimly suspected this, and like all lunatics, simply called all men lunatics except myself.

3

So I lived, abandoning myself to this insanity for another six years, till my marriage. During that time I went abroad. Life in Europe and my acquaintance with leading and learned Europeans confirmed me yet more in the faith of striving after perfection in which I believed, for I found the same faith among them. That faith took with me the common form it assumes with the majority of educated people of our day. It was expressed by the word 'progress'. It then appeared to me that this word meant something. I did not as yet understand that, being tormented (like every vital man) by the question how it is best for me to live, in my answer, 'Live in conformity with progress', I was like a man in a boat who when carried along by wind and waves should reply to what for him is the chief and only question, 'whither to steer', by saying, 'We are being carried somewhere'.

I did not then notice this. Only occasionally – not by reason but by instinct – I revolted against this superstition so common in our day, by which people hide from themselves their lack of understanding of life. . . . So, for instance, during my stay in Paris, the sight of an execution revealed to me the instability of my superstitious belief in progress. When I saw the head part from the body and how they thumped separately into the box, I understood, not with my mind but with my whole being, that no theory of the reasonableness of our present progress could justify this deed; and that though everybody from the creation of the world had held it to be necessary, on whatever theory, I knew it to be unnecessary and bad; and therefore the arbiter of what is good and evil is not what people say and do, nor is it progress, but it is my heart and I. Another instance of a realisation that the superstitious belief in progress is insufficient as a guide to life was my brother's death. Wise, good, serious, he fell ill while still a young man, suffered for more than a year, and died painfully, not understanding why he had lived and still less why he had to die. No theories could give me, or him, any reply to these questions during his slow and painful dying. But these were only rare instances of doubt, and I actually continued to live professing a faith only in progress. 'Everything evolves and I evolve with it: and why it is that I evolve with all things will be known some day.' So I ought to have formulated my faith at that time.

On returning from abroad I settled in the country and chanced to occupy myself with peasant schools. This work was particularly to my taste because in it I had not to face the falsity which had become obvious to me and stared me in the face when I tried to teach people by literary means. Here also I acted in the name of progress, but I already regarded progress itself critically. I said to myself: 'In some of its developments progress has proceeded wrongly, and with primitive peasant children one must deal in a spirit of perfect freedom, letting them choose what path of progress they please.' In reality I was ever revolving round one and the same insoluble problem, which was: how to teach without knowing what to teach. In the higher spheres of literary activity I had realised that one could not teach without knowing what, for I saw that people all taught differently, and by quarrelling among themselves only succeeded in hiding their ignorance from one another. But here, with peasant children, I thought to evade this difficulty by letting them learn what they liked. It amuses me now when I remember how I shuffled in trying to satisfy my desire to teach, while in the depth of my soul I knew very well that I could not teach anything needful for I did not know what was needful. After spending a year at school work I went abroad a second time to discover how to teach others while myself knowing nothing.

And it seemed to me that I had learnt this abroad, and in the year of the peasants' emancipation (1861) I returned to Russia armed with all this wisdom, and having become an Arbiter I began to teach, both the uneducated peasants in schools and the educated classes through a magazine I published. Things appeared to be going well, but I felt I was not quite sound mentally and that matters could not long continue in that way. And I should perhaps then have come to the state of despair I reached fifteen years later had there not been one side of life still unexplored by me which promised me happiness: that was marriage.

For a year I busied myself with arbitration work, the schools, and the magazine; and I became so worn out – as a result especially of my mental confusion – and so hard was my struggle as Arbiter, so obscure the results of my activity in the schools, so repulsive my shuffling in the magazine (which always amounted to one and the same thing: a desire to teach everybody and to hide the fact that I did not know what to teach), that I fell ill, mentally rather than physically, threw up everything, and went away to the Bashkirs in the steppes, to breathe fresh air, drink kumys,* and live a merely animal life.

Returning from there I married. The new conditions of happy family life completely diverted me from all search for the general meaning of life. My whole life was centred at that time in my family, wife and children, and therefore in care to increase our means of livelihood. My striving after self-perfection, for which I had already substituted a striving for perfection in general, i.e. progress, was now again replaced by the effort simply to secure the best possible conditions for myself and my family.

So another fifteen years passed.

In spite of the fact that I now regarded authorship as of no importance, I still continued to write during those fifteen years. I had already tasted the temptation of authorship – the temptation of immense monetary rewards and applause for my insignificant work – and I devoted myself to it as a means of improving my material position and of stifling in my soul all questions as to the meaning of my own life or life in general.

I wrote: teaching what was for me the only truth, namely, that one should live so as to have the best for oneself and one's family.

So I lived; but five years ago something very strange began to happen to me. At first I experienced moments of perplexity and arrest of life, as though I did not know what to do or how to live; and I felt lost and became dejected. But this passed, and I went on living as before. Then these moments of perplexity began to recur oftener and oftener, and always in the same form. They were always expressed by the questions: What is it for? What does it lead to?

At first it seemed to me that these were aimless and irrelevant questions. I thought that it was all well known, and that if I should ever wish to deal with the solution it would not cost me much effort; just at present I had no time for it, but when I wanted to I should be able to find the answer. The questions however began to repeat themselves frequently, and to demand replies more and more insistently; and like drops of ink always falling on one place they ran together into one black blot.

Then occurred what happens to everyone sickening with a mortal internal disease. At first trivial signs of indisposition appear to which the sick man pays no attention; then these signs reappear more and more often and merge into one uninterrupted period of suffering. The suffering increases and, before the sick man can look round, what he took for a mere indisposition has already become more important to him than anything else in the world – it is death!

That was what happened to me. I understood that it was no casual indisposition but something very important, and that if these questions constantly repeated themselves they would have to be answered. And I tried to answer them. The questions seemed such stupid, simple, childish ones; but as soon as I touched them and tried to solve them I at once became convinced, first, that they are not childish and stupid but the most important and profound of life's questions; and secondly that, try as I would, I could not solve them. Before occupying myself with my Samara estate, the education of my son, or the writing of a book, I had to know *why* I was doing it. As long as I did not know why, I could do nothing and could not live. Amid the thoughts of estate management which greatly occupied me at that time, the question would suddenly occur: 'Well, you will have 6,000 *desyatínas** of land in Samara Government and 300 horses, and what then?' . . . And I was quite disconcerted and did not know what to think. Or when considering plans for the education of my children, I would say to myself: 'What for?' Or when considering how the peasants might become prosperous, I would suddenly say to myself: 'But what does it matter to me?' Or when thinking of the fame my works would bring me, I would say to myself, 'Very well; you will be more famous than Gogol or Pushkin or Shakespeare or Molière, or than all the writers in the world – and what of it?' And I could find no reply at all. The questions would not wait, they had to be answered at once, and if I did not answer them it was impossible to live. But there was no answer.

I felt that what I had been standing on had collapsed and that I had nothing left under my feet. What I had lived on no longer existed, and there was nothing left.

4

My life came to a standstill. I could breathe, eat, drink, and sleep, and I could not help doing these things; but there was no life, for there were no wishes the fulfilment of which I could consider reasonable. If I desired anything, I knew in advance that whether I satisfied my desire or not, nothing would come of it. Had a fairy come and offered to fulfil my desires I should not have known what to ask. If in moments of intoxication I felt something which, though not a wish, was a habit left by former wishes, in sober moments I knew this to be a delusion and that there was really nothing to wish for. I could not even wish to know the truth, for I guessed of what it consisted. The truth was that life is meaningless. I had as it were lived, lived, and walked, walked, till I had come to a precipice and saw clearly that there was nothing ahead of me but destruction. It was impossible to stop, impossible to go back, and impossible to close my eyes or avoid seeing that there was nothing ahead but suffering and real death – complete annihilation.

It had come to this, that I, a healthy, fortunate man, felt I could no longer live: some irresistible power impelled me to rid myself one way or other of life. I cannot say I *wished* to kill myself. The power which drew me away from life was stronger, fuller, and more widespread than any mere wish. It was a force similar to the former striving to live, only in a contrary direction. All my strength drew me away from life. The thought of self-destruction now came to me as naturally as thoughts of how to improve my life had come formerly. And it was so seductive that I had to be cunning with myself lest I should carry it out too hastily. I did not wish to hurry, because I wanted to use all efforts to disentangle the matter. 'If I cannot unravel matters, there will always be time.' And it was then that I, a man favoured by fortune, hid a cord from myself lest I should hang myself from the crosspiece of the partition in my room where I undressed alone every evening, and I ceased to go out shooting with a gun lest I should be tempted by so easy a way of ending my life. I did not myself know what I wanted: I feared life, desired to escape from it, yet still hoped something of it.

And all this befell me at a time when all around me I had what is considered complete good fortune. I was not yet fifty; I had a good wife who loved me and whom I loved, good children, and a large estate which without much effort on my part improved and increased. I was respected by my relations and acquaintances more than at any previous time. I was praised by others and without much self-deception could consider that my name was famous. And far from being insane or mentally diseased, I enjoyed on the contrary a strength of mind and body such as I have seldom met with among men of my kind; physically I could keep up with the peasants at mowing, and mentally I could work for eight and ten hours at a stretch without experiencing any ill results from such exertion. And in this situation I came to this – that I could not live, and, fearing death, had to employ cunning with myself to avoid taking my own life.

My mental condition presented itself to me in this way: my life is a stupid and spiteful joke someone has played on me. Though I did not acknowledge a 'someone' who created me, yet such a presentation – that someone had played an evil and stupid joke on me by placing me in the world – was the form of expression that suggested itself most naturally to me.

Involuntarily it appeared to me that there, somewhere, was someone who amused himself by watching how I lived for thirty or forty years: learning, developing, maturing in body and mind, and how, having with matured mental powers reached the summit of life from which it all lay before me, I stood on that summit – like an arch-fool – seeing clearly that there is nothing in life, and that there has been and will be nothing. And *he* was amused. . . .

But whether that 'someone' laughing at me existed or not, I was none the better off. I could give no reasonable meaning to any single action or to my whole life. I was only surprised that I could have avoided understanding this from the very beginning – it has been so long known to all. Today or tomorrow sickness and death will come (they had come already) to those I love or to me; nothing will remain but stench and worms. Sooner or later my affairs, whatever they may be, will be forgotten, and I shall not exist. Then why go on making any effort? . . . How can man fail to see this? And how go on living? That is what is surprising! One can only live while one is intoxicated with life; as soon as one is sober it is impossible not to see that it is all a mere fraud and a stupid fraud! That is precisely what it is: there is nothing either amusing or witty about it, it is simply cruel and stupid.

There is an Eastern fable, told long ago, of a traveller overtaken on a plain by an enraged beast. Escaping from the beast he gets into a dry well, but sees at the bottom of the well a dragon that has opened its jaws to swallow him. And the unfortunate man, not daring to climb out lest he should be destroyed by the enraged beast, and not daring to leap to the bottom of the well lest he should be eaten by the dragon, seizes a twig growing in a crack in the well and clings to it. His hands are growing weaker and he feels he will soon have to resign himself to the destruction that awaits him above or below, but still he clings on. Then he sees that two mice, a black and a white one, go regularly round and round the stem of the twig to which he is clinging and gnaw at it. And soon the twig itself will snap and he will fall into the dragon's jaws. The traveller sees this and knows that he will inevitably perish; but while still hanging he looks around, sees some drops of honey on the leaves of the twig, reaches them with his tongue and licks them. So I too clung to the twig of life, knowing that the dragon of death was inevitably awaiting me, ready to tear me to pieces; and I could not understand why I had fallen into such torment. I tried to lick the honey which formerly consoled me, but the honey no longer gave me pleasure, and the white and black mice of day and night gnawed at the branch by which I hung. I saw the dragon clearly and the honey no longer tasted sweet. I only saw the unescapable dragon and the mice, and I could not tear my gaze from them. And this is not a fable but the real unanswerable truth intelligible to all.

The deception of the joys of life which formerly allayed my terror of the dragon now no longer deceived me. No matter how often I may be told, 'You cannot understand the meaning of life so do not think about it, but live', I can no longer do it: I have already done it too long. I cannot now help seeing day and night going round and bringing me to death. That is all I see, for that alone is true. All else is false.

The two drops of honey which diverted my eyes from the cruel truth longer than the rest: my love of family, and of writing – art as I called it – were no longer sweet to me.

'Family' . . . said I to myself. But my family – wife and children – are also human. They are placed just as I am: they must either live in a lie or see the terrible truth. Why should they live? Why should I love them, guard them, bring them up, or watch them? That they may come to the despair that I feel, or else be stupid? Loving them, I cannot hide the truth from them: each step in knowledge leads them to the truth. And the truth is death.

'Art, poetry?' . . . Under the influence of success and the praise of men, I had long assured myself that this was a thing one could do though death was drawing near – death which destroys all things, including my work and its remembrance; but soon I saw that that too was a fraud. It was plain to me that art is an adornment of life, an allurement to life. But life had lost its attraction for me, so how could I attract others? As long as I was not living my own life but was borne on the waves of some other life – as long as I believed that life had a meaning, though one I could not express – the reflection of life in poetry and art of all kinds afforded me pleasure: it was pleasant to look at life in the mirror of art. But when I began to seek the meaning of life and felt the necessity of living my own life, that mirror became for me unnecessary, superfluous, ridiculous, or painful. I could no longer soothe myself with what I now saw in the mirror, namely, that my position was stupid and desperate. It was all very well to enjoy the sight when in the depth of my soul I believed that my life had a meaning. Then the play of lights – comic, tragic, touching, beautiful, and terrible – in life amused me. But when I knew life to be meaningless and terrible, the play in the mirror could no longer amuse me. No sweetness of honey could be sweet to me when I saw the dragon and saw the mice gnawing away my support.

Nor was that all. Had I simply understood that life had no meaning I could have borne it quietly, knowing that that was my lot. But I could not satisfy myself with that. Had I been like a man living in a wood from which he knows there is no exit, I could have lived; but I was like one lost in a wood who, horrified at having lost his way, rushes about wishing to find the road. He knows that each step he takes confuses him more and more, but still he cannot help rushing about.

It was indeed terrible. And to rid myself of the terror I wished to kill myself. I experienced terror at what awaited me – knew that that terror was even worse than the position I was in, but still I could not patiently await the end. However convincing the argument might be that in any case some vessel in my heart would give way, or something would burst and all would be over, I could not patiently await that end. The horror of darkness was too great, and I wished to free myself from it as quickly as possible by noose or bullet. That was the feeling which drew me most strongly towards suicide.

5

'But perhaps I have overlooked something, or misunderstood something?' said I to myself several times. 'It cannot be that this condition of despair is natural to man!' And I sought for an explanation of these problems in all the branches of knowledge acquired by men. I sought painfully and long, not from idle curiosity or listlessly, but painfully and persistently day and night – sought as a perishing man seeks for safety – and I found nothing.

I sought in all the sciences, but far from finding what I wanted, became convinced that all who like myself had sought in knowledge for the meaning of life had found nothing. And not only had they found nothing, but they had plainly acknowledged that the very thing which made me despair – namely the senselessness of life – is the one indubitable thing man can know.

I sought everywhere; and thanks to a life spent in learning, and thanks also to my relations with the scholarly world, I had access to scientists and scholars in all branches of knowledge, and they readily showed me all their knowledge, not only in books but also in conversation, so that I had at my disposal all that science has to say on this question of life.

I was long unable to believe that it gives no other reply to life's questions than that which it actually does give. It long seemed to me, when I saw the important and serious air with which science announces its conclusions which have nothing in common with the real questions of human life, that there was something I had not understood. I long was timid before science, and it seemed to me that the lack of conformity between the answers and my questions arose not by the fault of science but from my ignorance, but the matter was for me not a game or an amusement but one of life and death, and I was involuntarily brought to the conviction that my questions were the only legitimate ones, forming the basis of all knowledge, and that I with my questions was not to blame, but science if it pretends to reply to those questions.

My question – that which at the age of fifty brought me to the verge of suicide – was the simplest of questions, lying in the soul of every man from the foolish child to the wisest elder: it was a question without an answer to which one cannot live, as I had found by experience. It was: 'What will come of what I am doing today or shall do tomorrow? What will come of my whole life?'

Differently expressed, the question is: 'Why should I live, why wish for anything, or do anything?' It can also be expressed thus: 'Is there any meaning in my life that the inevitable death awaiting me does not destroy?'

To this one question, variously expressed, I sought an answer in science. And I found that in relation to that question all human knowledge is divided as it were into two opposite hemispheres at the ends of which are two poles: the one a negative and the other a positive; but that neither at the one nor the other pole is there an answer to life's questions.

The one series of sciences seems not to recognise the question, but replies clearly and exactly to its own independent questions: that is the series of experimental sciences, and at the extreme end of it stands mathematics. The other series of sciences recognises the question, but does not answer it; that is the series of abstract sciences, and at the extreme end of it stands metaphysics.

From early youth I had been interested in the abstract sciences, but later the mathematical and natural sciences attracted me, and until I put my question definitely to myself, until that question had itself grown up within me urgently demanding a decision, I contented myself with those counterfeit answers which science gives.

Now in the experimental sphere I said to myself: 'Everything develops and differentiates itself, moving towards complexity and perfection, and there are laws directing this movement. You are a part of the whole. Having learnt as far as possible the whole, and having learnt the law of evolution, you will understand also your place in the whole and will know yourself.' Ashamed as I am to confess it, there was a time when I seemed satisfied with that. It was just the time when I was myself becoming more complex and was developing. My muscles were growing and strengthening, my memory was being enriched, my capacity to think and understand was increasing, I was growing and developing; and feeling this growth in myself it was natural for me to think that such was the universal law in which I should find the solution of the question of my life. But a time came when the growth within me ceased. I felt that I was not developing, but fading, my muscles were weakening, my teeth falling out, and I saw that the law not only did not explain anything to me, but that there never had been or could be such a law, and that I had taken for a law what I had found in myself at a certain period of my life. I regarded the definition of that law more strictly, and it became clear to me that there could be no law of endless development; it became clear that to say, 'in infinite space and time everything develops, becomes more perfect and more complex, is differentiated', is to say nothing at all. These are all words with no meaning, for in the infinite there is neither complex nor simple, neither forward nor backward, nor better or worse.

Above all, my personal question, 'What am I with my desires?' remained quite unanswered. And I understood that those sciences are very interesting and attractive, but that they are exact and clear in inverse proportion to their applicability to the question of life: the less their applicability to the question of life, the more exact and clear they are, while the more they try to reply to the question of life, the more obscure and unattractive they become. If one turns to the division of sciences which attempt to reply to the questions of life – to physiology, psychology, biology, sociology – one encounters an appalling poverty of thought, the greatest obscurity, a quite unjustifiable pretension to solve irrelevant questions, and a continual contradiction of each authority by others and even by himself. If one turns to the branches of science which are not concerned with the solution of the questions of life, but which reply to their own special scientific questions, one is enraptured by the power of man's mind, but one knows in advance that they give no reply to life's questions. Those sciences simply ignore life's questions. They say: 'To the question of what you are and why you live we have no reply, and are not occupied with that; but if you want to know the laws of light, of chemical combinations, the laws of development of organisms, if you want to know the laws of bodies and their form, and the relation of numbers and quantities, if you want to know the laws of your mind, to all that we have clear, exact, and unquestionable replies.'

In general the relation of the experimental sciences to life's question may be expressed thus: Question: 'Why do I live?'

Answer: 'In infinite space, in infinite time, infinitely small particles change their forms in infinite complexity, and when you have understood the laws of those mutations of form you will understand why you live on the earth.'

Then in the sphere of abstract science I said to myself: 'All humanity lives and develops on the basis of spiritual principles and ideals which guide it. Those ideals are expressed in religions, in sciences, in arts, in forms of government. Those ideals become more and more elevated, and humanity advances to its highest welfare. I am part of humanity, and therefore my vocation is to forward the recognition and the realisation of the ideals of humanity.' And at the time of my weak-mindedness I was satisfied with that; but as soon as the question of life presented itself clearly to me, those theories immediately crumbled away. Not to speak of the unscrupulous obscurity with which those sciences announce conclusions formed on the study of a small part of mankind as general conclusions; not to speak of the mutual contradictions of different adherents of this view as to what are the ideals of humanity; the strangeness, not to say stupidity, of the theory consists in the fact that in order to reply to the question facing each man: 'What am I?' or 'Why do I live?' or 'What must I do?' one has first to decide the question: 'What is the life of the whole?' (which is to him unknown and of which he is acquainted with one tiny part in one minute period of time). To understand what he is, man must first understand all this mysterious humanity, consisting of people such as himself who do not understand one another.

I have to confess that there was a time when I believed this. It was the time when I had my own favourite ideals justifying my own caprices, and I was trying to devise a theory which would allow one to consider my caprices as the law of humanity. But as soon as the question of life arose in my soul in full clearness that reply at once flew to dust. And I understood that as in the experimental sciences there are real sciences, and semi-sciences which try to give answers to questions beyond their competence, so in this sphere there is a whole series of most diffused sciences which try to reply to irrelevant questions. Semi-sciences of that kind, the juridical and the social-historical, endeavour to solve the questions of a man's life by pretending to decide, each in its own way, the question of the life of all humanity.

But as in the sphere of man's experimental knowledge one who sincerely inquires how he is to live cannot be satisfied with the reply – 'Study in endless space the mutations, infinite in time and in complexity, of innumerable atoms, and then you will understand your life' – so also a sincere man cannot be satisfied with the reply: 'Study the whole life of humanity of which we cannot know either the beginning or the end, of which we do not even know a small part, and then you will understand your own life.' And like the experimental semi-sciences, so these other semi-sciences are the more filled with obscurities, inexactitudes, stupidities, and contradictions, the further they diverge from the real problems. The problem of experimental science is the sequence of cause and effect in material phenomena. It is only necessary for experimental science to introduce the question of a final cause for it to become nonsensical. The problem of abstract science is the recognition of the primordial essence of life. It is only necessary to introduce the investigation of consequential phenomena (such as social and historical phenomena) and it also becomes nonsensical.

Experimental science only then gives positive knowledge and displays the greatness of the human mind when it does not introduce into its investigations the question of an ultimate cause. And, on the contrary, abstract science is only then science and displays the greatness of the human mind when it puts quite aside questions relating to the consequential causes of phenomena and regards man solely in relation to an ultimate cause. Such in this realm of science – forming the pole of the sphere – is metaphysics or philosophy. That science states the question clearly: 'What am I, and what is the universe? And why do I exist, and why does the universe exist?' And since it has existed it has always replied in the same way. Whether the philosopher calls the essence of life existing within me, and in all that exists, by the name of 'idea', or 'substance', or 'spirit', or 'will', he says one and the same thing: that this essence exists and that I am of that same essence; but why it is he does not know, and does not say, if he is an exact thinker. I ask: 'Why should this essence exist? What results from the fact that it is and will be?' . . . And philosophy not merely does not reply, but is itself only asking that question. And if it is real philosophy all its labour lies merely in trying to put that question clearly. And if it keeps firmly to its task it cannot reply to the question otherwise than thus: 'What am I, and what is the universe?' 'All and nothing'; and to the question 'Why?' by 'I do not know'.

So that however I may turn these replies of philosophy I can never obtain anything like an answer – and not because, as in the clear experimental sphere, the reply does not relate to my question, but because here, though all the mental work is directed just to my question, there is no answer, but instead of an answer one gets the same question, only in a complex form.

6

In my search for answers to life's questions I experienced just what is felt by a man lost in a forest.

He reaches a glade, climbs a tree, and clearly sees the limitless distance, but sees that his home is not and cannot be there; then he goes into the dark wood and sees the darkness, but there also his home is not.

So I wandered in that wood of human knowledge, amid the gleams of mathematical and experimental science which showed me clear horizons but in a direction where there could be no home, and also amid the darkness of the abstract sciences where I was immersed in deeper gloom the further I went, and where I finally convinced myself that there was, and could be, no exit.

Yielding myself to the bright side of knowledge, I understood that I was only diverting my gaze from the question. However alluringly clear those horizons which opened out before me might be, however alluring it might be to immerse oneself in the limitless expanse of those sciences, I already understood that the clearer they were the less they met my need and the less they replied to my question.

'I know', said I to myself, 'what science so persistently tries to discover, and along that road there is no reply to the question as to the meaning of my life.' In the abstract sphere I understood that notwithstanding the fact, or just because of the fact, that the direct aim of science is to reply to my question, there is no reply but that which I have myself already given: 'What is the meaning of my life?' 'There is none.' Or: 'What will come of my life?' 'Nothing.' Or: 'Why does everything exist that exists, and why do I exist?' 'Because it exists.'

Inquiring for one region of human knowledge, I received an

innumerable quantity of exact replies concerning matters about which I had not asked: about the chemical constituents of the stars, about the movement of the sun towards the constellation Hercules, about the origin of species and of man, about the forms of infinitely minute imponderable particles of ether; but in this sphere of knowledge the only answer to my question, 'What is the meaning of my life?' was: 'You are what you call your "life"; you are a transitory, casual cohesion of particles. The mutual inter-actions and changes of these particles produce in you what you call your "life". That cohesion will last some time; afterwards the interaction of these particles will cease and what you call "life" will cease, and so will all your questions. You are an accidentally united little lump of something. That little lump ferments. The little lump calls that fermenting its "life". The lump will disinte-grate and there will be an end of the fermenting and of all the questions.' So answers the clear side of science and cannot answer otherwise if it strictly follows its principles.

From such a reply one sees that the reply does not answer the question. I want to know the meaning of my life, but that it is a fragment of the infinite, far from giving it a meaning, destroys its every possible meaning. The obscure compromises which that side of experimental exact science makes with abstract science when it says that the meaning of life consists in development and in co-operation with development, owing to their inexactness and obscurity cannot be considered as replies.

The other side of science – the abstract side – when it holds strictly to its principles, replying directly to the question, always replies, and in all ages has replied, in one and the same way: 'The world is something infinite and incomprehensible. Human life is an incomprehensible part of that incomprehensible "all".' Again I exclude all those compromises between abstract and experimen-tal sciences which supply the whole ballast of the semi-sciences called juridical, political, and historical. In those semi-sciences the conception of development and progress is again wrongly intro-duced, only with this difference, that there it was the development of everything while here it is the development of the life of mankind. The error is there as before: development and progress in infinity can have no aim or direction, and, as far as my question is concerned, no answer is given.

In truly abstract science, namely in genuine philosophy – not in that which Schopenhauer* calls 'professorial philosophy', which serves only to classify all existing phenomena in new philosophic categories and to call them by new names – where the philosopher does not lose sight of the essential question, the reply is always one and the same – the reply given by Socrates,* Schopenhauer, Solomon,* and Buddha.*

'We approach truth only inasmuch as we depart from life', said Socrates when preparing for death. 'For what do we, who love truth, strive after in life? To free ourselves from the body, and from all the evil that is caused by the life of the body! If so, then how can we fail to be glad when death comes to us?

'The wise man seeks death all his life and therefore death is not terrible to him.'

And Schopenhauer says:

'Having recognized the inmost essence of the world as *will*, and all its phenomena – from the unconscious working of the obscure forces of Nature up to the completely conscious action of man – as only the objectivity of that will, we shall in no way avoid the conclusion that together with the voluntary renunciation and self-destruction of the will all those phenomena also disappear, that constant striving and effort without aim or rest on all the stages of objectivity in which and through which the world exists; the diversity of successive forms will disappear, and together with the form all the manifestations of will, with its most universal forms, space and time, and finally its most fundamental form – subject and object. Without will there is no concept and no world. Before us, certainly, nothing remains. But what resists this transition into annihilation, our nature, is only that same wish to live – *Wille zum Leben* – which forms ourselves as well as our world. That we are so afraid of annihilation or, what is the same thing, that we so wish to live, merely means that we are ourselves nothing else but this desire to live, and know nothing but it. And so what remains after the complete annihilation of the will, for us who are so full of the will, is, of course, nothing; but on the other hand, for those in whom the will has turned and renounced itself, this so real world of ours with all its suns and milky way is nothing.'

'Vanity of vanities', says Solomon – 'vanity of vanities – all is vanity. What profit hath a man of all his labour which he taketh under the sun? One generation passeth away, and another generation cometh: but the earth abideth for ever. . . . The thing that hath been, is that which shall be; and that which is done is that which shall be done: and there is no new thing under the sun. Is there anything whereof it may be said, See, this is new? it hath been already of old time, which was before us. There is no remembrance of former things; neither shall there be any remembrance of things that are to come with those that shall come after. I the Preacher was King over Israel in Jerusalem. And I gave my heart to seek and search out by wisdom concerning all that is done under heaven: this sore travail hath God given to the sons of man to be exercised therewith. I have seen all the works that are done under the sun; and behold, all is vanity and vexation of spirit. . . . I communed with my own heart, saying, Lo, I am come to great estate, and have gotten more wisdom than all they that have been before me over Jerusalem: yea, my heart hath great experience of wisdom and knowledge. And I gave my heart to know wisdom, and to know madness and folly: I perceived that this also is vexation of spirit. For in much wisdom is much grief: and he that increaseth knowledge increaseth sorrow.

'I said in my heart, Go to now, I will prove thee with mirth, therefore enjoy pleasure: and behold this also is vanity. I said of laughter, It is mad: and of mirth, What doeth it? I sought in my heart how to cheer my flesh with wine, and while my heart was guided by wisdom, to lay hold on folly, till I might see what it was good for the sons of men that they should do under heaven the number of the days of their life. I made me great works; I builded me houses; I planted me vineyards: I made me gardens and orchards, and I planted trees in them of all kinds of fruits: I made me pools of water, to water therefrom the forest where trees were reared: I got me servants and maidens, and had servants born in my house; also I had great possessions of herds and flocks above all that were before me in Jerusalem: I gathered me also silver and gold and the peculiar treasure from kings and from the provinces: I got me men singers and women singers; and the delights of the sons of men, as musical instruments and that of all sorts. So I was great, and increased more than all that were before me in Jerusalem: also my wisdom remained with me. And whatever mine eyes desired I kept not from them. I withheld not my heart from any joy. . . . Then I looked on all the works that my hands had wrought, and on the labour that I had laboured to do: and, behold, all was vanity and vexation of spirit, and there was no profit from them under the sun. And I turned myself to behold wisdom, and madness, and folly. . . . But I perceived that one event happeneth to them all. Then said I in my heart, As it happeneth to the fool, so it happeneth even to me, and why was I then more wise? Then I said in my heart, that this also is vanity. For there is no remembrance of the wise more than of the fool for ever; seeing that which now is in the days to come shall all be forgotten. And how dieth the wise man? as the fool. Therefore I hated life; because the work that is wrought under the sun is grievous unto me: for all is vanity and vexation of spirit. Yea, I hated all my labour which I had taken under the sun: seeing that I must leave it unto the man that shall be after me. . . . For what hath man of all his labour, and of the vexation of his heart, wherein he hath laboured under the sun? For all his days are sorrows, and his travail grief; yea, even in the night his heart taketh no rest. This is also vanity. Man is not blessed with security that he should eat and drink and cheer his soul from his own labour. . . . All things come alike to all: there is one event to the righteous and to the wicked; to the good and to the evil: to the clean and to the unclean; to him that sacrificeth and to him that sacrificeth not; as is the good, so is the sinner; and he that sweareth, as he that feareth an oath. This is an evil in all that is done under the sun, that there is one event unto all; yea, also the heart of the sons of men is full of evil, and madness is in their heart while they live, and after that they go to the dead. For him that is among the living there is hope: for a living dog is better than a dead lion. For the living know that they shall die: but the dead know not any thing, neither have they any more a reward; for the memory of them is forgotten. Also their love, and their hatred, and their envy, is now perished; neither have they any more a portion for ever in any thing that is done under the sun.'

So said Solomon, or whoever wrote those words.

And this is what the Indian wisdom tells:

Sakya Muni, a young, happy prince, from whom the existence of sickness, old age, and death had been hidden, went out to drive and saw a terrible old man, toothless and slobbering. The prince, from whom till then old age had been concealed, was amazed, and asked his driver what it was, and how that man had come to such a wretched and disgusting condition, and when he learnt that this was the common fate of all men, that the same thing inevitably awaited him – the young prince – he could not continue his drive, but gave orders to go home, that he might consider this fact. So he shut himself up alone and considered it. And he probably devised some consolation for himself, for he subsequently again went out to drive, feeling merry and happy. But this time he saw a sick man. He saw an emaciated, livid, trembling man with dim eyes. The prince, from whom sickness had been concealed, stopped and asked what this was. And when he learnt that this was sickness, to which all men are liable, and that he himself – a healthy and happy prince – might himself fall ill tomorrow, he again was in no mood to enjoy himself but gave orders to drive home, and again sought some solace, and probably found it, for he drove out a third time for pleasure. But this third time he saw another new sight: he saw men carrying something. 'What is that?' 'A dead man.' 'What does *dead* mean?' asked the prince. He was told that to become dead means to become like that man. The prince approached the corpse, uncovered it, and looked at it. 'What will happen to him now?' asked the prince. He was told that the corpse would be buried in the ground. 'Why?' 'Because he will certainly not return to life, and will only produce a stench and worms.' 'And is that the fate of all men? Will the same thing happen to me? Will they bury me, and shall I cause a stench and be eaten by worms?' 'Yes.' 'Home! I shall not drive out for pleasure, and never will so drive out again!'

And Sakya Muni could find no consolation in life, and decided that life is the greatest of evils; and he devoted all the strength of his soul to free himself from it, and to free others; and to do this so that, even after death, life shall not be renewed any more but be completely destroyed at its very roots. So speaks all the wisdom of India.

These then are the direct replies that human wisdom gives when it replies to life's question.

'The life of the body is an evil and a lie. Therefore the destruction of the life of the body is a blessing, and we should desire it', says Socrates.

'Life is that which should not be – an evil; and the passage into Nothingness is the only good in life', says Schopenhauer.

'All that is in the world – folly and wisdom and riches and poverty and mirth and grief – is vanity and emptiness. Man dies and nothing is left of him. And that is stupid', says Solomon.

'To live in the consciousness of the inevitability of suffering, of becoming enfeebled, of old age and of death, is impossible – we must free ourselves from life, from all possible life', says Buddha.

And what these strong minds said has been said and thought and felt by millions upon millions of people like them. And I have thought it and felt it.

So my wandering among the sciences, far from freeing me from my despair, only strengthened it. One kind of knowledge did not reply to life's question, the other kind replied directly confirming my despair, indicating not that the result at which I had arrived was the fruit of error or of a diseased state of my mind, but on the contrary that I had thought correctly, and that my thoughts coincided with the conclusions of the most powerful of human minds.

It is no good deceiving oneself. It is all – vanity! Happy is he who has not been born: death is better than life, and one must free oneself from life.

7

Not finding an explanation in science I began to seek for it in life, hoping to find it among the people around me. And I began to observe how the people around me – people like myself – lived, and what their attitude was to this question which had brought me to despair.

And this is what I found among people who were in the same position as myself as regards education and manner of life.

I found that for people of my circle there were four ways out of the terrible position in which we are all placed.

The first was that of ignorance. It consists in not knowing, not understanding, that life is an evil and an absurdity. People of this sort – chiefly women, or very young or very dull people – have not yet understood that question of life which presented itself to Schopenhauer, Solomon, and Buddha. They see neither the dragon that awaits them nor the mice gnawing the shrub by which they are hanging, and they lick the drops of honey. But they lick those drops of honey only for a while: something will turn their attention to the dragon and the mice, and there will be an end to their licking. From them I had nothing to learn – one cannot cease to know what one does know.

The second way out is epicureanism. It consists, while knowing the hopelessness of life, in making use meanwhile of the advantages one has, disregarding the dragon and the mice, and licking the honey in the best way, especially if there is much of it within reach. Solomon expresses this way out thus: 'Then I commended mirth, because a man hath no better thing under the sun, than to eat, and to drink, and to be merry: and that this should accompany him in his labour the days of his life, which God giveth him under the sun.

'Therefore eat thy bread with joy and drink thy wine with a merry heart. . . . Live joyfully with the wife whom thou lovest all the days of the life of thy vanity . . . for this is thy portion in life and in thy labours which thou takest under the sun. . . . Whatsoever thy hand findeth to do, do it with thy might, for there is no work, nor device, nor knowledge, nor wisdom, in the grave, whither thou goest.'

That is the way in which the majority of people of our circle make life possible for themselves. Their circumstances furnish them with more of welfare than of hardship, and their moral dullness makes it possible for them to forget that the advantage of their position is accidental, and that not everyone can have a thousand wives and palaces like Solomon, that for everyone who has a thousand wives there are a thousand without a wife, and that for each palace there are a thousand people who have to build it in the sweat of their brows; and that the accident that has today made me a Solomon may tomorrow make me a Solomon's slave. The dullness óf these people's imagination enables them to forget the things that gave Buddha no peace – the inevitability of sickness, old age, and death, which today or tomorrow will destroy all these pleasures.

So think and feel the majority of people of our day and our manner of life. The fact that some of these people declare the dullness of their thoughts and imaginations to be a philosophy, which they call Positive, does not remove them, in my opinion, from the ranks of those who, to avoid seeing the question, lick the honey. I could not imitate these people; not having their dullness of imagination I could not artificially produce it in myself. I could not tear my eyes from the mice and the dragon, as no vital man can after he has once seen them.

The third escape is that of strength and energy. It consists in destroying life, when one has understood that it is an evil and an absurdity. A few exceptionally strong and consistent people act so. Having understood the stupidity of the joke that has been played on them, and having understood that it is better to be dead than to be alive, and that it is best of all not to exist, they act accordingly and promptly end this stupid joke, since there are means: a rope round one's neck, water, a knife to stick into one's heart, or the trains on the railways; and the number of those of our circle who act in this way becomes greater and greater, and for the most part they act so at the best time of their life, when the strength of their mind is in full bloom and few habits degrading to the mind have as yet been acquired.

I saw that this was the worthiest way of escape and I wished to adopt it.

The fourth way out is that of weakness. It consists in seeing the truth of the situation and yet clinging to life, knowing in advance that nothing can come of it. People of this kind know that death is better than life, but not having the strength to act rationally – to end the deception quickly and kill themselves – they seem to wait for something. This is the escape of weakness, for if I know what is best and it is within my power, why not yield to what is best? . . . I found myself in that category.

So people of my class evade the terrible contradiction in four ways. Strain my attention as I would, I saw no way except those four. One way was not to understand that life is senseless, vanity, and an evil, and that it is better not to live. I could not help knowing this, and when I once knew it could not shut my eyes to it. The second way was to use life such as it is without thinking of the future. And I could not do that. I, like Sakya Muni, could not ride out hunting when I knew that old age, suffering, and death exist. My imagination was too vivid. Nor could I rejoice in the momentary accidents that for an instant threw pleasure to my lot. The third way, having understood that life is evil and stupid, was to end it by killing oneself. I understood that, but somehow still did not kill myself. The fourth way was to live like Solomon and Schopenhauer – knowing that life is a stupid joke played upon us, and still to go on living, washing oneself, dressing, dining, talking, and even writing books. This was to me repulsive and tormenting, but I remained in that position.

I see now that if I did not kill myself it was due to some dim consciousness of the invalidity of my thoughts. However convincing and indubitable appeared to me the sequence of my thoughts and of those of the wise that have brought us to the admission of the senselessness of life, there remained in me a vague doubt of the justice of my conclusion.

It was like this: I, my reason, have acknowledged that life is senseless. If there is nothing higher than reason (and there is not: nothing can prove that there is), then reason is the creator of life for me. If reason did not exist there would be for me no life. How can reason deny life when it is the creator of life? Or to put it the other way: were there no life, my reason would not exist; therefore reason is life's son. Life is all. Reason is its fruit yet reason rejects life itself! I felt that there was something wrong here.

Life is a senseless evil, that is certain, said I to myself. Yet I have lived and am still living, and all mankind lived and lives. How is that? Why does it live, when it is possible not to live? Is it that only I and Schopenhauer are wise enough to understand the senselessness and evil of life?

The reasoning showing the vanity of life is not so difficult, and has long been familiar to the very simplest folk; yet they have lived and still live. How is it they all live and never think of doubting the reasonableness of life?

My knowledge, confirmed by the wisdom of the sages, has shown me that everything on earth – organic and inorganic – is all most cleverly arranged – only my own position is stupid. And those fools – the enormous masses of people – know nothing about how everything organic and inorganic in the world is arranged; but they live, and it seems to them that their life is very wisely arranged! . . .

And it struck me: 'But what if there is something I do not yet know? Ignorance behaves just in that way. Ignorance always says just what I am saying. When it does not know something, it says that what it does not know is stupid. Indeed, it appears that there is a whole humanity that lived and lives as if it understood the meaning of its life, for without understanding it it could not live; but I say that all this life is senseless and that I cannot live.

'Nothing prevents our denying life by suicide. Well then, kill yourself, and you won't discuss. If life displeases you, kill yourself! You live, and cannot understand the meaning of life – then finish it, and do not fool about in life, saying and writing that you do not understand it. You have come into good company where people are contented and know what they are doing; if you find it dull and repulsive – go away!'

Indeed, what are we who are convinced of the necessity of suicide yet do not decide to commit it, but the weakest, most inconsistent, and to put it plainly, the stupidest of men, fussing about with our own stupidity as a fool fusses about with a painted hussy? For our wisdom, however indubitable it may be, has not given us the knowledge of the meaning of our life. But all mankind who sustain life – millions of them – do not doubt the meaning of life.

Indeed, from the most distant times of which I know anything, when life began, people have lived knowing the argument about the vanity of life which has shown me its senselessness, and yet they lived attributing some meaning to it.

From the time when any life began among men they had that meaning of life, and they led that life which has descended to me. All that is in me and around me, all, corporeal and incorporeal, is the fruit of their knowledge of life. Those very instruments of thought with which I consider this life and condemn it were all devised not by me but by them. I myself was born, taught, and brought up thanks to them. They dug out the iron, taught us to cut down the forests, tamed the cows and horses, taught us to sow corn and to live together, organised our life, and taught me to think and speak. And I, their product, fed, supplied with drink, taught by them, thinking with their thoughts and words, have argued that they are an absurdity! 'There is something wrong', said I to myself. 'I have blundered somewhere.' But it was a long time before I could find out where the mistake was.

8

All these doubts, which I am now able to express more or less systematically, I could not then have expressed. I then only felt that however logically inevitable were my conclusions concerning the vanity of life, confirmed as they were by the greatest thinkers, there was something not right about them. Whether it was in the reasoning itself or in the statement of the question I did not know – I only felt that the conclusion was rationally convincing, but that was insufficient. All these conclusions could not so convince me as to make me do what followed from my reasoning, that is to say, kill myself. And I should have told an untruth had I, without killing myself, said that reason had brought me to the point I had reached. Reason worked, but something else was also working which I can only call a consciousness of life. A force was working which compelled me to turn my attention to this and not to that; and it was this force which extricated me from my desperate situation and turned my mind in quite another direction. This force compelled me to turn my attention to the fact that

I and a few hundred similar people are not the whole of mankind, and that I did not yet know the life of mankind.

Looking at the narrow circle of my equals, I saw only people who had not understood the question, or who had understood it and drowned it in life's intoxication, or had understood it and ended their lives, or had understood it and yet from weakness were living out their desperate life. And I saw no others. It seemed to me that narrow circle of rich, learned, and leisured people to which I belonged formed the whole of humanity, and that those milliards of others who have lived and are living were cattle of some sort – not real people.

Strange, incredibly incomprehensible as it now seems to me that I could, while reasoning about life, overlook the whole life of mankind that surrounded me on all sides; that I could to such a degree blunder so absurdly as to think that my life, and Solomon's and Schopenhauer's, is the real, normal life, and that the life of the milliards is a circumstance undeserving of attention – strange as this now is to me, I see that so it was. In the delusion of my pride of intellect it seemed to me so indubitable that I and Solomon and Schopenhauer had stated the question so truly and exactly that nothing else was possible – so indubitable did it seem that all those milliards consisted of men who had not yet arrived at an apprehension of all the profundity of the question – that I sought for the meaning of my life without it once occurring to me to ask: 'But what meaning is and has been given to their lives by all the milliards of common folk who live and have lived in the world?'

I long lived in this state of lunacy, which, in fact if not in words, is particularly characteristic of us very liberal and learned people. But thanks either to the strange physical affection I have for the real labouring people, which compelled me to understand them and to see that they are not so stupid as we suppose, or thanks to the sincerity of my conviction that I could know nothing beyond the fact that the best I could do was to hang myself, at any rate I instinctively felt that if I wished to live and understand the meaning of life, I must seek this meaning not among those who have lost it and wish to kill themselves, but among those milliards of the past and the present who make life and who support the burden of their own lives and of ours also. And I considered the enormous masses of those simple, unlearned, and poor people who have lived and are living and I saw something quite different. I saw that, with rare exceptions, all those milliards who have lived and are living do not fit into my divisions, and that I could not class them as not understanding the question, for they themselves state it and reply to it with extraordinary clearness. Nor could I consider them epicureans, for their life consists more of privations and sufferings than of enjoyments. Still less could I consider them as irrationally dragging on a meaningless existence, for every act of their life, as well as death itself, is explained by them. To kill themselves they consider the greatest evil. It appeared that all mankind had a knowledge, unacknowledged and despised by me, of the meaning of life. It appeared that reasonable knowledge does not give the meaning of life, but excludes life: while the meaning attributed to life by milliards of people, by all humanity, rests on some despised pseudo-knowledge.

Rational knowledge, presented by the learned and wise, denies the meaning of life, but the enormous masses of men, the whole of mankind, receive that meaning in irrational knowledge. And that irrational knowledge is faith, that very thing which I could not but reject. It is God, One in Three; the creation in six days; the devils and angels, and all the rest that I cannot accept as long as I retain my reason.

My position was terrible. I knew I could find nothing along the path of reasonable knowledge except a denial of life; and there – in faith – was nothing but a denial of reason, which was yet more impossible for me than a denial of life. From rational knowledge it appeared that life is an evil, people know this and it is in their power to end life; yet they lived and still live, and I myself live though I have long known that life is senseless and an evil. By faith it appears that in order to understand the meaning of life I must renounce my reason, the very thing for which alone a meaning is required.

9

A contradiction arose from which there were two exits. Either that which I called reason was not so rational as I supposed, or that which seemed to me irrational was not so irrational as I supposed. And I began to verify the line of argument of my rational knowledge.

Verifying the line of argument of rational knowledge I found it quite correct. The conclusion that life is nothing was inevitable;

but I noticed a mistake. The mistake lay in this, that my reasoning was not in accord with the question I had put. The question was: 'Why should I live, that is to say, what real, permanent result will come out of my illusory transitory life – what meaning has my finite existence in this infinite world?' And to reply to that question I had studied life.

The solution of all the possible questions of life could evidently not satisfy me, for my question, simple as it at first appeared, included a demand for an explanation of the finite in terms of the infinite, and vice versa.

I asked: 'What is the meaning of my life, beyond time, cause, and space?' And I replied to quite another question: 'What is the meaning of my life within time, cause, and space?' With the result that, after long efforts of thought, the answer I reached was: 'None.'

In my reasonings I constantly compared (nor could I do otherwise) the finite with the finite, and the infinite with the infinite; but for that reason I reached the inevitable result: force is force, matter is matter, will is will, the infinite is the infinite, nothing is nothing – and that was all that could result.

It was something like what happens in mathematics, when thinking to solve an equation, we find we are working on an identity. The line of reasoning is correct, but results in the answer that a equals a, or x equals x, or o equals o. The same thing happened with my reasoning in relation to the question of the meaning of my life. The replies given by all science to that question only result in – identity.

And really, strictly scientific knowledge – that knowledge which begins, as Descartes's* did, with complete doubt about everything – rejects all knowledge admitted on faith and builds everything afresh on the laws of reason and experience, and cannot give any other reply to the question of life than that which I obtained: an indefinite reply. Only at first had it seemed to me that knowledge had given a positive reply – the reply of Schopenhauer: that life has no meaning and is an evil. But on examining the matter I understood that the reply is not positive, it was only my feeling that so expressed it. Strictly expressed, as it is by the Brahmins* and by Solomon and Schopenhauer, the reply is merely indefinite, or an identity: o equals o, life is nothing. So that philosophic knowledge denies nothing, but only replies that the question cannot be solved by it – that for it the solution remains indefinite.

Having understood this, I understood that it was not possible to seek in rational knowledge for a reply to my question, and that the reply given by rational knowledge is a mere indication that a reply can only be obtained by a different statement of the question and only when the relation of the finite to the infinite is included in the question. And I understood that, however irrational and distorted might be the replies given by faith, they have this advantage, that they introduce into every answer a relation between the finite and the infinite, without which there can be no solution.

In whatever way I stated the question, that relation appeared in the answer. How am I to live? – According to the law of God. What real result will come of my life? – Eternal torment or eternal bliss. What meaning has life that death does not destroy? – Union with the eternal God: heaven.

So that besides rational knowledge, which had seemed to me the only knowledge, I was inevitably brought to acknowledge that all live humanity has another irrational knowledge – faith which makes it possible to live. Faith still remained to me as irrational as it was before, but I could not but admit that it alone gives mankind a reply to the questions of life, and that consequently it makes life possible. Reasonable knowledge had brought me to acknowledge that life is senseless – my life had come to a halt and I wished to destroy myself. Looking around on the whole of mankind I saw that people live and declare that they know the meaning of life. I looked at myself – I had lived as long as I knew a meaning of life. As to others so also to me faith had given a meaning to life and had made life possible.

Looking again at people of other lands, at my contemporaries and at their predecessors, I saw the same thing. Where there is life, there since man began faith has made life possible for him, and the chief outline of that faith is everywhere and always identical.

Whatever the faith may be, and whatever answers it may give, and to whomsoever it gives them, every such answer gives to the finite existence of man an infinite meaning, a meaning not destroyed by sufferings, deprivations, or death. This means that only in faith can we find for life a meaning and a possibility. What, then, is this faith? And I understood that faith is not merely 'the evidence of things not seen', etc., and is not a revelation (that defines only one of the indications of faith), is not the relation of man to God (one has first to define faith and then God, and not define faith through God); it is not only agreement with what has been told one (as faith is most usually supposed to be), but faith is a knowledge of the meaning of human life in consequence of which man does not destroy himself but lives. Faith is the strength of life. If a man lives he believes in something. If he did not believe that one must live for something, he would not live. If he does not see and recognise the illusory nature of the finite, he believes in the finite; if he understands the illusory nature of the finite, he must believe in the infinite. Without faith he cannot live.

And I recalled the whole course of my mental labour and was horrified. It was now clear to me that for man to be able to live he must either not see the infinite, or have such an explanation of the meaning of life as will connect the finite with the infinite. Such an explanation I had had; but as long as I believed in the finite I did not need the explanation, and I began to verify it by reason. And in the light of reason the whole of my former explanation flew to atoms. But a time came when I ceased to believe in the finite. And then I began to build up on rational foundations, out of what I knew, an explanation which would give a meaning to life; but nothing could I build. Together with the best human intellects I reached the result that o equals o, and was much astonished at that conclusion, though nothing else could have resulted.

What was I doing when I sought an answer in the experimental sciences? I wished to know why I live, and for this purpose studied all that is outside me. Evidently I might learn much, but nothing of what I needed.

What was I doing when I sought an answer in philosophical knowledge? I was studying the thoughts of those who had found themselves in the same position as I, lacking a reply to the question 'Why do I live?' Evidently I could learn nothing but what I knew myself, namely that nothing can be known.

What am I? – A part of the infinite. In those few words lies the whole problem.

Is it possible that humanity has only put that question to itself since yesterday? And can no one before me have set himself that question – a question so simple, and one that springs to the tongue of every wise child?

Surely that question has been asked since man began; and naturally for the solution of that question since man began it has been equally insufficient to compare the finite with the finite and the infinite with the infinite, and since man began the relation of the finite to the infinite has been sought out and expressed.

All these conceptions in which the finite has been adjusted to the infinite and a meaning found for life – the conception of God, of will, of goodness – we submit to logical examination. And all those conceptions fail to stand reason's criticism.

Were it not so terrible it would be ludicrous with what pride and self-satisfaction we, like children, pull the watch to pieces, take out the spring, make a toy of it, and are then surprised that the watch does not go.

A solution of the contradiction between the finite and the infinite, and such a reply to the question of life as will make it possible to live, is necessary and precious. And that is the only solution which we find everywhere, always, and among all peoples: a solution descending from times in which we lose sight of the life of man, a solution so difficult that we can compose nothing like it – and this solution we light-heartedly destroy in order again to set the same question, which is natural to everyone and to which we have no answer.

The conception of an infinite God, the divinity of the soul, the connection of human affairs with God, the unity and existence of the soul, man's conception of moral goodness and evil – are conceptions formulated in the hidden infinity of human thought, they are those conceptions without which neither life nor I should exist; yet rejecting all that labour of the whole of humanity, I wished to remake it afresh myself and in my own manner.

I did not then think like that, but the germs of these thoughts were already in me. I understood, in the first place, that my position with Schopenhauer and Solomon, notwithstanding our wisdom, was stupid: we see that life is an evil and yet continue to live. That is evidently stupid, for if life is senseless and I am so fond of what is reasonable, it should be destroyed, and then there would be no one to challenge it. Secondly, I understood that all one's reasonings turned in a vicious circle like a wheel out of gear with its pinion. However much and however well we may reason we cannot obtain a reply to the question; and o will always equal o, and therefore our path is probably erroneous. Thirdly, I began to understand that in the replies given by faith is stored up the deepest human wisdom and that I had no right to deny them on the ground of reason, and that those answers are the only ones which reply to life's question.

10

I understood this, but it made matters no better for me. I was now ready to accept any faith if only it did not demand of me a direct denial of reason – which would be a falsehood. And I studied Buddhism* and Mohammedanism* from books, and most of all I studied Christianity both from books and from the people around me.

Naturally I first of all turned to the Orthodox of my circle, to people who were learned: to Church theologians, monks, to theologians of the newest shade, and even to Evangelicals who profess salvation by belief in the Redemption. And I seized on these believers and questioned them as to their beliefs and their understanding of the meaning of life.

But though I made all possible concessions, and avoided all disputes, I could not accept the faith of these people. I saw that what they gave out as their faith did not explain the meaning of life but obscured it, and that they themselves affirm their belief not to answer that question of life which brought me to faith, but for some other aims alien to me.

I remember the painful feeling of fear of being thrown back into my former state of despair, after the hope I often and often experienced in my intercourse with these people.

The more fully they explained to me their doctrines, the more clearly did I perceive their error and realised that my hope of finding in their belief an explanation of the meaning of life was vain.

It was not that in their doctrines they mixed many unnecessary and unreasonable things with the Christian truths that had always been near to me: that was not what repelled me. I was repelled by the fact that these people's lives were like my own, with only this difference – that such a life did not correspond to the principles they expounded in their teachings. I clearly felt that they deceived themselves and that they, like myself, found no other meaning in life than to live while life lasts, taking all one's hands can seize. I saw this because if they had had a meaning which destroyed the fear of loss, suffering, and death, they would not have feared these things. But they, these believers of our circle, just like myself, living in sufficiency and superfluity, tried to increase or preserve them, feared privations, suffering, and death, and just like myself and all of us unbelievers, lived to satisfy their desires, and lived just as badly, if not worse, than the unbelievers.

No arguments could convince me of the truth of their faith. Only deeds which showed that they saw a meaning in life making what was so dreadful to me – poverty, sickness, and death – not dreadful to them could convince me. And such deeds I did not see among the various believers in our circle. On the contrary, I saw such deeds done by people of our circle who were the most unbelieving, but never by our so-called believers.

And I understood that the belief of these people was not the faith I sought, and that their faith is not a real faith but an epicurean consolation in life.

I understood that that faith may perhaps serve, if not for a consolation at least for some distraction for a repentant Solomon on his death-bed, but it cannot serve for the great majority of mankind, who are called on not to amuse themselves while consuming the labour of others but to create life.

For all humanity to be able to live, and continue to live attributing a meaning to life, they, those milliards, must have a different, a real, knowledge of faith. Indeed, it was not the fact that we, with Solomon and Schopenhauer, did not kill ourselves that convinced me of the existence of faith, but the fact that those milliards of people have lived and are living, and have borne Solomon and us on the current of their lives.

And I began to draw near to the believers among the poor, simple, unlettered folk: pilgrims, monks, sectarians, and peasants. The faith of these common people was the same Christian faith as was professed by the pseudo-believers of our circle. Among them, too, I found a great deal of superstition mixed with the Christian truths; but the difference was that the superstitions of the believers of our circle were quite unnecessary to them and were not in conformity with their lives, being merely a kind of epicurean diversion; but the superstitions of the believers among the labouring masses conformed so with their lives that it was impossible to imagine them to oneself without those superstitions, which were a necessary condition of their life. The whole life of believers was a confirmation of the meaning of life which their faith gave them.

And I began to look well into the life and faith of these people, and the more I considered it the more I became convinced that they have a real faith which is a necessity to them and alone gives their life a meaning and makes it possible for them to live. In contrast with what I had seen in our circle – where life without faith is possible and where hardly one in a thousand acknowledges himself to be a believer – among them there is hardly one unbeliever in a thousand. In contrast with what I had seen in our circle, where the whole of life is passed in idleness, amusement, and dissatisfaction, I saw that the whole life of these people was passed in heavy labour, and that they were content with life. In contradistinction to the way in which people of our circle oppose fate and complain of it on account of deprivations and sufferings, these people accepted illness and sorrow without any perplexity or opposition, and with a quiet and firm conviction that all is good. In contradistinction to us, who the wiser we are the less we understand the meaning of life, and see some evil irony in the fact that we suffer and die, these folk live and suffer, and they approach death and suffering with tranquillity and in most cases gladly. In contrast to the fact that a tranquil death, a death without horror and despair, is a very rare exception in our circle, a troubled, rebellious, and unhappy death is the rarest exception among the people. And such people, lacking all that for us and for Solomon is the only good of life and yet experiencing the greatest happiness, are a great multitude. I looked more widely around me. I considered the life of the enormous mass of the people in the past and the present. And of such people, understanding the meaning of life and able to live and to die, I saw not two or three, or tens, but hundreds, thousands, and millions. And they all – endlessly different in their manners, minds, education, and position, as they were – all alike, in complete contrast to my ignorance, knew the meaning of life and death, laboured quietly, endured deprivations and sufferings, and lived and died seeing therein not vanity but good.

And I learnt to love these people. The more I came to know their life, the life of those who are living and of others who are dead of whom I read and heard, the more I loved them and the easier it became for me to live. So I went on for about two years, and a change took place in me which had long been preparing and the promise of which had always been in me. It came about that the life of our circle, the rich and learned, not merely became distasteful to me, but lost all meaning in my eyes. All our actions, discussions, science and art presented itself to me in a new light. I understood that it is all merely self-indulgence, and that to find a meaning in it is impossible; while the life of the whole labouring people, the whole of mankind who produce life, appeared to me in its true significance. I understood that *that* is life itself, and that the meaning given to that life is true: and I accepted it.

11

And remembering how those very beliefs had repelled me and had seemed meaningless when professed by people whose lives conflicted with them, and how these same beliefs attracted me and seemed reasonable when I saw that people lived in accord with them, I understood why I had then rejected those beliefs and found them meaningless, yet now accepted them and found them full of meaning. I understood that I had erred, and why I erred. I had erred not so much because I thought incorrectly as because I lived badly. I understood that it was not an error in my thought that had hid truth from me so much as my life itself in the exceptional conditions of epicurean gratification of desires in which I passed it. I understood that my question as to what my life is, and the answer – an evil – was quite correct. The only mistake was that the answer referred only to my life, while I had referred it to life in general. I asked myself what my life is, and got the reply: an evil and an absurdity. And really my life – a life of indulgence of desires – was senseless and evil, and therefore the reply, 'Life is evil and an absurdity', referred only to my life, but not to human life in general. I understood the truth which I afterwards found in the Gospels, 'that men loved darkness rather than the light, for their works were evil. For everyone that doeth ill hateth the light, and cometh not to the light, lest his works should be reproved.' I perceived that to understand the meaning of life it is necessary first that life should not be meaningless and evil, then we can apply reason to explain it. I understood why I had so long wandered round so evident a truth, and that if one is to think and speak of the life of mankind, one must think and speak of that life and not of the life of some of life's parasites. That truth was always as true as that two and two are four, but I had not acknowledged it, because on admitting two and two to be four I had also to admit that I was bad; and to feel myself to be good was for me more important and necessary than for two and two to be four. I came to love good people, hated myself, and confessed the truth. Now all became clear to me.

What if an executioner passing his whole life in torturing people and cutting off their heads, or a hopeless drunkard, or a madman settled for life in a dark room which he has fouled and imagines that he would perish if he left – what if he asked himself: 'What is life?' Evidently he could get no other reply to that question than that life is the greatest evil, and the madman's answer would be perfectly correct, but only as applied to himself. What if I am such a madman? What if all we rich and leisured people are such madmen? and I understood that we really are such madmen. I at any rate was certainly such.

And indeed a bird is so made that it must fly, collect food, and build a nest, and when I see that a bird does this I have pleasure in its joy. A goat, a hare, and a wolf are so made that they must feed themselves, and must breed and feed their family, and when they do so I feel firmly assured that they are happy and that their life is a reasonable one. Then what should a man do? He too should produce his living as the animals do, but with this difference, that he will perish if he does it alone; he must obtain it not for himself but for all. And when he does that, I have a firm assurance that he is happy and that his life is reasonable. But what had I done during the whole thirty years of my responsible life? Far from producing sustenance for all, I did not even produce it for myself. I lived as a parasite, and on asking myself, what is the use of my life? I got the reply: 'No use.' If the meaning of human life lies in supporting it, how could I – who for thirty years had been engaged not on supporting life but on destroying it in myself and in others – how could I obtain any other answer than that my life was senseless and an evil? . . . It was both senseless and evil.

The life of the world endures by someone's will – by the life of the whole world and by our lives someone fulfils his purpose. To hope to understand the meaning of that will one must first perform it by doing what is wanted of us. But if I will not do what is wanted of me, I shall never understand what is wanted of me, and still less what is wanted of us all and of the whole world.

If a naked, hungry beggar has been taken from the cross-roads, brought into a building belonging to a beautiful establishment, fed, supplied with drink, and obliged to move a handle up and down, evidently, before discussing why he was taken, why he should move the handle, and whether the whole establishment is reasonably arranged – the beggar should first of all move the handle. If he moves the handle he will understand that it works a pump, that the pump draws water and that the water irrigates the garden beds; then he will be taken from the pumping station to another place where he will gather fruits and will enter into the joy of his master, and, passing from lower to higher work, will understand more and more of the arrangements of the establishment, and taking part in it will never think of asking why he is there, and will certainly not reproach the master.

So those who do his will, the simple, unlearned working folk, whom we regard as cattle, do not reproach the master; but we, the wise, eat the master's food but do not do what the master wishes, and instead of doing it sit in a circle and discuss: 'Why should that handle be moved? Isn't it stupid?' So we have decided. We have decided that the master is stupid, or does not exist, and that we are wise, only we feel that we are quite useless and that we must somehow do away with ourselves.

12

The consciousness of the error in reasonable knowledge helped me to free myself from the temptation of idle ratiocination. The conviction that knowledge of truth can only be found by living led me to doubt the rightness of my life; but I was saved only by the fact that I was able to tear myself from my exclusiveness and to see the real life of the plain working people, and to understand that it alone is real life. I understood that if I wish to understand life and its meaning, I must not live the life of a parasite, but must live a real life, and – taking the meaning given to life by real humanity and merging myself in that life – verify it.

During that time this is what happened to me. During that whole year, when I was asking myself almost every moment whether I should not end matters with a noose or a bullet – all that time, together with the course of thought and observation about which I have spoken, my heart was oppressed with a painful feeling, which I can only describe as a search for God.

I say that that search for God was not reasoning, but a feeling, because that search proceeded not from the course of my thoughts – it was even directly contrary to them – but proceeded from the heart. It was a feeling of fear, orphanage, isolation in a strange land, and a hope of help from someone.

Though I was quite convinced of the impossibility of proving the existence of a Deity (Kant* had shown, and I quite understood him, that it could not be proved), I yet sought for God, hoped that I should find Him, and from old habit addressed prayers to that which I sought but had not found. I went over in my mind the arguments of Kant and Schopenhauer showing the impossibility of proving the existence of a God, and I began to verify those arguments and to refute them. Cause, said I to myself, is not a category of thought such as are Time and Space. If I exist, there must be some cause for it, and a cause of causes. And that first cause of all is what men have called 'God'. And I paused on that thought, and tried with all my being to recognise the presence of that cause. And as soon as I acknowledged that there is a force in whose power I am, I at a once felt that I could live. But I asked myself: What is that cause, that force? How am I to think of it? What are my relations to that which I call 'God'? And only the familiar replies occurred to me: 'He is the Creator and Preserver.' This reply did not satisfy me, and I felt I was losing within me what I needed for my life. I became terrified and began to pray to Him whom I sought, that He should help me. But the more I prayed the more apparent it became to me that He did not hear me, and that there was no one to whom to address myself. And with despair in my heart that there is no God at all, I said: 'Lord, have mercy, save me! Lord, teach me!' But no one had mercy on me, and I felt that my life was coming to a standstill.

But again and again, from various sides, I returned to the same conclusion that I could not have come into the world without any cause or reason or meaning; I could not be such a fledgling fallen from its nest as I felt myself to be. Or, granting that I be such, lying on my back crying in the high grass, even then I cry because I know that a mother has borne me within her, has hatched me, warmed me, fed me, and loved me. Where is she – that mother? If I have been deserted, who has deserted me? I cannot hide from myself that someone bore me, loving me. Who was that someone? Again 'God'? He knows and sees my searching, my despair, and my struggle.

'He exists', said I to myself. And I had only for an instant to admit that, and at once life rose within me, and I felt the possibility and joy of being. But again, from the admission of the existence of a God I went on to seek my relation with Him; and again I imagined *that* God – our Creator in Three Persons who sent His Son, the Saviour – and again *that* God, detached from the world and from me, melted like a block of ice, melted before my eyes, and again nothing remained, and again the spring of life dried up within me, and I despaired and felt that I had nothing to do but to kill myself. And the worst of all was, that I felt I could not do it.

Not twice or three times, but tens and hundreds of times, I reached those conditions, first of joy and animation, and then of despair and consciousness of the impossibility of living.

I remember that it was in early spring: I was alone in the wood listening to its sounds. I listened and thought ever of the same thing, as I had constantly done during those last three years. I was again seeking God.

'Very well, there is no God', said I to myself; 'there is no one who is not my imagination but a reality like my whole life. He does not exist, and no miracles can prove His existence, because the miracles would be my imagination, besides being irrational.

'But my *perception* of God, of Him whom I seek,' I asked myself, 'where has that perception come from?' And again at this thought the glad waves of life rose within me. All that was around me came to life and received a meaning. But my joy did not last long. My mind continued its work.

'The conception of God is not God', said I to myself. 'The conception is what takes place within me. The conception of God is something I can evoke or can refrain from evoking in myself. That is not what I seek. I seek that without which there can be no life.' And again all around me and within me began to die, and again I wished to kill myself.

But then I turned my gaze upon myself, on what went on within me, and I remembered all those cessations of life and reanimations that recurred within me hundreds of times. I remembered that I only lived at those times when I believed in God. As it was before, so it was now; I need only be aware of God to live; I need only forget Him, or disbelieve Him, and I died.

What is this animation and dying? I do not live when I lose belief in the existence of God. I should long ago have killed myself had I not had a dim hope of finding Him. I live, really live, only when I feel Him and seek Him. 'What more do you seek?'

exclaimed a voice within me. 'This is He. He is that without which one cannot live. To know God and to live is one and the same thing. God is life.'

'Live seeking God, and then you will not live without God.' And more than ever before, all within me and around me lit up, and the light did not again abandon me.

And I was saved from suicide. When and how this change occurred I could not say. As imperceptibly and gradually the force of life in me had been destroyed and I had reached the impossibility of living, a cessation of life and the necessity of suicide, so imperceptibly and gradually did that force of life return to me. And strange to say the strength of life which returned to me was not new, but quite old – the same that had borne me along in my earliest days.

I quite returned to what belonged to my earliest childhood and youth. I returned to the belief in that Will which produced me and desires something of me. I returned to the belief that the chief and only aim of my life is to be better, i.e., to live in accord with that Will. And I returned to the belief that I can find the expression of that Will in what humanity, in the distant past hidden from me, has produced for its guidance: that is to say, I returned to a belief in God, in moral perfection, and in a tradition transmitting the meaning of life. There was only this difference, that then all this was accepted unconsciously, while now I knew that without it I could not live.

What happened to me was something like this: I was put into a boat (I do not remember when) and pushed off from an unknown shore, shown the direction to the opposite shore, had oars put into my unpractised hands, and was left alone. I rowed as best I could and moved forward; but the further I advanced towards the middle of the stream the more rapid grew the current bearing me away from my goal and the more frequently did I encounter others, like myself, borne away by the stream. There were a few rowers who continued to row, there were others who had abandoned their oars; there were large boats and immense vessels full of people. Some struggled against the current, others yielded to it. And the further I went the more, seeing the progress down the current of all those who were adrift, I forgot the direction given me. In the very centre of the stream, amid the crowd of boats and vessels which were being borne down stream, I quite lost my direction and abandoned my oars. Around me on all sides, with mirth and rejoicing, people with sails and oars were borne down the stream, assuring me and each other that no other direction was possible. And I believed them and floated with them. And I was carried far; so far that I heard the roar of the rapids in which I must be shattered, and I saw boats shattered in them. And I recollected myself. I was long unable to understand what had happened to me. I saw before me nothing but destruction, towards which I was rushing and which I feared. I saw no safety anywhere and did not know what to do; but, looking back, I perceived innumerable boats which unceasingly and strenuously pushed across the stream, and I remembered about the shore, the oars, and the direction, and began to pull back upwards against the stream and towards the shore.

That shore was God; that direction was tradition; the oars were the freedom given me to pull for the shore and unite with God. And so the force of life was renewed in me and I again began to live.

13

I turned from the life of our circle, acknowledging that ours is not life but a simulation of life – that the conditions of superfluity in which we live deprive us of the possibility of understanding life, and that in order to understand life I must understand not an exceptional life such as ours who are parasites on life, but the life of the simple labouring folk – those who make life – and the meaning which they attribute to it. The simplest labouring people around me were the Russian people, and I turned to them and to the meaning of life which they give. That meaning, if one can put it into words, was as follows: Every man has come into this world by the will of God. And God has so made man that every man can destroy his soul or save it. The aim of man in life is to save his soul, and to save his soul he must live 'godly' and to live 'godly' he must renounce all the pleasures of life, must labour, humble himself, suffer, and be merciful. That meaning the people obtain from the whole teaching of faith transmitted to them by their pastors and by the traditions that live among the people. This meaning was clear to me and near to my heart. But together with this meaning of the popular faith of our non-sectarian folk, among whom I live, much was inseparably bound up that revolted me and seemed to me inexplicable: sacraments, Church services, fasts, and the adoration of relics and icons. The people cannot separate the one from the other, nor could I. And strange as much of what entered into the faith of these people was to me, I accepted everything, and attended the services, knelt morning and evening in prayer, fasted, and prepared to receive the Eucharist: and at first my reason did not resist anything. The very things that had formerly seemed to me impossible did not now evoke in me any opposition.

My relations to faith before and after were quite different. Formerly life itself seemed to me full of meaning and faith presented itself as the arbitrary assertion of propositions to me quite unnecessary, unreasonable, and disconnected from life. I then asked myself what meaning those propositions had and, convinced that they had none, I rejected them. Now on the contrary I knew firmly that my life otherwise has, and can have, no meaning, and the articles of faith were far from presenting themselves to me as unnecessary – on the contrary I had been led by indubitable experience to the conviction that only these propositions presented by faith give life a meaning. Formerly I looked on them as on some quite unnecessary gibberish, but now, if I did not understand them, I yet knew that they had a meaning, and I said to myself that I must learn to understand them.

I argued as follows, telling myself that the knowledge of faith flows, like all humanity with its reason, from a mysterious source. That source is God, the origin both of the human body and the human reason. As my body has descended to me from God, so also has my reason and my understanding of life, and consequently the various stages of the development of that understanding of life cannot be false. All that people sincerely believe in must be true; it may be differently expressed but it cannot be a lie, and therefore if it presents itself to me as a lie, that only means that I have not understood it. Furthermore I said to myself, the essence of every faith consists in its giving life a meaning which death does not destroy. Naturally for a faith to be able to reply to the questions of a king dying in luxury, of an old slave tormented by overwork, of an unreasoning child, of a wise old man, of a half-witted old woman, of a young and happy wife, of a youth tormented by passions, of all people in the most varied conditions of life and education – if there is one reply to the one eternal question of life: 'Why do I live and what will result from my life?' –

the reply, though one in its essence, must be endlessly varied in its presentation; and the more it is one, the more true and profound it is, the more strange and deformed must it naturally appear in its attempted expression, conformably to the education and position of each person. But this argument, justifying in my eyes the queerness of much on the ritual side of religion, did not suffice to allow me in the one great affair of life – religion – to do things which seemed to me questionable. With all my soul I wished to be in a position to mingle with the people, fulfilling the ritual side of their religion; but I could not do it. I felt that I should lie to myself and mock at what was sacred to me, were I to do so. At this point, however, our new Russian theological writers came to my rescue.

According to the explanation these theologians gave, the fundamental dogma of our faith is the infallibility of the Church. From the admission of that dogma follows inevitably the truth of all that is professed by the Church. The Church as an assembly of true believers united by love and therefore possessed of true knowledge became the basis of my belief. I told myself that divine truth cannot be accessible to a separate individual; it is revealed only to the whole assembly of people united by love. To attain truth one must not separate, and in order not to separate one must love and must endure things one may not agree with.

Truth reveals itself to love, and if you do not submit to the rites of the Church you transgress against love; and by transgressing against love you deprive yourself of the possibility of recognising the truth. I did not then see the sophistry contained in this argument. I did not see that union in love may give the greatest love, but certainly cannot give us divine truth expressed in the definite words of the Nicene Creed. I also did not perceive that love cannot make a certain expression of truth an obligatory condition of union. I did not then see these mistakes in the argument and thanks to it was able to accept and perform all the rites of the Orthodox Church without understanding most of them. I then tried with all the strength of my soul to avoid all arguments and contradictions, and tried to explain as reasonably as possible the Church statements I encountered.

When fulfilling the rites of the Church I humbled my reason and submitted to the tradition possessed by all humanity. I united myself with my forefathers: the father, mother, and grandparents I loved. They and all my predecessors believed and lived, and they produced me. I united myself also with the millions of the common people whom I respected. Moreover, those actions had nothing bad in themselves ('bad' I considered the indulgence of one's desires). When rising early for Church services I knew I was doing well, if only because I was sacrificing my bodily ease to humble my mental pride, for the sake of union with my ancestors and contemporaries, and for the sake of finding the meaning of life. It was the same with my preparations to receive Communion, and with the daily reading of prayers with genuflections, and also with the observance of all the fasts. However insignificant these sacrifices might be I made them for the sake of something good. I fasted, prepared for Communion, and observed the fixed hours of prayer at home and in church. During Church service I attended to every word, and gave them a meaning whenever I could. In the Mass the most important words for me were: 'Let us love one another in conformity!' The further words, 'In unity we believe in the Father, the Son, and Holy Ghost', I passed by, because I could not understand them.

14

It was then so necessary for me to believe in order to live that I unconsciously concealed from myself the contradictions and obscurities of theology. But this reading of meanings into the rites had its limits. If the chief words in the prayer for the Emperor became more and more clear to me, if I found some explanation for the words 'and remembering our Sovereign Most-Holy Mother of God and all the Saints, ourselves and one another, we give our whole life to Christ our God', if I explained to myself the frequent repetition of prayers for the Tsar and his relations by the fact that they are more exposed to temptations than other people and therefore are more in need of being prayed for – the prayers about subduing our enemies and evil under our feet (even if one tried to say that *sin* was the enemy prayed against), these and other prayers, such as the 'cherubic song' and the whole sacrament of the oblation, or 'the chosen warriors', etc. – quite two-thirds of all the services – either remained completely incomprehensible or, when I forced an explanation into them, made me feel that I was lying, thereby quite destroying my relation to God and depriving me of all possibility of belief.

I felt the same about the celebration of the chief holidays. To remember the Sabbath, that is to devote one day to God, was something I could understand. But the chief holiday was in commemoration of the Resurrection, the reality of which I could not picture to myself or understand. And that name of 'Resurrection' was also given to the weekly holiday. And on those days the Sacrament of the Eucharist was administered, which was quite unintelligible to me. The rest of the twelve great holidays, except Christmas, commemorated miracles – the things I tried not to think about in order not to deny: the Ascension, Pentecost, Epiphany, the Feast of the Intercession of the Holy Virgin, etc. At the celebration of these holidays, feeling that importance was being attributed to the very things that to me presented a negative importance, I either devised tranquillising explanations or shut my eyes in order not to see what tempted me.

Most of all this happened to me when taking part in the most usual Sacraments, which are considered the most important: baptism and communion. There I encountered not incomprehensible but fully comprehensible doings: doings which seemed to me to lead into temptation, and I was in a dilemma – whether to lie or to reject them.

Never shall I forget the painful feeling I experienced the day I received the Eucharist for the first time after many years. The service, confession, and prayers were quite intelligible and produced in me a glad consciousness that the meaning of life was being revealed to me. The Communion itself I explained as an act performed in remembrance of Christ, and indicating a purification from sin and the full acceptance of Christ's teaching. If that explanation was artificial I did not notice its artificiality: so happy was I at humbling and abasing myself before the priest – a simple, timid country clergyman – turning all the dirt out of my soul and confessing my vices, so glad was I to merge in thought with the humility of the fathers who wrote the prayers of the office, so glad was I of union with all who have believed and now believe, that I did not notice the artificiality of my explanation. But when I approached the altar gates, and the priest made me say that I believed that what I was about to swallow was truly flesh and blood, I felt a pain in my heart: it was not merely a false note, it was a cruel demand made by someone or other who evidently had never known what faith is.

I now permit myself to say that it was a cruel demand, but I did not then think so: only it was indescribably painful to me. I was no longer in the position in which I had been in youth when I thought all in life was clear; I had indeed come to faith because, apart from faith, I had found nothing, certainly nothing, except destruction; therefore to throw away that faith was impossible and I submitted. And I found in my soul a feeling which helped me to endure it. This was the feeling of self-abasement and humility. I humbled myself, swallowed that flesh and blood without any blasphemous feelings and with a wish to believe. But the blow had been struck and, knowing what awaited me, I could not go a second time.

I continued to fulfil the rites of the Church and still believed that the doctrine I was following contained the truth, when something happened to me which I now understand but which then seemed strange.

I was listening to the conversation of an illiterate peasant, a pilgrim, about God, faith, life, and salvation, when a knowledge of faith revealed itself to me. I drew near to the people, listening to their opinions on life and faith, and I understood the truth more and more. So also was it when I read the Lives of Holy Men, which became my favourite books. Putting aside the miracles and regarding them as fables illustrating thoughts, this reading revealed to me life's meaning. There were the lives of Makarius the Great,* the story of Buddha, there were the words of St John Chrysostom,* and there were the stories of the traveller in the well, the monk who found some gold, and of Peter the publican. There were stories of the martyrs, all announcing that death does not exclude life, and there were the stories of ignorant, stupid men, who knew nothing of the teaching of the Church but who yet were saved.

But as soon as I met learned believers or took up their books, doubt of myself, dissatisfaction, and exasperated disputation were roused within me, and I felt that the more I entered into the meaning of these men's speech, the more I went astray from truth and approached an abyss.

15

How often I envied the peasants their illiteracy and lack of learning! Those statements in the creeds which to me were evident absurdities, for them contained nothing false; they could accept them and could believe in the truth – the truth I believed in. Only to me, unhappy man, was it clear that with truth falsehood was interwoven by finest threads, and that I could not accept it in that form.

So I lived for about three years. At first, when I was only slightly associated with truth as a catechumen and was only scenting out what seemed to me clearest, these encounters struck me less. When I did not understand anything, I said, 'It is my fault, I am sinful'; but the more I became imbued with the truths I was learning, the more they became the basis of my life, the more oppressive and the more painful became these encounters and the sharper became the line between what I do not understand because I am not able to understand it, and what cannot be understood except by lying to oneself.

In spite of my doubts and sufferings I still clung to the Orthodox Church. But questions of life arose which had to be decided; and the decision of these questions by the Church – contrary to the very bases of the belief by which I lived – obliged me at last to renounce communion with Orthodoxy as impossible. These questions were: first the relation of the Orthodox Eastern Church to other Churches – to the Catholics and to the so-called sectarians. At that time, in consequence of my interest in religion, I came into touch with believers of various faiths: Catholics, Protestants, Old-Believers,* Molokans,* and others. And I met among them many men of lofty morals who were truly religious. I wished to be a brother to them. And what happened? That teaching which promised to unite all in one faith and love – that very teaching, in the person of its best representatives, told me that these men were all living a lie; that what gave them their power of life was a temptation of the devil; and that we alone possess the only possible truth. And I saw that all who do not profess an identical faith with themselves are considered by the Orthodox to be heretics, just as the Catholics and others consider the Orthodox to be heretics. And I saw that the Orthodox (though they try to hide this) regard with hostility all who do not express their faith by the same external symbols and words as themselves; and this is naturally so: first, because the assertion that you are in falsehood and I am in truth is the most cruel thing one man can say to another; and secondly, because a man loving his children and brothers cannot help being hostile to those who wish to pervert his children and brothers to a false belief. And that hostility is increased in proportion to one's greater knowledge of theology. And to me, who considered that truth lay in union by love, it became self-evident that theology was itself destroying what it ought to produce.

This offence is so obvious to us educated people who have lived in countries where various religions are professed and have seen the contempt, self-assurance, and invincible contradiction with which Catholics behave to the Orthodox Greeks and to the Protestants, and the Orthodox to Catholics and Protestants, and the Protestants to the two others, and the similar attitude of Old-Believers, Pashkovites (Russian Evangelicals),* Shakers,* and all religions – that the very obviousness of the temptation at first perplexes us. One says to oneself: it is impossible that it is so simple and that people do not see that if two assertions are mutually contradictory, then neither of them has the sole truth which faith should possess. There is something else here, there must be some explanation. I thought there was, and sought that explanation and read all I could on the subject, and consulted all whom I could. And no one gave me any explanation, except the one which causes the Sumsky Hussars to consider the Sumsky Hussars the best regiment in the world, and the Yellow Uhlans to consider that the best regiment in the world is the Yellow Uhlans. The ecclesiastics of all the different creeds, through their best representatives, told me nothing but that they believed themselves to have the truth and the others to be in error, and that all they could do was to pray for them. I went to archimandrites, bishops, elders, monks of the strictest orders, and asked them; but none of them made any attempt to explain the matter to me except one man, who explained it all and explained it so that I never asked any one any more about it. I said that for every unbeliever turning to belief (and all our young generation are in a position to do so) the question that presents itself first is, why is truth not in Lutheranism* nor in Catholicism, but in Orthodoxy? Educated in the high school he cannot help knowing – what the peasants do not know – that the Protestants and Catholics equally affirm that their faith is the only true one. Historical evidence, twisted by each religion in its own favour, is insufficient. Is it not possible, said I, to understand the teaching in a loftier way, so that from its height the differences should disappear, as they do for one who believes truly? Can we not go further along a path like the one we are following with the Old-Believers? They emphasize the fact that they have a differently shaped cross and different alleluias and a different procession round the altar. We reply: You believe in the Nicene Creed,* in the seven sacraments, and so do we. Let us hold to that, and in other matters do as you please. We have united with them by placing the essentials of faith above the unessentials. Now with the Catholics can we not say: You believe in so and so and in so and so, which are the chief things, and as for the Filioque clause and the Pope – do as you please. Can we not say the same to the Protestants, uniting with them in what is most important?

My interlocutor agreed with my thoughts, but told me that such concessions would bring reproach on the spiritual authorities for deserting the faith of our forefathers, and this would produce a schism; and the vocation of the spiritual authorities is to safeguard in all its purity the Greco-Russian Orthodox faith inherited from our forefathers.

And I understood it all. I am seeking a faith, the power of life; and they are seeking the best way to fulfil in the eyes of men certain human obligations. And fulfilling these human affairs they fulfil them in a human way. However much they may talk of their pity for their erring brethren, and of addressing prayers for them to the throne of the Almighty – to carry out human purposes violence is necessary, and it has always been applied and is and will be applied. If of two religions each considers itself true and the other false, then men desiring to attract others to the truth will preach their own doctrine. And if a false teaching is preached to the inexperienced sons of their Church – which has the truth – then that Church cannot but burn the books and remove the man who is misleading its sons. What is to be done with a sectarian – burning, in the opinion of the Orthodox, with the fire of false doctrine – who in the most important affair of life, in faith, misleads the sons of the Church? What can be done with him except to cut off his head or to incarcerate him? Under the Tsar Alexis Mikhaylovich* people were burned at the stake, that is to say, the severest method of punishment of the time was applied, and in our day also the severest method of punishment is applied – detention in solitary confinement.

And I turned my attention to what is done in the name of religion and was horrified, and I almost entirely abjured Orthodoxy.

The second relation of the Church to a question of life was with regard to war and executions.

At that time Russia was at war. And Russians, in the name of Christian love, began to kill their fellow men. It was impossible not to think about this, and not to see that killing is an evil repugnant to the first principles of any faith. Yet prayers were said in the churches for the success of our arms, and the teachers of the Faith acknowledged killing to be an act resulting from the Faith. And besides the murders during the war, I saw, during the disturbances which followed the war, Church dignitaries and teachers and monks of the lesser and stricter orders who approved the killing of helpless, erring youths. And I took note of all that is done by men who profess Christianity, and I was horrified.

16

And I ceased to doubt, and became fully convinced that not all was true in the religion I had joined. Formerly I should have said that it was all false, but I could not say so now. The whole of the people possessed a knowledge of the truth, for otherwise they could not have lived. Moreover, that knowledge was accessible to me, for I had felt it and had lived by it. But I no longer doubted that there was also falsehood in it. And all that had previously repelled me now presented itself vividly before me. And though I saw that among the peasants there was a smaller admixture of the lies that repelled me than among the representatives of the Church, I still saw that in the people's belief also falsehood was mingled with the truth.

But where did the truth and where did the falsehood come from? Both the falsehood and the truth were contained in the so-called holy tradition and in the Scriptures. Both the falsehood and the truth had been handed down by what is called the Church.

And whether I liked or not, I was brought to the study and investigation of these writings and traditions – which till now I had been so afraid to investigate.

And I turned to the examination of that same theology which I had once rejected with such contempt as unnecessary. Formerly it seemed to me a series of unnecessary absurdities, when on all sides I was surrounded by manifestations of life which seemed to me clear and full of sense; now I should have been glad to throw away what would not enter a healthy head, but I had nowhere to turn to. On this teaching religious doctrine rests, or at least with it the only knowledge of the meaning of life that I have found is inseparably connected. However wild it may seem to my firm old mind, it was the only hope of salvation. It had to be carefully, attentively examined in order to understand it, and not even to understand it as I understand the propositions of science: I do not seek that, nor can I seek it, knowing the special character of religious knowledge. I shall not seek the explanation of everything. I know that the explanation of everything, like the commencement of everything, must be concealed in infinity. But I wish to understand in a way which will bring me to what is inevitably inexplicable. I wish to recognise anything that is inexplicable as being so not because the demands of my reason are wrong (they are right, and apart from them I can understand nothing), but because I recognise the limits of my intellect. I wish to understand in such a way that everything that is inexplicable shall present itself to me as being necessarily inexplicable, and not as being something I am under an arbitrary obligation to believe.

That there is truth in the teaching is to me indubitable, but it is also certain that there is falsehood in it, and I must find what is true and what is false, and must disentangle the one from the other. I am setting to work upon this task. What of falsehood I have found in the teaching and what I have found of truth, and to what conclusions I came, will form the following parts of this work, which if it be worth it and if anyone wants it, will probably some day be printed somewhere.

1879.

The foregoing was written by me some three years ago, and will be printed.

Now, a few days ago, when revising it and returning to the line of thought and to the feelings I had when I was living through it all, I had a dream. This dream expressed in condensed form all that I had experienced and described, and I think therefore that, for those who have understood me, a description of this dream will refresh and elucidate and unify what has been set forth at such length in the foregoing pages. The dream was this:

I saw that I was lying on a bed. I was neither comfortable nor uncomfortable: I was lying on my back. But I began to consider how, and on what, I was lying – a question which had not till then occurred to me. And observing my bed, I saw I was lying on plaited string supports attached to its sides: my feet were resting on one such support, my calves on another, and my legs felt uncomfortable. I seemed to know that those supports were movable, and with a movement of my foot I pushed away the furthest of them at my feet – it seemed to me that it would be more comfortable so. But I pushed it away too far and wished to reach it again with my foot, and that movement caused the next support under my calves to slip away also, so that my legs hung in the air. I made a movement with my whole body to adjust myself, fully convinced that I could do so at once; but the movement caused the other supports under me to slip and to become entangled, and I saw that matters were going quite wrong: the whole of the lower part of my body slipped and hung down, though my feet did not reach the ground. I was holding on only by the upper part of my back, and not only did it become uncomfortable but I was even frightened. And then only did I ask myself about something that had not before occurred to me. I asked myself: Where am I and what am I lying on? and I began to look around, and first of all to look down in the direction in which my body was hanging and whither I felt I must soon fall. I looked down and did not believe my eyes. I was not only at a height comparable to the height of the highest towers or mountains, but at a height such as I could never have imagined.

I could not even make out whether I saw anything there below, in that bottomless abyss over which I was hanging and whither I was being drawn. My heart contracted, and I experienced horror. To look thither was terrible. If I looked thither I felt that I should at once slip from the last support and perish. And I did not look. But not to look was still worse, for I thought of what would happen to me directly I fell from the last support. And I felt that from fear I was losing my last supports, and that my back was slowly slipping lower and lower. Another moment and I should drop off. And then it occurred to me that this cannot be real. It is a dream. Wake up! I try to arouse myself but cannot do so. What am I to do? What am I to do? I ask myself, and look upwards. Above, there is also an infinite space. I look into the immensity of sky and try to forget about the immensity below, and I really do forget it. The immensity below repels and frightens me; the immensity above attracts and strengthens me. I am still supported above the abyss by the last supports that have not yet slipped from under me; I know that I am hanging, but I look only upwards and my fear passes. As happens in dreams, a voice says: 'Notice this,

this is it!' And I look more and more into the infinite above me and feel that I am becoming calm. I remember all that has happened, and remember how it all happened; how I moved my legs, how I hung down, how frightened I was, and how I was saved from fear by looking upwards. And I ask myself: Well, and now am I not hanging just the same? And I do not so much look round as experience with my whole body the point of support on which I am held. I see that I no longer hang as if about to fall, but am firmly held. I ask myself how I am held: I feel about, look round, and see that under me, under the middle of my body, there is one support, and that when I look upwards I lie on it in the position of securest balance, and that it alone gave me support before. And then, as happens in dreams, I imagined the mechanism by means of which I was held; a very natural, intelligible, and sure means, though to one awake that mechanism has no sense. I was even surprised in my dream that I had not understood it sooner. It appeared that at my head there was a pillar, and the security of that slender pillar was undoubted though there was nothing to support it. From the pillar a loop hung very ingeniously and yet simply, and if one lay with the middle of one's body in that loop and looked up, there could be no question of falling. This was all clear to me, and I was glad and tranquil. And it seemed as if someone said to me: 'See that you remember.'

And I awoke.

1882.

NOTES

Notes from Underground

p.3 Imitation and parody are frequently encountered in Dostoyevsky. Many echoes of Gogol and Chernyshevsky have been detected in this work, but its opening page seems to parody the English historian Henry Thomas Buckle (1821–62), whose *History of Civilisation in England* (1857–61) is certainly one of Dostoyevsky's targets. Buckle is a great user of footnotes, and this one may be a parodic reminder of his pernickety academic habit. He also makes a number of references to the liver, which may have been in Dostoyevsky's mind when opening this work; the most interesting disquisition on this subject appears at the end of vol. I, chap. 3 – in a protracted footnote ('The gland most universal among animals . . . is the liver . . .').

p.6 'The great and the beautiful' is a concept deriving from the philosopher I. Kant (1724–1804), much discussed in Russia during the 1830s and 1840s along with other aspects of German aesthetic theory and idealistic philosophy.

p.11 descended from an ape: Charles Darwin's theory of evolution through natural selection is clearly under attack here; his *Origin of Species* had appeared as recently as 1859.

p.15 to mistake approximate and secondary causes for primary: The concept of primary causes is dear to Buckle's heart (see the third chapter of his book), and alien to Dostoyevsky's. The several references to this idea are clearly directed against the Englishman.

p.17 'Chateau Lafitte' (properly Laffitte): A high-quality French red wine.

p.20 Napoleon – the great Napoleon and the modern one: The writer has in mind the numerous bloody campaigns of Napoleon I (Bonaparte) (1769–1821) and Napoleon III (1808–73), who became dictator by a violent coup d'état in 1851.

p.20 North America: This concerns the brutal Civil War which had begun in 1861 and would not be resolved until 1865, one year later. The Battle of Gettysburg had taken place in 1863, the previous year.

p.20 Schleswig-Holstein: The neck of land to the south of Denmark separating that country from what is now Germany. Danish claims to sovereignty over this region led to war with Austria and Prussia, which broke out in late 1863.

p.21 Attila: King of the Huns (died 453), notorious for his invasion of Europe with much vandalism and cruelty.

p.21 Stenka Razin (properly Stepan Razin): A Don Cossack leader of popular uprisings in southern Russia during the period 1667–71, and famous in folk-song for drowning his bride following taunts from his men that he was going soft; he was betrayed and executed in 1671.

p.21 Cleopatra: The seventh Egyptian queen of that name (69–30 BC), celebrated for her beauty and charm, but also capricious and cruel.

p.21 nature's laws, and ... tables of logarithms: These are further taunts levelled against Buckle, who believed that fundamental laws would one day be discovered to explain everything in nature and human history. For this purpose arithmetic would be used to compute and collate all facts and actions. Laws of nature are considered in the first few pages of Buckle's treatise; the first arithmetical references come along only about ten pages later.

p.21 calendar: The idea of constructing a great calendar controlling all human affairs also derives from Buckle, but is seen at its most interesting as the Table of Hourly Commandments established for this purpose in the One State depicted in Yevgeniy Zamyatin's science-fiction novel *We* (1924), itself an important precursor of Huxley's *Brave New World* (1932), Orwell's *1984* (1949), Bradbury's *Fahrenheit 451* (1953) and Margaret Atwood's *The Handmaid's Tale* (1987). Dostoyevsky's influence on this fascinating twentieth-century school of literature (deriving both from this work and from the 'Legend of the Grand Inquisitor' in *The Brothers Karamazov*) is of the profoundest importance.

p.22 the Crystal Palace: The huge, cathedral-like building constructed of iron and glass to house artefacts from all over the world for London's Great Exhibition of 1851. It was intended as a celebration both of British inventiveness and of technology in general. Dostoyevsky saw it as the great symbol of mid-century materialism. It was repellent in every way, but most of all because it was considered sacrosanct, and virtually worshipped, by so many people. The reference may also be considered a jibe at the expense of Chernyshevsky since Vera, the heroine of his novel *What is to be Done?*, in her 'Fourth Dream', sets up a vision of a future socialist society housed in a great palace of iron and crystal. It is not without significance that several of the future worlds envisaged by science fiction writers are located under great glass domes (e.g., Star City in V. Bryusov's *The Republic of the Southern Cross* and the One State in Zamyatin's *We*).

p.26 Colossus of Rhodes: One of the Seven Wonders of the World, this gigantic statue of Helios (the Greek sun god) was built on the island of Rhodes in the third century BC.

p.34 Heine: Heinrich Heine, born Chaim Harry Heine (1797–1856), was a German poet and satirical journalist of Jewish origin.

p.35 Rousseau: Jean-Jacques Rousseau (1712–78) was the French philosopher and writer whose posthumously published *Confessions* were written towards the end of his life as an exercise in self-analysis and self-justification.

p.37 Nekrasov: Nikolay Nekrasov (1821–78): was a leading advocate of civic poetry, believing that literature should be used in the service of society as a scourge of injustice. This extract from an early poem, 'Kogda iz mraka zabluzhden'ya . . .' (1845), is a very good choice. It is appropriate in itself, since it is addressed with sympathy to a fallen woman and therefore anticipates what is to come in Part II. It was also a particular favourite of Chernyshevsky's and therefore a suitable target for attack by Dostoyevsky. Finally, it is awful poetry, technically insipid and embarrassingly sentimental. The author relishes the idea of giving prominence to such a feeble effort and enjoys a nice joke in quoting less than half the poem before ending with dots and a triple 'etc.', as if to say (with a yawn) that there is much more drivel where this came from but he can't be bothered to go on with it.

p.40 King of Spain: A reference to Poprishchin in Gogol's story *Notes of a Madman* (1835), who imagined himself to be the King of Spain.

p.43 Lieutenant Pirogov: A character in Gogol's story *Nevsky Prospect* (1835), who tried to complain to the authorities after being beaten.

p.44 grivennik: A low-value coin worth ten kopecks.

p.44 *Notes of the Fatherland:* An important journal which, in the 1840s, became a rallying point for the liberal-minded Westernising tendency. After a quiet decade in the 1850s, following government intervention, by the time of this reference it was regaining some of its old fire, and beginning to discuss social issues once again.

p.45 Nevsky Prospect: The main thoroughfare of St Petersburg, often a place for strolling, arranging meetings or simply showing oneself to society.

p.50 Manfredian style: The hero of Byron's *Manfred* (1815) was still remembered by the Russians for his aloofness, pride and disregard for danger.

p.50 Austerlitz: In December 1805 Napoleon Bonaparte defeated the armies of Russia and Austria in a famous battle at Austerlitz in Moravia.

p.52ff The old school 'friends' are given rather funny names, perhaps after Gogol, following a common eighteenth-century tradition. Simonov's is fairly neutral, since he is reasonably agreeable; perhaps it carries some slight biblical overtones. Trudolyubov (Mr Industrious) is aptly named because of his narrow-mindedness. Ferfichkin (Mr Fopkin) is made to sound ridiculous; ugly and hateful, this 'friend' was a bitter enemy at school. Zverkov (Mr Beast) is the worst of the lot, a man whose attitude and behaviour are truly bestial. We can hardly imagine that Dostoyevsky is trying to be funny at this point; the Underground Man must have renamed his old acquaintances, each according to the degree of dislike entertained for them.

p.59 uniform: This is not military; civil servants went to work in uniform.

p.73 Silvio: The dashing, sardonic hero of *The Shot*, one of Alexander Pushkin's *Tales of Belkin* (1830).

p.73 Masquerade: A melodramatic play by Mikhail Lermontov (1835), closely imitative of Shakespeare's *Othello*.

p.77 Haymarket: Not the most salubrious area of St Petersburg. The proximity of the Haymarket is cited on the second page of *Crime and Punishment* as one of the reasons why the area in which Raskolnikov lives is so run-down and filthy.

p.97 George-Sandian subtleties: George Sand was the pen name of Lucile-Aurore Dupin (1804–76), a French writer as famous for her love-affairs (especially with Musset and Chopin) as for her writing, though this was also sensational, dealing with such controversial issues as the unfair treatment of women and free love.

p.97 Into my house . . . : The lines quoted are those which conclude the Nekrasov poem at the head of this section (see note to p.37 above).

p.98 Alexander of Macedon: Better known as Alexander the Great, this conqueror of all the civilised world lived only to the age of 33 (356–323 BC). He is remembered not only for his military prowess, but also for nobility of manner, personal courage and generosity.

A Confession

p.117 Voltaire: Pen-name of François Marie Arouet (1694–1778), French philosopher, satirist and creative writer famous for his biting wit and his antipathy towards organised religion.

p.125 kumys: A healthy drink made from fermented mare's milk.

p.126 desyatínas: A *desyatína* was land-measure roughly equal to 2 3/4 acres.

p.137 Schopenhauer: German philosopher characterised by extreme pessimism. He believed that human life consists only of suffering and that the only remedy would be for humanity to achieve extinction by managing to overcome the appalling will-to-live which is its birthright. Schopenhauer himself lived to the age of seventy-two (1788–1860).

p.138 Socrates: Greek philosopher known to posterity not through any surviving writings, but via those of Plato, Aristotle and Xenophon. A man of great wisdom, he had a special interest in ethical conduct, believing in particular that wickedness arose from ignorance.

p.138 Solomon: The wisest of all the Kings of Israel as recorded in the Old Testament, especially the Book of Kings.

p.138 Buddha: This name, meaning 'enlightened', was assumed by the Indian Siddhartha Gautama, at the age of thirty-six, on the attainment of 'perfect truth'. The founder of the religious system known as Buddhism, he died (reputedly) in 544 BC.

p.149 Descartes: The French mathematician and philosopher René Descartes (1596–1650) is considered the founder of the modern scientific method. Applying this to metaphysical speculation, he formulated what he took to be the only unchallengeable philosophical certainty: 'I think, therefore I am' ('Cogito, ergo sum').

p.149 Brahmins: Members of the priestly meditative order of Hinduism.

p.153 Buddhism: A religious system created by the Buddha in India in the sixth century BC. According to its four 'Noble Truths' the pain of human existence, created by the sin of birth, is to be ended only by faith, perfect behaviour and right meditation leading to a state of oblivion known as 'Nirvana'.

p.153 Mohammedanism: Another name for Islam, the religious system founded by the prophet Mohammed (also Mahomet or Muhammad) (570–632 AD), whose adherents are known as Muslims (Moslems, Mussulmans). Islam (meaning 'submission to the will of God') imposes strict rules of behaviour, including daily prayer, the observance of Ramadan (a month of fasting) and the determination to make a pilgrimage to Mecca.

p.159 Kant: The German philosopher Immanuel Kant (1724–1804) attempted to define the nature, and the limitations, of human reason. His rejection of outright empiricism and atheism appealed to Tolstoy, who is particularly interested here in Kant's assertion that morality and religion are serious phenomena existing outside the province of knowledge and calculation.

p.167 Makarius the Great [1482–1563]: Metropolitan of Moscow from 1542, who placed Orthodox Church affairs on a stronger footing by repressing locally based heretical movements and by strengthening links with the rulers of Russia, especially Ivan IV. He founded the nation's first printing press.

p.167 4 St John Chrysostom [345-407 AD]: Patriarch of Constantinople from 398, Chrysostom preached asceticism, charity and obedience to the Scriptures. He also established the basis of the liturgy adopted by the Orthodox Church.

p.168 Old-Believers: Dissenters within the Russian Orthodox Church (*staroobryadtsy*, later known as *raskolniki* (schismatics)) who rejected the seventeenth-century liturgical reforms of Patriarch Nikon. Their greatest champion was the priest Avvakum, whose sufferings on their behalf are described vividly in his autobiography.

p.168 Molokans: A religious sect originating in the eighteenth century, greatly opposed to Orthodox Church hierarchy, sacraments and ritual. Much persecuted by Tsarist governments, they withdrew into remote regions in order to pursue an agrarian way of life.

p.169 Pashkovites: A religious sect similar in its beliefs to the Molokans (see preceding note), named (in 1784) after its founder, Colonel V. A. Pashkov.

p.169 Shakers: A celibate religious sect, formed originally in England in the eighteenth century but soon transferred to the USA. The name was first created in order to ridicule the contortions performed by adherents during religious dancing.

p.169 Lutheranism: The movement formed by supporters of Martin Luther (1483-1546), the German religious reformer whose 'Ninety-five Theses', nailed to the church door at the castle of Wittenberg on 31 October, 1517, marked the beginning of the Reformation. Luther believed that church ritual was a hypocritical distraction from the true business of religion, which was personal faith.

p.170 Nicene Creed: A confession of faith published after the first ecumenical council of the Christian Church convoked by Constantine the Great at Nicaea in 325 AD in order to discuss, and reject, the views of Arius concerning the non-divine nature of Jesus Christ. With only minor changes the Creed survives today in the liturgy of the Established Church and the general doctrine accepted by most Protestants.

p.170 Alexis [Aleksey] Mikhaylovich [1629-76]: Tsar of Russia from the age of sixteen (in 1645), Aleksey ruled during a period of substantial progress for his country. Russian law was brought into proper codification (*ulozhenie*), much neighbouring territory was absorbed and the troublesome Cossack rebellion led by Stepan Razin was put down. Atrocities certainly took place, but this was not a reign of exceptional barbarity. Tolstoy's reference to it seems rather arbitrary.

_____

Notes from Underground

D. S. Mirsky's succinct remarks, in *A History of Russian Literature* (New York, 1960), define *Notes from Underground* as a work of philosophy, a great mystical revelation and 'a strong poison'.

> *Memoirs from Underground*, the work that introduces us, chronologically, to the 'mature' Dostoyevsky, contains at once the essence of his essential self. It cannot be regarded as imaginative literature pure and simple. There is in it quite as much philosophy as literature. It would have to be connected with his journalistic writings were it not that it proceeded from a deeper and more significant spiritual level of his personality. The work occupies a central place in the creation of Dostoyevsky. Here his essential tragical intuition is expressed in the most unadulterated and ruthless form. It transcends art and literature, and its place is among the great mystical revelations of mankind. The faith in the supreme value of the human personality and its freedom, and in the irrational religious and tragic foundation of the spiritual universe, which is above reason, above the distinction of good and evil (the faith, ultimately, of all mystical religion), is expressed in a paradoxical, unexpected, and entirely spontaneous form. The central position of *Memoirs from Underground* in the work of Dostoyevsky was first discerned by Nietzsche and Rozanov. It stands in the center of the writings of Shestov, the greatest of Dostoyevsky's commentators. Viewed as literature, it is also the most original of Dostoyevsky's works, although also the most unpleasant and the most 'cruel.' It cannot be recommended to those who are not either sufficiently strong to overcome it or sufficiently innocent to remain unpoisoned. It is a strong poison, which is most safely left untouched.

In *Dostoevsky: His Life and Work* (Princeton, 1967), Konstantin Mochulsky relates *Notes from Underground* to Dostoyevsky's four great subsequent novels, and defines this work as 'the greatest attempt at a philosophy of tragedy'. He also regrets the censoring of a vital chapter and wonders why the author never reinstated the original version.

Notes from Underground is a 'strange' work. Everything in it is striking: the structure, style, the subject. The first part consists of the underground man's confession in which the most profound problems of philosophy are examined. As for strength and daring of thought, Dostoevsky yields neither to Nietzsche nor Kierkegaard. He is near to them in spirit, he is 'of their kin.' The second part is the tale Apropos of the Wet Snow. The underground man, having explained his credo, relates his memoirs. The tie between the philosophical considerations and the shameful 'anecdotes' from the hero's life seems utterly artificial. Only in the end is their organic unity disclosed. . . .

The underground man's confession is the philosophical preface to the cycle of the great novels. Before Dostoevsky's work is disclosed to us as a vast five-act tragedy (Crime and Punishment, The Idiot, The Devils, A Raw Youth, and The Brothers Karamazov), Notes from Underground introduces us to the philosophy of tragedy. In the bilious and 'unsightly' chatter of the paradoxalist the Russian philosopher's greatest insights are expressed. Through the sharpened edge of analysis the sickness of consciousness is uncovered, its inertia and dichotomy, its inner tragedy. The struggle against reason and necessity leads to impotent 'weeping and gnashing' – to the tragedy of Nietzsche and Kierkegaard. Investigation of the irrational blind will, being cast about in void self-formation, reveals the tragedy of personality and freedom. Finally, the critique of socialism concludes with an assertion of the tragedy of historical process, purposeless and bloody, and the tragedy of world evil, which cannot be cured by any socialistic 'earthly paradise.' In this sense Notes from Underground is the greatest attempt at a philosophy of tragedy in world literature. The malicious despair and intrepid cynicism of the underground man unmasks all the idols, all the 'sublimating frauds,' all the 'noble and beautiful,' all the comforting illusions and salutary fictions, everything by which man has enclosed himself from the 'dark abyss.' Man is on the brink of a precipice – here is the paysage of tragedy. The author leads us through terror and destruction, but does he bring us to mystical purification, to a catharsis? Is it possible that 'sitting with arms folded' and 'intentional pouring water through a sieve' are the final word in his skeptic philosophy? To consider the Notes as an expression of 'metaphysical despair' would mean not to observe what is most important in their design. The force of the underground man's revolt stems not from indifference and doubt, but from a passionate, exalted faith. He contends so vehemently with falsehood because a new truth has been opened for him. He still cannot find a *word* for it and is forced to speak in hints and circumlocutions. The underground man, 'this acutely conscious mouse' – is nonetheless better than the tedious *homme de la nature et de la vérité*; the underground is nonetheless better than the socialist anthill. . . .

The underground man is a *disenchanted idealist and a humanist put to shame*. He only alludes to his new faith. But these allusions are revealed to us in the light of one of Dostoevsky's letters to his brother regarding the publication of *Underground* in *Epoch*. 'I must also complain about my article,' he writes.

> The misprints are terrible, and it would have been better not to print the next to last chapter at all (the most important one, where the essential thought is expressed), than to print it as it is, i.e., with sentences torn out and full of self-contradictions. But what can be done now! Those swines of censors – where I mocked at everything and sometimes *blasphemed for form's sake* – that's let pass, but where from all this I deduced the *need of faith and Christ* – that is suppressed.

The 'next to last chapter,' the tenth – which, in the form abridged by the censor, runs only a page and a half – is deemed by the author 'the most important.' . . . The mockery and blasphemy are only 'for form's sake,' for the heightening of contrast, to lend as much reinforcement as possible to the negative argumentation. In answer to it there had to appear a religious affirmation: 'the need of faith and Christ.' . . .

The censor distorted the design, but, strange as it might be, the author never reestablished the original text in subsequent editions. Dostoevsky's 'philosophy of tragedy' has remained without its mystical consummation.

Richard Peace, discussing the spirit of rejection which directs *Notes from Underground*, relates it to contemporary Russian politics and literature. The following is from his examination of the major novels, *Dostoyevsky* (Cambridge, 1971).

The whole fabric of *Notes from Underground* is permeated by a spirit of rejection; not least, the author is rejecting his own early work. Thus there are strong indications that in the person of the underground man Dostoyevsky wished to portray a disillusioned idealist from his own generation – the generation of 'the forties'. In an introductory note he describes his hero as: 'A character of the recent past. He is one of the representatives of the generation which is still with us.' The 'Schillerism' of the forties, or in the words of the underground man himself: ' "All that is beautiful and lofty", as we used to call it at one time', is a recurrent motif in the work: it still has a claim on this soured idealist.

The rejection of the forties, its romantic idealism and its literary clichés, is particularly prominent in Part II. Here the underground man launches into an attack on romanticism, and makes constant ironic use of the phrase: 'all that is beautiful and lofty' as he picks out the Russian romantics for special condemnation. He accuses them of insincerity, of professing high ideals whilst having their sights firmly fixed on material things (there is even an apparent sneer at Turgenev for having gone off to Germany to preserve his romanticism intact).

The ironic title given to Part II: 'Apropos of Sleet' is intended to suggest the writings of the 'natural school' of the forties – those followers of Gogol with whom Dostoyevsky himself had been classified, and the first incident which the underground man here relates reads like a pastiche on Gogol's story *The Greatcoat*. Here, as in Gogol, a downtrodden civil servant (the underground man himself) endures privations so that he may have clothes which are better than his means allow (in particular a showy fur for his greatcoat). In both stories clothes are treated as a symbol of human dignity, but in Dostoyevsky's version the sentimentalised submissiveness attributed to Gogol's hero has been replaced by the malicious self-assertiveness of the underground man. Dostoyevsky's hero needs his clothes, not to satisfy the basic demands of everyday existence, but those of his own psychological perverseness: he needs them so that *on one occasion* he may confront as an equal some officer whom he chooses to think has insulted him. The underground man is the very inversion of Gogol's pathetic hero: Dostoyevsky's downtrodden civil servant is not merely a victim, he in turn is a tyrant; he is the underdog in rebellion against the literary cliché which up to now has sought to confine him. He refuses to be treated as an *object*, he too is a *subject* in his own right. After the underground man Dostoyevsky's male representatives of 'the humble and the downtrodden' can never be the same: Marmeladov, Lebedev, Lebyadkin, Snegirev are all his spiritual heirs.

The continuation of Part II (the underground man's encounter with his 'friends') jeers at the noble ideas on friendship current in the forties and culminates in an incident with a prostitute which is an open revision of the verses by Nekrasov which the underground man takes as his epigraph. 'When from the gloom of erring ways' was written in 1846, the year after Nekrasov's 'discovery' of Dostoyevsky himself. Its ideas are thus closely linked to Dostoyevsky's youth. The theme of the redemption of a fallen woman, typifies the 'beautiful and lofty' humanitarian ideals of the forties.

Nekrasov was an idealist, who as a successful literary *entrepre-*

neur certainly had his sights fixed on material things, and the ironic way in which Dostoyevsky introduces this poem (cf. the bathetic ending 'Etc., etc., etc.' matched again in chapter nine by the comment 'from the same poetry') prepares the reader for a polemical treatment of this 'beautiful and lofty' theme. But the underground man's perverse attempt to rescue Liza is not only a comment on the sentimental humanism of Nekrasov's poem, it may also be taken, in a certain sense, as a revision of the platonic sexual relationship between an older man and a younger girl portrayed by Dostoyevsky in his own *Poor Folk*. Dostoyevsky in renouncing the Schilleresque values of the forties is also renouncing his own youth.

The polemics of *Notes from Underground*, however, are being waged on two fronts: the greater part of the underground man's philosophising is directed against ideas current at the actual time of writing – the ideas of 'the sixties'. These two periods of the 1840s and the 1860s were high points in Russian cultural life. Between them stretched the barren waste of Tsar Nicholas's 'barrack-room régime' at its worst. The difference between the gentle, aesthetically orientated humanism of the older generation and the new stridently utilitarian and 'ethically' preoccupied attitude of the younger men is clearly expressed in Turgenev's novel *Fathers and Children*. Dostoyevsky, who had been whisked away at the height of the forties to return to the new social ferment of the sixties, was able to see the contrast clearer than anyone. The theme of the generations is one which we shall encounter more than once in his later writing.

In this extract, from *Dostoevsky: The Stir of Liberation*, 1860–1865 (London, 1987), Joseph Frank shows the influence of *Notes from Underground* on modern culture, and stresses its parodic and satirical purpose.

Few works in modern literature are more widely read than Dostoevsky's *Notes from Underground* or so often cited as a key text revelatory of the hidden depths of the sensibility of our time. The term 'underground man' has become part of the vocabulary of contemporary culture, and this character has now achieved – like Hamlet, Don Quixote, Don Juan, and Faust – the stature of one of the great archetypal literary creations. No book or essay dealing with the precarious situation of modern man would be complete without some allusion to Dostoevsky's explosive figure. Most important cultural developments of the present century – Nietzscheanism, Freudianism, Expressionism, Surrealism, Crisis Theology, Existentialism – have claimed the underground man as their own or have been linked with him by zealous interpreters; and when the underground man has not been hailed as a prophetic anticipation, he has been held up to exhibition as a luridly repulsive warning.

The underground man has thus entered into the very warp and woof of modern culture in a fashion testifying to the philosophical suggestiveness and hypnotic power of this first great creation of Dostoevsky's post-Siberian years. At the same time, however, this widespread notoriety has given rise to a good deal of misunderstanding. It has led critics and commentators to enlist the underground man in the service of one or another contemporary point of view, and then to proclaim their particular emphasis to be identical with Dostoevsky's own (though, even more recently, it has become fashionable to profess a total unconcern about the need to establish any such identification). Most readings, in any case, exhibit a tendency to overstress one or the other of the work's two main aspects: either the conceptual level is taken as dominant (the first part has even been printed separately in an anthology of philosophical texts), or the emphasis has been placed on the perverse psychology of the main character. In fact, however, the text cannot be properly understood without grasping the interaction between these two levels, which interpenetrate to motivate both the underground man's ideas and his behavior.

Notes from Underground attracted very little attention when first published (no critical notice was taken of it in any Russian journal), and only many years later was it brought into prominence. In 1883, N. K. Mikhailovsky wrote his all-too-influential article 'A Cruel Talent,' citing some of the more sadistic passages of *Notes from Underground* and arguing that the utterances and actions of the character illustrated Dostoevsky's own 'tendencies to torture.' Eight years later, writing from an opposed ideological perspective, V. V. Rozanov interpreted the work as essentially inspired by Dostoevsky's awareness of the irrational depths of the human soul, with all its conflicting impulses for evil as well as for good. No world order based on reason and rationality could possibly contain this seething chaos of the human psyche; only religion (Eastern Orthodoxy) could aid man to overcome his capricious and destructive propensities. Rozanov, to be sure, comes much closer than Mikhailovsky to grasping certain essential features of the text; but no notice at all is taken of the artistic strategy that Dostoevsky employs – a strategy, as we shall see, that makes the attack on 'reason' far more subtle than the sort of head-on confrontation Rozanov thinks it to be. . . .

Another highly influential view of *Notes from Underground* was the one proposed by Lev Shestov, who read it in the context of Russian Nietzscheanism. The underground man dominates and tyrannizes everyone with whom he comes into contact; and Shestov interprets this as Dostoevsky's personal repudiation of the sentimental and humanitarian ideals of his early work, which have now been replaced by a recognition of the terrible reality of human egoism. Egoism finally triumphs in *Notes from Underground*, thus expressing Dostoevsky's acceptance of a universe of cruelty, pain, and suffering that no ultimate moral perspective can rationalize or justify. For Shestov, the essence of the work is contained in the underground man's declaration: 'Let the world go smash as long as I get my tea every day' – a profession of sublime selfishness in which, according to Shestov, Dostoevsky proclaims his reluctant but courageous acceptance of a philosophy of amoralism 'beyond good and evil.' Shestov's analysis unquestionably points to an important aspect of the underground man's character; but he simply takes him to be Dostoevsky's mouthpiece, and fails to understand how the figure is used to realize a more complex artistic purpose.

It was evident from the day of publication that Dostoevsky's *Notes from Underground* was an attack, particularly in Part I, on Chernyshevsky's philosophy of 'rational egoism'; but interpreters at the turn of the century paid very little attention to this ancient quarrel, which was considered quite incidental and of no artistic importance. Up to the early 1920s, the usual view of *Notes from Underground* assumed that Dostoevsky had been stimulated by opposition to Chernyshevsky, but had used radical ideas only as a foil. Chernyshevsky had believed that man was innately good and amenable to reason, and that, once enlightened as to his true interests, he would be able, with the help of reason and science, to construct a perfect society. Dostoevsky may have also believed man to be capable of good, but he considered him equally full of evil, irrational, capricious, and destructive inclinations; and it was *this* disturbing truth that he brilliantly presented through the underground man as an answer to Chernyshevsky's naive optimism.

Although such a view may seem quite plausible at first reading, it can hardly be sustained after a little reflection. For it would require us to consider Dostoevsky as just about the worst polemicist in all of literary history. He was, after all, supposedly writing to dissuade readers from accepting Chernyshevsky's ideas. Could he really have imagined that anyone in his right mind would *prefer* the life of the underground man to the radiant happiness of Chernyshevsky's denizens of Utopia? Obviously not; and since Dostoevsky was anything but a fool, it may be assumed that the invention of the underground man was not inspired by any such self-defeating notion. In reality, as another line of interpretation soon began to make clear, his attack on Chernyshevsky and the radicals is far more intricate and cunning than had previously been suspected.

The first true glimpse into the artistic logic of *Notes from Underground* appears in an article by V. L. Komarovich, who in 1921 pointed out that Dostoevsky's novella was structurally dependent on *What Is To Be Done?* Whole sections of the work in the second part – the attempt of the underground man to bump into an officer on the Nevsky Prospect, for example, or the famous encounter with the prostitute Liza – are modeled on specific episodes in Chernyshevsky's book, and are obvious *parodies* that inverted the meaning of those episodes in their original context. . . .

The uncovering of such parodies in *Notes from Underground* opened the way to a new approach, and suggested that the relation to Chernyshevsky was far from being merely ancillary to what was, in substance, the portrayal of an aberrant personality. But while Komarovich pointed to the use of parody in the second part of the text, he continued to regard the imprecations of the underground man against 'reason' in the first part simply as a straightforward argument with Utilitarianism. The underground man, in other words, was still speaking directly for Dostoevsky and could be identified with the author's own position.

A further decisive advance was made a few years later by another Russian critic, A. Skaftymov, who focused on the problem of whether, and to what extent, the underground man could be considered Dostoevsky's spokesman in any straightforward fashion. Without raising the issue of parody, Skaftymov argued that the negative views of the underground man could in no way be taken to represent Dostoevsky's own position. As Shestov had also pointed out, such an identification would constitute a flagrant repudiation of all the moral ideals that Dostoevsky was continuing to uphold in his journalism. 'The underground man in *Notes*,' wrote Skaftymov, 'is not only the accuser but also one of the accused,' whose objurgations and insults are as much (if not more) directed against himself as against others, and whose eccentric and self-destructive existence by no means represents anything that Dostoevsky was approving without qualification. Skaftymov also perceptively remarked (but only in a footnote, and without developing the full import of his observation) that Dostoevsky's strategy is that of destroying his opponents 'from within, carrying their logical presuppositions and possibilities to their consistent conclusion and arriving at a destructively helpless blind alley.'

These words provide an essential insight into one of the main features of Dostoevsky's technique as an ideological novelist; but Skaftymov does not properly use his own aperçu for the analysis of *Notes from Underground*. Although fully aware that the novella is 'a polemical work,' he mentions Chernyshevsky only in another footnote and fails to see how this polemical intent enters into the very creation of the character of the underground man. Skaftymov's analysis of the text thus remains on the level of moral-psychological generalities, and while accurate enough as far as it goes, does not penetrate to the heart of Dostoevsky's conception. This can be reached, in my view, only by combining and extending Komarovich's remarks on the parodistic element in *Notes from Underground* with Skaftymov's perception of how the underground man dramatizes within himself the ultimate consequences of the position that Dostoevsky was opposing. In other words, the underground man is not only a moral-psychological type whose egoism Dostoevsky wishes to expose; he is also a social-ideological one, whose psychology must be seen as intimately interconnected with the ideas he accepts and by which he tries to live.

Dostoevsky, it seems to me, overtly pointed to this aspect of the character in the footnote appended to the title of the novella. 'Both the author of the *Notes* and the *Notes* themselves,' he writes, 'are of course fictitious. Nonetheless, such persons as the author of such memoirs not only may, but *must*, exist in our society, if we take into consideration the circumstances that led to the formation of our society. It was my intention to bring before our reading public, more conspicuously than is usually done, one of the characters of our most recent past. He is one of the representatives of a generation that is still with us' (italics added).

Dostoevsky here is obviously talking about the formation of Russian ('our') society, which, as he could expect all readers of *Epoch* to know – had he not explained this endlessly in his articles in *Time*, most recently and explicitly in *Winter Notes*? – had been formed by the successive waves of European influence that had washed over Russia since the time of Peter the Great. The underground man *must* exist as a type because he is the inevitable product of such a cultural formation; and his character does in fact embody and reflect two phases of this historical evolution. He is, in short, conceived as a parodistic persona, whose life exemplifies the tragic-comic impasses resulting from the effects of such influences on the Russian national psyche. His diatribes in the first part thus do not arise, as has commonly been thought, because of his rejection of reason; on the contrary, they result from his acceptance of *all* the implications of reason in its then-current Russian incarnation – and particularly, all those consequences that advocates of reason such as Chernyshevsky blithely chose to disregard. In the second part Dostoevsky extends the same technique to those more sentimental-humanitarian elements of Chernyshevsky's ideology that had revived some of the atmosphere of the 1840s.

Dostoevsky's footnote thus attempted to alert his audience to the satirical and parodistic nature of his conception; but it was too oblique to serve its purpose. Like many other examples of first-person satirical parody, *Notes from Underground* has usually been misunderstood and taken straight. Indeed, the intrinsic danger of such a form, used for such a purpose, is that it tends to wipe out any critical distance between the narrator and reader, and makes it difficult to *see through* the character to the target of the satire. A famous example of such a misunderstanding in English literature is Defoe's *The Shortest Way with Dissenters*, in which the dissenter Defoe, ironically speaking through the persona of a fanatical Tory, called for the physical extermination of all dissenters. But the irony was not understood, and Defoe, taken at his word, was sentenced to a term in the pillory as punishment. This danger can be avoided only if, as in *Gulliver's Travels*, the reader is disoriented from the very start by the strangeness of the situation, or if in other ways – linguistic exaggerations or manifestly grotesque behavior – he is made aware that the I-narrator is only a convention and not a genuine character. Although Dostoevsky makes some attempt to supplement his footnote in this direction, these efforts were not sufficient to balance the overwhelming psychological presence of the underground man and the force of his imprecations and anathemas against some of the most cherished dogmas of modern civilization. As a result, the parodistic function of his character has always been obscured by the immense vitality of its artistic embodiment, and it has, paradoxically, been Dostoevsky's very genius for the creation of character that has most interfered with the proper understanding of *Notes from Underground*.

It is not really difficult to comprehend why, in this instance, the passion that Dostoevsky poured into his character should have overshadowed the nature of the work as a satirical parody. Time and again we can hear Dostoevsky speaking about himself through his fictional guise, and he unquestionably endowed the underground man with some of his deepest and most intimate feelings. As the underground man belabors his own self-disgust and guilt, was not Dostoevsky also expressing his self-condemnation as a conscience-stricken spectator of his wife's death-agonies, and repenting of the egoism to which he confessed in his notebook? The self-critical references to the underground man's school years in the second part certainly draw on Dostoevsky's own unhappy sojourn long ago in the Academy of Engineers; and the frenzy of the character's revolt against a world of imprisonment by 'the laws of nature' imaginatively revived all the despair and torment of the prison years. Besides, what a release it must have been for Dostoevsky, after all his guarded temporizing and cautious qualifying, finally to fling his defiance into the teeth of the radicals and expose the disastrous implications of their 'advanced' ideas! No wonder he could not resist the temptation to impart more depth and vitality to his central figure than the literary form he had chosen really required!

These personal taproots of his inspiration, however, all flow into the service of an articulate and coherent satirical conception. *Notes from Underground* has been read as the psychological self-revelation of a pathological personality, or as a theological cry of despair over the evils of 'human nature,' or as a declaration of Dostoevsky's supposed adherence to Nietzsche's philosophy of 'amoralism' and the will to power, or as a defiant assertion of the revolt of the human personality against all attempts to limit its inexhaustible potentialities – and the list can easily be continued. All these readings, and many more, can plausibly be supported if certain features of the text are singled out and placed in the foreground while others are simply overlooked or forgotten. But if we are interested in understanding Dostoevsky's own point of view, so far as this can be reconstructed, then we must take it for what it was initially meant to be – a brilliantly Swiftian satire, remarkable for the finesse of its conception and the brio of its execution, which dramatizes the dilemmas of a representative Russian personality attempting to live by the two European codes whose unhappy effects Dostoevsky explores. And though the sections have a loose narrative link, the novella is above all a diptych depicting two episodes of a symbolic history of the Russian intelligentsia.

A Confession

D. S. Mirsky (*A History of Russian Literature*) extols the aesthetic quality of *A Confession*, its tight construction, oratorical energy, perfect style and simple language.

A Confession itself may without exaggeration be called in some ways his greatest artistic work. It is not a disinterested, self-contained 'representation of life' like *War and Peace* or *Anna Karenina*; it is 'utilitarian,' it is 'propaganda work,' and in this sense it is less 'pure art.' But it possesses 'æsthetic' qualities that are not present in the great novels. It is *constructed*, and constructed with supreme skill and precision. it has an oratorical movement difficult to expect from the author of *War and Peace*. It is more synthetic and universal, and does not rely for its action on little homely and familiar effects of realism, so abundant in the novels. Its analysis is simple, deep, courageous – and there is nothing in it of that 'psychological eavesdropping' (the phrase is Leontiev's) which repels many readers in his earlier works. *War and Peace* and *Anna Karenina* have been compared, somewhat farfetchedly, with the poems of Homer. *A Confession* might with more appropriateness be placed by the side of no less supreme 'world's books' – Ecclesiastes and the book of Job. So it is quite wrong to affirm that in any literary sense the change that overcame Tolstoy about 1880 was a fall. He remained forever, not only the supreme writer, but the supreme craftsman of Russian letters. Even the most dryly dogmatic of his treatises is a masterpiece of literary ability and of the best Russian. For all that, the fact remains that henceforward Tolstoy ceased to be a 'writer,' in the sense of a man who writes for the sake of producing good literary work, and became a preacher. And when he turned, as he did very soon, towards imaginative narrative, he wrote stories that, like everything else, were strictly subordinate to his dogmatic teaching and intended to illustrate and to popularize it.

The first of Tolstoy's works in which he preached his new teaching was *A Confession* (begun in 1880 and completed in 1882). *A Confession* is altogether on a higher level than the rest – it is one of the world's masterpieces. It is a work of art, and Tolstoy's biographer would give proof of too much simple-mindedness if he used it as biographical material in the strict sense of the word. But the work is more important to us than the facts that led up to it. The facts have been, and are no more. Their history in *A Confession* remains as a perfect work, a living entity. It is one of the greatest and most lasting expressions of the human soul in the presence of the eternal mysteries of life and death. To give the argument in one's own words would be presumption, to quote passages would be to destroy. For it is a wonderful whole, built with marvelous precision and effectiveness. Every detail, every turn of thought, every oratorical cadence, is in its right place to contribute to the one supreme effect. It is the greatest piece of oratory in Russian literature. But it is not conventional eloquence. Its rhythm is a logical, mathematical rhythm – a rhythm of ideas – and Tolstoy scorns all the devices of traditional rhetoric. It is sustained in the simplest of languages, in that wonderful language of Tolstoy, whose secret has not yet been caught, and which is naturally lost in a translation. A good translation (like Aylmer Maude's) will preserve the oratorical movement of the original, for this is based on the succession of ideas and large syntactical units, not on the sound and quantity of words. But the effect of Tolstoy's Russian cannot be reproduced in any of the literary languages of the West, for all of them are too far divorced from their spoken forms, and the spoken languages too full of slang. Russian alone has this felicity – that it can use everyday speech to produce effects of Biblical majesty. And Tolstoy's favorite device in *A Confession*, of illustrating his idea by a parable, is in complete keeping with the general tone of the work. Tolstoy's language was largely his own creation. He achieved in *A Confession*, for the language of abstract thought, what he had attempted in his pedagogical articles and achieved for narrative prose in his novels – the creation of a new literary language free from the bookish traditions of contemporary literature and based entirely on the language actually spoken. The language thus evolved is beyond doubt the best vehicle yet used in Russian for the expression of abstract thought. The extent of Tolstoy's innovation in the literary language is singularly great – it is almost a different language from that of his contemporaries. Many of the principal terms of his teaching are words that had not been used before Tolstoy in literary Russian, and were borrowed by him from the colloquial speech of his class. Such, for instance, is one of his most frequent words – *durno* – bad.

In *Tolstoy* (London, 1977), T. G. S. Cain describes the triumph of the life force over Tolstoy's obsession with death and attraction to suicide.

[Tolstoy] was too much of a rationalist to accept for good the vague theology he had given to Pierre and Levin: only when his belief had a firm ground of reason could he feel secure in it, and *A Confession* was the first and most important step in that direction.

Why he should have felt so strong a compulsion to move in that direction, why the need for an explanation in religious rather than materialist terms was so pressing, is largely accounted for by the obsession with death which we see running through all his work. As he grew older the question of *how* to live, the problem of happiness, gave way more and more to the question of *why*, the problem of death. The prospect of a complete annihilation as the inevitable end of all that he might achieve was an agonising one: that he was simply moving towards death seemed to him to rob all that he did of meaning and value, to make a cruel joke of his life, a life which he saw above all as a struggle towards meaning and truth. If there was no other end than death to his activities as artist, father, landowner, teacher, then it was better not to struggle. The vision of a terrible pointlessness is seen again and again in his diaries, letters, stories and novels, and in the pages of *A Confession*, and it is in the latter that it finds its most stark and concentrated expression, as he describes how the questions 'What is it for? What does it lead to?' drove him to the very edge of suicide. . . . The agony of annihilation was so terrible for Tolstoy partly because life had given him so much, not only in his birth and material success, but in his enormous vitality. He was so much more alive than most men that death was all the greater an enemy: what it took from him would be more than it took from others. His pride and egoism were aspects of this vitality: that he, Lev Nikolayevich Tolstoy, should cease to exist seemed absurd and terrible, all the more so because the search for meaning and significance, for the purpose of it all, had become his *raison d'être*. Thus it is that more and more in the years before *A Confession* his remorseless rationalism returned him to the question 'why?', worrying the problem like a tenacious dog, and again and again coming to the same, terrifying conclusion: that life had no meaning in the face of death, that even his boundless energies and appetites could not give it such a meaning, that it was simply a cruel joke, and that the only worthy way of escape was not to submit to the joke, but to stop living – to commit suicide. Tolstoy's respect in *A Confession* for those who, finding themselves in such a position, do have the courage to kill themselves casts an interesting light on Anna's suicide. For Anna's clear vision of life as she drives to the station, the book she reads 'filled with anxieties, deceptions, grief, and evil', is very close to that view of life as a cruel joke which Tolstoy holds to be the logical view of anyone who has no faith. Not only do we come to understand better the respect with which he viewed Anna's suicide, but it seems likely that he put into the utter nihilism of her newly enlightened vision something of his own most desperately bleak moments at this time.

Without underrating this despair – indeed, it is impossible to do so when we look at Anna, or at Levin's fears that he may kill himself – it seems doubtful if suicide was ever quite so close for Tolstoy as *A Confession* maintains. The 'irresistible power' which drew him away from life seems to have been matched by that instinctive belief in life which was, after all, the ultimate cause of his troubles. And in the end it is that force of life that wins in *A Confession*, though only at a great cost to itself. It drives him to construct a rational religion that will enable him to go on living, but in the process the old, generous vitality, the love that is not based on principle or theory, is itself forced into a rational straitjacket, from which it is only to emerge in flashes in the later work, and only finally to reassert itself in the posthumously published *Hadji Murat*.

In his volume on the author, also called simply *Tolstoy* (Harmondsworth, 1988), A. N. Wilson warns us not to be deceived by Tolstoy's rhetoric; *A Confession* should be seen as a work of self-deception, titanic arrogance and peculiar destructiveness.

A Confession, which has been described as 'the finest of all Tolstoy's non-fiction works' and 'one of the noblest and most courageous utterances of man', was probably begun in 1879. For some time, the juices had been gnawing at an emptied imagination, the stomach wall having to exercise its usual digestive function of turning experience into fiction. In the previous summer of 1878, he had toyed with the idea of writing a proper autobiography and jotted down some reminiscences of his childhood, but, like his attempt to expurgate his ancestral past in *The Decembrists*, it came to nothing.

Approaching *A Confession* 'blind', the reader will indeed be arrested by its overpowering emotional force, and might even mistake its apparently ratiocinative thrust, its burning intellectual sincerity, for a piece of argument. But for those who have followed Tolstoy's life and work in a chronological order, its ninety or so pages give off disconcerting impressions. It is not the book which its author intends us to read. Doubtless, while he was writing it, *A Confession* felt as noble and courageous as some modern readers have found it; and there is – unquestionably – a high nobility about it. But it is not, as Tolstoy so heart-rendingly believes, the record of a mind clearing, of a troubled soul coming at last to peace. Newman's *Apologia* in a different way gives off highly comparable danger signals. His insistence that joining the Roman Church was 'like coming into port after a stormy sea' (a strange way of describing the anguish he had felt ever since becoming a Catholic) is highly comparable to Tolstoy's claim at the end of *A Confession* that he has found the secret which will give his soul peace. Tolstoy's *A Confession* is outwardly the story of a thoughtless sensualist, who had put all thoughts of God, the meaning of life, soul or goodness aside. He had pursued first, as a young soldier, the sins of the flesh, and the cruel pleasures of war. Then, as a literary man, he had pursued fame and money, and had enjoyed the didactic role thrust upon the Russian writer, even though he had nothing to teach. Then he had got married and become wholly absorbed in his family. He had, however, been haunted by a terrible sense of the pointlessness of existence in upper-class society. He had known both the anguish of *ennui* so profound that he had often been tempted to commit suicide; and on the other hand, or at the same time, a terror of death which poisoned his whole life. He had turned this way and that for a solution to the questions Who am I? and What is the point of living? Philosophy (Kant and Schopenhauer) had been as impotent to help as had natural science. Finally, he had discovered that while the pampered intelligentsia and aristocracy were leading lives which were indeed pointless, and which led only to despair, there was a huge category of persons who had faith, who were able to live and who did, apparently, know life's secret. These were the peasants. He had thrown himself into adopting their Holy Orthodox faith, but he had been unable to resist thinking about it and going into it, and the more he went in, and the more he thought, the more obvious it became to him that the Orthodox Church was founded on a lie, that its insistence upon such esoteric or improbable doctrines as the Trinity, the Ascension, or the miracles of the saints, was as blasphemous as its refusal to take seriously the central moral teachings of Him whom they claimed to be the second person of the Trinity. But this liberation from the Church, this discovery that the monks and the archimandrites and the bishops and the theologians had got everything wrong, did not shake Tolstoy's faith in the honest Christianity of the peasants. Nor did it drive him back into a pure Voltairean negativism. On the contrary, it was when he realised that being Orthodox was incompatible with true Christianity that he felt a true peace, and he resolved to practise the five great commandments given by Christ in His Sermon on the Mount. Henceforth, like Levin at the end of *Anna Karenina*, he would live by this simple creed, and he would achieve salvation, that is, not some mystical or supernatural benefit bestowed upon him by the Church, but the inner certainty that he was leading a life as it was meant by God to be led.

Such, in essence, is *A Confession*. The violence of its similes, his life as a boat careering down a fast river as he tries to row against the stream, knowing that the bank is God, or the man about to fall into the dragon jaws of death, pausing to lick two drops of honey, is a taste of the Tolstoy who was now struggling to be born. They reflect the appalling conflicts which were going on inside him; and they suggest that he had undergone, or was undergoing, what in slightly outmoded modern jargon would be termed a mental 'breakdown'. Every bit of his life is seen as an aching torment. There are various moments when the unconscious egoism of a man who is lying back on the analyst's couch shows a sign of painful dislocation. For example, in section eleven, where it suddenly dawns on him that 'life is evil and an absurdity' (a generalisation applying to the whole of humanity) is not necessarily true because 'my particular life of senseless indulgence of desires was senseless and evil'. Or again, in a slightly different mood, when he describes his anger with the scientists for being unable to answer the question 'Why do *I* live?'

Tolstoy writes in such a frank and readable manner that his rhetoric can deceive us into thinking that such a proposition makes some sort of sense. But who are these scientists and why should 'they' have devoted their minds either to the rather nebulous question of whether life has a meaning (not their job) or to the more specialised question of why Lev Nikolayevich should exist?

Once one is alerted to the danger signals, *A Confession*, precisely because of its artless sincerity, is revealed as a transparent piece of self-deception: transparent, that is, to everyone except the author. It simply is not true, for example, that at earlier phases of life Tolstoy thought only of sensualism, or only of fame, or only of money. Throughout his life, he had been troubled by a conflict between an unyielding, intellectual rationalism and a passionately religious temperament. He had often thought of amending his life along the lines of some simplified form of Christianity, purged of its 'dogmas'. He had often flirted with the Orthodoxy of his boyhood, yearned to lead a simple life, and to imitate the peasants. He had always – except for brief crazes and intervals – preferred the country to the town. So the picture of his slow turning-away from the life of the urban intelligentsia towards rural piety is a totally false one. Nor does his picture of, for example, the St Petersburg intelligentsia bear any relation to what it had actually been like at the time. His claim that they were all burning to teach their readers great moral truths was as untrue of Turgenev as it was of Tolstoy's great friend, Fet, an unwavering devotee of art for art's sake.

Just as *Childhood* bore less relation to his actual childhood than it had done to the period when the book was being written, so these 'memories' of St Petersburg society when Tolstoy was a young man are actually direct responses to what was happening at the time he was writing his confession. He is referring not to Fet and Turgenev, but to Dostoyevsky's challenge, 'Men such as the author of *Anna Karenina* are teachers of society.'

The most extraordinary claim of all is that in the early years of his marriage he regarded authorship as being of no possible importance, and that he only wrote 'insignificant work' for the sake of monetary reward. Does this describe the fervent energy with which he wrote and wrote and recorrected Sofya's copies of *War and Peace*? Apparently, it is meant to. Even if there had been no financial reward, there could have been no greater possible satisfaction for a novelist than to have written *War and Peace* which is indeed one of the 'noblest utterances . . . of man'. Tolstoy's capacity to forget had blotted it all out. Moreover, in describing his state of mind upon finishing *Anna Karenina* he reveals his extraordinary, and surely psychotic, ability to find dissatisfaction precisely in the areas which should have given the greatest and the noblest forms of pleasure. ' "Very well," he had said to himself; "you will be more famous than Gogol or Pushkin or Shakespeare or Molière, or than all the writers in the world – and what of it?" And I could find no reply at all.' The reason he could find no reply is that it was not a rational question. It is almost unimaginable that Pushkin, Molière or Shakespeare would have asked themselves such a question. Tolstoy thinks that by asking it he reveals his indifference to literature. In fact, it reveals quite the reverse. It shows that he had seen it all as a competition: a competition which, moreover, he had won. Having decided implicitly that he was in fact the greatest literary genius in the world, it was not like him to rest on his laurels. Having got some laurels, he proceeded to tear them leaf from leaf. There is nobility, there is grandeur here.

But there is also titanic arrogance, and a peculiar destructiveness which is all Tolstoy's own. Tolstoy's question suggests that so long as there were these geniuses, his own was to be rebuked; and this attitude was to harden over the coming years as he developed his theories of art. But, once more, there is a genius whose name very conspicuously does not appear in the list, and we almost expect to hear it later on in *A Confession* when he tells us that having failed to find anyone among his own class who understood the meaning of life, his eyes were opened. 'And of such people, understanding the meaning of life and able to live and to die, I saw not two or three or tens, but hundreds, thousands and millions. And they all – endlessly different in their manners, minds, education, and position as they were – all alike, in complete contrast to my ignorance, knew the meaning of life and death, laboured quietly, endured deprivations and sufferings, and lived and died, seeing therein not vanity but good.'

What is this if it is not the voice of the Devil who speaks to Ivan Karamazov in his dream: 'I would surrender this super-celestial life, all ranks and honours, if only I could become incarnate in the soul of a seven-pood merchant's wife and put up candles to God.'

It may be that part of the unconscious, motivating force for the conversion of Tolstoy was a panic-stricken longing not to be Dostoyevsky. For having steered so firmly in the direction of a seven-pood merchant's wife, and having put up candles to God, Tolstoy became convinced, and devoted the next five years of his writing life to proving that, while the peasant worshipper had somehow or other got hold of the secret of life, his or her faith was actually based on lies and misconceptions. But one must emphasise that any part Dostoyevsky played in all this must have been marginal, and unconscious. The figure who was about to be passed through the digesting machine of Tolstoy's imagination was none other than Christ Himself, and the theological outpourings which now came from Tolstoy's pen reflect his famed genius for 'making it strange'.

Dostoyevsky and Tolstoy Compared

In this final extract, again from *A History of Russian Literature*, D. S. Mirsky provides an illuminating comparison of the two authors, in the course of which he mentions only two works by name: *Memoirs from Underground* (*sic*) and *A Confession*.

Both psychologically and historically Dostoyevsky is a very complex figure, and it is necessary to distinguish not only between the various periods of his life and the various currents of his mind, but between the different *levels* of his personality. The higher – or rather, deeper – level is present only in the imaginative work of his last seventeen years, beginning with *Memoirs from Underground*. The lower – or rather, more superficial – level is apparent in all his work, but more particularly in his journalistic writings and in the imaginative work of before 1864. The deeper, the essential, Dostoyevsky is one of the most significant and ominous figures in the whole history of the human mind, one of its boldest and most disastrous adventures in the sphere of ultimate spiritual quest. The superficial Dostoyevsky is a man of his time, comparable – and not always favorably comparable – to many other Russian novelists and publicists of the age of Alexander II, a mind that had many rivals and that cannot be placed in any way apart from, or above, Herzen, Grigoriev, or Leontiev. The other one, the essential Dostoyevsky, for the profundity, complexity, and significance of his spiritual experience, has only two possible rivals in the whole range of Russian literature – Rozanov and of course Tolstoy, who, however, seems to have been given to the world for the special purpose of being contrasted with Dostoyevsky.

The comparison between Tolstoy and Dostoyevsky has for many years been, with Russian and foreign critics, a favorite subject of discussion. Much has been said of the aristocratic nature of the former and the plebeian nature of the latter; of the one's Luciferian pride and the other's Christian humility; of the naturalism of the one and the spiritualism of the other. Apart from the difference of social position and education, a main difference between the two is that Tolstoy was a puritan, and Dostoyevsky a symbolist. That is to say that for Dostoyevsky all relative values were related to absolute values and received their significance, positive or negative, from the way they reflected the higher values. For Tolstoy the absolute and the relative are two disconnected worlds, and the relative is in itself evil. Hence Tolstoy's contempt for the meaningless diversity of human history, and Dostoyevsky's eminently historical mode of thinking, which relates to all the main line of higher Russian thought – to Chaadayev, the Slavophils, Herzen, Grigoriev, Leontiev, and Soloviev. Dostoyevsky is one of them: his thought is always historically related. Even in their most purely spiritual form, his problems are not concerned with an eternal, static, and immutable law, but with the drama that is being played out in human history by the supreme forces of the universe. Hence the great complexity, fluidity, and many-sidedness of his thought as compared to the rigidly geometrical and rectilinear thinking of Tolstoy. Tolstoy (in spite of his sensitiveness to the infinitesimals of life) was in his moral philosophy, both on the high level of *A Confession* and on the much lower level of his anti-alcoholic and vegetarian tracts, a Euclid of moral quantities. Dostoyevsky deals in the elusive calculus of fluid values. Hence also what Strakhov so happily called the 'purity' of Tolstoy and what may be called the obvious 'impurity' of Dostoyevsky. He was never dealing with stable entities, but with fluid processes; and not seldom the process was one of dissolution and putrefaction.

On a more social and historical plane it is also important to note that while Tolstoy was an aristocrat and (alone of his literary contemporaries) culturally had his roots in the old French and eighteenth-century civilization of the Russian gentry, Dostoyevsky was, to the core, a plebeian and a democrat. He belonged to the same historical and social formation that produced Belinsky, Nekrasov, and Grigoriev, and to this is due, among other things, that absence of all grace and elegance, whether internal or external, which characterizes all his work, together with an absence of reserve, discipline, and dignity, and an excess of abnormal self-consciousness.

SUGGESTIONS FOR FURTHER READING

The following studies incorporate further material relating to *Notes from Underground* and *A Confession*, while also placing the two works biographically, historically, and with reference to the longer and more celebrated works by the two authors.

Dostoyevsky

J. Catteau, *Dostoyevsky and the Process of Literary Creation* (Cambridge, 1989)

J. Frank, *Dostoevsky* (Princeton, 1976–) [Three volumes of a planned five-volume literary biography are available]

R. L. Jackson, *The Art of Dostoyevsky: Deliriums and Nocturnes* (Princeton, 1981)

J. Jones, *Dostoevsky* (Oxford, 1983)

M. Jones, *Dostoyevsky: the Novel of Discord* (New York, 1976)

G. Kjetsaa, *Fyodor Dostoevsky: a Writer's Life* (London, 1988)

W. J. Leatherbarrow, *Fedor Dostoevsky* (Boston, 1981)

K. Mochulsky, *Dostoevsky: His Life and Work* (Princeton, 1967)

R. A. Peace, *Dostoevsky's 'Notes from Underground'* (Bristol, 1993)

Tolstoy

J. Bayley, *Tolstoy and the Novel* (London, 1966)

T. G. S. Cain *Tolstoy* (London, 1977)

R. Christian, *Tolstoy: a Critical Introduction* (London, 1969)

E. Crankshaw, *Tolstoy: the Making of a Novelist* (New York, 1974)

H. Gifford (ed.), *Leo Tolstoy* (Harmondsworth, 1971)

A. Maude, *The Life of Tolstoy*, 2 vols (New York, 1910)

W. W. Rowe, *Leo Tolstoy* (Boston, 1986)

E. J. Simmons, *Leo Tolstoy* (Boston, 1946)

——*Tolstoy* (London, 1973)

E. Wasiolek, *Tolstoy's Major Fiction* (Chicago, 1978)

Dostoyevsky and Tolstoy

G. Steiner, *Tolstoy or Dostoyevsky: an Essay in the Old Criticism* (New York, 1959)

TEXT SUMMARIES

Notes from Underground

Part I The Underground

1 The Underground Man presents himself. Forty years old, ill and spiteful, he has retired from the civil service and now lives in a wretched basement flat.
2 He revels in his own degradation.
3 He rejects the laws of mathematics and science.
4 Pain as a source of pleasure.
5 Primary and secondary causes.
6 Positive and negative idleness.
7 The role of self-interest, reason and science in human affairs.
8 The limits of reason.
9 The unreliability of science and good sense. $2 \times 2 = 5$.
10 The awfulness of the Crystal Palace.
11 Normality, repression and reasons for writing.

Part II Apropos of the Falling Sleet

1 Recollections of childhood, work in the civil service and an insult avenged.
2 Dissipation and dreams of heroism. A visit to an old school-friend.
3 Reunion with four old boys, and a planned farewell dinner for one of them.
4 The disastrous dinner, followed by a proposed trip to a brothel.
5 A dreamt-of duel does not materialise. He meets a girl at the brothel.
6 He speaks to her, Liza, about early death, her job and family relationships.
7 Further such talk brings her near to despair, but wins her confidence.
8 Dreadful relations with his servant. Fear that Liza may visit him. She does.
9 Their roles are reversed. She pities him; he feels both attraction and hatred.
10 Love is impossible. She leaves for ever. He reflects on the writing of his notes.

A Confession

1 Tolstoy tells of his early disillusionment with Orthodox religion.
2 Debauchery, army life and writing provide no lasting satisfaction.
3 Neither do marriage, travel, journalism, teaching or raising a family.
4 The emptiness and absurdity of life lead to thoughts of suicide.
5 The inadequacy, in these circumstances, of science and philosophy.
6 The great thinkers merely confirm the vanity of human life.
7 Apart from ignorance or epicureanism, only weakness prevents suicide.
8 The masses live on enviably, but their faith goes against reason.
9 Ergo: reason is inadequate. The need to return to faith and God's will.
10 The poor people provide a better example for living than the educated rich.
11 The need for passivity, acceptance and altruism. Questioning kills action.
12 The search for God: God is life, faith and love.
13 Intellectual pride can be tamed. A return to the Church.
14 The unacceptability of Church ceremony, especially the Eucharist.
15 Growing doubts about the inadequacy and falseness of the Church.
16 Doubts are dispelled, but Orthodoxy has to be abandoned. Living on in the Christian spirit, without seeking an explanation for everything.

ACKNOWLEDGEMENTS

The Publishers are grateful for permission to reproduce extracts from the following publications in the endmatter of this volume:

T. G. S. Cain, *Tolstoy* (Paul Elek, 1977).

Joseph Frank, *Dostoevsky: The Stir of Liberation,* 1860–1865 (Robson Books, 1987); copyright Princeton University Press.

D. S. Mirsky, *A History of Russian Literature* (Alfred A. Knopf, 1960).

Konstantin Mochulsky, *Dostoevsky: His Life and Work*, trans. Michael A. Minihan (Princeton University Press, 1967).

Richard Peace, *Dostoevsky: An Examination of the Major Novels* (Cambridge University Press, 1971).

A. N. Wilson, *Tolstoy* (Penguin Books, 1988).

CLASSIC NOVELS
IN EVERYMAN

A SELECTION

The Way of All Flesh
SAMUEL BUTLER
A savagely funny odyssey from joy-
less duty to unbridled liberalism **£4.99**

Born in Exile
GEORGE GISSING
A rationalist's progress towards love
and compromise in class-ridden
Victorian England **£4.99**

David Copperfield
CHARLES DICKENS
One of Dickens' best-loved novels,
brimming with humour **£3.99**

The Last Chronicle of Barset
ANTHONY TROLLOPE
Trollope's magnificent conclusion
to his Barsetshire novels **£4.99**

He Knew He Was Right
ANTHONY TROLLOPE
Sexual jealousy, money and
women's rights within marriage –
a novel ahead of its time **£6.99**

Tess of the D'Urbervilles
THOMAS HARDY
The powerful, poetic classic of
wronged innocence **£3.99**

Wuthering Heights
and Poems
EMILY BRONTE
A powerful work of genius – one of
the great masterpieces of literature
£3.50

Tom Jones
HENRY FIELDING
The wayward adventures of one of
literatures most likable heroes **£5.99**

The Master of Ballantrae
and Weir of Hermiston
R. L. STEVENSON
Together in one volume, two great
novels of high adventure and family
conflict **£4.99**

£3.99

£2.99

£3.99

AVAILABILITY
All books are available from your local bookshop or direct from
**Littlehampton Book Services Cash Sales, 14 Eldon Way, LinesideEstate,
Littlehampton, West Sussex BN17 7HE.** PRICES ARE SUBJECT TO CHANGE.

To order any of the books, please enclose a cheque (in £ sterling) made payable to
Littlehampton Book Services, or phone your order through with credit card details (Access,
Visa or Mastercard) on 0903 721596 (24 hour answering service) stating card number and
expiry date. Please add £1.25 for package and postage to the total value of your order.

WOMEN'S WRITING
IN EVERYMAN

A SELECTION

Female Playwrights of the Restoration
FIVE COMEDIES
Rediscovered literary treasures in a unique selection **£5.99**

The Secret Self
SHORT STORIES BY WOMEN
'A superb collection' *Guardian* **£4.99**

Short Stories
KATHERINE MANSFIELD
An excellent selection displaying the remarkable range of Mansfield's talent **£3.99**

Women Romantic Poets 1780-1830: An Anthology
Hidden talent from the Romantic era, rediscovered for the first time **£5.99**

Selected Poems
ELIZABETH BARRETT BROWNING
A major contribution to our appreciation of this inspiring and innovative poet **£5.99**

Frankenstein
MARY SHELLEY
A masterpiece of Gothic terror in its original 1818 version **£3.99**

The Life of Charlotte Brontë
MRS GASKELL
A moving and perceptive tribute by one writer to another **£4.99**

Vindication of the Rights of Woman and The Subjection of Women
MARY WOLLSTONECRAFT
AND J. S. MILL
Two pioneering works of early feminist thought **£4.99**

The Pastor's Wife
ELIZABETH VON ARNIM
A funny and accomplished novel by the author of *Elizabeth and Her German Garden* **£5.99**

£4.99

£2.99

£5.99

POETRY
IN EVERYMAN

A SELECTION

Silver Poets of the Sixteenth Century

EDITED BY
DOUGLAS BROOKS-DAVIES
A new edition of this famous
Everyman collection **£6.99**

Complete Poems

JOHN DONNE
The father of metaphysical verse in
this highly-acclaimed edition **£4.99**

Complete English Poems, Of Education, Areopagitica

JOHN MILTON
An excellent introduction to
Milton's poetry and prose **£6.99**

Selected Poems

JOHN DRYDEN
A poet's portrait of Restoration
England **£4.99**

Selected Poems

PERCY BYSSHE SHELLEY
'The essential Shelley' in one
volume **£3.50**

Women Romantic Poets 1780-1830: An Anthology

Hidden talent from the Romantic era,
rediscovered for the first time **£5.99**

Poems in Scots and English

ROBERT BURNS
The best of Scotland's greatest lyric
poet **£4.99**

Selected Poems

D. H. LAWRENCE
A newly-edited selection spanning
the whole of Lawrence's literary
career **£4.99**

The Poems

W. B. YEATS
Ireland's greatest lyric poet
surveyed in this ground-breaking
edition **£6.50**

£5.99

£4.99

£3.50

AVAILABILITY

All books are available from your local bookshop or direct from
**Littlehampton Book Services Cash Sales, 14 Eldon Way, LinesideEstate,
Littlehampton, West Sussex BN17 7HE.** PRICES ARE SUBJECT TO CHANGE.

To order any of the books, please enclose a cheque (in £ sterling) made payable to
Littlehampton Book Services, or phone your order through with credit card details (Access,
Visa or Mastercard) on 0903 721596 (24 hour answering service) stating card number and
expiry date. Please add £1.25 for package and postage to the total value of your order.

SHORT STORY COLLECTIONS
IN EVERYMAN

A SELECTION

The Secret Self
Short Stories by Women
'A superb collection' *Guardian* **£4.99**

Selected Short Stories
and Poems
THOMAS HARDY
The best of Hardy's Wessex in a
unique selection **£4.99**

The Best of
Sherlock Holmes
ARTHUR CONAN DOYLE
All the favourite adventures in one
volume **£4.99**

Great Tales of Detection
Nineteen Stories
Chosen by Dorothy L. Sayers **£3.99**

Short Stories
KATHERINE MANSFIELD
A selection displaying the
remarkable range of Mansfield's
writing **£3.99**

Selected Stories
RUDYARD KIPLING
Includes stories chosen to reveal the
'other' Kipling **£4.50**

The Strange Case of
Dr Jekyll and Mr Hyde
and Other Stories
R. L. STEVENSON
An exciting selection of gripping
tales from a master of suspense **£3.99**

Modern Short Stories 2:
1940-1980
Thirty-one stories from the greatest
modern writers **£3.50**

The Day of Silence and
Other Stories
GEORGE GISSING
Gissing's finest stories, available for
the first time in one volume **£4.99**

Selected Tales
HENRY JAMES
Stories portraying the tensions
between private life and the outside
world **£5.99**

£4.99

£6.99

AVAILABILITY
All books are available from your local bookshop or direct from
**Littlehampton Book Services Cash Sales, 14 Eldon Way, LinesideEstate,
Littlehampton, West Sussex BN17 7HE.** PRICES ARE SUBJECT TO CHANGE.

To order any of the books, please enclose a cheque (in £ sterling) made payable to
Littlehampton Book Services, or phone your order through with credit card details (Access,
Visa or Mastercard) on 0903 721596 (24 hour answering service) stating card number and
expiry date. Please add £1.25 for package and postage to the total value of your order.